Bewitched Shadows

Autumn Blake

Copyright © 2022 Autumn Blake

All rights reserved. Without limiting the rights under copyright reserved above, no part of this publication may be reproduced, stored in, or introduced into a retrieval system, or transmitted in any form or by any means (electronic, mechanical, photocopying, recording, or otherwise) without prior written permission of the copyright owner. The only exception is brief quotations in printed reviews.

This book is a work of fiction. The names, characters, places, and incidents are the product of the author's imagination or are used fictitiously. Any resemblance to actual events, business establishments, locales, or persons living or dead is entirely coincidental.

Cover design by @saintjupit3rgr4phic

Editing: Ashley Olivier

All rights reserved.

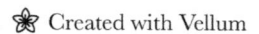

❀ Created with Vellum

NOTE TO READERS

This book contains depictions of sexually explicit scenes, grief, PTSD, and violence. It contains mature language, themes, and content that may not be suitable for all readers. Reader discretion is advised.

To my husband:
You pushed me to follow my dreams, motivating me to keep going whenever I wanted to give up.
I love you.

1
EMBER

The Coven always warned that a ruby-red blood moon foretold a terrible omen. I couldn't ignore the warning brewing in the pit of my stomach to remain cautious, despite the warm glow emanating through my body.

As the granddaughter of the Coven's High Priestess, my attendance was mandatory, so here I stood, sweating in the Louisiana humidity as I surveyed the field of supernatural creatures.

The hedonistic vampires' attempts at a Grecian Bacchanal barely disguised the Council's pathetic attempts at harmony within New Orleans's growing supernatural community. As if I wanted to choke on the stench of incense and blood while playing the role of a dutiful witch.

The drink table provided better enticement in my current mood. My sisters would kill me for already swaying on my feet under the effects of the imported Fae wine, but desperate times called for desperate measures.

Alerted to a presence behind me, I stiffened, knowing who stood at my back without having to turn towards his annoyingly handsome face. Over the cacophony of shouts and laughter, I side-eyed Killian with a saccharine smile, my well-practiced southern manners a quick defensive against his oncoming attack. "Having fun ogling me, demon? Take a picture. I'm sure it would last you longer."

I poured myself another hefty glass of shimmery pink Fae wine, ignoring the demon stalking me with his signature frown and black ensemble to better hide in the shadows.

His impenetrable gaze sent delicious shivers down my spine.

And *not* in a good way, I scolded myself.

I took in the rest of his face with a silent sigh of discontent. Thick, inky black hair ruffled around his neck, looking at once perfect and effortless, while his tanned skin glowed under the moonlight, emphasizing the scar running from his left eye to his ear. It was his one imperfection, and it only added to his overall roguish appeal. *Bastard.*

When he caught me staring, I ignored the knowing slant of his firm mouth and took in the evening's spectacle instead. But though there was much to observe, I glanced over my shoulder at him once more with a twinkle of excitement.

His amber eyes glowed as he stepped closer. "This brings back memories of our first meeting in the marsh, don't you agree? I'm surprised you're sober this late into the evening. Though, by the looks of it, you'll be stripped nude and dancing in the woods in no time."

I turned a bright shade of puce as embarrassment coursed through me. I suppose my reputation proceeded me, with Killian subjected to many of my wild exploits this past summer.

The demon looked as if he wouldn't know fun if it bit him in his sublimely firm ass.

I raised a dark brow. "While I'm sure you often fantasize about naked women, you would have to possess some fragment of a personality to lure one into your bed."

He smirked, lifting the scarred skin of his cheek. "Do you often think about me in bed, sweetheart?"

I looked away from his smug face, biting my lip to hide a smile. "What are you doing here, anyway? Carreau forcing you to play nice with the other creatures in Gaia for once?"

Though a demon sat on the Louisiana Council of Supernaturals, they remained reviled by most of the community. Unlike witches, shifters, and vampires, they held no lands on our plane, forced to remain in Hell.

Killian's amused eyes hardened at the mention of Carreau, and I knew I had touched a nerve. "I'm not here for your precious Council. I have other business tonight that does not concern impetuous witches."

His tone cut, and yet his unwavering attention followed my every movement, brushing along my skin like shadows bleeding through light. Humiliating memories from that afternoon in the marsh floated to the surface. Buoys impossible to ignore.

I fought the urge to fan my overheated cheeks under his scrutiny. "As for thinking about you in bed, I only think about you when I imagine Hell on Gaia."

His brows lifted, and I fought a foul curse at my lame retort. I needed to get away from him before more word vomit expelled from my lips, adding another embarrassing exchange to wallow about as I lay restlessly in bed each night.

I turned on my heel without another word and trudged back to my sisters' table, leaving him alone with his victory. Passing through the black satin-covered tables surrounded by crowds of various creatures, I forced the demon from my mind, refusing to turn back for a last look.

Instead, I focused on what mattered: getting shitfaced on free booze and having a night to *not* remember.

Creatures I knew from across the state were in attendance, whether it be through the force of the Council or the desire to intermingle and make new alliances. While I often enjoyed such gatherings of immortals as a respite away from hiding my true nature from humans, tonight, I merely sought oblivion.

I gulped from my flute, kicking my legs as my silk bedsheet-turned-toga tried to trip me onto the dewy grass. Thankfully, most of the ground was covered in expensive European rugs the wealthy vampires had shipped out for this event.

Prince Alexei and his Court of pompous bloodsuckers who immigrated to New Orleans from across Europe at various phases in their immortal lives remained in the Crescent City as a constant foreboding presence. They sipped on glasses of thick blood; their exotic, inhuman beauty too magnificent to look upon as they gazed at the rest of the creatures with mild contempt.

My sisters sat around an empty table near some of the Coven, though they didn't mingle. I danced over, my cheeks flushed despite the warm October breeze. I adjusted the laurel wreath around my head as it tipped precariously, nearly poking an eye out as I swung my arms around Audra's bare shoulders.

Her amusement crinkled the corners of her emerald eyes. "I see you found the Fae wine. Have mercy on us and stay away from the pack tonight."

I fought an eyeroll. It was one little Fae wine induced orgy, not a murder. Yet the mention of the pack cooled my excitement as I cast a quick glance around the creature-filled tables. "I have no intention of dallying with any of their ilk after how they treated me at the Mabon celebration. They're dead to me, most especially Wren fucking Boudreaux."

Wren and I had been an on and off again item since high school, an arrangement that worked well for me as the years passed. But because of his father's meddling, I was no longer welcome on pack lands or with any of its members. And *good riddance*. Shifters were insufferable on their best day.

Audra snorted, sending wisps of her red tinged hair near the flickering candles. "Okay, Ember." She smirked. "Until one of the wolves crooks a finger at you with that Cajun accent and you fall to your knees and drop trou. You must work on your self-control, dearest."

I had spent my fair share of evenings within the arms of a sexy male or two, and I didn't regret one night with them. New Orleans was a melting pot of creatures and mortals from across the world, and I took it as my civic duty to sample to my heart's content.

My lips twitched. "What can I say? Muscles and gargantuan dicks are my weakness."

Jade smacked both Audra and me with her beaded purse as her green eyes narrowed in frustration. "Will the two of you be quiet? Isla is right there with her friends. She'll know what hussies her older sisters are."

Audra and I shared a look before we burst into laughter, causing Jade's scowl to deepen.

"If you're not getting any, Jade, just say that. This is a judgement free zone," Audra spoke around her straw.

Jade sniffed, not bothering to respond as she adjusted the dark curls spilling from her haphazard braid.

Our lackluster love life was only the tip of the iceberg in this family.

Watching our youngest sister dance with an uninhibited innocence sent a stabbing pain through my chest. "Poor Isla." My eyes prickled with sudden emotion. "No parents to guide her in the world. Just three fuckups with no plans, no dreams, no hope."

As if to punctuate my out-of-control emotions, my fingers sparked with tiny flickers of fire.

Jade's calming presence centered me as her hand summoned soil and debris from under the table to act as an extinguisher if need be. "Get it together, Em. No outbursts tonight. Happy thoughts."

"Happy?" I whispered, wiping away my tears with shaky hands, still aflame.

Audra groaned, startling me from my outburst. "*Goddess save me.* Are we jumping straight to the morose stage of drunkenness tonight? Because that's definitely what I had in mind for a Bacchanal revel."

Jade tucked a lock of my chestnut hair away from the firecrackers flickering from my fingers. "There's been some wins this week, Ember. You didn't explode anything or embarrass Grandmother at last week's sabbath. I could tell your restraint impressed her."

With watery eyes, I peeked through the fingers covering my face and found Grandmother. She sat with the elders of the Coven, all wearing identical expressions of distaste at the vampire's sensual displays atop velvet cushions.

Pride was not the first emotion I would assert to Grandmother's perceptions of me.

Audra rubbed my back. "And we're not *total* fuckups. We're the hottest witches in attendance tonight and, without a doubt, the most powerful. Between all our affinities, we've got a major edge over the creatures here pretending to make nice with each other."

Jade snorted. "Y'all say that like it's a good thing. We know what Grandmother wants. I wouldn't doubt if she forced us to attend training with the rest of the witches vying for a spot on the elder's chair one day."

I paled at the thought of being forced to display my magick in front of others within the Coven. "Grandmother wouldn't do that, would she?"

"Wouldn't do what?" Isla sang from behind Jade, her electric-blue eyes and golden hair braided with flowers in a crown atop of her head, like a real-life fairy princess.

Audra answered, her lips quirking with amusement, "Grandmother wouldn't force Ember into advanced spell work she isn't ready for. She may be an icy bitch, but she's not cruel. She allowed us to remain at home, though she would rather keep us under her thumb at the estate."

Jade pursed her lips, whatever knowledge she garnered from her training with Grandmother belying the comforting words.

With the fire blazing and the music pulsating through the field enchanted to ward away curious mortals, my head swam with the memories I fought with every waking breath.

I decided I'd had enough of serious talk.

From the corner of my eye, I spotted Killian lurking in the shadows once more. From a safe distance, I let my gaze linger over his impressive six-and-a-half-foot frame of lean muscle, without fearing his mockery. He may be an ass, but he was sexy as Hell. Too bad his personality ruined it for him.

Audra waved her hand in front of my face. "Hello? Gaia to Ember. You're drooling, sister. It's quite embarrassing."

I snapped back to her grinning face and flushed at being caught ogling the demon. Only he and I knew all the gory details about our humiliating encounter all those months ago, and I wanted to keep it that way.

Jade glanced over to where Killian stood, but her attention snapped to the Vampire Prince instead. Her lips curled with disgust as she watched him spread across a velvet cushion with a bevy of buxom females trailing kisses down his body. "We've got nothing in common with these creatures other than immortal life, unfortunately for us."

A distraction was needed. I hailed over a vampire waiter, who eyed me with derision as I downed the rest of my drink. "Shots!" I yelled.

Jade turned back to me with growing exasperation, rubbing her temples. "Ember, I swear to the Goddess, if you blow something up tonight or hex anyone, I *will* disown you."

Isla laughed and kissed me on the cheek, sweet as pie. "I'll never disown you, Em. Especially when Jade knows you've been working to control your power."

She meant the words as a compliment, but my stomach clenched. My gaze wandered to the sultry dancing around the bonfire, illuminating the dark field in shadows to distract my growing nausea. This argument grew tiresome after hearing it on repeat. It wasn't that I hadn't *tried* to be a better witch. No matter how much training, yoga, meditation, or energy healing I committed myself to, there seemed to be a block inside me, hindering my ability to control my magick.

A tray of purple smoking shots arrived, and I grabbed two, double-fisting them, before drinking them in one go. I lifted my arms above my head, my golden bracelets clinking along my arms. "Let's dance!" I shouted over the music.

Audra immediately gripped my hand as we ran into the grassy field to join the rave.

The fire brought out the scarlet tones in her hair, and I couldn't help but pull on a long strand as I absorbed the fire's energy, siphoning power from its glow. I threw my arms around her and spun, giggling as the alcohol took effect.

Jade's scowl from across the field captured my attention, and I felt some of my giddiness wither. "It's not like I try to infuriate her, but her expectations are too much for me to live up to," I slurred, my words coming more jumbled after my fevered dancing.

"I know, she can be as much of a haughty bitch as Grandmother. It's because she's perfection itself and her magick always came easy to her. She can't understand how you haven't mastered yours yet. Plus, she's under a lot of pressure being next in line as High Priestess."

I whirled and stared up at the stars, Audra's words a balm against my bruised ego. Plus, I felt a selfish relief that it wasn't me who was the eldest sister in our family, the one responsible for keeping our power within the Coven as the next High Priestess.

A sudden prickle along the back of my neck made my witch intuition tingle. I turned, getting caught in Killian's impenetrable stare.

He moved in and out of his shadows, his lips curled with something like contempt as he watched me lose myself to the night's revel. But along with his distaste, his gaze also held a tendril of desire. A feeling I knew all too well.

My bare toes curled into the grass as he watched me dance, my hips moving to the slow beat. I ran my hands over my body, luxuriating in the feel of silk, before fisting them into my dark, loose hair, imagining for a moment all the ways he could make me scream.

Heat radiated from him, just as searing hot as the fire crackling.

Audra snorted, breaking the spell. "The demon looks like he's unsure whether he wants to fuck you or stab you."

Surprise lit within me, and I grinned wickedly. Despite how much I pretended otherwise, I had once wanted to enjoy the carnal possibilities between us. But Killian had made it clear how he felt about my advances. His grated insults still stung, no matter how desperately I sought to bury them.

As his attention moved from my body to my victorious smile, he shook himself before whipping his head away from me. A cold dismissal, but it came too late.

I knew I had won this round as he stormed away into the night, losing himself in the darkness. It should bring me pleasure, but my smile withered away. I knew not to let his scorn faze me, but with the blood moon highlighting all my hidden wants and fears, the lie tasted bitter on my tongue.

Audra threw her arms around me, spinning me further into the jumble of bodies. "Fret not, young Ember. The male was not worthy of your beauty anyhow."

I pouted, knowing she was right. Demons and witches mixed like vinegar and water, our relationship a parasitic one. I would do well to remember why he rejected me that reckless evening in the marsh.

And why I was wrong to still fantasize about his hands and mouth worshipping me.

My eyes drifted back across the field, and I watched him approach a wolf from Wren's pack hooking up with two vampires. Killian watched them for a beat, and I felt a prickle of jealousy as I noticed how stunning the females were.

When a vampire's hands pulled me back into his chest, I allowed it, swerving my hips with delight. I blocked all thoughts of the demon from my mind, my eyes drifting shut as I lost myself in the beats of the music once more.

2

KILLIAN

The witch would be my downfall. Moving in my shadows, I forced the visual of a writhing and beautiful witch from my mind—and the murder I wanted to inflict on the creatures who dared watch her with covetous expressions of lust.

It wasn't the first time she had distracted me from my duties here on Gaia, and I knew it wouldn't be the last. With one heated glance or quirk of her lips, she managed to both bewitch and blind me with frustration.

My attention refocused on my target. I watched with bored disgust as he lay tangled betwixt two vampires, their fangs submerged into the shifter's meaty thigh while he groaned with desire.

Mercifully, I let him enjoy their bite for a second longer before I hauled him off the rug.

The females screeched as I pulled him into my shadows, but I paid them no mind. A long-suffering sigh escaped my lips. "You have been naughty, Baron. Two hundred thousand gold stolen from the Devil, and you thought you could flee his reach?"

I usually savored when the target knew the jig was up.

When all the lamented regrets and broken hopes withered away on their faces like apparitions. But tonight, I was eager to have this task finished. At least the fool had the decency to submit to my smokey chains as I transported him to Hell.

Upon bursting into the Realm of Pride, frigid air slapped against my cheeks as I approached Satan's castle, Infernos. It stood like a shiny beacon of golden light with elaborate, gilded details carved into the snowcapped mountaintops. The palace spilled into the dark forest beneath the mountain and into Satan's lands, giving an illusion of wealth and power.

A lie Satan exploited to garner the respect he craved from the other demon lords.

Instead of taking Baron through the castle's main entrance and attracting unwanted attention, I materialized into the prisons below the castle's surface, carved deep inside the gloomy caverns of the mountain, thick with steaming fog.

With a lift of my chin, I ignored the pointed looks of the demon sentries who stared at me with looks of fear or disgust, their beady eyes trailing from my scarred visage to the shifter in my grasp.

After twenty years working as the Scourge, my father's mercenary and assassin, I had yet to earn any respect in their eyes, despite my royal lineage. The realm favored beauty, and I was an ugly blight on that image of perfection. No matter that I kept a heavy stream of the worst souls of humanity feeding our realm.

"Another soul, Charon," I called with a bored air, throwing the shifter into the arms of the armored guards. The male's skin grew gray as his grim future settled into reality. "I believe my father allocated his punishment to ten years on the docks."

"Very well, Killian," the demon sighed, his skeletal hands trailing over his braided grey beard. With another wave, he sent Baron off to the dungeons to await his servitude along the

River of Death, connecting all seven demon realms together within the plane.

He marked my job as complete on the Scroll of Debts before he shot me a questioning glance over his spectacles. "I suppose I'll be seeing you again soon, my lord?"

I flinched at the title and turned away, ready to be free from this plane once more. "There are always more souls my father will depose me to reap, Charon. I'll return once he has decided my next victim."

In the next breath, I flashed above to the great hall lined with father's trophies of past conquests—weaponry, armor, and the heads of his enemies. The smell of roasted meat and stale demon brew assaulted my senses before I noticed the crowd.

Too late to flee, I squared my shoulders as I stalked towards them with my head lifted high.

My father sat perched on his throne, a bejeweled crown tilted off to one side of his golden head. When he sensed my approach, his merriness cleared away from his face like cobwebs, sullen disappointment replacing it. "Oh, it's you, Killian. What news do you bring from the mortal realm?"

The surrounding demons tittered like starving birds, their nourishment Satan's supercilious regard. I felt a moment of hot shame as their eyes wandered over my mutilated face and dark, inky hair, so unlike my father and his former lady's ethereal beauty.

There was too much of my mother's darkness, not only her dark hair and golden eyes, but her cool disdain for everything the Lord of Pride revered. To the realm, and most especially my father, I would always be the unwanted bastard son obligated to wear the crown out of necessity.

I avoided the curious eyes in favor of studying my father. "Another soul brought to the prisons. We remain on track to meet our quota before my succession."

Though I attempted my usual unaffected tone, my father's

eyes narrowed on mine with anger, as I knew they would whenever I mentioned his impending retirement.

He waved away the crowd with a sniff. "Clear the room."

When we were alone, he dropped his unbothered superiority, the fire he hid inside unfurling as he gripped the edge of his throne. "You mock me before all again and I will ensure your century within this realm remains filled with torment. Do not forget the power I hold over these demons—and how much they despise you."

My hackles rose with renewed anger. "It is because of you that I am reviled. I have known since I arrived at this keep how unwanted I was by you. Your mate and children died, and instead of wallowing in your grief alone, you sought a pretty demoness who begot me. You are responsible for my existence, and yet I am the one paying for your crimes."

My father's eyes grew haunted, as they often did at the mention of Hana and their sons. He swallowed the pain before cracking his knuckles, returning to his usual sneer.

Had I any sympathy for the male, I could understand the tragedy of his situation, but any emotion other than hatred long fled my soul when I viewed my father.

Agitated, he leaned back against his gilded chair. "And what news of Carreau and the ridiculous Council he sits upon?"

I contained a snort of amusement. "It appears New Orleans has been functioning in a state of peace under the Council's reign. Carreau and the other creatures populating the city work together to keep harmony between the various factions, self-regulating their own and socializing with each other where the mortals are not present to observe."

Before creatures hid behind their illusions or glamours, they lived amongst the humans without fear of discovery. However, the mortals' minds were weak and unwilling to evolve. Creatures found it easier to blend in with them—or deceive them—allowing free rein over the bountiful plane they inhabited.

I continued, despite my father's bored focus shifting to a bowl of violet berries. "The witches' impenetrable shields conceal much of their doings while the vampires use their wealth to pay off governments and media. It appears to be working for them, especially considering the city's notoriety for the supernatural. They hide in plain sight."

My father scoffed. "Ridiculous notion, cohabitating with those foul creatures. I am gladdened for our plane beneath Gaia. I would slit my throat if I had to live amongst those animals."

Thoughts of Gaia only brought on a cascade of thoughts of the witch with her siren's lips and fiery attitude all wrapped up in a sexy as sin bow. She set my body alight like no other, and I *hated* her for it.

My first glance of her all those months ago, with long, soft brown hair swirling in the wind as she perched on the edge of the murky bayou, her buxom breasts pushed together in her ridiculously miniscule bikini, had my trousers tightening.

Though the shifter males swam nearby, their wild scents rolling off her silky skin in waves, I crept closer for a better look at the creature who had bewitched me. In the darkening evening sun, she saw me through my shadows. She quirked those plump lips into a sultry smile. "Now who might you be, handsome?"

I grew infuriated with her, convinced she taunted me for my ugly facade. But then I caught the irresistible scent of her desire—sweet and heady—the want clear in her sultry blue eyes.

At that moment, I would have given anything for her approval. I would have sacrificed my title, my kingdom, my honor for a taste of her sweet lips. But then I noticed the glassiness in her eyes and the marks along her neck and shoulder: love bites.

She would never be mine, not when her options were endless and far more favorable than what I offered. I was in line for the throne, an irrefutable job the realm would force me to submit to, and she was a fun-loving witch. It was an impossibility.

At her flirtatious appraisal of me and a come-hither crook of her finger, I hardened myself as I turned away from her lusts. "I would not fuck a witch for any amount of gold, harlot. Find another of your lovers to slake your needs."

My words were scathing and cruel. Lies. And yet, the effect was immediate and pervasive.

She despised me, and I told myself that it was for the best. Even when months later, she still consumed my every waking thought. I grew weary of it.

I forced myself back to the present at my father's deep sigh, full of the long-suffering disappointment I knew well. He waved me away with his hand. "Leave me, Killian. I have no desire to endure your presence any longer."

I backed away from my father's dais with clenched teeth.

Satan cleared his throat, and I froze my steps at his next words. "Do not keep me waiting much longer for the next soul you reap. I want our stores full before you steal my throne, and you won't like the consequences if you continue to disappoint much longer."

My gut churned as I portaled back to Gaia.

The deadline of my succession continued forward, and yet I felt nowhere near prepared for ruling, least of all when I could still scent Ember's vanilla fragrance in my nose like the sweetest of tortures.

But I was quite good at burying my true feelings, and I wouldn't start failing in that now.

3
EMBER

Audra and Jade held me upright as we began the long walk back to our car from the Bacchanal field. Surrounded by dark woods, every step became more tedious, my heels catching on rocks and uneven dirt.

"Slow down! My feet are broken," I slurred, my mobility growing more difficult.

Jade's nails dug into my arm as she held me upright. "Ember, if you don't shut the Hell up, I'll magick you to sleep and drag your sorry ass the entire way home."

Even in my current state of drunkenness, I could sense Jade's pervasive wrath. She was more irritable than usual, and I knew I was the cause.

"Just let us do the work. Stop fighting," Audra groaned as she dodged my wayward elbow.

Bile rose, and I knew I wouldn't make it to the car before I was sick. At least Isla had left the party hours ago with her friends, so she wouldn't witness her disastrous sister.

A strange lump lay in the brush, and I squinted in the near blackness to make it out. "Is that a dead deer?" My face fell, moisture leaking from my eyes. "Who would hit such a beautiful creature? Just drive slower."

The tears were coming full force now, and Jade ground her teeth in annoyance.

"What *is* that?" Audra muttered, her words underscored with urgency. "It doesn't look like a deer."

When we creeped closer, the smell hit us. The road stunk of overripe fruit with the faint twinge of ammonia. Strong emotional echoes left a scent all creatures could detect.

This was fear. Not just fear, but raw, undiluted *terror*.

Jade realized what lay before us and gasped in horror. Her hands dropped me, and I stumbled.

Audra held onto my shoulder to keep me upright, sagging under my weight. "Goddess, you're heavy," she groaned before her words died off.

We were upon it now. Or rather, her.

Garnet, congealing blood along pale skin, swam in my vision before my stomach revolted.

Shocked nausea surfacing, I pulled free from Audra's grip and gagged before spewing wine into the grass below my feet.

Audra gripped my hair in one hand while she kept me standing with the other, her eyes trained on the dead vampire. "Holy shit, it's Rosalind Vasilyev."

But I was no longer listening. Instead, I was eighteen years old, staring down at my mother and fathers' wide, glassy, unblinking stares, ruby-blood welts torn into their flesh, severing their necks like a macabre necklace.

I heaved again, my stomach cramping as tears ran over my cheeks, suffocating me.

"She's dead," were the last words I heard before I passed out, the blackness consuming me.

☽☾

"Who did this to her?"

"What are we supposed to do about the Samhain festival? Will the Council cancel it?"

"What is the plan for finding the one responsible?"

I tuned out the voices of the angry witches and warlocks and sipped on my healing tonic seeped with cinnamon, praying to the Goddess I wouldn't vomit on Grandmother's expensive Persian rug.

By the overwhelming smell of ash and myrrh circulating in the meeting room, I could tell the Coven was fired up for vengeance. Or at least concerned with their own self-interests about what the murder would mean for them.

Unlike the more exclusive Covens, New Orleans blended witches and warlocks from all over the world. It sometimes made us disjointed and quick to argument, but also something unique.

Fleur's shock of silver hair caught my attention. I sidled up beside her, my steps slow with exhaustion. We had been friends since we were children, though in the years since my parents' deaths, our relationship had dwindled more to drinking buddies.

"Hey, girl. Where were you last night?" I asked, sitting on the settee next to her.

Her deep skin was smooth of any worries, but her stormy grey eyes revealed her underlying emotions. She angled her head towards her older sister seated with the elders. "Tabitha forced me to stick around the estate working on spells with her. As if that would impress your grandmother." She looked at me with sickening realization. "But that could have been any of us last night."

"Do you know who she was?" My legs twitched with nervous energy.

After stumbling into the vampire's slain body, I had drifted in and out of nightmares, waking to vomit and shake on the floor like a leaf. The details were hazy from my panic attack and the copious amounts of hallucinogenic wine. Not to mention Jade's silent treatment this morning on during the drive to the estate.

My stomach seized as I imagined the female's cold, grey skin and the grisly gash spanning from ear to ear, so like the way I found my parents years ago.

I took another hefty gulp of tea.

Fleur's full lips thinned. "It was Rosalind Vasilyev."

I gaped, nearly choking on the warm liquid. "The prince's cousin? Someone must have balls of steel to come after one of theirs. Aren't they like the Russian Mafia, but vampiric?"

Fleur muffled a tired laugh, her voice hushed as she glanced around the stifling room to be sure no one overheard. "Pretty much. Such an insult won't stand, and the vampires have their own form of justice. *If* they can discover who was behind the attack."

At the front of the room, Grandmother stood on a small platform. "Silence," she commanded, her hand lifting to quiet the room with a cool glance.

The room grew still, and I twisted in my seat for a better view.

Her golden hair and sapphire eyes reminded me of looking at an older version of my mother, but with none of her warmth. "By now, you all know what occurred at the Bacchanal. We need to deal with this matter with a level mind. Rushing into rash actions will be the downfall of our Coven and could put more witches' lives at stake." She clasped her hands in front of her, the picture of calm ease. "Now, when we found Rosalind, she was lying hidden near the woods, away from the revelry. Either someone lured her away or they ambushed her. There were bruises along her arms, signaling she fought off her attacker."

"Do the vampires have any suspects?" asked Everett Domingue, one of the last remaining warlocks descended from

New Orleans Voodoo Priestess Marie Laveau's powerful line. He swept his fingers through his grey hair, the dark skin around his eyes wrinkling with concern.

Rebecca's mien crinkled with irritation at the interruption. "Alexei and his family are well connected and have ties to dangerous creatures. Alistair remains at his royal seat in Slovenia, but he tasked Alexei with discovering the murderer. There were no known enemies in the city, but whoever did this crime must have had reason to target her."

Everett and his sister, Rosemary, whispered, their faces close together, clearly unimpressed with Grandmother's response.

Other than the Domingues, I could sense the relief coursing through the room as the immediate panic and tension eased. The alternative to such a simple explanation was unthinkable. The Coven would be more than happy to distance themselves from the vampires and their Court's politics, regardless of the uneasy truce we shared under the Council.

Grandmother continued with a sniff, "At the Council meeting early this morning, we gained the vampire's guest list and will inquire into who in attendance could have made this attack on our people."

Eve Barstow, another elder with prominent roots in Salem, stood, her eyes twinkling with malicious glee. "But Rebecca, that could be half the city's creatures. The vampires aren't known for their acquired tastes. Nor should it be our concern. Let the vampires deal with their own mess."

I hid a smile at Grandmother's restrained snarl.

She responded through clenched teeth. "The Coven operates within the Council for events such as these. Any chance of criminality should receive swift justice. It will be challenging to sort this out, and Alexei knows creatures will need enticement. Which brings me to our last discussion: Alexei has offered a reward for whoever finds and brings forward the creature responsible for his cousin's death. And not a monetary prize."

The air around the room froze as the Coven leaned in. Self-interests aside, a good competition and reward would spur any witch into action.

Grandmother continued with a flat smile, "Alexei has offered a priceless heirloom from his family's vault to whomever discovers the killer: the amulet of Davorina. The necklace is a mystical talisman stolen from the witches of Bled. It's said to siphon magick and make the wearer more powerful, like our own talismans, but far more potent."

I perked up in my seat, my mind whirling with the possibilities. This could be the opportunity I had waited for!

With such an item, I could control my magick and prove to my Coven that there was more to me than just partying and exploding shit with my lack of control.

The crowd burst into a cacophony of chatter, the question on everyone's lips—how did the vampires come into possession of such a trinket, and how would we take it from them?

Grandmother fielded off the witches, but I heard little of what she said as the plan unfurled in my mind. Without the resources of the elders or the knowledge of the shady underground of the supernatural realm, I would need a way behind the curtain.

Unfortunately, I knew the perfect candidate for such an endeavor.

And he hated my eternal guts.

Fleur's voice broke through the haze in my mind. "You would think the Coven had never heard of mystical heirlooms falling into the wrong hands before. We've been fucked over for centuries, used for our power." She shook her head with annoyance. "Tabitha and my dad are leaving, so I'm going to bounce. I'll see you at work later this week?"

"Sure thing," I responded, distracted by my thoughts.

I pushed through the crowd of impassioned witches, seeking my sisters. Jade, Audra, and Isla stood beside Grandmother, their eyes dark and red-rimmed from our sleepless night. I caught the tail end of their conversation as I took my place at Audra's side.

"Girls, I'll try once again to convince you. Come and stay at the estate. I hate the idea of the four of you all alone in that big house."

Oh, Hell no.

I stared beseechingly at Jade, and her face grew pinched. "Grandmother, we appreciate the concern, but I promise we're fine at home. We place protective charms around the house every night, and we don't take any chances with strangers."

From the glint in Grandmother's eyes, I knew where her mind had wandered. She didn't say the words aloud, but I could hear them in my mind all the same.

Charms and protective spells didn't save your parents from getting butchered in their own backyard.

Rebecca sighed, her calm mask slipping as she watched us huddle together. Like this, she almost appeared like the grandmother who would spoil us with café au laits and beignets on afternoon adventures in the French Quarter. But in a blink, the mask of the High Priestess returned. "Very well. But if anything happens to you girls, I want you here, no questions asked. Understood?"

We nodded in agreement before she began making her rounds through the room, doing her duty as our leader.

Isla's eyes were dark, her mood dimmed by the disturbing discovery the night before.

Jade placed a hand on her shoulder. "Let's grab some fresh ingredients from the farmer's market and make some red beans and rice for dinner. We've got a lot to do before the Samhain festival."

The three of us groaned as we piled filed out of the white

colonial estate, the forest-green French doors slamming shut behind us. Walking down the winding driveway lined by sweeping oaks filled with cars, we piled inside our father's old SUV.

I listened to their easy chatter as we drove away from the Coven estate, but inside, I made my plans. No matter the cost, I would win the amulet from Prince Alexei and prove to everyone in this Goddess-damned city just how greatly they underestimated me.

4
KILLIAN

Icy rage suffused my being as I unsheathed my blade, pushing past wide-eyed demons to enter Inferno's fighting rings. The Forest of Pride, forever blanketed in crystal-white snow and sharp spears of ice, trapped the incensed shouts of anger and pain as the castle's soldiers trained and fought in their own prideful battles of strength at the bottom of the mountain range.

Taliah, one of Satan's elite soldiers—and my oldest friend—watched my progression with unease, her lithe movements slowing as she led the new recruits through defensive drills. Freed from her usual battle armor, her fighting leathers bore mud stains from hours in the yard, while her black hair lay plaited into tight braids.

Instead of greeting her, I stripped my shirt and jumped inside the ring, allowing my demon to unleash himself in a flash of smoke. Through blackened eyes, I watched my first opponent, a young demon with stunted horns and a smug mouth, approach me at the center of the ring.

They were all the same—desperate demons seeking a name for themselves, and who better than Satan's scarred bastard to prove their might? He soon lost his smile as he shielded my sword with stilted backward jumps.

My blade weaved in wide, masterful arcs. The clanging sounds of steel centered my contempt. I pushed my body through the battle techniques drilled into my blood, honed over two decades.

My heavy ebony wings unfurled, the sharp points stabbing through the demon's shoulder blade with a sickening crunch.

He shouted, his dagger poised to stab the sensitive membranes, but I pulled my talons back, spurting blood along the ring's mucky ground. Collapsing onto his knees, he met the cold steel of my blade along his vulnerable neck.

"Next," I called, watching with cool disdain as two demons hauled off his broken body to see the healer.

My neck corded with tension, nowhere near calmed from my earlier anger.

After my meeting with Satan, I had returned to the Bacchanal, lingering in the shadow dimension, unseen by the masses, only to discover the bloody aftermath of the slain vampire. Nausea swirled in the pit of my stomach at the female's horrified scream, frozen forever in death.

I could not banish the image from my mind, nor could I forget my shameful reaction of stark, knee-shattering relief as I realized the murdered female wasn't my witch.

The witch. Not *mine*.

The untainted mountain air cleared away the stench of Gaia.

I cracked my neck from side to side, finally harnessing my rage after a few hours of getting roughed up inside the pit. The sixth and final demon slated to fight against me tapped out, retching against the ground after a swift kick to his overfull abdomen.

I had lost myself once more, and the demons around the ring watched with unwilling respect at my display of unbridled violence. My body glistened with a sheen of sweat and mud, though I paid it no mind.

Clarity shone through, and I realized I had made a mistake in getting close with her this past year. My duty was here—my succession only a month away. I had a career, a reputation that kept the pompous courtiers away from me. Mixing with the creatures above would only make my life harder after I took my father's seat, prohibiting me from leaving this plane again until my time on the throne was complete.

I took a deep breath to harness my demon back inside, my wings furling back with a pop as my eyes cleared of the demon rage. When my eyes returned to their usual gold, Taliah wandered over, her raven braids swinging as she clapped.

The demons scattered at her approach, and she leaned against the wooden trough filled with fresh spring water. She assessed my mood with pursed lips. "I take it something happened while you were away gallivanting in Gaia?"

I shot her a warning look as I jumped from the ring, stalking to the bathing hut to rinse off the blood and grime. As I passed the healing tent, the hushed whispers died off, and the demons glared at my retreating back.

Not that I cared about any of the creatures here. The disgust was mutual.

Unruffled by my mood, Taliah entered behind me. Her dark eyes trailed over my bruised and filthy chest, silently judging my actions in the ring.

But I didn't require a lecture.

I stripped my pants and stepped into a metal tub, my breath hissing out as I touched a tender area near my thigh. "Like what you see?" I gritted out through my teeth, knowing it would irritate her and distract her from questioning me further.

She lurched forward and punched me in my shoulder, my breath stuttering out at the sharp pain. "Don't you dare speak to me that way, Killian Infernos. You're not the Lord of the Realm yet. Now, stop moaning and tell me what's happened."

I suppressed a laugh. Taliah and I had met during my early days in Satan's Court when we were both mere children, starved for both nurturing and comfort. We bonded over our mutual love of fighting and revenge.

Regardless of our similarly murky parentage, we rose in the ranks together until we forced the other demons to respect us. Unlike me, Taliah was far more deserving of her ascension. Had I not possessed Satan's blood, I would have never escaped the fighting pits.

Often, I wondered which was the worse fate.

Ice-cold water trailed over me, and I grimaced, more discomforted by her knowing eyes than my shriveling skin. "Nothing new with my father. Just more orders to reap souls in his last vestiges of power over me. I'm meeting a new contact in Gaia tomorrow night to discover who has been making ill-advised pacts," I trailed off, smiling ruefully. "The Scourge never sleeps, as you well know."

Taliah's eyes flashed with fury as the poisonous barbs slipped past her lips after a quick glance to ensure we were alone. "He is a rat bastard. He pretends your succession was a surprise when our realm has followed the traditions of the original fallen for over a millennium. Why must he hold you accountable for something you had no say in?"

My father may be Satan, but he wasn't the original Fallen. Like a mantle passed down through the bloodline, Satan was a moniker, a means to hold the power of the seraphim who had absconded from the Beyond all those years ago.

Now, the line had reached its end with my father's beloved wife and true born children dying off in petty civil battles. All he had left was a bastard begotten from a demoness he used to diminish his grief. Whom he had relished torturing for birthing me in secret.

Taliah looked as if she would continue arguing with me, but her lips snapped shut. "Where are you going? Back to New Orleans?"

I wrapped a towel around my hips. "With Carreau on the Council, it makes it easier for me to do my job. Not to mention the pre-established safeties in place to remain discreet. I'm meeting her at a bar called Low Road. It's in neutral territory outside of the Council's boundaries."

"Be cautious, Killian. Peace in Gaia is precarious, and you have much to lose." Taliah crossed her arms, her face stiffened from the mention of Carreau. "He is as bad as your father, his own self-interest fueling the deals he makes on behalf of our people with the Council. He'll do whatever the witches or vampires tell him, and he'll do so with a smile. We cannot consider Carreau a loyal ally."

The fragile bond between Hell and Gaia stood intact so long as the demons did nothing to interfere with their laws or cause human detection. One wrong move could spell destruction to that peace.

I nodded, redressing quickly so I could escape to my rooms

We stalked back towards the keep, my exhausted body crying out at the steep flight back to the castle entrance. Desperate to collapse into my bed after the long day, I almost missed the newcomers.

"Who are they?"

Taliah's eyes grew stormy once more, her hands clenched against the railing. Looking down at the cliff side road leading into the castle gates, she gritted out, "New recruits. Your father continues to force villagers into joining his armies. He has stretched his reach to the Isle of Remembering to find demons with battle skill fit enough to his liking." Noting the young women and children with lean bodies, her lips curled with disgust. "There are some who he intends to train or keep for the city's pleasures."

And I thought the demon lord couldn't fall any lower in my esteem.

"They look young," I muttered, noting the gaunt faces and malnourished bodies struggling to hold their packs and hulking weaponry.

"At least they will eat better here than in their villages."

The realm's misbalanced wealth spread far and wide. Watching the hunger and hope in the young demons' eyes made my chest pang with remembered emotions. I, too, had entered those golden gates, assuming my life would change for the better after my mother's death. But then I discovered Satan's true nature, and all my hopes withered like ashes in the wind.

I cleared my suddenly thick throat. "I'll call you tomorrow if I need any help."

"Consider it done, my friend."

No longer able to stomach another moment in this realm, I flashed away from Hell back to Gaia. My splashy townhome along a quiet street in the French Quarter was an extravagance I kept secret from even Taliah.

The brick home adorned with black shutters kept curious eyes away and had been my sanctuary in the years since becoming the Scourge, paid for with the gold I earned in my mercenary jobs. Not sparing a glance at the sparse living room or kitchen, I kicked off my boots, lamenting the mud stains I would need to clean from the hardwood in the morning.

Living in muck for most of my life cured me of any desire to live in filth, and I took pride in keeping my home immaculate.

I whipped off my shirt and hobbled up the creaking steps to the loft bedroom overlooking the vacant street below. It was currently empty of tourists who would soon flock to the city and disrupt my peace with lit-up Hand Grenades and drunken shouts.

Not that I would be here to experience it, I realized with a deepening frown. This oasis was one of many personal luxuries I was soon to lose with my succession.

Too exhausted to strip down further or down a quick demon brew that would suppress painful nightmares, I collapsed onto my fresh, silky sheets with a muffled groan.

I would pay for my fighting tomorrow, but for now, I let the aches pull me into a deep, troubled sleep where I definitely didn't dream about the witch smirking at me with a humorous sparkle in her eyes before pulling me down for a lush kiss.

5

EMBER

With a nervous gust of breath, I placed the final black candle along the edge of my salt circle. I stepped back to admire my handiwork and felt reluctant pride at my efforts. The circle was neat and perfectly ordered with black obsidian and salt to protect me from the demon I sought to summon. He wouldn't be easily manipulated, and he would definitely be furious at my actions. If not downright murderous.

I fought a gleeful grin at the thought.

After spending the afternoon brewing spelled tonics for our birth control and weaving dried herb bundles to be sold at the Samhain festival, I had finally worked up the courage to find the spell for a demonic summoning in our family grimoire.

The spells copied from our ancestors' ancient tomes spanned throughout the centuries. They described rites for ritualistic sex and ceremonial magicks, hexes and curses that made the hairs on the back of my neck stick up with fear, as well as the more basic folk herb recipes for a witch's everyday comforts.

I had waited until Jade grew distracted with Isla's homework to steal a picture of the incantation and ingredients before making my preparations.

With the girls out of the house on an evening coffee run, I knew it was now or never to act on my plan to uncover Rosalind's murder, and therefore win the respect and freedom I craved.

Bolstered by my motivations, I crushed a handful of dried sage leaves with a few drops of moon water in my mortar and pestle. I glanced over the spell one more time for good measure before I sliced my silver serpent athame dagger across my fingertip, dripping a few drops of my blood into the slimy concoction.

While my fire magick remained volatile and unreliable, a basic spell casting shouldn't be too much of a strain. Just in case, I stored a fire extinguisher near my bed for such emergencies.

With a grimace, I spread the mixture over the small handkerchief I once stole from the demon for such an auspicious occasion.

Who even carried handkerchiefs anymore?

Spine steeled, I turned off my overhead lights, the room plunging into darkness with only the flickering flames around my circle to see. I clutched the handkerchief and my fire opal charm bracelet—the mystical talisman that harnessed my fire magick—that emanated a warm glow as I chanted the spell.

Ego te daemonium
Ingredere in gyrum meum et alligatus factus est mihi
'Non nocere vel malitiae
Ego te voco

The vowels rolled off my tongue and my eyes drifted closed as I repeated the spell, my mind envisioning Killian's glowering face. The surrounding energy shifted into an oppressive and inky jet, curling around my face like smoke.

I brought the handkerchief to the flame of the candle in front of me and let the fire burn the edges, the smell of brimstone and pine wafting through the air.

There was a moment of calm. The room emptied of sound, with only the void surrounding me. Then, the space between planes opened with an audible crack to allow the demon inside my sacred space. When he appeared, the room snapped back, the void closing behind him like a locked door, trapping him within the line of salt and flame until I allowed him to leave.

Silence greeted me, and I narrowed my eyes at the empty circle before me. "I know you're there, demon. No sense hiding in your shadows all night."

Killian appeared in a blink, spinning around the circle, his sharp fangs gleaming with malice as if wakening from a nightmare. For a moment, his demonic form appeared, his horns and wings flickering in the candlelight before disappearing back into the shadow dimension.

I didn't get a good look, but from what I saw, he was *magnificent*.

His eyes were tired, his hair haphazard, and I realized he had been asleep. My eyes dipped to his bare chest, and I gulped with unbidden desire. *Goddess, he was fit.* All bulk and muscles he hid beneath his shadows.

Surprisingly, his lips curled at my hungry gaze, our eyes locked in a heated standoff before he seemed to awaken. All softness snapped away as he took in my chaotic bedroom and my summoning circle with a snarl.

The promise of violence in his eyes as he stepped forward caused goosebumps to break out over my heated skin. Realizing my spell trapped him, he stepped back from the circle's edge. "Foolish witch. You don't know how dead you are."

His voice was as silky and rough as I remembered, his face more alluring in the darkness as anger transformed it. He reminded me of one of my favorite quartz crystals—hard lines and edges that could be off-putting upon first glance, but you couldn't help but feel mesmerized and lean closer for a second look. His slightly crooked nose was another unspoken tell of a violent youth if the silver scar on his cheek wasn't enough of a sign. Though he kept his shiny raven hair to his collar to hide the flesh of his cheek, it peeked through when he shook his head in frustration.

But I hadn't summoned him here to ogle his impressive form. I cleared my throat, my anger rising to the surface. He was not the innocent victim in this situation and had he been free, I would lay dead in a pool of my blood.

I must never forget what he was and what he was capable of.

"I believe what you mean to say is how may I service you, daughter of Hecate?" Smirking at him, I enjoyed the fume seeping from his pores. "Unless you have lost your sense of sight or whatever limited brain capacity resides in that thick skull of yours, you're in *my* circle, demon. To do with as I please."

I held out his handkerchief, waving it in front of him like a bull. "You should be careful how easily you allow witches to steal a personal item. It's sloppy demon-ing."

His eyes bled with black as his demon came out to play. When he next spoke, his voice was rougher, mirroring the monster within him. "I know that once I deny you the deal you seek to make, you will be mine to do with as I see fit. And I don't take kindly to surprise summonings from spoiled witches."

A serpent grin flashed across my face. "I'll make it quick

then. I'm sure you've heard about the death at last night's party. What conclusions have you come to?"

"Conclusions about the murder?"

I fought an eyeroll at his false obtuseness. "Yes, demon. About the murder. Do you have any professional opinions, considering killing is kind of in your job description?"

He glared at me, looking as if he wished he could squash me under his boot like an insect. "I don't kill my targets unless they deserve to die. If you're accusing me of something, get on with it."

I straightened, my eyes hardening at the half-remembered memory through the Fae wine haze of the night before. When it popped into my mind, crushing disappointment had sought to drown me. "I saw you with Rosalind."

His eyes narrowed to slits. "I don't know what you're referring to."

Lie.

Facing off against each other, I stared into the black depths of Killian's eyes and silently pleaded with him not to be the monster who slashed Rosalind and left her in a field like trash. We enjoyed our verbal battles, but beneath our pointed insults, I never considered him to be a stone-cold killer.

Not really. At least not of anyone who was innocent.

But now, I wasn't so sure.

"I find it curious that after you pull her away from her shifter lover, she ends up slain in the grass like some sort of pagan sacrifice."

"You would know about those, witch," be bit back.

"Merely stating the facts. You slunk from your shadows and pulled a shifter male away from two vampire females before disappearing. One of those females was Rosalind Vasilyev, who is now dead. Seems suspicious."

I strode forward, fire blazing in my hands as my magick sparked to life, a tell of the rising emotion inside of me. I knew

I needed to cool it before I set the house on fire, but my mind was past logical thought as I approached him.

His gaze dipped to my fingers before his gaze returned to mine, lips thinned.

"Did you have anything to do with the murder of the vampire at last night's Bacchanal? Answer truthfully." I imbued as much authority as I could muster. The call of my magick and the circle's charms would prevent him from causing harm, but it was the powdered calamus root sprinkled into the salt ring deterring the demon from speaking deceptions.

"No," he gritted out, bound by my spell. "I didn't touch her, nor did I order another to do so. Happy now, witch?"

"Actually, yes." I puffed out my cheeks, unwilling to admit why I felt a rush of immense relief he wasn't a psycho killer.

He sucked in a ragged breath, his eyes returning to their molten caramel as he leashed his demon before my eyes. He had more control over the beast inside of him than any other demon I had come across.

I rubbed my hands together, feeling almost euphoric at this turn of events. "Now, we can move on to the fun part of the night's business."

He stared at me for a beat before his glacial expression melted into the sly amusement I had grown to know well. "Are you planning on attempting to seduce me again?"

Though his words were teasing, his eyes roamed over my black leggings and velvet halter top with unbidden desire. He realized he was staring at my tits at the same moment I did, and he looked away. But not fast enough.

"No seduction plans tonight." I grinned. "Tonight, you and I are going to make a deal."

He stared blankly before bursting into surprised laughter.

It wasn't a typical display of emotion for the demon, yet it made him even more attractive, sending a pulse of my heat through me.

He crossed his arms, highlighting his bulging biceps. "I believe I already told you my answer on that front. But in case the brain inside your skull is not following our conversation, the answer is no."

Stumped, I studied my nails, the picture of nonchalance, though my insides were churning with uncertainty. This was not my most well-thought-out plan.

If I let him leave this circle without a bargain struck, I would be in serious shit. Having to tell Jade I not only summoned a demon but fucked it up and needed help to protect the family from his wrath made me feel physically sick.

I didn't expect Killian to cause us any physical harm, but one couldn't be too careful. He *was* a mercenary warrior for Hell, after all.

"There must be something you want. I'm the granddaughter of the High Priestess, and I have many connections in the city. We could make it an equal exchange."

He watched me with a strange expression crossing his face. "And what do you want badly enough to summon a demon?"

"Easy—help me find who killed Rosalind, so I can win the reward from Prince Alexei. Oh, and of course, vow not to harm me or my family." I added the last part under my breath, and he appeared offended at the tacked-on forethought about his violent tendencies.

But then his face grew sharp with anger. "You are not to get involved with this murder, witch."

"And who are you to give me orders?" I demanded, my hands pressed over my hips.

His eyes grew predatory, as if realizing how much he wanted to give me orders. In bed.

Unfortunately, his irritation with me was stronger than his lust. "This will be dangerous. Creatures from across the city will attempt to win the prize, and I promise you they won't care about who gets harmed. Without your magick, you will be defenseless."

My excitement dwindled to icy fear as his words hit me like a slap across the face. "How do you know about that?"

He frowned, further illuminating the deep planes of his handsome face. "Everyone in the city knows, witch. Though immortal, supernatural beings have nothing better to do than gossip."

Wonderful. Not only was I fighting against my Coven's perception of me, but the entire city knew about my magick issues. It couldn't get any more humiliating.

My cheeks flushed, and I fought the urge to press my hands against them. I steeled my resolve, more determined than ever to win the amulet. "I'm going to find the killer with or without you, so are you in or not?"

A risk. I held my breath as I watched him consider me.

After a long beat of silence, he muttered, "No deal, witch."

I fought my instant rage. If he would not help me, I would find someone who would.

"Begone demon. Leave my circle and return to whence you came." I waved my hand, expelling him from the circle with bitter disappointment before he could utter another word.

We stared at each other from across the boundary, and my breath caught in my throat.

How was he still here?

His smile was slow to come, but when it did, it spread wide across his stony face. "Wrong decision, little witch. Now, we play by my rules."

I gaped as he stepped over the edge of my circle, smudging the line of salt with a disdainful kick.

Perhaps I should have read the spell through instead of skimming the actual summoning bits.

Oh, I was in so *much Goddess-damned trouble.*

6

KILLIAN

I spread out over the witch's dark floral comforter, my hands resting behind my pounding head, watching her glance between me and the bedroom door, her legs tensing to run for it.

"I'll only follow you," I warned her, fighting an eyeroll at her dramatics.

The room was not what I expected from the wild party witch. The southern charm of the historic Queen Anne-style home remained intact, with the original hardwood floors cracking ominously underfoot. There was a hint of smoking sage bundles and incense in the air, with an overwhelming number of crystals of various sizes and colors stacked along most surfaces.

It was cozy, and undeniably the home of a family of witches.

A witch I was in no mood to play nice with.

"Now," I drawled, "we're going to talk this out like calm, logical creatures and then, you're going to stay out of this murder business."

Fire flared in her eyes, and her feet shifted away from the door to square off against me. "Get out of my bed, demon."

"I thought you wanted me in your bed?"

Her cheeks grew flushed as her hands shook, her fingers sparking with fire once more. "Will I never live that night down? It was one stupid mistake after enough Yaeger bombs to kill a mortal. A mistake I don't plan on repeating. So, move on and get out of my house."

By the end of her tirade, she was pulling me by my legs, intent on dragging me away.

The memory of the night in question lingered in my mind, erasing all my good humor. I inhaled sharply and moved away from her, leaning against her antique dresser scattered with fragrant perfume oils and bright, eclectic jewelry. Feeling more collected, I asked, "Why don't we return to the topic at hand? Why do you care so much about this female's death? And don't tell me you want the vampire's reward because I'll tell you now, it will be something you'd be better off not possessing."

Her eyes darted, revealing the inner workings of her strange mind.

Oh, she wanted that reward. Badly enough to put herself at risk.

She took a deep breath, looking as if she already regretted her next words. "I want my family to get off my back about how I choose to live my life. If I can earn my Coven's respect despite my love of Fae wine and wild sex, then my life will be much easier."

At the mention of sex, the air inside the bedroom became thick with tension. The heated chemistry between the two of us was undeniable. Even I could admit to it, though I was loath to.

I wanted to learn her luscious body, explore all the ways I could make her scream into the night with pleasure. My eyes dipped to her pouty lips before shaking free from her spell. Gods, I needed to put this attraction behind me before I acted any more foolish than I already had.

"I am not overstating when I tell you this will become dangerous. And trust me, the amulet will not be an asset in proving your worth to your Coven."

Pain glittered in her eyes before she hid it. "Oh yes, because you know so much about witches and our way of life. Don't condescend to me. You underestimate my determination and what I'm willing to do in order to win."

I looked her over with a raised brow, stepping closer to feel the heat of her skin. "And what is that? Kiss them to death? Challenge them to a beer pong competition?"

We were now toe to toe, her chest heaving as we faced off.

I shouldn't antagonize her like this, but she looked so lovely when she was furious that I couldn't resist. My eyes followed the curving dips of her body and lingered on the swirls of green swimming within the blue of her eyes. An ocean I wanted to lose myself within and never recover from.

Her breath panted out as she leaned closer. "What will I do to win? I'll simply do this," she whispered, before blowing a handful of salt into my face. "Begone, demon!"

For a moment, I froze in shock before I coughed, wiping the white dust off my face and chest. "Really, witch?" My anger simmered. Her lack of knowledge would one day get her hurt. Sooner rather than later, at this rate. "Do you know nothing about demons?"

She huffed, stalking away from me towards her circle as if I were in the wrong. "I figured it was worth a shot."

I shook my head in disbelief. She was confounding, especially when in the next breath, she grabbed her serpent athame dagger from the floor and attempted to stab me in the heart with it.

Dematerializing into a cloud of shadow, I reappeared behind her, grasping her hand to dislodge it as my other hand gripped her neck.

She stomped down on my foot, her heeled boots stabbing

into my toes, as she elbowed low against my gut. The sensitive wound from the fighting ring gave her the edge as she dislodged my grip, spinning around to kick my stomach.

I grabbed her leg and used her momentum to toss her to the floor, my thighs caging her squirming body, straddling her hips, as I yanked the dagger from her grip.

Without proper training with the weapon, she would only injure herself.

Before she could surge upward, I trapped her arms beneath mine. My demon grew far too excited at the threat of sex or violence. Possibly both.

Her small, supple body lay tense beneath mine, realizing that all her plans had failed.

My nose flared, catching her addictive scent. She smelled of spicy, caramelized peaches with hints of cinnamon and cardamom, an exotic dessert I wanted to consume.

"Do you surrender, witch?" I purred, my eyes beginning to flood with black at our current position.

"Not on your life, demon." Her lips curled into a brief, belligerent smile I wanted to kiss away.

I leaned closer to her, my ragged breath fanning across her cheek, lifting the sun-lightened tendrils of hair escaping her braid. "Did you actually believe you could best me? I'm a mercenary. A warrior of Hell with years of battle under my belt."

She stared up at the ceiling as her mouth tightened with frustration. "It's not like my sisters and I make a habit of socializing with your kind, so pardon me for my ignorance of Hell's inhabitants."

"*Your kind?*"

Saucy witch. I eased one hand away from her arm to grip the end of her braid, pulling on the strands to get her eyes back on mine. "Here's a brief lesson about *my kind*. Salt does little to harm me unless it's a part of a devious witch's spell. Now, are you finished sulking? I grow weary of tutoring uneducated daughters of Hecate."

She bit her lip as her eyes focused back on me, captivating me. Her freed hand lifted to a fallen tendril of dark hair that slipped into my eyes. She brushed it away tenderly. "You could always teach me more about demons while you help me find the killer."

I laughed low, the sound raspy from unuse. My eyes grew warm with amusement as I beheld her hopeful smile.

She may be an impulsive hell cat, but she had a fiery determination unlike any other creature I had met before. I found myself desperate for a taste of it.

My face transformed as hunger lit within her eyes. Staring at each other in silence, the moment grew heady, the months of suppressed lust and want rising to the surface in a fiery rush.

I leaned down until our lips hovered an inch apart.

Our breaths echoed in the quiet room as I fought with every ounce of my self-control not to give in, somehow knowing it would be the end of my life as I knew it.

The witch, unbidden by such issues, decided for me. Her lips met mine with a gasp, her hand twining in my hair and pulling me down to rest against her lush chest.

I froze for only a moment, my mind fighting against the allure of the soft laps of her tongue against my lip, begging for entrance as I luxuriated in her body beneath me.

She let out a small, impetuous sigh, and I knew it was over.

Groaning, I surrendered, helpless to deny her what I could provide. I gripped the witch's hips, pulling her lithe body closer to mine.

She moaned into my mouth, her legs parting to allow me into the warm cradle of her thighs, before wrapping them around me to hold me as a willing prisoner.

Her tongue tasted of spiced wine and wicked female as we fought each other for dominance.

My shadows curled around her wrist, yanking it away from my hair, and secured it with her other hand to the floorboards.

She bit down on my lip as punishment. Hard enough to draw a drop of blood.

I huffed a laugh. "Now, that's not very nice, witch."

She narrowed her eyes, struggling against my shadow's hold. Her little tongue reached out and licked away the blood and my body responded viciously.

Our lips collided again, battling each other. It was savage and a little clumsy, our need more important than practiced skill.

As we kissed, seconds or minutes could have passed. My hands explored her body, reaching beneath her to clutch her ass before following the smooth line of her back to better angle her body to mine. I let a finger trail to the curve of her breast, bulging beneath the confines of her top, toying with the flesh without giving her what she desired.

She pulled away from my mouth and bared her teeth, unwilling to be denied her pleasure.

I chuckled, my eyes dancing with mirth when a loud door slamming shut downstairs reached through our haze of lust.

Horror dawned as reality resurfaced. I released her hands at the shift in mood and stood, the fire between us extinguishing in a cold rush. I couldn't decide who I was more annoyed with—her or myself. "What the Hell was that, witch?"

"What are you talking about? You kissed me," she hissed, jumping up from her position on the floor.

I felt desire burn through me like acid, my demon responding to her unspoken call. My chest pounded as a sheen of sweat formed over my brow. Staggering, I caught myself on the edge of her dresser, her knickknacks clanging as the furniture tipped.

My demon clamored to explode out of me, and I fought it

with every ounce of strength I possessed, though it proved much stronger than ever before.

She gasped, glancing up at my horns with awe and slight alarm. "Killian?"

I narrowed my eyes, red hot rage replacing my overwhelming lust. "What spell did you put over me, witch?" I couldn't stop myself, my hands trailing over her arms, the need to feel her skin against me, all-consuming. "I am fucking *ravenous* for you."

Her eyes glazed over as my lips collided back to hers, biting at her lip with the confusing mix of emotions. I didn't know whether I wanted my kiss to soothe or hurt.

With my demon out of control for her, it made me think of Satan and his volatile emotions after losing his mate. *Mate.*

Panic surged through me, and I dragged myself away.

No, she couldn't be my mate.

Her hoarse voice reached past my wall of confusion. "I didn't put a spell over you."

The sound soothed and enticed, like melting chocolate. I curled my fingers into fists to avoid reaching out for her once more. "*Liar*," I hissed.

There was no other explanation for my blood heating into a molten river as I beheld her face. The need coursing through me was impossible to deny. She *had* to have hexed me.

"Remove your spell or I will make you pay the consequences."

"I didn't do anything," she insisted, her brows furrowing as uncertainty danced across her pretty face. "At least I don't *think* I did. I definitely didn't mean to."

I scoffed. "Typical. The unaccomplished witch spells me and doesn't know how to fix her mistakes. Why am I not surprised?"

Her teeth ground together as my words found their mark. I

felt a moment of regret at the hurt in her eyes before I staunched it.

"I may be ignorant of demonic rules, but you underestimated the power of the daughters of Hecate if you found yourself summoned by one."

The sounds of footsteps came closer.

I needed to get away from her before I did something I regretted. Like drag her down to Hell with me and never let her go.

Viper-fast, I moved through my shadows, hulking over her as my fingers grazed over the wild pulse at her neck. Gripping her nape, I brought her face close to mine. "Don't worry. I don't make the same mistakes twice. The next time I find you, you better have a better answer than *I don't know*."

I released her before I did something idiotic like kiss her again.

As I portaled away to Hell, I felt as if slavering, fanged Hell Hounds were on my trail. But one thought rose to the fore of my frenzied mind—why was it so difficult to leave the witch behind if there *wasn't* a spell at play?

7

EMBER

Throughout the night, I paced around my room. Every creak or groan sent me further into the depths of despair. After the girls had gone to bed, I had lingered outside their doors, biting my nails with fear over their safety. All because I couldn't control my impulses.

When I couldn't bear the confines of my room any longer, I crept downstairs and settled into my father's leather reading chair. The lingering scent of parchment and his favorite tobacco flower cologne was long gone, but whenever I closed my eyes, I could almost picture him here once more, his bespectacled eyes following my mother as she brewed sun tea in the kitchen with a book in her hand.

Usually, it brought me comfort to sit here, but tonight, I only felt doom.

When the sun brightened the darkness with warm orbs of light, I unfolded my sleep-deprived body, groaning at the cracks and pops as I stretched. I could hear Jade already moving around upstairs, so I wandered into the kitchen to brew some much-needed coffee.

I was pouring my second cup when Jade hurried down the stairs, dressed for her training at the estate with Grandmother.

She missed the last step as she noticed my eerie presence hunched over the kitchen counter, the dark circles under my eyes making me look like a phantom. "You scared the crap out of me," she gasped, her eyes taking in my appearance with a wrinkled brow. "Trouble sleeping again? Did you take your tonic?"

My night terrors began in the days following our parents' deaths. When I closed my eyes, all I could see was my parents' mangled bodies laid strewn across the grass. My dreams tormented me with visions of my mother's wide, lifeless eyes staring up at me and my father's mangled boot, twisted as if he fought to save my mother with every last ounce of energy he had.

Wearied, I forced myself back into the present and wrapped the well-worn wool blanket closer to my chilled body. "Are you leaving soon?"

Jade poured herself a mug of coffee and pulled out a packet of oatmeal, leaning against the counter. "Yeah, after I drop off some supplies at Get Hexed. Why? Did you want to come with?"

I topped off my mug, ignoring Jade's concerned frown. "No. I'm going to hang around the house today and clean. Maybe go out with Fleur later tonight."

It wasn't a lie. I needed to find another way to win this reward if Killian would not be useful. Fortunately, I knew where I needed to go.

Jade sighed, turning back to her breakfast. "Maybe you should lay off the alcohol for a while. Last night could've gone a lot differently had it been you wandering off alone."

My cheeks heated with shame and indignation. How I dealt with my trauma was my business, but I understood Jade's fears. "If someone wanted to kill me, they could do it whether I was sober or wasted. I have everything under control."

"Fine. Do what you want." She picked up her bag and

stuffed it with her supplies. "Tell Audra to meet me at the library after lunch."

Without another word. she slammed the door behind her.

I winced as the door rattled, echoing through the kitchen.

I was who I was. Jade would never understand. But maybe with my magick under control, everything would change for the better.

My coffee turned bitter on my tongue, but I forced myself to work on preparations for tonight's adventure. This time, I would not leave the house until I had a solid plan in place. Especially when I knew my intended snooping grounds would be rife with supernatural activity.

Regardless of the risks, the amulet would be mine, no matter how dangerous it turned out to be.

<hr />

Perched on a high-top table, I watched the crowd with intrigue as I sipped on a glass of cheap Chardonnay. Low Road's appeal factored in its location outside of Council territory and seclusion from the mortals within city limits. Unfamiliar creatures mingling with sweltering glasses of alcohol watched the TV screens broadcasting supernatural sports games or the pretty nymphs dancing near the DJ stand.

To my dismay, I caught sight of some of the Boudreaux pack playing pool and shooting darts at the rear of the bar where the patio opened to the Mississippi River.

I did my best to remain unseen, my face growing flushed with anxiety at the confrontation that would unfold. To say Wren and I left things on a sour note would be an understatement. The pack hated my guts out of loyalty to him and their distaste for witches.

After slinking in my chair for a few more minutes, I grew frustrated. I would learn nothing about Rosalind's killer hiding in my chair all night. I downed my glass and jumped down, aiming for the rowdy group of shifters.

There was no time like the present to rip off the band-aid and let this wound heal.

My heeled boots clacking on the sticky concrete floors announced my presence before the wolves scented me. With one whiff, the pack growled low, their eyes stalking my approach with enough malice to make me second guess my impulsive decision.

"Howdy, guys. Fancy seeing you here tonight."

Most of the group were wolves I knew after years spent on the pack lands deep in the bayou. Their roguish, rough charm made immortal—and mortal—hearts pound, and that was before the wolves spoke in their drawling Cajun accents, tempting even the coldest of hearts.

I nodded to the unsmiling males with false cheer. "Brent, Travis, Aaron, what's up?"

Like Wren, his closest pack members were the sons of other high-ranking wolves in the pack. Of the three, Aaron was the only one to offer me a small smile. "Evening, Cher. Good seeing you again."

Brent and Travis shot him cool looks before the two sneered down at me, their eyes flashing yellow with their beasts. A warning.

"Leave. Before things get outta hand," Travis growled.

Aaron bit his lip, beseeching me with his eyes to follow orders considering Travis's mood, but I was never good at playing submissive.

I perched myself on the pool table, my long legs crossing to display my smooth skin. "There's no need to be rude, wolf. I'm here to ask you guys a few questions."

Travis snorted, his eyes trailing across my body with equal parts desire and disgust. "Da answer is no, saloppe; we won't be fucking you again. Dat answer your question?"

The wolves howled with laughter, the Cajun insult flying over my head.

As other patrons shifted their eyes to us with curiosity, my nails dug into the wood below me. I forced myself to smile; the southern woman's defensive. "I've already fucked you, Travis, and it wasn't worth a repeat."

The smile wiped clear from his face, and he growled low, his chest rumbling with fury. "You sure screamed out a lot dat night. Den again, you also fucked Wren, Aaron, and Brent, so who's to say you had feeling 'tween your legs after dat ride?"

My cheeks heated with embarrassment—not at my actions, but at the callous words he'd spoken loud enough for the entire bar to hear. I was not ashamed of my sexual experiences, though many resulted from drunken nights seeking to disappear from my grief.

Aaron pushed in between Travis and me, his auburn locks falling into his eyes as he tried to diffuse the tension. "Just leave it, ami. Ember, say your peace, den go before it gets heated."

I forced my lips to curl into a smile, refusing to let them see Travis's words got to me.

He was right; this wasn't a social call.

I leaned back onto the table, licking my lips. "I have questions about the night of the Bacchanal." Not missing the quick glances they shot each other, I perked up. "I know the Council already questioned y'all, but do you have any insight that would help me find her attacker?"

Aaron's eyes shuttered with worry. "I don't know if you should mess around in dis, Em."

Travis rolled his eyes. "Who cares? One less witch would make da world a better place."

I stood from my perch on the pool table, my eyes glowing with fire as I stalked towards the irritating wolf who had gotten on my last nerve. "Say it again, Travis."

Brent, silent until now, pulled my arm, dragging me away from the table before we caused a scene. His black eyes glared down at me, and his claws tore the fabric of my dress. Leaning down to my ear, he hissed, "Get out of here before you explode something. And stay da fuck out of dis investigation or you're going to get your ass hurt. And not in da way you like."

He shoved me away, and I stumbled in my heeled boots.

The bar watched me with varying looks of pity and fear, and I realized my hands were sparking from my emotional outburst.

Fucking Hell. I glanced over to the back patio doors and rushed towards them, seeking an escape. The night air hit my heated cheeks, and I leaned forward, my hands braced on my knees as I fought to breathe. The salty air calmed my mind, my heartbeat slowing as I watched the quiet murky water below, crickets chirping a soothing sound.

I hadn't been so close to a public panic attack in months. Maybe Aaron and the others were right. Maybe I didn't have what it took to solve this case.

A quiet moan broke me out of my self-pity, and I looked over to the shadowed corner of the patio where a male caged in a female who writhed in his arms with delight.

Lucky girl. I wanted nothing more than a bottle of red and a night of getting my world rocked after the weekend I had.

I glanced back inside the bar window for a moment, torn.

When the male stiffened, sensing their private moment interrupted, I called out an apology.

I paused with my hands grasping the door handle, not ready to face the crowd once more.

With an annoyed curse, I turned back to the dark corner

and froze. A cold sweat formed on my brow with growing horror and more than a little jealousy as glowing amber eyes stared back at me in surprise.

Oh, *shit*.

8

KILLIAN

Low Road was busy for a weekday night. I pulled my baseball hat low on my head, wanting to stay under the radar. I took in the crowd, grimacing when I noticed the werewolves playing pool, their eyes trained on the comely nymphs. They could become a problem if they knew I was behind one of their brethren's recent disappearance.

Instead of walking through the bar to the outdoor patio, I exited and slipped into my shadows, circling around the brush to remain undetected. From the corner of the enclosed patio, I could see my contact walk into the bar, her sheer, gauze-like dress hiding little in the low lighting.

The night air held a bite. It felt nowhere near as chilled as Pride, but a foreshadowing of the colder weather Louisiana would soon have.

Amarisa perched herself on the wooden gate overlooking the Mississippi, and I closed in. Her knees widened, an invitation for me to get closer, but I held my ground a short distance away. She trailed a finger down my chest as the moonlight brushed over her luminous skin, highlighting her curves like a gentle lover. "Looking good tonight, Killian."

I caught her hand before it could move down to my trousers. "Were you seen?"

She simpered, her teeth dragging through her glossy lips. "Oh, I am often seen. How could I not be?" She gestured to her beautiful dress and body. "But the supernaturals here know to be discreet, considering I know every powerful creature in this city."

From the gleam in her eyes, I knew she had her hands in the pants of many across New Orleans. An asset when one wanted to uncover secret dealings behind the scenes.

She continued with a spark in her lavender eyes. "If the Scourge has deigned to seek my company, I knew it must be serious indeed."

I stiffened at the use of my moniker. It appeared my reputation was well-known past the gates of Hell. My stomach sunk with a sickening twist at the thought of what else she may be privy to.

"Have you heard any news about the recent murder at the Bacchanal?" she asked, twirling a strand of pale pink hair around her finger.

"Murder?" I feigned ignorance.

Her pale eyes grew wet with unshed tears. "Rosalind Vasilyev, the vampire prince's cousin. They found her with her neck severed."

"And was anyone taken by the Council for questioning?"

Indignation diffused her sorrow. "Oh, the Council moved swiftly and diligently, but it appears they are at a loss. A grand reward is being offered by the Vampire Court for the identity of the killer, which only shows how little information they have."

Hm. It did not surprise me the Council had little information. Though they pretended to hold leadership over the city, it only took one evening under the veil to discover the seedy underbelly. But the nymph's emotions surprised me. "This seems personal to you."

Her expression tightened as she glanced around the empty patio. "It's not just the vampire who has died under suspicious circumstances. A few years ago, there were unsolved murders. Two witches, a vampire, a shifter, and a Fae. All creatures who belonged to prominent families of Council members. They covered the deaths up out of fear of human discovery or appearing weak to the community. Now, I fear the killings have begun once more. The vampire's death is the same manner as the prior killings."

I held back my disbelief at her tale. The odds of the same killer waiting years to murder again were slim. Shaking my head, I put aside the new tidbit for later. "I doubt Rosalind's death had anything to do with the Council. An ex-lover or domestic dispute, I'm guessing. Now, do you have a name for me?"

My next target would need to be quickly dispatched to keep my father's temper balanced. His threat still lingered in my mind, and I would not allow his revenge on Gaia.

"If you say so, Killian." She pouted and leaned back, putting her ample breasts on display. "You know nothing in this world is free. What will you give me for it?"

I pulled the stack of cash and a single black rose from Satan's Garden from my bag. A priceless gift. "Will this suffice?"

She brought the inky petals to her nose, the fragrance unlike any flower on the mortal plane, rich and seductive and yet still sweet. Her eyes crinkled with innocent delight. "This will suffice, in addition to a kiss. To seal the deal."

"Fine," I sighed with irritation. "But I want the name and location first."

She leaned in with a sly glance, her lips brushing against the shell of my ear. "Wren Boudreaux is part of the shifter pack. You'll find him at Tony's Riverboat Casino—a supernatural harbor boat docked on the edge of town and bespelled to remain invisible to the humans."

My brows furrowed at the knowledge that my second target this month belonged to the Boudreaux pack living along the bayous. The wolves who socialized with a certain witch I sought to avoid.

It begged the question—why was the pack making deals with demons when they claimed to despise us?

"Are the wolves acting beyond the Council? I find it hard to believe Hunt would let such a thing happen under his nose."

"Hunt grows weary of pretending to play nice with the others. Unlike witches and vampires, all they can offer is muscle, which means their people are often on the line. His seat on the Council and the benefits it affords him are the only reasons he hasn't gone rogue."

It wasn't much information to go on, but at least I had a task—something to take my mind away from the dreams keeping me awake each night. And my impending nightmare in Hell.

"Thank you for your information. I hope we can continue to do business together." I handed her the cash, which she slid inside her purse alongside her flower which she weaved into her hair.

She perked up and wrapped her arms and legs around me like a tree. "Now for my kiss."

I fought an eyeroll and leaned in, prepared to give her a simple, close-mouthed kiss and return to the bar to spy, but the nymph was stronger than she looked.

Her lips pressed into mine, her tongue searching, despite my stiffening shoulders. She moaned as she crushed my body to hers.

It wasn't a bad kiss. I had suffered through far worse as a lad. Any other night, a willing, beautiful female would be easy fodder to fuck some of the tension away. While others fought for a chance to lie with such a being, I found the risk outweighed the rewards. A nymph who could be bought would sell my secrets in a heartbeat, and I had far too many of those.

"Oh. Sorry to interrupt." An all-too familiar voice broke through my mind's wanderings.

I pulled away from Amarisa and turned back to find the witch.

Her eyes widened with alarm as she realized who stood before her. With a squeak, she fled, disappearing into the loud bar without a glance back.

I extricated myself from the nymph's grip, my face hardening with a wave of inexplicable anger and regret. Why should I care that she caught me with another when she had done far worse to me?

Amarisa caught my arm, her pink hair swirling around her face in the wind. "Be careful. The witch may seem inexperienced, but her power is immense."

I stifled an aggravated groan. "You be careful, too. These are dangerous times," I told the nymph as I walked back into the light, eager to find the witch.

She smiled, a flash of white in the darkness. "Always am, Killian. Always am."

🌙

When Ember noticed my presence, she groaned low, slamming her bedroom door shut behind her. She ignored me as she disappeared into the adjoined bathroom.

With a flourish, I moved from the bed and watched from the door frame as she twisted the groaning metal faucet of her clawfoot tub. Lavender and eucalyptus filled the air from the bewitched salts she dumped into the steaming water.

She turned her attention to me with a sullen frown. "What do you want, demon? It's been a long day, and I want to relax and get some sleep before work tomorrow."

"You work?" The skepticism in my voice had her shoulders stiffening.

"Yes," she bit out through her teeth. "I work at my Coven's storefront in the Quarter. Now, tell me what you want and leave."

I pursed my lips, refusing to portal back to my townhouse until I had this matter settled. I felt a strange need to explain my earlier actions, though I had no reason to. Her spell at work, no doubt. "Have you discovered a means to undo your spell?"

Arms crossed, she hissed, "First, there isn't a spell. Second, if there was a spell, there is no way in Hell I could have discovered a way to break such a complex cast in less than twenty-four hours. Now, go find the dirty hole you crawled out of or you're getting a show."

I ground my teeth. "I'm not leaving here until we've settled this."

"Fine."

She didn't spare me another glance as she undressed, unbothered by my silent gawking. Turning to face the tub, she unhooked her lacy black bra, the flash of pale skin seizing my attention.

My feet shuffled before I trained my eyes on the wall above the tub, her perfect body a distraction I couldn't afford. I heard her dip a toe in the water to test the temperature before she sank into the tub, sighing at the effects of the salts on her body.

My body grew tense at the small sound.

The witch was bold. And devious.

I grew annoyed with her, and myself, as my body responded to hers. "Your spell is at work once more," I growled low.

She glanced over at my pants with an arched brow. "Or I'm devastatingly seductive and you can't help but fall prey to my beauty and charm. It's okay to admit you're smitten, demon. We're amongst friends here. Oh, wait. Never mind. It's embarrassing for you, after all."

Humor flashed through me before I could halt it. I cleared my throat, stepping closer to the tub. "I have a proposition for you, witch."

She peeked through her lashes, the bubbles and dried petals settling around her chest like gauze. "Are you suggesting we make a deal? After you denied me earlier?"

The idea had come to me after she fled from Low Road. With her spell still pervading my senses, riling my demon into thinking she was his, I needed to keep her safe. I could discover the villain behind the vampire's death and force her to remove her spell before my presence would be required in Hell.

Her spell remaining was not an option. "I'm willing to open up negotiations once more now that I have some stake in the terms."

She let out a snort. "And what would be your terms?"

"Same as before. I will help you find the creature behind the vampire's death if you remove your spell from me."

She hummed, her eyes far more scrutinous than I expected from her. "That's not the only reason you made a one-eighty here. Spill."

I bit back an irritated retort. "It was a mere rumor I heard tonight. About murders five years ago and how Rosalind's cause of death was similar."

Her voice puffed out on a shocked breath. "Creatures are saying it's connected?"

Interest perked through me. So the witch knew of these crimes too? Perhaps I had dismissed Amarisa's fears too soon. "Things have changed. If there's even a possibility of the rumors being true, New Orleans is more dangerous than before."

The witch grew pale, her body sinking lower in the water.

I paused at her harrowed expression, my demon clamoring inside of me to soothe her.

Her hands grasped a bar of soap, lathering herself over as a distraction from the troubling revelation. The air perfumed with magick, and I watched her with curiosity as her tells became clearer the more time I spent in her presence.

"And what's the cost of such a deal?"

My eyes darkened. "If you cannot remove your spell before the eve of Samhain, your soul will be mine as forfeit."

Her eyes grew wide before they hardened into slits. "I don't think so, demon. I'm not selling my soul like some maiden in a village signing the Devil's book in exchange for some goats."

I studied the rug at the base of the tub, my lips quirking with mischief. "Only Lucifer in the Realm of Wrath makes his contracts in the old ways. Our pact will be much more streamlined, with terms benefiting both parties."

"That still doesn't account for my soul being forfeit—whatever that means." She shook her head, sending droplets of water onto my pant legs. "No deal."

I leaned closer, my hands gripping the porcelain. "Either way, you're going to remove your spell. If I must threaten every member of your Coven to do it, so be it. This way, you at least get something out of it for yourself."

She swallowed, and I could sense her rising indecision. "Why my soul, though? Surely, you can understand my hesitation."

I sat back on my haunches, a kneeling brute next to this beautiful creature. "Because I don't trust you. Witches are known deceivers, using demons to do their dirty work for centuries. Your soul is collateral, so I know you'll make good on your promises."

"And what about demons' trustworthiness? You claim we have used demons for our own selfish desires, but the demons keep coming in droves, tricking mortals and creatures into their deceptive deals, sucking their souls dry like dementors."

My brows furrowed at her strange reference. "You have never made a deal with a demon before, so let me make myself clear. I'm sacrificing much by entering this pact with you. Your soul may be forfeited if you renege, but so is mine. If a demon does not complete the terms of the pact, you will have power over me, free to hex me further to your heart's content."

She settled back into the water, her fingers dancing along the surface as she considered my offer. "This is all moot if I haven't put a spell on you. If I did, I wouldn't know where to start in identifying it, let alone how to remove it."

Her shoulders dipped into the water, dispersing the bubbles. Her revealed body made my mouth water with desire.

My eyes narrowed, the irises flooding with black. "Believe me, the spell is there. It's making my demon consider you his. Waiting is not an option."

Shock and rising horror etched on her face as my words sunk in. "As in, the demon living inside you thinks I'm his mate?"

"Yes, so you can see why it is imperative you remove the spell."

Her brows furrowed as she realized the extent of the problem. She nodded her ascent with a hard look. "I will investigate the matter and do my best to remove the spell. But I have a stipulation."

I let out a raspy laugh. She was more impetuous than I first believed. "Of course you do, witch."

She washed the suds from her arms as she spoke, but I could sense her underlying apprehension. "You must vow to protect my sisters from harm. I don't want a single hair from their heads harmed in our mission. Do you understand?"

As if I had any reason to harm the witches in her home. "I vow it." My solemn words alone were as much of a pact as any bargain.

After a gulp of fear, she held out her arm, the smooth, wet skin glistening. "Okay, let's make a deal."

Not giving her a chance to change her mind, my silver dagger materialized from my shadows, and I sliced the blade down my palm before doing the same to hers.

She yelped in shock before her eyes grew wide at our hands joined in a morbid embrace.

There was a sizzle, a stab of pain as our blood mingled together.

Fire and ice.

Oil and water.

We were enemies, two creatures who, by the laws of nature, should never be together.

But I only held her hand tighter, my eyes razing over her face. "Repeat after me: I, Ember Belle, vow to remove the spell I placed before midnight on Samhain. In exchange, Killian will help me uncover the identity of the killer from the Bacchanal. If matters are resolved before the deadline, all previous terms are undone. If we do not meet the terms, the other's soul is forfeit."

She breathed through her nose before repeating the pact, her voice clear of any fear.

At her last whispered words, I felt it.

Brimstone and her spiced sugar scent filled my senses as our pact locked into place. The demon mark appeared on her bare forearm like a tattoo, the shape curling like a brand on her, claiming her as mine.

"The mark reflects my ties to the Realm of Pride," I told her, my voice catching at the sudden onslaught of feelings as our bond settled into place.

Her eyes met mine as the air between us shimmered, our

souls connecting and tying together, an irrevocable bond until the end of our pact.

Within my chest, I could feel her reaching towards me, the strange emotions calling to her. I stood, putting some distance between our physical bodies, though the closeness within our souls remained. "As part of our pact, we will sense each other. Powerful emotions, near-death experiences. Anything that could affect the terms of our bargain."

She shivered; her gaze fascinated as she turned her arm to better see her new marking. "It's strange. I can feel you, but it's through a fog."

"That's because I fortified my walls to keep curious witches out. I would urge you to do the same," I rasped. "The accepted bond confirms a spell exists."

She blanched, her emotions sparking from disappointment to grim acceptance through the bond.

My own frenzied thoughts sought a way to release the pressure. I stopped myself from snapping my fangs at her and turned to leave, but she stopped me with a delicate tug along the mental bond.

Her face was wearied, her eyes dull with panic. "This changes nothing, demon. We're still enemies."

A pulse of hurt radiated through my chest before reason returned, along with my anger.

"Don't worry, witch. I would never forget that fact."

9
EMBER

Get Hexed sat on a quiet block next to Jackson Square, its black awning and iron fencing both alluring and disturbing to mortals who wandered around with wide eyes and curious touches. Bundles of dried, fragrant herbs hung from the low ceilings, brushing against shoppers' heads as they ducked and descended the stairs. The space flickered with candlelight while the scent of burning incense could feel oppressive to outsiders.

As I looked around at the merchandise, I couldn't take much credit for the array of spelled bath and cosmetic products, alchemical elixirs and dusts, kitchen witchery cookbooks, or casting tools. My brief stint into the capitalization of my magick had sent customers screaming from the store, only to be caught and spelled by a panicked Jade to forget what they witnessed. As a result, they demoted me to cashier duty.

With the demon pact hidden under the sleeves of my lightweight sweater, my leg shook underneath the table. Jade had noticed my strange attitude this morning, so now I would buzz with nervous energy all day. I imagined the look on her face when she realized what her impulsive sister had done this time and felt sick.

I drummed my fingers on the countertop, and flipped through protective charms and tokens I gathered from a shelf to create witch's ladders for protection. As I glanced down at the family Book of Shadows, I strung branches of rowan wood with small crystals and iron nails. Despite Killian's promise, it would ease some of my anxiety, knowing the ladders—hidden somewhere inside my sisters' bedrooms—kept away creatures with ill intent.

At the sound of a whispered argument, I glanced up at the two human women, tourists by the strings of colorful Mardi Gras beads and the "I Heart NOLA" t-shirts with bedazzled Fleur de lis. They hovered over a table of smudge sticks and sage bundles as they gossiped about a mutual friend back home and the bad negative energy they planned to expel from her asshole boyfriend.

If only my problems could be smudged away.

Under the cash register, I moved my finger in a small circle, my magick trickling out to infuse the ladders, sealing the spell with a flash of orange, flickering light. It wasn't enough power to catch anything on fire, but enough to make the charms do their job.

The human women glanced over at me in mild disconcertment, seeking the strange flicker of flame once more.

I pasted on a fake smile and shrugged, casting my hand around the store with a laugh. "Just the friendly neighborhood shop ghost causing trouble again."

They tittered as if I had said something amusing.

No wonder we found it easy to blend with the mortals. The poor creatures had zero sense of self preservation. Most humans preferred to disbelieve the strange oddities they couldn't explain away through logic.

The bell pinged, announcing their hasty departure with no spending. As they walked through the invisible border of the shop, the spell to wipe memories of mystical sights shimmered as it did its work. Now, the women would only remember the quirky shop as eccentric.

Before I could settle into my coffee before the next tourist rush, Killian materialized beside me with without warning.

I jumped, shooting him an annoyed glare before I took in his outfit. He wore a loose white shirt with the sleeves rolled up to his elbows and leather trousers that hugged him in all the right places. His sword sat strapped to his chest, and his tousled hair smelled of his masculine pine scent. He looked as if he belonged atop a horse with a sword and shield, and *it was doing it for me.*

My brows lifted, not bothering to hide my ogling. "What is this, medieval times?"

He walked around the shop with his arms crossed, taking in the occult goods with curiosity. He poked at a basket stuffed with cloth voodoo dolls with a grimace. "When you said you had a job, I can't deny a part of me thought it may include dancing on a bar top or hexing small children in a basement somewhere. I had to see for myself."

"This is New Orleans. There are no basements," I muttered, my words halting as his eyebrows crept up to his hairline. "And that was your attempt at a joke. I'm shocked; the cold demon has a humorous side."

I stood, closing the Book of Shadows with a snap. Leaning against the counter, I brought my hands to my hips, surveying him with pursed lips.

"I'm just your average shopkeeper, nothing wild or scary about that. You, on the other hand? Pray tell. Are you sidelining as an actor in your downtime? Or better yet, a stripper? Because if so, I have plenty of friends who would pay good money for a piece of that." I gestured to the bulge of his legs and ass in his sublimely tight pants.

He glowered, his eyes the color of molten caramel ice cream. "I was fight training. When one's job involves the violent exchange of fists and weaponry, one practices said skills."

I nodded sagely. "Oh, I'm sure you practice plenty of skills in your leathers."

He stalked closer until we were toe to toe. His lips twitched as he fingered a strand of my hair. "For such a malicious witch, you need to work on your insults."

"Yeah, I'll get right on that, Zorro. Now, why are you bothering me?"

He raised his brows, releasing my hair from his grip. "We have our first assignment tonight."

After tense silence, I rolled my eyes at his silent routine. "And that would be?"

"It's a need-to-know basis. And you don't."

"That's bullshit. We're partners in this!" I exclaimed, my cheeks heating with irritation. I slapped away his hand as he tried to lift one of the protection ladders for closer inspection.

"I believe I agreed to help you find the killer. Nothing about being partners in crime."

Though I wanted to argue, I held my tongue. I would discover his secret soon enough.

He pushed away from the register. "Be ready in a few hours. And wear something nice, not whatever this look is."

He disappeared as suddenly as he had appeared, leaving me fuming over his insult.

"Asshole," I muttered, glancing down at the leggings I rolled out of bed in.

Flustered, I snatched a box of my favorite mystical chocolates, a preemptive gift to myself for dealing with the demon. The silky, dark cacao infused with chili and sex magick gave the consumer a euphoric high rivaling a fiery night in bed with a skilled lover. They were a necessity as far as I was concerned.

Before I could dwell further on the night's activities, the door chimed, announcing another customer. I glanced up to find Audra, her fiery hair bouncing against her bared shoulders as she flounced over to me.

She eyed the empty store with a wince, jumping into the chair next to me. "Slow day?"

I shrugged. "You know how it is early in the season. It'll pick up in no time. Especially considering all the ghost and vampire tours the Council has been pushing."

Hiding in plain sight sometimes benefited us in the Big Easy.

Audra crossed her legs and slanted a knowing look at me. "Now that it's just us, spill. What's going on with you?"

I side-eyed her, knowing she would be far more perceptive than Jade. "I already told you, I'm fine. Still reeling from the Bacchanal."

Her eyes grew soft, and she draped her hand over mine. "I know. I've felt the same. Seeing her with the same wound as Mom and Dad brought up a lot of memories we'd all rather forget."

My shoulders tensed, and I brushed off the sweeping emotion that threatened to break me. I realized I had two options here. I could lie about Killian and try to keep our involvement around the city quiet. Or I could get ahead of this thing and make it more palatable for the coming weeks. I preferred the latter.

"I'm seeing someone new."

Her eyes widened with surprise. "*What?* Is it one of the pack? I thought you swore off Wren and the wolves." Her voice trailed off as suspicion rose in her wise depths.

I straightened my shoulders. "His name is Killian. He's a demon living in the city."

Audra had lifted my coffee to her mouth before spitting the hot beverage all over the counter. "The mercenary demon?" she gasped when she could speak again. "Do you know what they call him? The Scourge. As in a punishment, a weapon. Someone you steer clear of and run the opposite way from."

Stalling, I pulled away my protective charms, drying the spill with receipt paper. I hadn't realized he had a gruesome moniker known throughout the city. Killian was moody and a soul reaper from Hell, but he didn't seem *that* bad.

"Wait." She stopped cold, her eyes growing round. "Tell me this isn't the demon from the Bacchanal you were making slutty eyes at across the bonfire all night."

My cheeks pinkened, the description far too apt for my liking.

Her eyes flickered with emotion. "There is *something* between the two of you, and it is *not* romance."

"Maybe I'm not looking for romance. He's good in bed, and that's enough for me."

Her lips curled with disgust. "You can get laid anytime you want. You don't have to lower yourself to a demon. I mean, he's hot in a rugged way, but you could tag team an entire Fae Court and it would still be less icky than being with one of them."

I pulled on one of her curls. "Don't be so dramatic. Demons aren't that bad."

She eyed me like I had lost my mind. "Dude, they literally suck out souls. Why do you think the Council refused to let them integrate into the city like the other factions? Only Carreau and a few others live here. Because they're *dangerous*." She grimaced with disgust. "I don't know how you can bear to be in his company for more than a few minutes. He seems tedious."

My insides prickled with guilt as I lied straight through my teeth, "You have nothing to worry about. I've got everything under control." The winds picked up outside, beating against the shop windows like an omen. "And he's not a bad guy. He's very protective of me," I quietly added.

She cocked her head. "Whatever you say, Em." Picking up the protective charms I was working on, she raised a brow. "And you're crafting these because?"

My gaze darted away. "Practicing my casting. If I'm going to drive Grandmother to an early grave with my wild sex life, I may as well make up for it by not being a total disaster with my magick."

"You know that's not true, right? Just because you've struggled more with your gifts, doesn't make you a fuck-up."

Her voice was gentle, but I didn't deserve her kindness. I snickered to hide the pain behind my words, "I'm the literal definition of a fuck-up."

Audra didn't take the bait. She pulled one of my plaits, her green eyes narrowed into slits. "Snap out of it, Em. Pity parties are beneath you. What we're going to do is take steps towards self-improvement without knocking ourselves down."

I nodded, huffing out a laugh.

I needed to pull myself together. The demon pact and murder seemed like easy challenges compared to proving everyone that I was worthy of my magick and the Coven's respect.

Audra stood, readjusting her miniskirt. "You should invite your new demon boytoy over to the house for dinner. It may help cool some of Jade's future ire if we got to know him."

I shuddered at the thought of having to introduce Jade to Killian and as my demon boyfriend. If Audra's reaction was any indication, Jade's rage would be catastrophic.

"See you later. And save some of those chocolates for me, you hoarder." She winked before leaving me alone once more.

My smile slipped as I pulled my sleeve up, exposing the ink on my arm. I trailed a finger over the inky moon and stars wrapped around a vicious serpent, the physical evidence of my impulsiveness.

I needed the amulet now more than ever.

Without it, I would be hopeless in undoing whatever fucked-up spell I had cast on Killian, which, considering my recent outbursts, was becoming more likely to be true.

Whatever he had planned tonight, I hoped it brought me closer to claiming it and making good on my promises to be better. Or I would disappoint everyone again; a fate I needed to avoid.

10

EMBER

Instead of luring me into a back alley to suck out my soul, the demon brought me to the place that topped my list of terrible experiences: a riverboat casino. Despite my better than average genetics as a witch, I still succumbed to seasickness as prolifically as any mortal. As a resident of the city below sea level my entire life, it was especially humiliating to be so green at the gills after only thirty minutes on a stationary boat.

Killian sat me at the bar while he stalked off and did whatever it was demons did.

I was two gin martinis in before happy hour ended and regretting every choice that brought me to this point. The bartender, at least, had no issue chatting with me while I waited for Killian to return.

My attention drifted around the ship at the striking males with roughened features. I could admit there was an appeal of this cursed ship. More mythological creatures sat aboard the docked casino boat than I had ever seen at Council events. An actual satyr sat amongst a group of water wraiths, his stumpy hooves hidden beneath his loose trouser legs.

With a sardonic grin, I faced the bartender once more.

"On a scale of one to ten, how would you rate your job? Asking for a friend."

His mouth quirked, lifting his thin blond mustache as he dropped another olive into my drink. "Darling, you don't have it in you to deal with the shit I get up to."

I didn't doubt it.

With a sigh, I leaned over the bar, searching for Killian. Why would he invite me if he intended on sitting me in timeout the entire night? Easily enough, I caught sight of his black hair and tall form towering over most aboard the boat. I observed his terse exchange with the cherubic male demon with interest.

The demon was attractive in an almost too-perfect way. His eyes drifted over to mine, catching me staring, and he brightened.

Killian glanced over at me and scowled, snapping a finger in front of his friend's face.

I gulped more gin to hide my smile. When the two approached, I downed the rest, knowing I would need the liquid courage for whatever awaited me.

"My, my. And who might you be?" the demon drawled, an exaggerated southern twang slurring his words as he held out a tanned hand.

I shook it, accentuating my accent in return. "Ember Belle. Em to my friends."

"Em, then, because we're going to be fast friends."

The demon shouldered in next to me, his skin glowing under the dim lights. "I'm Carreau, by the way. Since my dear friend Killian here is being so rude."

My face froze as I realized the demon from the Council stood before me. Unlike Hunt or Grandmother, the demon was young and hot, nothing like what I expected for the head of the demon species here on this plane.

At the spike of emotion through the bond, Killian's entire

countenance grew even stiffer. I couldn't help but exaggerate my response to annoy him. "Pleasure's all mine, Carreau. That's an interesting name. Does it mean anything?"

His grin widened, showing off his dimples. "My father, Gressil, gave it to me."

I knew next to nothing about demon hierarchies or important figures, but from the emphasis on his father's name, the cut of his suit, and his effortless charm, it was easy to assume he came from money and power.

Killian, who looked as though he scraped through life by the skin of his teeth, wore the evidence of his struggles for all to see.

I softened more to him and eased back on my blatant flirting.

Killian's body radiated cold tension, glowering before taking away my martini glass and handing it back to the bartender. "If you two are done, we have somewhere to be."

Carreau gave him a mocking salute before grabbing my hand and dropping a kiss on the back of it. "Until next time, sweet Em."

In a flash of smoke, he disappeared into the shadow dimension.

Killian's thunderous expression focused on me as he pulled me up from the barstool. "Let's go."

Piqued, he dragged me behind him through the gaming tables before plopping me in a quiet corner near the back of the boat.

"Don't manhandle me again, dickhead," I hissed, adjusting my low-cut top to distract from the fire burning in his amber eyes.

Unbothered with my irritation, he eased into the chair next to me and shuffled a deck of cards he conjured from his shadows. "We're going to play a few rounds while I watch the crowd for my guy."

Curiosity overpowered my irritation. On a sigh, I begrudgingly asked, "Who are you looking for?"

But Killian would not be easily deterred. Ignoring my question, he said, "Do you know Piquet?"

I quirked a brow. "No, because I'm not one hundred years old. My card skills end at Crazy Eights."

He tsked, dealing out the cards. "Blackjack, then."

I glanced down with frustration. *Two fours.* "Hit me," I sighed.

He placed another card down.

An eight. "Again."

He raised a sardonic brow but dealt me my last card. Flipping it over, I grinned at the black four. He turned over his own cards and a scowl grew over his face. *Eighteen.*

"Don't feel bad, demon. My witch's intuition makes me an incredible card shark. It's how I made most of my booze cash throughout high school."

He growled low. "Again."

What a sore loser. I laughed aloud at the look of concentration on his face.

Shuffling the deck once more, we played a few rounds as he watched the crowd. After what seemed like hours, he perked up upon spotting a male from across the boat.

I snuck a glance in the direction he stared at and froze.

Oh. *Fuck.* I brushed my hair over my shoulder, attempting to hide my face in the curtain of my shining locks.

Wren Boudreaux forced his long legs into a chair next to two busty nymphs, who flushed with lust as they watched the delicious werewolf male in his prime. There was no flare of jealousy, only annoyance, as I watched him flirt with the women, his eyes settling over their cleavage bursting from their low tops.

"What do you want with him?" I asked.

His eyes missed nothing. Scowling, he glanced between the two of us. "Will this be a problem?"

"He's my ex. And not the killer."

The demon's face was blank as he dealt another hand, though he never looked at the cards. "I need to get some information from him. Since you know him, you can help me get it. Would you prefer violence or manipulation?"

I balked until I realized he was being serious. I sat straighter in my chair. "Neither! What is this about, if not the murder?"

"A side mission. Your ex-lover has gotten his paws into some naughty shit he shouldn't have toyed with."

The pack would see anything offensive as an act of warfare. No matter what Wren had gotten himself into. Getting involved with pack matters went beyond my pay grade.

"If I help you, then you'll owe me a favor."

He glared down at me. "This entire ploy between us is because of your spell. You dare ask for more?"

I raised my brows. "If you want me to be your accomplice in getting information from my ex, which has nothing to do with our pact, then yes. Payment is owed."

He cursed, surprising me with his alacrity. "Fine," he growled. "One favor."

"Perfect." I jumped up, ready to get this over with, when he pulled me back down into my chair by the back of my leather jacket.

"We'll let him drink a bit more and get comfortable before we attract his attention and coerce him into leaving. We'll corner him outside without witnesses."

That meant we could have hours to kill. This was turning into an all-night endeavor.

I thought about sending a quick text to Audra before thinking better of it. She would only get curious and scry for my location, if she hadn't already.

My curiosity sparked as I wondered what Wren could have done that was so terrible. "You know, I'm great at keeping secrets. What did Wren do to get on your radar?"

He shook his head at my attempt at stealth before leaning back into his chair and raising his hand to the waitress for another round.

I rolled my eyes. With a heavy sigh, I crossed my arms and prepared myself for a night of utter boredom.

But what else did I expect from the cold demon?

☽◉☾

The next few hours dragged as I monitored my phone's clock. Killian remained focused on Wren, retreating to the bar to get us drinks to better blend in as more and more guests arrived on the boat. I moaned with annoyance every time he brought back water.

My attention kept returning to Wren. Over the past year, he had become harder, more volatile than the boy I had spent my summers swimming in the marsh with, or the friend I had lost my virginity to. His dusky dark blond hair and piercing steel-grey eyes, along with fabulous genetics, meant he always stood out in a crowd with his golden-boy good looks. Even now, he raked in female attention from creatures as he wasted thousands of his father's cash on the card tables. Had I missed all the signs of his downfall while I wallowed in my pain?

Wren drained his beer and stumbled to his feet. His steady flow of Corona and whiskey would have hindered his shifter senses, but he would still be deadly in a fight.

At his movement towards the bar, Killian stood and gestured for me to follow.

The plan we hacked together was simple. Make sure Wren had a visual of Killian and me locked in a romantic embrace, stage a terse encounter, and force him to flee to the dark streets below.

Simple enough. Except the part where Killian and I would be in each other's arms again.

I bit my lip hard enough to sting to snap myself out of lusty panic coursing through my blood. No doubt the bastard could feel every humiliating trickle of emotion through the cursed bond.

I snuck a look from the curtain of my hair and found him terse.

Killian wrapped his arm around my shoulder, and I leaned close to his chest, my nose brushing against the stiff fabric of his shirt as his delectable scent hit my senses.

Arousal danced under my skin despite myself. As we walked around the full tables, I forced myself to laugh like he had said something funny.

Killian shot me a pained expression before leaning his plump mouth to my ear. "You sound like a dying hyena. Just act natural, witch."

A genuine chuckle burst free at the look on his face and my cheeks grew warm when his lips quirked in response.

Perhaps I had misjudged the uptight demon.

Wren had refilled his glass when he caught sight of us.

Focused on our act, my eyes avoided eye contact with the wolf as I leaned on my tip toes to whisper into Killian's ear. "I can't wait to get you home. I'm going to fuck you so hard you won't be able to portal straight."

Killian's sharp intake of breath was the only outward sign of my heated words before his hands drifted down my arms to my hips. He pulled me onto the high-top barstool, stepping in between my legs until they wrapped around his waist.

Oh, we were making a scene all right.

Other patrons stole desirous glances at our performance, which strangely titillated me.

I yanked on Killian's belt, hungry for more of his mouth's attention.

His lips quirked at the fire in my eyes, and he leaned forward, his lips hovering near mine. He skirted my mouth and licked a warm trail up my neck towards my ear. I shivered, my body breaking into goosebumps at the sensation of his tongue along my skin. My lust rippled through me, the heady ball of fire in my core aching with the need to get the demon alone and show him what he had been missing.

When he reached a sensitive spot on my neck that made my toes curl, I grasped his raven locks and forced his head back up to mine. His eyes were black as I brought him closer. My lips tingled with anticipation as our breath mingled. Our mouths grazed, the softness of his lips teasing, when Wren sidled up beside me, his wolf growling low.

"What da fuck is dis?"

Growing rigid, Killian pulled away, though my grip in his hair didn't let him get far. At the loss of Killian's touch, I bit back a moan before remembering this was all an act. A brief trickle of hurt and embarrassment pierced through my erotic fog.

Killian turned to Wren with an arrogant smile. "Do I know you?"

Wren's teeth flashed as he looked between the two of us with anger and disgust. "Yes, dat's my girl you're touching right now."

That snapped me out of my daze. My head whipped to his, giving me whiplash. I fought a delirious burst of laughter. "I'm not your girl, Wren. In case you forgot, we broke up a month ago after you banged a vampire, so don't be a hypocrite."

Wren's lips curled up in an ugly snarl, as if he would argue the point with me.

The audacity of this prick.

Another reason I would never entangle with a werewolf

again was their irrational possessiveness. I wasn't Wren's mate, yet because he and I were once an item, he thought he owned my body. Which meant him and his friends, if everyone was willing.

The injustice of it made my fingers spark with renewed fury.

Killian wrapped his arm around my shoulder, the smirk still teasing his lips. "I believe the lady has spoken. Ember, let's go. I think you promised me something to do with your bed and a fucking hard enough to affect my dematerialization."

I swayed in my heels. My name flowing from his lips with that dark, sexy tone made butterflies flutter within my stomach. It made me want to know how it would sound deep in the throes of a hard fucking when I rocked his motherfucking world.

From both Wren and Killian's flared nostrils, they could pick up on the direction of my thoughts from my scent.

Lovely. I grasped Killian's large hand, his fingers dwarfing mine. "Let's go, demon. See you never, Wren."

I knew we had baited the wolf when I felt his eyes, along with most of the other creatures', follow our exit off the casino boat. We wouldn't have to wait long for him to follow us into the dark street below.

And then, I only hoped Killian didn't kill him too badly.

11

KILLIAN

"Whatever happens, vow you will stay out of it," I rumbled to the witch before the wolf attacked.

His body hit mine like a linebacker. I shifted him away from Ember's gawking form. Using my shadows, I moved in a blur, pushing the werewolf against a truck bed, the metal groaning under our combined weight.

"She's *my* female," Wren growled, his eyes flashing an eerie yellow with his wolf at the fore.

My body shot tight at the words. I fought the urge to tear out his throat as my demon prowled inside, ready to be unleashed upon the idiot who thought to claim what was mine. "She's not your mate, so what makes you think you can claim her?"

Wren attempted to bite my neck with his canines, set on staking his dominance.

My shadows were quicker. Unfurling into restraints, I bound him to the truck, my control slipping as I fought to keep my demon at bay.

Wren struggled beneath my hold, his face twisting from rage to baffled indignity. "Ember wouldn't stoop to a demon unless you were forcing her. I'm protecting her."

I laughed low. The shifter was delusional and getting on my last nerve. "Did she look like she was being forced? From my view, she couldn't wait to get me alone for a ride. But Ember is not why we're here, wolf."

"What are you talking about?" he sputtered, fear sparking in his eyes.

Wren's struggles slowed, and I used it to my advantage. I tightened my grip on my shadows, making him wince in pain. My voice dipped to a lethal growl. "I think you know what I speak of. The son of the alpha should know better than to make deals with the Devil. Now, the Devil wants his due."

Wren's amber skin leached color under the harsh streetlights. "No, no. I just needed more time."

The wolf's deal mattered not to me. "You fucked up, wolf. But I will give you an opportunity to complete the transaction for a favor."

Though powerful and aggressive, the wolf was no match for my shadows, my honed skills. I savored the regret and bitter acceptance shifting over his face.

"Fine," he gritted. "What do you want?"

I smiled, knowing the wolf was mine. "When I come to your pack's boxing tournament this weekend, I want you to show me your lands, a stretch near the bayou where a dryad was found years ago. After, you'll assist me in any way I need until after Samhain."

His eyebrows furrowed in confusion at my request.

I had dug into the murder streak, not finding much beyond the death of a dryad. Arabelle was a Fae creature who embodied the forest. Despite her lineage as daughter of King Oberon, someone left her brutalized in the marshes along the Boudreaux property.

Wren stiffened, his blue eyes flickering with fear once more. "You ask too much. Open-ended bargains are a fool's game."

The wolf wasn't a *complete* idiot then.

I raised a brow, the breeze from the river cooling my ire. "Very well, your favor will entail assisting me in a non-life-threatening manner. How is that, wolf?"

His lips twisted with defeat before he bared his canines in a grim smile. "Fine, you have a deal."

I fought my own answering grin of triumph. I was *that* good at my job.

Unlike with the witch, I had no intention of binding my soul to one of his kind. Instead of pulling out my dagger and completing a pact, I would hold the wolf to his word. "Then the deal is struck. Know if you renege on the terms, I will cart your hide down to Hell faster than you can say puppy chow."

I released my shadows and stepped away, turning to Ember, who hid beneath the streetlight, glancing around for witnesses.

Wren glanced over at Ember with a sneer. "Enjoy my seconds, demon. She surely has gotten around most of da males in dis city. You two deserve each other."

Black coated my vision as my demon raged inside at the wolf's insult. My fist flew, punching his irritating face so hard, the wolf collapsed back onto the wet pavement with a sickening thud. I cracked my knuckles, glaring down at his body before stalking away.

I walked to the witch, her eyes as wide as saucers.

"Is he dead?"

From the look in her eyes, I couldn't hold back my jealous growl. Her concern for the asshole grated almost as much as his previous words. "Just stunned. Let's go."

We stalked away, into the busy nightlife and towards her car in silence. Though the night sky above us was dark, the bright neon lights of bars lit up the streets as if it were daytime. Drunken tourists in low-cut tops and polo shirts held lit-up alcoholic drinks and smoked pungent substances, while punchy jazz music blasted from storefronts.

My senses felt invaded by the overload of stimuli, as much as from the reek of piss and stale beer daily road cleaners couldn't clear away. While I preferred stalking around the city in my shadows, I didn't mind taking in the night's chaos with the witch by my side.

I half expected her to clamor for a drink at the nearest pub, but she seemed happy enough to trail through the crowds with a cloaked expression in her eyes.

We slowed at a crosswalk as a vampire holding a clipboard and megaphone guided a group of mortals through a tour of the haunted buildings surrounded by iron. Steeped full of violence, most of the city's lore was unfortunately true.

Ember snorted, her cheeks flushed with humor at the tale the vampire spun to the wide-eyed group who listened while snapping photos on their phones. "It's pretty genius, using NOLA's history to sensitize the masses to the supernatural. Maybe one day we can be open about who we are."

Her words were wistful and full of hope. She glanced up at me, her face clear of her earlier tension. "Well? What did Wren say?"

Of course, the wolf still lingered in her mind. Visions of the two of them twined together on the grassy marsh coursed through me like poison. My teeth clenched, all my prior anger returning. "I got what I needed. That's all you need to worry about."

Two women wearing painted carnival masks stumbled into us, and we moved aside on the uneven road to let them pass. I pulled the keys to her SUV from my pocket and dangled them in front of her. "Where are you parked?"

Her lips dropped open as she looked between my face and the keys. "How did you—? Never mind. Just give me the keys and let me go home. I'm so sick of this back and forth with you. One minute you're a decent male and I think we're having an okay time, and the next you're cold as ice."

Fire roared within her eyes, and I inhaled sharply, awed by the rise of passion in her lovely face. My life boiled down to reaping souls and fighting, with brief interludes of pleasure that never cleared my need for vengeance. But with her, those worries slipped away into the background, with only her bright eyes and sly smile at the fore.

In the end, it didn't matter. She was not for me, and my feelings resulted from a spell she cast over me to meet her own ends. "Just tell me where your car is," I bit out.

Looking as if she would argue, she snapped her teeth before turning on her heel and leading me towards a parking garage. We didn't speak again, the silence taut with our charged anger.

I opened the passenger door and lifted her inside, the brush of her skin against mine feeling like electric shocks. Broken laughter echoing in the cavernous space distracted me long enough to take a calming breath.

I was wound tight. My demon still needed a release, unsatisfied from the fight with the wolf.

Until the witch was home, that would have to wait.

Her peach and vanilla scent lingered in the enclosed space, and my body vibrated with tension. Glancing at her out of the corner of my eye, I thought about how easy it would be to spread her legs open and touch the sweet flesh calling to me.

Remembering her heated words and touches from the boat, my hands white-knuckled the steering wheel.

She peeked over at me and bit her lip, her legs crossing and uncrossing before she adjusted the vents to blow air on her flushed cheeks.

I realized, with mild horror, when she looked at me like that—unsure yet consumed with need—I would do about anything she asked.

I blasted the radio and drowned out all my lust as I drove her home.

Soon she would release me from her spell, and whatever was permeating the air between us would be gone with it. I had everything under control.

☽☉☾

All my suspicions were confirmed as I approached the Belle's family home. Their house resided within an affluent area of town, close to the Coven estate—hardly unexpected for the prominent family. A massive oak tree's roots cracked through the sidewalk near their iron fence, the leaves brushing along the second-story windows that overlooked the street.

It looked how I expected from a family of witches: jet-black and eldritch. They painted every surface dark except for the original wooden door adorned with a floral wreath that I detected magick emanating from.

Every light was lit from within, illuminating the cozy, familial space, and the faces of three witches. The moment I parked, they flew outside. Their steps faltered to a swift halt when they noticed who stood beside their sister.

"Who the fuck is this?" the older witch with dark hair gritted through her teeth.

A spike of panic surged through the bond. Ember leaned into my side, her sweet breath fanning along my neck as she whispered into my ear, "Remember how you owe me one from earlier? This is it. You're going to pretend to be my boyfriend, so my sisters don't kill either of us."

I wanted to growl low, to fight her right here and now on the driveway, but her sisters were now upon us.

Ember wrapped her hand around my waist, her fingers pinching into my side. "Hey, y'all. This is Killian."

Ember's smile did not fool the dark-haired witch. "Where have you been all night? We've been worried sick. We called

Fleur, who hasn't seen you at all today. I thought you were dead in a ditch," she ground out.

Unexpected approval flowed through me. Ember's elder sister reminded me of Taliah with her furrowed brow and an air of superiority. Not to mention her fierce loyalty.

The petite blonde witch smiled up at me, her eyes the same startling shade of blue as Ember's. "Sorry for my sister's rudeness. I'm Isla, and this is Audra and Jade. We're so happy to meet you."

My heart stuttered at the pure innocence and joy on the girl's face.

With the four sisters standing together, it was impossible to not see the similarities between their fair complexions and bright eyes. They clearly loved each other deeply, their bond tangible as they huddled together on the pavement.

I felt a sudden stab of jealousy.

Isla sidled up to me. "Well, let's not stand out here in the street all night. Come in, come in."

She threw her sisters a glare before grabbing my arm, attempting to pull me inside with another wide grin. "Ember's never invited a boy home before. Tell us everything about yourself, Killian."

I glanced back at Ember with alarm, but she was engaged in a silent battle with her two other sisters, the one with fiery hair smirking with concealed glee.

Ember sighed and looked at me, her eyebrows furling. "Isla, sweetness, Killian has other business to attend tonight. We'll schedule a raincheck, okay?"

Isla released my arm, her wide, guileless eyes filling with embarrassment. "Sorry! Now, I'm the rude one."

I forced myself to soften, my lips curling into a rusty smile. "Don't mention it. Thank you for your warm welcome, and I'm sure I'll see you all again."

Her eyes cleared of her meek shyness and crinkled at the corners with happiness. "Sounds great. We'll hold you to that."

I stepped away from the witches, who watched me with curiosity. My back hunched over as I skimmed my lips against Ember's cheek. "Be ready for the pack's tournament on Saturday." I stood back to my full height. "Goodnight, ladies."

Curiosity gleamed in Ember's eyes, but I already turned away from her stunning face.

"Night, Killian," Isla sang, her smile wide as she wrapped her arm through Ember's, dragging her inside the house.

The older witch looked as if she wanted to curse or banish me, but Audra whispered into her ear something that made her spine stiffen. She turned with a sniff and trailed behind her sisters into the house without a backwards glance; the enchanted doors locking resolutely behind them.

This complicated matters.

With a final glance at the house, I dematerialized into my shadows and portaled back to Hell. There was much to do, and I couldn't afford any more distractions. Especially none from witch with pretty eyes I wanted to spend an eternity within.

12
EMBER

Not for the first time, I thanked the Goddess for Merlot. I chugged the glass of wine in front of me like a lifeline. Our dining room table transformed into a battle zone, with Jade on one side and me on the other. Thankfully, Audra and Isla circled in and out, running interference.

Jade shook her head, disgust rolling off her in waves. "How could you be so irresponsible? Your actions were beyond reckless. Think about the safety of your sisters. Demons are not domestic pets; they are wild animals not suitable for the home."

Audra winced, looking guilty as she sat at the table and twirling her scrying dagger. "He's a demon. Can you trust him? He may be a panty-melter in bed, but he's still a literal being of Hell. Caution is warranted when moving forward with one of his ilk."

So much for our talk this morning. The traitor.

"Well, I thought he was super nice and charming. You can't judge an entire species off of a few bad eggs," Isla chimed in, coming to my side. "And we can take care of ourselves. We're not damsels in distress here."

Audra rolled her eyes and refilled everyone's glasses, except Isla, who sipped iced moon tea with sugared lemon.

I took a deep breath. I knew this recent development would disturb my sisters, but Jade's vitriol took me aback. Witches and demons notoriously hated each other, but the chemistry between Killian and me was undeniable. "Isla's right. Killian isn't at all like the stories we've heard about their species. He takes care of me."

"What about Grandmother? How will she react when she learns her granddaughter is seeing one of those vile creatures?" Jade asked, her eyes growing weary.

Clarity struck as I realized where Jade's anger stemmed from. "You just don't want to appear weak in front of Grandmother and the Coven. This has nothing to do with Killian and everything to do with you and your ambitions!"

Jade's eyes withered at me. "Unlike you, there is no choice for me. I will be the High Priestess someday and must follow tradition. And maybe the elders were right. The Council doesn't even trust the demons with unmitigated access to Gaia. We don't know what they are capable of."

I forced myself to shrug my shoulders, feigning nonchalance. "We're still two consenting adults, and Killian is allowed access here. Doesn't that count for something?" Pulling out my trump card, I studied my chipped nail polish with an air of boredom. "I met Carreau earlier tonight, and he seemed fine with our relationship. If Grandmother takes issue with it, then who cares? I'm already a disappointment in her eyes, so there's not much farther I can fall."

Isla frowned. "You know that's not true, Emmy."

Jade said nothing, her eyes stormy as she gazed at me.

She didn't have to—I knew she agreed. I crossed my arms tightly around my ribs. "Grandmother has more on her plate to worry about than who I'm dating. Rosalind's attacker is still out there, and no one seems capable of finding who's responsible."

Audra's brow furrowed. "It is strange, isn't it? My intuition is telling me there's more here than meets the eye, but I can't figure out how."

Jade took a hefty sip from her glass. "Fine, I will keep your dalliance with the demon between us for now. But I don't want him sneaking around our house without me present."

I collapsed back against my chair, thankful that the screaming portion of the night's events were ending. "That won't be a problem. Look, I'm beat. We have tea with Grandmother tomorrow, and I need to mentally prepare. I know this is a lot all at once. Can we call a truce for tonight and talk about this later?"

Audra raised her glass in a mock toast, her smile turning sinister. "To Ember and her random demon boyfriend. We promise not to bite… much."

Isla giggled and kissed Jade's cheek, walking to the kitchen to put away her glass. "I have school tomorrow, so I'm going to head to bed."

I followed behind her, escaping Jade and Audra's curious eyes.

A pang of panic lurched through me, and I almost told them the truth. Glancing back down the stairs, I sent out a silent prayer my actions wouldn't have consequences that would affect my sisters.

☽☉☾

The gardens at the Coven estate were my favorite place in the entire world. As children, Jade, Audra, and I would run through the expansive hedge maze, getting lost for hours until our mother would cast a scrying charm sending a golden spool of thread to each of us to follow back into her arms. Now, it was the only part of the estate I felt her presence, despite our parents' gravestones inside the estate cemetery.

The scent of roses, eucalyptus, and rosemary was heady in the cool air. I settled into the metal picnic table, my red floral sundress stark against the lively greens and pinks not quite wilted from the colder weather.

"Ladies, happy tidings." Grandmother and her cloud of musk perfume settled into her seat across from me, her hair pulled back into a chignon. "How are your studies coming? Have you girls been practicing your spell work?"

It was the only rule she had set out when Jade insisted we stay at our family home alone.

Jade sipped the oolong mint tea from her teacup with a stiff smile. "Audra has been working hard in the libraries, studying to earn a place at Dragomire. And Isla is at the top of her class, as you well know."

I fought an eyeroll at the obvious shift in her behavior around Grandmother. With Jade as Miss Perfect, it only made me look more of a mess in comparison.

Grandmother's eyes hovered over me, and my back stooped lower into my chair. "And you, Ember? What have you been up to?"

"Not much," I sighed. "Still working at Get Hexed a few days a week, and the rest of the time, I work on personal development. Digging deep into who I am and my place with the divine."

Though she still smiled, her voice cut. "And what have you discovered about yourself? Do you plan to take any action on said self-improvement?"

Ouch. Touché, Grandmother.

"Yes," I lied. "I was planning on checking out the library here on at the estate before I left today to bring home some reading material. I figured it was time to learn more about my fire magick since we don't have anyone else in the Coven who can help me."

My mother and I were the last fire witches for years after my grandfather's death, and now I was alone. I couldn't count the number of times I had snuck into their old bedroom and let my fingers graze over mother's Book of Shadows, knowing she would have the answers I sought. And every time, I let my fingers drift away, not quite ready to open those pages still smelling of her gardenia perfume.

Grandmother's eyes lit up. "I think that's a wonderful idea, Ember. And you know you can always come to me. I don't have your mother's affinity, but I raised her. As you girls know, our family's disposition for spirit affinities often manifests years after puberty. It would behoove you girls to train with Rosemary in case it manifests."

Audra and I shared a glance. Spirit magick had always seemed creepy to me, always being able to sense the spirits who hadn't passed to the Beyond. Possessing such magick seemed a bit much to ask of a witch.

Clearing my tight throat, I searched my mind for a distraction and realized I could try to garner more information about Rosalind and what the Council knew so far. "Have you heard anything knew about the murder?"

Grandmother's entire mien shifted, her eyes shuttering. "The Council is not unaware of the rumors whispered around the city about the similarities between the death of poor Rosalind and the murders five years ago. I want you girls to know we do not consider the two crimes to be linked."

Just like before with Killian, my stomach bottomed out, the visions creeping in uninvited while I tried not to vomit the hot tea and spiced apple muffins.

Jade brushed aside her long hair, her cheeks flushed with angry splotches. "Is that what people are saying? That whoever killed Mom and Dad and the other creatures have started their massacre once more?"

Grandmother nodded. "Unless the killer strikes again, I don't see how they're connected."

"So, we sit back and wait for another murder victim to show up somewhere, their neck slit?" Audra bit out.

I was with her. It seemed irresponsible not to get ahead of this thing. It was another reason, other than securing the amulet for myself, that drove me to pursue the killer. I couldn't allow this to happen to another family.

"We have no suspects, as before. There were no clues left behind, nor any mystical fingerprints. The bodies kept both their blood and their souls. We have no trail to follow." Grandmother stood, adjusting her blazer with a weary sigh. "And on that note, I have business to take care of. You girls okay finishing up alone?"

We nodded and watched her return through the French doors into the house.

Jade downed the rest of her tea and stood. "Audra and I are going to practice some spell work. Did you want to come, Ember?"

I shook my head. "I wasn't lying to Grandmother earlier. I'm going to head to the library to find some books to borrow. Meet at the car in an hour?"

We split up, and I hurried down the hallway into the heart of the house. The library was quiet. A plethora of spelled candles flickered over dark mahogany reading tables and rich burgundy couches sat empty near a fireplace that rarely lit up, considering the Louisiana heat.

My fingers brushed against shelves, dust settling over my fingertips before I wiped them on my dress. The bookcase I sought hid near the back of the room, the protective spell surrounding it shimmering in the dim light. Unlike the other texts, these were the Coven's most precious and rare tomes, only to be accessed under elder supervision.

I knocked my thumb on my scrying blade and pressed a drop of blood against the shield, unlocking the hidden latch with my ancestral genetics. With a click, it sprang open, and I felt a pulse of magick from the books.

They smelled of resin and frankincense, the smooth spines emanating ancient, dark magicks.

A fine sheen of dust coated most of the books from unuse, however, one book sat on the bottom shelf, hidden away as if it wanted to remain unseen. The worn black spine seemed to call to me, and I plucked it out and examined the cover with a shiver. Etched with designs and ancient sigils I couldn't identify, the most obvious being the deep scarlet pentacle with the demonic skeleton horns rising above it, I knew this had to be what I sought.

I hid the grimoire inside my bag, my shaking hands shutting the cabinet with a soft click.

If anyone discovered I had pilfered from the forbidden shelves—and dared to take this from the estate—I would be in heaps of trouble.

As I walked back into the main reading area, a dark form hovered in the shadows. My shriek echoed in the silent room as I noticed the witch perched on a leather reading chair, her eyebrows raised with glee.

"And what do we have here?"

My hand flew to my heart, my eyes narrowing on Fleur with accusation. "That was cruel and beneath you."

She laughed, crossing the room with a wide smile. "Apologies. Though it isn't my fault you're skulking around the library like a thief in the night. What are you doing in here?"

"Just hiding from Grandmother and my sisters," I joked, hoping my laughter didn't sound forced.

Fleur snorted, "I feel you. Tabitha dragged me here so she

could get an early start on her training. Your sister should be careful. Tabitha has her eyes set on High Priestess."

I chortled, imagining our older sisters fighting for the mantle while Fleur and I watched from the sidelines with mouths full of popcorn.

Fleur fished her phone from her pocket. "Guess what?" she sang, her white hair fluttering around her shoulders as she jumped up and down with excitement.

"What?" I asked, my heart still bouncing around my chest as I attempted to not appear guilty as fuck.

"I got us invitations to the Faerie party inside the Autumn Court!" she squealed, holding up the animated email displaying the address and password to enter the Fae plane along a ley line running through the city.

My smile froze. Any other time, I would be jumping right alongside her considering the Fae were picky with their invites, but now, I only felt lingering fears about my demon pact and my ever present need to win the amulet.

Sensing my lack of enthusiasm, Fleur's grey eyes narrowed with suspicion. "Did you not hear me? We have a key into Faerie. We've been waiting for this since we were teenagers."

I forced myself to smile, though I knew it rang false by the set of her jaw. "No, I'm excited. I've just been so stressed with everything going on that I'm feeling a bit off. When is it?"

Her expression cleared as sympathy replaced her ire. She wrapped her arm around my shoulders, pressing into me with a small hug. "Sorry, Em. I keep forgetting how close to home the Bacchanal must have been for you. The party is next weekend. A rager under the crescent moon." She waggled her brows at the implication.

I huffed out a laugh. "Inhibitions be damned."

She cocked her hand to her hip. "You know it. So, you down?"

I took a deep breath, already regretting my decision. "Of course, I'm down. But first, we need to find the perfect outfits."

Distracted, we returned to the main room to wait for my sisters. I tried to listen to her plans, but my mind remained rooted on the book hidden inside my bag and the trip to the pack lands Killian and I would make the next day.

With a sinking feeling building inside my stomach, I forced myself to set aside my worries and focus instead on the here and now. I was the MVP of bottling my emotions and pushing my troubles to tomorrow rather than ruining today.

13

EMBER

The werewolf den sat on the edge of the city through the isolated, waterlogged bayous and marshes. It worked well for the shifters who preferred their distance from mortals and needed ample private lands to run free in their wolven forms. The secluded, oversaturated grounds felt oppressive before I even set eyes on the wolves.

Upon exiting the car, I breathed in the wet soil, earthy and grounding. Noting the pack's watchful, predatory gaze, I held my spine straighter as I stepped onto the grass, my boots sinking into the ground. Cicadas sang an ominous tune, and I swatted away a swarm of mosquitos seeming to enjoy my sweet, witchy blood.

Killian held out his arm, and I took it, dislodging my heel from the mud as we walked through the imposing compound gate encircling their lands, keeping outsiders away.

The massive house stood on cinder blocks after the last hurricane came through, destroying much of their property. Even the sweeping tree branches coated in Spanish moss seemed to gnarl and creep closer to the ground as if weighted down by the foreboding streak of bad luck the wolves seemed to possess.

My eyes trailed across the wrap-around porch filled with rocking chairs and tables often filled with pack members who felt like a large family. Familiar faces watched from their perch on the porch railing, and I swallowed thickly at their expressions of distrust.

Fortunately, there were no signs of Wren as we made our way around the back of the Boudreaux's expansive home and into the detached boxing rings held in the steel-enclosed garages spanning as far as a football field.

Killian raised his brows at the baneful glares cast my way, leaning to whisper in my ear, "Why am I not surprised you have a reputation around these parts? And I thought I would be enemy number one. What did you do? Murder someone's first-born?"

Though his tone was at ease, his eyes remained trained on the shifters, quiet violence radiating off him in waves.

I flushed. Images of Travis and Brent spreading whispers of my past deeds to the demon made me wither inside, however, I refused to be ashamed of my past. I jutted my chin up and shrugged with a noncommittal sound.

From the shouting and muffled groans echoing through the marsh, the fighting matches had already begun, blood and sweat permeating the early dusk air. We walked into the chaotic mass of bodies, Cajun French shouts distracting me as Killian sought Martha, Wren's mother, and the alpha's mate.

It was easy enough to spot her in the crowd with her firecracker red hair and the frown etched on her otherwise lovely face. When she noticed our approach, she stiffened.

Killian stepped forward, his face neutral. "Good evening, Mrs. Boudreaux. We're here to see the alpha. I believe he's expecting us."

She angled her head at him, her eyes flicking over to mine, before turning on her heel with a sniff. "Mais la," she bit out,

"Follow me. He's in da armory working on pack business 'fore Wren's fight."

Armory?

I shot Killian a glare. We were totally getting murdered and dumped in the swamps.

The armory comprised a warehouse behind the house at the edge of the property, filled with stockpiled supplies for the pack. As part of the Council negotiations, the shifters provided muscle and hands-on combat whenever necessary, and they took their role seriously. Blades, guns, and other archaic-looking tools presented an alarming backdrop for the alpha.

Hunt Boudreaux's low growl emanated from deep in his chest. He ignored the demon's presence, focusing his eerie yellow eyes on me. "My boy tells me a demon wants to speak about dose murders. He said nothing about you coming to my lands."

Killian cocked a sardonic brow, but his grip tightened on my arm, as if he would rip me away from the alpha if need be. "We only need a few moments of your time. Could you spare one of your pack members familiar with the stretch of land where the dryad was found?"

Hunt's thick brows drew together. "I don't see what purpose you'd have in dredgin' up old merde. Dat was five long years ago, no? Da land's been cleared and used by my pack since den."

"Be that as it may, Wren gave me permission to view the land for a boon. We'll get out of your hair."

I fought a chuckle at his play on words before I noticed Hunt's rising beast.

Hunt's canines lengthened, his eyes shifting back and forth from his usual blue to eerie yellow. "Boon? What business you have with my boy?" He turned to me with a restrained snarl. "Did you get my boy into dis?"

Killian's eyes narrowed, his face darkening as he pushed me

behind him. "Wren's business is with me, not her. As to why we want to see the land, I'm sure you've heard the whispers about the past murders aligning with the vampire's recent death at the Bacchanal. We want the murderer found as much as I'm sure you do."

Hunt growled low, "You dare question my loyalty? I was dere, demon scum. I saw da attacks, how easily da killer slipped away. From da brutality of it, I'd say it was one of yours dat did the killing. I'd be careful 'bout throwing accusations around dese parts."

A sneer curled his lips as he refocused his anger on me. "And what 'bout you, Ember? You aren't my boy's bele anymore. I want you off my lands."

Straightening my spine, I faced Hunt's fury head on. "Look, Mr. Boudreaux, some nasty shit is happening in the city that could affect not just the pack's safety, but other creatures as well. I know you don't care much for me, but you can see keeping this away from the mortals is tantamount to our continued survival in the city."

Hunt shook his head. "You always had a knack for findin' your way into trouble. I see things haven't changed a bit."

My cheeks flamed, but I resisted glancing up to surmise Killian's reaction. I shouldn't care what the demon thought of me and yet, my magick tingled along my fingertips. Talking with Hunt was like talking to a brick wall. He would never see me or any other creature as anything other than an enemy.

After a stilted moment, Killian spoke, his tone hard. "As fascinating as this all is, we're wasting time. It'll take us only minutes to view your land, and then we'll leave."

Hunt crossed his arms, his meaty arms an unveiled threat. "I'll send Wren to show you da way and then I want you two gone, never to return."

Killian nodded, and we left the warehouse.

A few steps behind Hunt, my eyes seemed drawn to the

strange barrels tucked away behind a workbench, which glowed when Hunt cranked off the lights.

I gave myself a mental shake. This next hour would be misery, and I needed to remain focused on the mission. For the amulet, I could endure an awkward walk in the marsh with my ex. What was the worst that could happen?

)☾(

Wren ushered us into the darkening woods, his blue eyes avoiding mine. I expected some mention of the encounter on the riverboat, but Wren seemed content to ignore our presence. After our conversation with Hunt, I was relieved for the moment of quiet.

I shivered at the slight drop in temperature, wishing I had brought a jacket. I knew part of the chilliness came from the strained air between me and my former boyfriend. Well, that and the unspoken hatred lingering between him and Killian.

The only sounds for several minutes were our boots crunching on dead leaves and twigs and the mournful howl of the wind echoing through the spindly cypress trees, rooted into the murky water spotted with bright green algae.

I fought the urge to open my mouth and fill the silence. "Is it much farther?" I mumbled when I could bear it no longer.

Wren shook his head, still facing away from me. "Just up here near da water."

His golden skin bared to the night air glistened, showcasing his preparations for the night's matches. Once upon a time, these Saturday nights had been the highlight of my week, the promise of alcohol and masculine energy a heady call. How quickly everything changed.

We fell into another dead silence.

I snuck a look through the curtain of my hair at Killian,

who watched the two of us with an unreadable expression. "Was there anything in particular you were looking for out here?"

Killian shrugged, turning back to the terrain. "Violence leaves an echo in the shadow dimension. I'm going to determine if someone murdered the dryad here or dropped her after the crime."

"You can see from so long ago?" I asked with confusion. Witches could also feel the echoes of violence, but our power was limited to the recent past unless you used strong magick.

"Perhaps. Truly violent deeds can linger for centuries. For a gruesome murder, five years would be nothing and could lead us to a clue about the creature responsible."

Wren glanced over at Killian with a deepening frown. "Are you implying one of mine killed da dryad?"

Killian stepped over a squirrel carcass, glancing at his boots with a grimace. "I never said that, but it makes one wonder why she was left on Boudreaux lands."

Wren growled low, tensing as if to fight.

I stepped forward to break the growing tension. "It's the same M.O. as the previous murders." At Wren's furrowed brow, I sighed, not wanting to get into it again. "People are saying Rosalind's death is like the murders years ago."

Wren's harsh face grew softer, all traces of animosity falling away. "Sorry, Em," he ground outspoke gruffly.

I shivered, clasping my arms around my body as if to hold my heart in place.

Killian had not discovered the link between me and the murders yet, and I intended to keep it that way.

He glanced at me questioningly, but I kept my lips sealed. Until the demon planned on sharing his secrets, I would keep mine. I shot a look at Wren, warning him to do the same.

His brows dipped lower as he looked between the demon and me. "How did you come to be involved in dis, Ember?"

Before I could reply, Killian cut in, "She's with me."

The biting words brokered no questions.

Wren made a noncommittal chuff, hurrying his steps, desperate to be away from us. "Well, here t'is." He pointed to an ordinary stretch of muddy banks with spongy moss floating along the top of the brown water like a film.

Killian leaned closer, his hand brushing lightly touching the wet ground. He disappeared in a wisp of shadow, leaving Wren and I to stand, avoiding each other's eyes.

"So, you and da demon, huh?" he asked, after the silence became too much.

"Why do you care?" My voice was defensive, and I fought to control my aggrieved expression. I was not the bitter sort of woman, especially not for a male who had disrespected me and allowed his friends to do the same.

He cleared his throat, still turned away from me. "I wanted to apologize, Em. For da other night and how everything went down with Leya."

The mention of the vampire female I caught him with resurfaced all those raw feelings. My volatile jumble of emotions sought an outlet to express itself. "Don't worry about it, Wren. It's in the past. I've moved on."

The words weren't untrue. Any feelings I had towards the wolf other than our onetime friendship and our healthy sex life had flown away long before the breakup. However, I couldn't deny the humiliation and betrayal still prickled.

"I know you don't care. You never did."

The bitterness in his tone gave me pause, and I shot a glare at his back.

That was it! After this past month of Hell, I couldn't take one more backhanded comment about how I was to blame for everything once again. My fire exploded from me, a cylindrical sphere pulling on all my rage, thrown at Wren's head.

His shifter instincts kicked in and he ducked in time for the fireball to explode against the tree behind him. He kicked the embers before they could spread. Snarling at me, his canines lengthened in his mouth. "Da fuck was dat, Em? You could've set our land on fire!"

My finger pointed at him with accusation. "That was a warning. You and your pack need to keep my name out of your mouths. I'm done with this crap. You fucked a vampire, but somehow, I'm the villain for trying to move on?"

Wren growled, "I never spoke a word 'bout you other than da truth. Travis told me all about da other night at Low Road. Do you have no shame, hitting on my pack members?"

I sucked in a breath and then chortled, frustrated tears streaming down my heated cheeks. "Travis is full of shit. And unless you forgot, you were all too willing to share me with them once upon a time. And then afterward you acted like I sickened you."

His eyes flashed yellow, his wolf visible under the surface. "It had nothing to do with da sex and everything to do with what happened later dat night. My father warned me dat your Coven was rotten to da core, and I defended you and your sisters. But dat night, you almost killed us with your magick, and I realized da truth."

My heart pounded inside my chest as I struggled to find my breath. It was another blackout night of drugs and booze among many. I had no recollection of the aftermath of the night, but somehow, I knew Wren spoke the truth.

He shook his head, leashing his wolf and retreating from me. "I'm not doing dis with you tonight." He paused. "Is da demon coming back soon? I have a fight to get to."

Killian materialized beside me, a blank expression on his face.

Turning on his heel, Wren ran to escape us.

Killian whistled low, his gait slowing to keep pace with me as I followed the path back to the compound. "You certainly know how to clear a room, witch," he whispered, his warm breath a calming caress on my chilled skin.

I swallowed with embarrassment, wondering what the demon had seen or heard, but I forced myself to laugh. "What can I say? I'm a riot."

Wren's shoulders rose at the sound of my laughter, but he didn't utter another word as we returned to the fighting ring.

The shouting reached us long before the bright lights from the open garage. Glancing back at Killian, a violent gleam entered Wren's eyes. "You can try a round in da ring, demon. Unless you're afraid."

"I don't think that's a great idea," I added hastily, huffing when they ignored me.

Killian tilted his head to the side. "Was the other night's beating not enough? Very well, wolf. Though I'll warn you, I'm quite good at what I do."

I sent Killian a pleading look while my thighs tensed to escape back to the car. But I knew by the set of his jaw that he would fight tonight.

I gulped as I followed behind them. This would not end well.

14

EMBER

"Oh, this is so fucked," I breathed from the sidelines of the fighting cage, my pulse jumping as Killian dodged Wren's flying fists. Sweat misted along my face from the mass of creatures crammed inside the bright garage with only small fans blowing warm air.

With dread sinking in my stomach, I watched the fight unfolding within the ring. I'd attended hundreds of matches over the years with Wren and the pack, and I knew how brutal it could be. The thought of Killian getting hurt sent strange prickles of fear through my body.

A commotion near my back briefly distracted me from Wren's viscous uppercut, nearly smashing open Killian's face. Travis, Brent, and Aaron formed a crescent around me, with Aaron taking the protective spot at my back.

As if he could do anything to stop his friends if they wanted to hurt me.

"Can I help you?" I muttered to the wolves, annoyed at the feral glances aimed at me. No doubt a result of Travis's big mouth.

Travis sneered. "We wanted to watch your face as Wren pummels your new boo."

I rolled my eyes. "The demon isn't my boyfriend."

"Dat's not what we've heard." Travis's eyes trailed over my ass in my tight jeans. "You sure have a knack for finding da worst kinds of monsters to align yourself with, don't you?"

I ground my teeth. "It's okay to admit you consider yourself a monster, Travis. We all have insecurities to work through. I'm sure with enough time and therapy, you can strive to become a better person."

Ignoring his hiss of anger, I shifted my gaze back towards the fight.

Killian blocked another strike with his muscled arm, with not even a bead of sweat on his brow. The demon stuck close to the perimeter, allowing Wren to take the offensive as he studied the shifter's fighting style weaknesses. His movements were effortless and unhurried, almost sensual.

I couldn't help but feel impressed watching Killian's strategic skills. The memory of my attempts to fight him off in my bedroom whirled in my mind. He was right; I never stood a chance.

Something strange seemed to come over Wren, a gleam in his eyes I never saw before. His fist landed on Killian's cheek as his wolf exploded out of him, canines and claws extended.

I sucked in a breath and leaned closer to assess the damage. I had seen Wren's wolf many times, especially in this very ring, but there seemed to be something off about him tonight. He appeared almost rangy, unpredictable and sloppy with his movements.

Travis and Brent chuckled beside me, the shifters shouting curses at the demon who wiped away the speck of blood from his mouth with a small, imperious grin.

There was a crack, a flash, and then Wren flew backwards, slamming into the gate on the opposite side with a low groan.

Killian stood at the center of the ring, not a hair out of place as he cracked his neck, horns and wings materializing from the shadow dimension. His wings unfurled, displaying the midnight membranous tissue like a bat, far too wide for the expanse of the cage.

When he shifted his stance, I gasped. His wings were *massive*. Spread in flight, they would be the width of an eighteen-wheeler.

I felt a sudden desire to lift a finger to touch them and feel their shape and weight in my palms. My eyes trailed up his chest moving with quiet breaths and up to the horns emerging from the back of his head. With fangs elongated like the shifters, the canines looked sharp and pronounced. Black diffused his eyes with his demon at the fore.

He glanced over his shoulder to find me, a feline grin in place.

He looked like a brutal warrior from Hell—the Scourge.

I sucked in a deep breath with surprise. I realized it wasn't disgust or fear pulsing through my veins as I looked at his true form, but *lust*.

By the quirk of his lips, I could tell he knew how much his form affected me.

Before I could look away in embarrassment, he returned his attention to Wren. The noises from their bodies colliding sickened my stomach. In their supernatural forms, their speed and agility were too fast for my witch eyes to pick up on, but the pervasive stench of blood grew heady in the humid air.

Killian didn't need long to defeat Wren. After a well-aimed, vicious punch, the wolf slumped onto the dirt. Killian's hands bracketed his throat, holding the wolf at an impossible angle.

Wren snarled, but there was unwilling surrender in his eyes.

The arena grew silent as Killian stood to his full height, his wings and horns retreating into the shadow dimension. He turned to watch Hunt Boudreaux enter the stifling garage. Killian smirked at the alpha, taunting him as he exited the cage. "I suppose I'll see myself out now."

Hunt's face grew thunderous. "Don't come here again, demon, or it'll be an act of war." He glanced over to where I stood, his teeth bared. "And take the witch with you."

The surrounding shifters grew silent, but Travis snorted, grabbing my arm hard enough to leave a mark. "Maybe she'd prefer to stay for another night in the marsh. You'd like dat, wouldn't you, Ember?"

Killian froze, his face turned towards Travis with a low growl.

By the set of his shoulders and lack of emotion on his face, I almost believed the demon to be bored, but the black jets of his eyes and the cold fury radiating through our bond told me all I needed to know.

I didn't have a second to stop him before he was airborne.

Their impact shook the floor beneath me as he took Travis to the ground, raining punches and blows. He snarled, animalistic in his anger.

Aaron pushed me back when I tried to get between them. "Absolutely not, Ember. They'll crush you in seconds."

I watched with rising horror as the entire arena witnessed Killian fight a high-standing member of the pack on my behalf like some damsel in distress. "Killian, let's go. He's not worth it," I ordered, my magick rising to the surface as a full-on panic attack blackened my vision.

Killian released the wolf with a low growl at the smell of flames erupting from my fingertips. His eyes hardened at Aaron's grip around my arm.

Aaron released me, lifting his hands up in surrender. "Sorry, man, just trying to keep her from getting crushed."

Killian stalked over to me, his shadows surrounding me as he glared at the creatures mutinously. "You should learn to watch your mouths. I won't be so lenient the next time I hear you disrespect the witch."

Side by side, we walked towards the doors, heads lifted

high. Creatures shuffled out of the demon's way with looks of fear and unwitting respect.

I forced my feet to slow and not run for the car and hide when the pack's eyes followed our movements. I waited until we were down the road, out of pack territory, before I let myself break. "You shouldn't have done that. I didn't need your help."

He snorted, his eyes still slightly crazed from the violence. But then he forced his breath to calm. "Are you alright?"

Tears of shame and frustration rolled past my barriers, but I forced myself to suppress my emotions. I would swallow them down and secure them in the pit inside that held all my grief and embarrassment.

The demon would not see my weakness.

We weren't friends; we weren't lovers. We were unwitting partners.

Necessity brought us together, not any true feeling, and I would do well to remember that.

My cool mask locked in place. "Just get me home, demon."

15

KILLIAN

Conflicting emotions flooding through me, I portaled back to Hell despite my demon screaming at me to return to Ember and offer her comfort after the disastrous outing with the wolves. While my instinct was to barrel into the training yard to fight until I spent my rage, instead I wandered to the weaponry hall.

Taliah sat at her work table, tinkering away at a new spear prototype that shot poisoned barbs across a battlefield. Her confident russet hands held her tools with precision while her dark brows furrowed with concentration.

"Am I interrupting?"

Her head shot up, and she moved aside her magnifying orb to smile at me. "Killian. How did it go on the mortal plane?"

My grunt echoed in the hall as I showed her my bloodied hands.

"That good?" She raised her brow, throwing me some gauze from her station.

I wrapped my bleeding fists with the fresh wrappings as I spilled all the details from the past few days.

Taliah listened as I related the results from the wolf den. She guffawed, her russet skin glowing with mirth as she clutched her sides. "Killian, please tell me you're joking. I would have given every ounce of gold I possess to see you in a shifter fighting ring."

"Believe me, I wish I was. Foul, backwards creatures." My eyes blackened as I remembered the crude words and deplorable behavior of the shifters. As well as the shame Ember couldn't disguise through the bond.

"Why did you bring a witch with you? One who seems to have such a rocky relationship with the wolves, at that."

I winced, knowing it was time to reveal the truth. "She summoned me to do her bidding and then spelled me in retaliation when I refused to pact with her. I made a deal with her to get her spell removed before Samhain in exchange for helping her find the murderer in Gaia."

Taliah's eyes grew wide before she stood in a rush and knocked aside her chair. "A spell? What are the specifications? Are we killing her? Let me grab my sword."

I lifted my hand to stop her retreat as the battle strategy unfurled in her mind. "The spell isn't antagonistic or causing me serious harm. But it makes my demon consider her my mate. I agreed to this pact and will see my task through. There will be no murdering the witch."

Just the thought of Taliah lifting a hand towards her in violence had my fangs lengthening in my mouth.

Her eyes grew wide. "Are you going beast mode on me right now? Seriously?"

"Can't help it," I panted. "My mate. Threat."

I fought to keep my demon at bay, but he prowled within my mind, claws swiping against my mental shields, trying to force his way free.

She crossed her arms, watching me struggle to leash my demon. "And you're one hundred percent sure this is a spell, and she's not your mate?"

I gritted my teeth at the suggestion. "I've been around her

several times during the past few months and never felt my demon react to her like this. It must be a spell at work."

"That's not necessarily a useful gauge. What were you doing when you felt the mate bond lock into place?"

"We kissed," I muttered after a lengthy pause. I knew how the words sounded and avoided her amused grin. "But she cannot be my mate. Not only are we incompatible, but I am taking over my father's seat as lord of the realm in mere weeks. My place here in Hell is absolute. Fate would not be so cruel as to bind me to someone I could never have."

Taliah snorted, her eyes growing cold as she lost herself in her own bitter memories. "That's hilarious coming from you. Fate is cruel above all else. But what if this is fate's way of showing you a different path, outside of your father's shadow, where you could be happy?"

I let myself ruminate on the image she painted. Never returning to this pit of a realm that only held pain and suffering and instead moving through Gaia with a partner, a friend, a lover. The fantasy tempted me. But I was the scarred, brutal demon set on revenge, and she was a luminescent witch who relied on her Coven. Whatever this bond was, it wasn't *real*.

Shaking loose from my bitter thoughts, I walked to the window overlooking the courtyard. "That's not all. I learned something very interesting when I viewed the land where the dryad died years ago."

Her curiosity sharpened. "Do tell."

"The killer did not dump the dryad on the shifters' lands like the wolves claimed. They murdered her there. I couldn't see who she fought, but she gave it her all before she was bound down and massacred."

The blistering fury still lingered in my soul after witnessing the echoes of such brutality.

Taliah's face showed similar disgust. "Who would injure a

creature such as the dryads? They are peaceful, benevolent creatures. Not to mention she was a daughter of King Oberon. That's a grave offense."

I shook my head, sending inky strands into my eyes. "I don't know, but I'm going to find out."

Before, this was transactional, a means to an end to have the spell removed. But now, I felt tied to this case. If the creature who killed the young dryad had returned, I would find them and make them pay for their crimes. "I need you to do some research for me on the witch and her family. The creatures in New Orleans are loyal and fearful towards the Coven. Find out what happened to her parents and why the Coven is so secretive about it."

Taliah studied me, her eyes giving away nothing. "I will ask my spies, but be honest with me. Are you being forced against your will into doing something because of her spell?" Her beautiful face transformed with malice. "Because if so, I can show the witch how kindly we take to non-consenting bitches around here."

My fingers flexed as I tied off the bandage. My encounters with the witch challenged many of my previous beliefs about their kind. She was young and foolish, but not a bloodthirsty heathen, as I had originally suspected. "I made the terms of our pact airtight. She has sworn to remove her spell by Samhain or pay the consequences."

Taliah considered me. "There's no shame in a demon pact, my friend. I know you have sworn never to compact with a soul, but you had no other choice."

My stomach twisted with guilt. "There's always a choice."

I knew agreeing to a demon pact would wear on my conscience, but I didn't expect the vulnerability I would feel as our souls connected. It was strange being aware of the witch's emotions. Her soul was a warm light, unblemished from the deeds that blackened my own.

She returned to her chair to its upright position with an aggrieved sigh. "In the meantime, use your witch to sort this case out. The sooner you finish, the more time you have to enjoy your last days of freedom."

Narrowing my eyes, I stood, towering over her with a flash of my teeth. "She's not my witch. But I'll get it taken care of."

"You still have three weeks until the succession. That's more than enough time to get this settled. Just swear to me that if anything happens or feels off, you'll call me."

"I promise, Tal. Now, let's go get some food. I'm famished."

☽☉☾

I was on my second plate of fragrant, tender meat when the demon tapped me on my shoulder, announcing Satan sought my presence in his quarters. Ignoring the curious stares and whispered retorts of the surrounding court, I stalked off without another look back.

The demons would never dare to speak insults outright to me considering my upcoming ascension as lord, but there was power in quiet discontent.

The hallways were silent, and I felt another pang of loneliness. Splendor abounded, and yet none of its sparkle could hide the seedy underbelly of the demons living within. At my father's gilded door, his harried assistant glared at me, as if I were to blame for my father's newest crisis.

I swallowed any lingering annoyance as I approached my father, posing for a portrait in his grand, velvet curtain-covered clawfoot bed bejeweled with gems pilfered from various planes.

Clearing my throat, my gaze shifted away from his nude body, settling instead out the crystal window overlooking Pride's forests.

My father shooed away the young artist and the giggling

females who lazed around him with their silken nightgowns covering little of their shapely bodies. His gaze hardened on me as he sat up, pulling the sheet higher around his groin. A small mercy. "You are behind schedule. I need more souls by the end of the week to complete my mission in the Realm of Greed. Mammon's forces grow bold, and without proper ammunition, our borders will fold."

My eyes sharpened on his. "What happened to the last half a dozen souls I brought to you? Souls aren't coins you stick in a candy machine at your whim."

His demon rage surfaced, the black spheres glaring up at me. "You dare speak to me about such matters. I am the Lord of the Realm."

I grinned, showing him my fangs. "As I will be soon. This is as much my kingdom as it is yours, though you may wish it otherwise."

My father spat. "I wish to the gods I never touched your mother. A mistake made during the depths of my despair at the loss of Hana and one I will never stop paying for. The two of you have brought me nothing but torment. Now, I'm left with a filthy bastard to claim my legacy."

I absorbed his cruelty, his tirade nothing I hadn't heard before. The fact remained that my father's time of glory was ending, and he *hated* me for it. "And yet, here I am, claiming your legacy before it falls to whichever courtier would be next in line after you. You should be thankful you at least have a bastard with your blood who will continue in your name."

I didn't allow him to contradict me, wanting this business finished. "I spoke with Wren Boudreaux and made it clear that until he repaid what he borrowed, it would cost him his soul."

My father's demon rage subsided, yet his frosty glare remained. "We are not in the business of charity, boy. I want my souls, and I want it done now. *Today*."

I stiffened, a sheen of sweat forming on the back of my

neck. "I'll bring you a soul by the end of the week," I managed, my voice rough, knowing Wren was now an impossibility under my new bargain.

"You will do better than that." He glowered. "I want at least five or I'll send another in your stead."

The thought of my father's generals on Gaia made me wither with fear. If anyone discovered my ties to Ember, she would be in grave danger. I would need to make another trek to Charon to be sure her name remained wiped clear from the Scroll of Debts.

Satan clapped, dismissing me, and the demons returned to the room. The females' laughter and perfume grated on my senses.

Resentment flowed through me as I returned to my bed chambers. My mind focused on my never-ending list of tasks while I packed my satchel. My mission would bring me across the state as I collected the five souls, and I felt a moment's hesitation about leaving the witch unattended.

A photo I still had of my mother caught my attention. My eyes traveled over the torn clipping of her face before I put the photo inside my bag, hidden in the depths as I tried to summon the deadened mask of the Scourge to the fore.

Just like my father, I would become Satan and lose my humanity to Hell until my time on the throne ran to its end. I was foolish to think I would ever amount to anything other than a killer.

16

EMBER

The night of the Faerie party, my stomach twisted into nervous knots. I swigged another shot from the bottle of Jose Cuervo I kept at my bedside table as Fleur tightened the laces on my new vintage corset embroidered with pink and red budding roses. I couldn't breathe, but my tits looked incredible.

Any lingering trepidation about entering the Faerie Court had faded in the days following my humiliation at the wolf den. I had waited for Killian to show up and confide what he had learned about the dryad, but he hadn't said a word.

And it pissed me off to no end.

Whatever time I spent not wallowing in self-pity, I used to attempt reading from the stolen grimoire. My eyes blurred from the text seeped full with demonic runes and languages. What I had translated about the different Realms of Hell piqued my interest. It depicted Pride as the most enchanting of all the sinful divisions with its wintry mountains and forests.

Not that I was reading up on Killian to discover more of his secrets.

"There, you're gorgeous." Fleur smiled.

I shimmied the corset over my rosy nipples trying to escape the low-cut top and dusted a copious amount of shimmery powder onto my cleavage and pouted in the mirror. "Well, if the night doesn't end with a Fae male's face pressed against my tits, I'll be disappointed." I smirked, swiping a final coat of lip gloss before grabbing my beaded bag from the bed.

As a contrast to my femme fatale ensemble, Fleur chose an understated but lovely peasant dress with pale lavender accents, bringing out the cool silver tones in her hair and eyes. She followed behind me as I crept down the stairs with my heels in hand. "Did you want to tell your sisters goodbye?"

I shook my head, my finger pressed to my lips.

They would murder me if they knew where I was going tonight. Faerie was dangerous—a captivating, delicious experience, but still ripe with risks.

When we were out of the house, I let out a breath and threw my shoes in the backseat of my car. "They would only convince us not to go," I reasoned to Fleur with a wink. "And I'm not missing this party for anything."

As we drove through the city, the car bumped over potholes while we sang to songs on the radio at the top of our lungs. Pulling up to the ley line, I parked in the grass next to the other creatures before we wandered into the field.

There was a ripple in the air as movement between the planes shifted to allow the doorway to open. Unlike the movies, there wasn't smoke or a giant wormhole exploding into the air.

The Fae female stepped from nothingness into the surrounding space, a sharp zap startling me back a few steps. Her hair fell down her back in pale blue tendrils floating around her smoky, midnight skin like snakes. She smiled, and razor-sharp teeth gleamed under the swath of moonlight. "Invitations," she called out in a lilting voice.

Creatures lined up with their phones pressed forward.

Once she determined we were all on the list, she opened the portal once more. "Move quickly and quietly. Any stops along the way or failure to return by night's end will spell your doom."

At her ominous words, Fleur grasped onto my hand and led me into the space beside the Fae. I swallowed a choked scream as we walked into the portal, the air bubbling and sparkling like champagne bubbles.

Time stretched as we walked forward. So much so that I wasn't sure if we had been walking for seconds or hours. Fleur's hand in mine kept me from descending into panic, and I breathed a sigh of relief when the journey through planes was over.

The air tasted luscious and spicy. An awed grin stretched across my face as I took in the Autumn Court for the first time. All the Faerie Courts embodied the natural world with their own spectacles and beauty, but the Autumn seemed to hypnotize. The sky blended bright oranges and deep umber reds like a milky galaxy among the stars, lighting the path ahead. A crescent moon shone, spreading wide across the strange sky in a golden glow.

Whereas the blood moon stretched over the sky of the Bacchanal spelled doom, this moon seemed to wink and crook a finger, pulling us closer.

Walking towards the palace, I gasped, captivated by the intricate wooden moat etched with ancient carvings. It stretched over sapphire blue waters, leading to the bronze castle on the other side. I watched entranced as water wraiths danced under the waves, their skin radiating pale light beneath the depths like bioluminescence.

"Come on, Em," Fleur spoke beside me, and I stepped away from the beauty to follow her to the palace gates.

The castle was adorned with elaborate burnished leaves and barren trees, making my jaw drop at its beauty. A melee of Autumn's soldiers stood with crossbows and staffs pointed at the group of newcomers, their expressions warm and inviting, despite the weaponry.

"Welcome, guests. A word of warning—do not harm any of the creatures in these lands, or else you risk the wrath of King Oberon. Once the clock strikes two, you must return to the ley line or else risk getting lost in Faerie until it pleases us to return you."

His slow grin caused a shiver to spread down my spine.

I felt a moment's pause as I reconsidered stepping inside. Still, when the gates opened, I stepped through, watching with trepidation as they closed them behind us like a locked door.

Fleur led me towards the main hall filled with Fae from all over the plane and other assorted creatures who ventured to Fae for the celebration. Vast mountains of delectable food and overflowing wine glasses beckoned like a gentle tugging hand while musicians played from the rafters, an enchanting tune I couldn't help but move my body to.

Before I lost myself, I glanced back at the wooden bolstered doors one last time.

Maybe this was a mistake.

Fleur handed me a glass of sparkling Fae wine and, with my first sip, my worries trickled away as the night's delights descended upon me. I let myself forget all thoughts of the demon, the murder, and my humiliation for a time. And it was glorious.

"Ember, come dance with me," Fleur squealed, her arms twisting above her head as she twirled beneath the open ballroom.

The strange night sky and moon twinkled down upon us.

I downed another glass of Fae wine, having lost count of

how many I'd already drunk. My movements were slow and dizzied as the world around me spun. I lifted my hand to my forehead and missed, catching the air beside me instead. "I don't feel so good," I slurred to no one in particular as Fleur got lost in another dance.

A Fae male trailed after me all evening, his tawny hair shimmering like metal with laughing eyes that watched me like a fox. His arm pulled me from my current path, guiding me to a quiet corner of the room before escaping into the crisp night air.

Another glass of wine was pushed into my hand as we walked along a mossy glen littered with sharp rocks. A honeyed voice whispered into my ear, "Drink, pretty witch. Drink the Fae's nectar and feel the power of Faerie singing within your blood."

Tipping the glass to my lips, the tart, lip-tingling sweetness tasted just as delicious as the first time I sipped it. I could feel the liquid slosh in my stomach, and I felt a trickle of nausea. "I think I need some food. I'm getting pretty toasted."

The male handed me a small platter of ripe, delectable fruits and desserts, meticulously and ornately designed like minor works of art.

I lifted a purple grape to my lips, eyes widening with awe as the juice burst upon my tongue like magick. "Oh, my Goddess," I moaned, my eyes shutting in ecstasy. "I've never tasted anything so delicious."

The male laughed, his lips trailing along my décolletage. "I think these berries will be even sweeter upon my tongue," he purred.

While any other time I would pull my breasts free, letting the sexy male have his way with me, a prickling at the back of my neck had me hesitating. I turned my face away as his lips moved to mine.

Unbothered, he brushed his mouth against my cheek, his

eyes devious as he grasped a piece of melon from the platter. "Open those luscious lips for me, witch."

My eyes widened. The Fae's whispered words had sounded so much like the demon's smoky voice, I almost believed it was him beside me, his sexy horns brushing against my collar as he tasted the skin of my neck.

"No, wait," I murmured, my hands clasping my head as I tried to focus. "Give me a minute."

The pulsating moon above sent shivers of energy through my body like a drug, and I responded to its call. I laid back onto the plush grass and let my hands wander over the budding flowers of the garden I lay in; the petals cool under my fingertips.

The male leaned over me, his lips lifting in a sly grin. "You look like Selene—a goddess, my darling witch. I want to make you scream into the night. The other Fae will cry with jealousy."

I snorted, not drunk enough I could let a corny line go by without a response. I pulled a scarlet rose from the bush beside me, my finger scraping on a sharp thorn. Hissing, I sucked on the cut, my salty blood coating my tongue.

The iron tang brought the Fae wine's potency to a halt.

My eyes widened as I took in the scene with fresh eyes. The garden I lay upon was dead, the petals falling onto the ground below in drooping, browned curls. The fruit still on my tongue was no longer sweet, but cloying, past ripe, and sticking to the back of my throat. I gagged, but forced myself to breathe through my nose.

When the threat of vomit had passed, I glanced up at the Fae beside me and shrieked. His handsome visage floated away, his broken glamour revealing a deer creature with antlers stretched over me, while his teeth sharpened to deadly points in a macabre smile.

He clucked his tongue, his clawed hand pushing against my

lips to silence any sound. "You shouldn't have done that, little witch."

I sat up—too fast—my head rushing with a flood of blood, making my vision swim with black.

The Fae's brown claws dragged through my hair, pulling and snagging on the curls Fleur had spent an hour perfecting.

Tears sprung to my eyes at the sting. I curled my feet under me in preparation, my eyes shifting to the grounds around me for an exit. The bastard had lured me away from the palace, deeper into the forest than I had intended. The lights and shouting of partygoers dimmed into a near whisper.

At the shot of fear singing through my blood, the Fae's eyes grew hooded, the copper depths flashing with hunger. His hand drifted back to my lips, the claw dragging across my skin like a silky threat. "It'll be over soon, my love. Best close your eyes."

Oh, that would not be happening.

I shot from the ground, my fist smacking into the male's mouth as magick sparked out of me, sending the creature flying backwards. My magick felt dulled under the brevity of the crescent moon, so instead of attempting to fight, I turned and ran back towards the Court.

My feet stumbled on tree roots while branches scratched and tore at my skin.

The trees closed in on me like gnarled demons as terror settled into my bones, making my steps less steady. I could hear the Fae behind me, not bothering to speed his hulking advance.

He knew I was his to devour, the castle too far for my sluggish legs to carry me.

On my next step, my feet were snagged from beneath me, the tree roots an accomplice in his pursuit to eat me.

He dashed forward, swooped me into his arms.

I held my breath against the smell of decay and death on him as he ran back towards his den. I screamed as the beast dragged his stiff mouth over mine, his teeth digging into my lips and drawing blood.

"Shh, my love. Don't fight this."

Before I could lash out with another panicked, last-ditch pulse of magick, a voice spoke from behind me. "I believe the lady said no," Killian's voice thundered in the silent forest. His wings and horns were a terrifying sight in the shadows as he stepped forward under the moonlight.

My blood heated as pure, unadulterated relief pulsed in my bones. With the Fae distracted with protecting his prey from the new predator, I elbowed him in his sunken ribs.

He dropped me to the rocky forest floor, making me wince with pain.

Killian moved in a flash, tossing the male across the glen, his wings unfurling like a whip. He charged the Fae, his horns locking with its antlers as they fought for dominance.

Killian was larger by several inches, but the Fae was devious, his claws scratching down Killian's chest with a maniacal laugh. "It won't be long until you fall, demon. My poison will curdle your organs and make your flesh ripe for eating."

My stomach heaved, and I spewed the Fae wine from my stomach, gasping as I retched.

Killian's demon only grew more infuriated, his claws swiping across the Fae's face, marring its wicked beauty with gore.

The male screamed, piercing the night and as quickly as the horror had begun, it ended. The Fae's skin withered away, leaving behind only the skeletal bones of his body, his flesh hanging off in weathered strips.

All the while, he screamed at a decibel making that made my ears bleed.

My stomach hurled once again, and I wondered what the male had fed me under the moonlight. The thought was too foul to consider.

Killian's steps slowed as the poison took effect. The Fae, still struggling beneath Killian's hold, butted his antlers into Killian's side, causing a dark ruby stain to mar his grey shirt. Killian gasped out in pain but kept his firm grip with a clenched jaw.

I couldn't stand here while the demon fought the Fae alone. Not when this was my fault to begin with.

I wiped my mouth with the back of my hand and staggered forward, kicking the straps of my heels off my feet. I summoned my magick, weak as it was on this plane, and sent it towards the Fae in a burst of flame.

A sigh of relief broke free when it missed Killian's head.

Killian rammed his horns into the Fae's heart, the sharp point ripping the black organ free from his chest. He let out a hollow wail, his body contorting grotesquely before it exploded into pieces, bones and skin scattering along the dirt, only to be swallowed whole by the earth.

We both gaped as the trees came to life with the fresh offering presented before the ancient roots. I almost lost the contents of my stomach once more when I heard the squelching of organs and crushing bones, the thick roots feeding the Fae's body into the gaping hole at the base of the tree.

Eyes vacant, I screeched, my feet running towards the castle before my brain could catch up.

The demon caught me, sweeping me into his arms, his mouth a flattened line. "Hang on tight," he snarled, before we disappeared into a cloud of smoke and into the shadow dimension.

Choking, I squeezed his neck until we landed back into Gaia, my lungs seizing with the rush of clean air unpolluted by Faerie. "Wait. Fleur. She'll be worried or think someone kidnapped me," I spoke through panicked breaths as Killian carted me back to my car.

He growled low, depositing me into the passenger seat with an icy glare. "Do not move an inch."

In a flash, he was gone, and I took an uneasy breath in the silence.

Killian had been unsteady on his feet while the poison still coursed through him. I felt a moment of sheer panic he would die because of my actions.

My head pounded, and I could still feel the lingering effects of the wine in my blood. I lowered the passenger mirror and groaned at the state of my appearance. My lips were bruised and coated in thick blood while the rest of me looked like I had gone to battle, which I suppose I had.

In the next breath, Killian and Fleur came barreling back into our plane.

Fleur screeched and teared at Killian's face with her nails and teeth.

"Fleur," I shouted in alarm, "it's okay. He's with me."

She looked between the two of us with a furrowed brow, her eyes widening as she grasped what I looked like.

"Did he do that to you?" she fumed, her eyes flashing silver as the dirt and grass danced beneath her feet with her earth magick.

"No, no," I hurried to explain. "Killian saved me. This is the result of a handsy Fae who had plans to eat me. And not in the sexy way."

My attempt at humor failed as both Fleur and Killian narrowed their eyes at me.

Fleur sat in the back seat, her eyes wary, while Killian got into the driver's seat. His face looked deathly pale and creased with pain.

"Are you okay?" I whispered to him, eyeing the marks on his chest and arms with alarm.

He gritted his teeth. "I'll be fine. I'll find some hemlock and oak bark when I get to your house. It takes away the effects of Fae poison."

I took a deep breath and settled deeper into my seat, wishing I could disappear.

No one spoke a word for the rest of the drive.

When we arrived at the house, Fleur sent me a questioning glance. "Did you want me to stay?"

I shook my head, my emotions a wreck. "I'll be fine. See you at the Coven meeting later this week."

She nodded and got into her car, driving away with another concerned glance back at me and the demon.

Killian guided me into the house. Rummaging in the kitchen, he grabbed a handful of herbs for his healing tonic. He picked up Jade's mortar and pestle and ground the two herbs together, forming a thick paste. Lifting his shirt, he rubbed the paste onto the bloody wound, unfazed at the audible sizzle when it touched his skin.

I gasped at the vicious wound along his ribs, swollen and bubbling as the poison affected the tissues of his skin.

Bile rose, but I choked it down.

Once he finished, and I knew he would be okay, I allowed myself to crack. Sweat dotted my brow as the effects of the night reached a fever pitch. "Thanks for your help, but I've got things covered from here."

He hissed low, and I could feel his cold fury through our bond. "Not another fucking word, witch."

He led me up the stairs to my bedroom, the house dark and quiet. Without speaking, Killian walked to my bathroom and ran the bath while I stood frozen in the center of my room.

My brain was pudding, my emotions frazzled.

I was going to have a full-blown panic attack and needed the demon gone, so I could suffer through it alone. Killian's presence beside me kept me tethered as he guided me to the water, undressing me with militant movements.

Kneeling beside me, his hands tenderly brushed through the snarls while I wept. After the blood and grime and glitter ran clean down the drain, he lifted me up and toweled me off. He wrapped the fluffy softness of my robe around me and carried me back into the bedroom without a word. "Which side do you sleep on?"

I cleared my throat, the words strangled, "Left."

My mind and body felt wrecked. Why was he being so kind to me after everything I put him through? It made little sense.

He lowered my blankets, nestling me inside with a loaded sigh. It said everything he didn't speak aloud, and I felt a well of hot shame fill inside my chest.

He straightened his spine, ready to leave, when I grasped his arm beneath the shredded shirt.

"Please stay?" I whispered. I knew the nightmares would soon come, and I realized I didn't want to be alone anymore with my grief.

His eyes flickered, a strange expression crossing his face, before he walked to the other side of the bed, kicking off his boots. He eased onto the bed beside me, taking care to keep a distance between us.

I curled onto my side. "Th-Thank you," I slurred, my eyes falling shut from exhaustion.

He was silent, and as I drifted into the blackness, I heard him from a distance, his voice the shining light mooring me from the wild, turbulent sea. "Sleep, witch. You're safe now."

17
KILLIAN

Throughout the night, my mind whirled over the events of the past few days, but the question that remained was: How had the witch found trouble after only three days away?

My blood boiled as I fought to keep my demon contained, my volatile emotions feeding into hers through the bond until I felt myself a hair-trigger away from returning to Faerie and razing the entire plane to the ground. The witch's panicked breaths and my healing wound were the only holds barring me to the Belle house.

Beside me, Ember tossed and turned, kicking off the blankets for the hundredth time.

I fought the urge to touch her clammy skin with a gentle graze of my fingertips. Though compassion for her suffering rolled through me, I couldn't deny that I was furious with the witch.

Furious at her for putting herself in such a position.

Furious with her for not fighting back hard enough.

Furious at her for almost dying, alone on a miserable patch of Faerie where no one would find her bones to bury.

All that anger needed a release, but I had no outlet to

unleash it, so instead, I remained as Ember's protector. A role I found myself too eager to fill.

When the morning dew kissed her window and the sun's rays shone inside, I rose from the bed, stretching my tight muscles. I could hear her sisters moving around the house, preparing for their day, and I felt an itch of longing for the normalcy and love the four sisters shared.

A text from Carreau lit up the screen of my phone, and I growled low at his message.

Urgent. Come to the Riverfront now.

Whatever the demon wanted, it wouldn't be pleasant if he was bothering me this early in the morning. My fingers twitched as I realized Oberon may seek justice for the dead Fae. Would they be able to find his bones after the tree swallowed him whole? Did I care?

My gaze returned to the sleeping witch. I wasn't eager to leave her behind, but I needed to get this meeting over with.

I portaled straight to the Riverfront, a quiet part of the city away from tourists, and flinched at the stench of seafood and frying oil from the restaurants along the Mississippi River wafting towards me with the wind. A bright red trolley car moved over the tracks and the dusky blue riverboat casino Ember and I visited stood ported nearby, camouflaged under the High Priestess's disguising spell.

Rebecca Graves stood with Carreau and Hunt Boudreaux along the murky waterline. As I approached the trio of Council members, I observed their expressions. From their identical scowls, I knew it couldn't be good.

My spine straightened with unease as I noticed Hunt's livid scowl, his beast close to the surface. I wondered if this was retaliation for the other night at his compound. However, Carreau looked at once smug and bored with his golden blond hair shining in the early sunlight, so I doubted any repercussions would come today.

I walked over to where they stood, my eyes drifting down into the water.

The blood drained from my head when I saw the body.

Fuck.

Carreau motioned me over, his sunglasses hiding whatever emotion hid beneath. "Killian, thanks for meeting us here. I'm afraid we have bad news."

I could agree a shifter body floating face first in the river was, in fact, bad news.

"Is that—?"

Carreau nodded, cutting me off with a grimace. "Travis Porter. Son of Hunt's second. I believe you became acquainted with him last week."

Double fuck. Of course, the one male I beat into a pulp ended up murdered near the seedy casino boat.

I forced my voice to remain calm and collected, though inside I cursed blackly. "I am aware the shifters witnessed the altercation between us, but I can assure you I had nothing to do with this."

Hunt's eyes flashed with outrage, but Carreau wrapped his arm around my shoulder. "I've told them you wouldn't have been so sloppy if you killed him. Especially considering the cause of death."

My teeth ground together. "Slit neck?"

Rebecca huffed, her white teeth gleaming as she bared them at me. "Yes. We have passed the point of claiming Rosalind's death was a coincidence. We now have ourselves a serial killer on the loose."

With another close look of the scene, I realized we were within the vampires' boundaries. "Has Alexei been informed?"

Carreau nodded. "We sent news to the Vampire Court; however, we are going straight there to meet with the prince since he can't leave the confines of his manor until sundown.

We're here to oversee the clean-up. But that's not why we invited you here today."

Nonplussed, I quirked a brow. "It's not?"

Hunt and Rebecca turned their faces away, before Carreau dropped his bombshell. "We want you to help us look into these crimes and find the killer before the Samhain festival."

I fought to keep the surprise off my face, while thoughts of Ember's scheme ran through my head. "Why me? What happened to Alexei's manhunt using his mystical reward for the creature who finds the killer?"

A cloud of agitated fury rose above the High Priestess at the mention of the stolen object. But she merely crossed her slender arms and glared at me as if I were to blame for her misfortunes. "This has gone past Alexei's own personal vendetta. This affects us all, therefore we cannot take any more chances for violence. And according to Carreau, you're our best bet."

Her lips curled as if the compliment pained her.

Carreau's wide grin stretched farther with delight. "We need an impartial judge to determine who could be behind these attacks. With Rosalind killed near a ley line and the shifter killed on the vampires' lands, we are dealing with someone who does not distinguish between creatures. Your skillset as Pride's mercenary is legendary. You're our best bet at getting this solved quickly and efficiently."

Finished with his counterparts' performance, Hunt stalked towards me with violence radiating from his hulking frame. "I don't care what y'all say. I don't trust dis demon. Don't you know who his pere is?" he growled, his anger from the previous night's events still blatant, as well as suspicion. "Dis demon killed Travis in retaliation."

My throat tightened as I forced myself to grin, aloof. "And where's your proof, wolf? I may be born into Satan's lineage, but I do not follow his ethical code, unlike the pups in your litter."

Spittle flew from his lips. "You collect his souls! And everyone saw you fight him. You only finished da job."

I fought a sneer, breathing through my nose to calm myself. "Collecting souls is merely business. If creatures would stop making pacts, then I wouldn't remain in your city. And for the last time—I never touched that wolf beyond the incident at the den."

"Enough!" Rebecca spat, her heels sliding free of the damp earth as she walked back to the concrete sidewalk. With a fiery glare at Hunt, she turned to me. "Can you do it, yes or no?"

"And what would be in it for me?" I asked her as I edged closer.

I looked for signs of Ember in the witch yet could not see the resemblance—in looks or temperament. She had Isla's blonde hair, still bright and youthful in the morning sun, and the severe frown marring her face resembled the eldest Belles' pique. There was none of Ember's humor, only her fire.

Carreau's dry hands settled over my shoulder. "What would you like? Territory here in the city? Though, I suppose you won't have use of it soon enough. Gold? Jewels? Tell us and we can make it work."

I paused, thinking hard on the arrangement. With Ember's pact, I would be compacted to solve the murder regardless of their ploys. However, the chance to acquire a reward for my future reign? That could make this ordeal worthwhile. "I'll take a favor to be repaid when and where I desire."

Rebecca and Hunt hissed, but Carreau's brows furrowed in thought.

There always contained a risk in entering an open-ended bargain, but they were desperate.

A fact we all knew.

Carreau held out his hand in agreement. "You have a deal.

I would start with the vampires, considering the location of the shifter's death. I'll get you in contact with Alexei to schedule a meetup. After that, you can arrange a meeting with Rebecca, and I'll force Oberon to remain on our plane long enough for you to interview him."

I shook his hand. "That should work."

Aggrieved, Hunt and Rebecca stalked away, while Carreau wandered to the clean-up crew that arrived to deal with Travis.

I watched them removed his body from the murky waters, my brows drawn pensively. His dark blood stained the surface, but all of his limbs remained intact. He was lucky the gators hadn't got to him yet.

But why leave him here? What was the killer's motive?

Alexei and the vampires would be out a pretty penny in covering up any mortal witnesses who may have seen his body. Everyone within the Council had something to lose were creatures to be discovered.

It made no sense, which only captured my curiosity more.

I turned and walked along the grassy road alongside the river, wondering how I would juggle all my tasks now. Especially when the witch realized her reward would be out of reach. All compliancy would go out the window if she knew there was nothing in it for her.

Unless I *didn't* tell her. She would certainly be more biddable if she still thought she could earn Alexei's trinket.

Thoughts of the witch and the night prior set my teeth on edge, and I found myself anxious to return to her home. With a final glance back at the port, I portaled away, ready to have it out with Ember once and for all.

Ember sat in bed surrounded by sticky, powdery beignets and a mug the size of her face filled with steaming chicory coffee. She flipped through the television in her fluffy robe, the house otherwise silent.

I watched her from my shadows as my anger finally reached its peak. "I see you're alive, though you don't deserve to be after your actions last night."

She shrieked, sending a plume of white sugar over her black comforter. "Holy shit, what is wrong with you?" She stared down at the mess with a moan and attempted to wipe away the powder, only to spread it further around.

"What's wrong with *me*?" I grated, shaking with my rage.

She rolled her eyes. "You know what I mean. Don't linger where I can't see you. Give a girl some warning."

Her obvious deflection gave me pause. Though her words were lighthearted and full of her normal sarcasm, I could see the deadness in her eyes. I took a breath before I kneeled, picking up a greasy donut from the floor. I dropped it in the paper bag on her night table, the brief respite away from her haunted eyes centering my emotions.

When she spoke, her voice was tight. A barely restrained sob lurked near the back of her throat. "You don't need to lecture me; I know how much I fucked up and what the cost could have been without you there to save me."

"Then why do you continue to put yourself at risk? Do you have a death wish?"

She shook her head, a lone tear splashing onto her chest. "It's complicated."

Frustrated by her non-answer, I ground my teeth. "Then enlighten me."

She pulled her legs into her chest with a huff. "You share nothing with me, so why should I confide in you?"

With her startling blue eyes focused on me, my breath stuttered. I turned, breaking her stare, and walked to her window overlooking the street below. Leaning against the ledge, I studied the oak tree, my eyes tracking the waterfall of leaves covering the ground in brown bracken.

Resigned, I cleared my throat. "What do you want to know?"

"Oh, I don't know? Why did you disappear for days without a word? What did you discover in the Boudreaux pack lands? Where did you go this morning? Those could be swell places to start."

Her questions were valid, and as was her agitation. It didn't mean I would share all my secrets, nor would I allow her to distract me from the root of our issues—her impulsiveness and lack of self-preservation.

Moving to her dresser scattered with her belongings, I settled my back against the drawers. My fingers grazed her jewelry and a stained tarot deck, cataloguing everything that she deemed worthy to display on her altar. "I didn't intentionally set out to ignore you or keep you away from the case. Nor did I disappear. My father sent me on a mission to acquire souls who were indebted to him, which kept me away from the city for a few days," I finally muttered when the silence continued.

"Your father?" she asked with a furrowed brow.

A hollow breath escaped. What was the point of keeping it a secret any longer? If the Council knew, the entire city was soon to follow. Regardless of the icy set to my shoulders, my voice still sounded defensive. "Satan, the Lord of Pride."

She gaped, her wane face paling further. "As in—"

"The anti-Christ, the Devil? Yeah, that's the one," I muttered, carefully observing her reaction. My heart thudded at her heaving chest, the slice of terror through the bond.

"And you're his son?"

My voice contained thirty years' worth of bitterness. "Unfortunately." I turned to look out the window, the memories suffocating. "As for your other questions, I didn't call because I had nothing concrete to go on. I will not speculate with you and have you impulsively acting without me. Which, considering last night, was a good call on my part." My eyes darkened to slits. "Now, it's your turn. What happened last night?"

I watched her face in the glass's reflection.

She was the loveliest creature I had ever seen. I wanted to shake her and then hold her close for upending my life and holding hers with so little value. Tears gleamed in her bright blue eyes, but she bravely fought them back. "This time of year isn't easy for me. They were my parents, the two witches that died five years ago."

My body froze. How the fuck had I missed this?

Sorrow and heartache soared through my chest. I wasn't sure if it was hers or mine, but I felt it keenly. After my shock wore off, dread settled low in my stomach. I hadn't yet heard from Taliah, but I knew whatever her spies dredged up would reveal this ugly truth.

No wonder she had such a personal stake in this.

I should have known this was more than her foolish perception of her Coven and a stolen vampire relic. This was personal to her, which made her dangerous.

All the fight drained from me as I watched the pain on her face. Dark, demented memories of my own swam to the surface. The bloody spike, a broken wail. *No.*

I swallowed, forcing my demon back as I focused on the present. For once, I was at a loss for words. Unsure of how to act.

My eyes drifted back to her dresser, the ancient tome nestled next to her stack of candles. I could sense the ancient magick from here, like a siren calling to me, as well as the ashy scent of brimstone. Stepping closer, I ran my fingers over the spine, a chill settling over my back.

I lifted the book, my eyes widening at the surprising heft before I read the title. "Do you know what this is?"

She jumped from the bed. "You weren't supposed to see that," she muttered.

With a frown, I moved the book away from her reaching grip. "Why do you have this?" I asked. As I flipped through the musty pages, the hairs on the back of my neck stood up.

There were dark, evil spells in here.

Spells capable of trapping and killing demons, not to mention ancient histories of my kind.

Undeterred, she shrugged. "Not going to lie. I was researching more about you and your people. This daughter of Hecate refuses to allow your pact to dictate my life without understanding the rules."

A surprising flash of pride glowed through me before I could quell it. But the grim risk of such a text in the hands of a desperate witch took root despite my approval at her proactive thinking.

I crossed my arms, satisfied that at least sorrow no longer suffused her bright eyes. "I'm pleased you're taking this seriously. Though you've gone to your best efforts to throw away your life. Which brings me to what I discovered this morning. There's been another death. A shifter."

Her eyes grew round as her apprehension rose to the surface once more. I nearly kicked myself at my lack of delicacy, but we had no time to ease her into this. Especially now that the stakes had just risen.

"Who?"

My voice grew clipped. "Travis."

"Oh, Goddess," she croaked, swaying on her feet. "How did he die?"

From the hard glint in my eyes, she knew before the words escaped my mouth. "Slashed throat. Same as the others."

She bit her lip, collapsing onto the bed with a bounce,

sending a fluff of powdered sugar around her like a cloud. Her head dropped into her hands, her hair fanning around her like silk. "What do we do?"

My mercenary training kicked in, and I gratefully allowed myself to refocus on the mission. "I'll organize a meeting with the Vampire Prince. Until then, I want to train you."

"Train me?" Cautious weariness spread over her face.

I assessed her thin arms and pale skin. This experience in Faerie weakened her, but I would not allow her recklessness to endanger her life again. "I'll teach you how to fight. I don't want another repeat of last night. If you can't use your magick, you sure as Hell will use your fists to get away from creatures who won't take no for an answer."

Her eyes filled with tears once more. "I'm not sure I have that kind of fight in me right now."

"Don't sell yourself short, witch. You have fire within you; you just need to learn how to channel it. And how to control yourself." I shifted into my shadows, needing an escape from the vulnerable emotions creeping through my steel walls. "I've got to go, but I'll return soon."

The witch's uncertain smile was almost my undoing. "I don't think I said it last night, but thank you for saving me. And for staying."

I swallowed thickly. Not trusting my voice, I gave her a nod before I portaled away.

All while my heart pounded in my chest like a frenzied drum.

18

EMBER

As I waltzed up the pathway to the Coven estate, Mr. Rollings held the door open with a scowl. His white hair gleamed under the flickering candelabras, and I suppressed a grin at his vigilant gaze. I set one measly piece of art on fire and now I was enemy number one.

It hardly seemed fair.

"You're late," he hissed, leading us to the meeting room with a huff.

Witches and warlocks sat spread around our formal dining room, already helping themselves to seafood gumbo and rice. The mood was lively and familiar with the sounds of laughter and soft jazz playing in the background.

I spotted Everett Domingue and his sister Rosemary sporting bright decorative shawls. As if sensing my appraisal, Rosemary met my eyes and winked, causing me to miss my next step. A powerful seer, with the allusive spirit affinity, she was one of the strongest witches in the country.

Vaguely worried, I wondered what secrets of mine she may have seen. And if she would share anything she learned through her visions.

Mr. Rollings came around with flutes of champagne

decorated with small arils of pomegranate, and my instinct was to rush him for a glass of liquid courage. However, the memories of the Fae's wandering hands and putrid mouth against mine held my hand back from reaching forward for a glass

I ignored my sisters' gaping mouths at my uncommon restraint and searched the crowded room for Fleur instead. It wasn't like her to avoid me after a night of partying, and I grew worried when I noticed her father seated alone.

Rebecca cleared her throat, standing on the elevated stage with a cool smile. "Witches and warlocks, happy tidings."

"Happy tidings," we intoned as one, though the various accents made the sound less creepy.

Grandmother's face trailed over the Coven with little warmth. "Before we begin our evening, let's discuss the elephant in the room. I'm sure all of you have heard about the most recent murder discovered near the Riverfront. Along with our lack of any credible suspects."

Tension rolled through the room like an oppressive cloud at her proclamation

Perhaps I was still in shock. That I was more relieved another creature hadn't won the amulet outweighed any sadness over Travis's death, which probably spoke volumes about me. It wasn't as if I *hated* the wolf. He was a real piece of shit, but before our animosity, we had been friendly. And now, because of this psycho killer, he would never run with his pack or howl under the full moon again.

Rebecca continued on, despite the uneasy whispers stretching across the table. "Before we begin, I must stress the importance of showing strength in the community for our Samhain festival. Though we are strong in our numbers and with our power, we still lack answers to the recent deaths and must keep these matters away from the mortals. We must remain vigilant. These festivals are not just for our Coven's pleasure. Samhain serves a much more important purpose: our continued ability to thrive and prosper in this city."

One of the younger warlocks stood, his fists clenched at his sides. "What does the festival matter? If the murders have begun again, we could all be in grave danger. Are we going to allow the creature responsible to get away with this and put our lives at stake once more?"

Rebecca stiffened with disapproval as the crowd murmured in agreement. "The Council has done everything within its means to discover the villain, but with no credible evidence or suspects, we can do little but continue to keep vigilant in our own circles."

The red-faced warlock sat down in a huff while the aggrieved witches quieted under the pressure of Grandmother's icy gaze.

I noticed Rosemary and her brother watching the Coven with pursed lips. Their family brought many powerful spells and rituals from the shamans of old when their ancestors first immigrated to New Orleans. When Grandfather's family arrived from Salem, fleeing the witch trials, many of the Voodoo practitioners chose to either join the Coven or remain independent. From the looks of displeasure on the siblings' faces, Grandmother's approach to this recent development disappointed them.

When no one else spoke, Rebecca moved on to lighter topics.

I took a deep breath, sending a covert glance at the back door. Turning to Audra, I leaned close to whisper in her ear. "I'm going to find the restroom. If Grandmother asks, tell her I'm not feeling great and will join them soon."

Jade's eyebrows pinched, and she leaned over Audra to search my face. "Are you okay? Have you been taking your birth control tonic?"

I waved away her worry. "Of course, I never miss my doses. My stomach's just upset from the beignets I ate earlier."

Audra hid a laugh with a delicate cough. "That's what you get for stealing my breakfast, bitch."

Isla opened her purse and placed a small vial into my hand with a smile. "I always carry healing tonics when you're around." She smirked. "Let me know if you need more."

"Thanks, sweetness." My cheeks reddened as I stood, sneaking out of the room. I glanced back to ensure I wasn't followed and ran to the library, shutting the heavy door behind me.

Like before, the room was eerily quiet.

With my efforts to translate the demonic grimoire reaching a stand-still, I sought another text to aid me in my quest to discover a way out of my pact. My serpent dagger twirled in my hand as I walked back to the hidden book cabinet. But as I neared the darkened corner, I jolted as I realized I wasn't alone.

Tabitha Harlow stood over the shelves, her silvery brown hair a protective curtain around her face. She was the golden witch Grandmother wished we would become, the ambitious brown-noser who would just love to catch me out doing something nefarious.

I shuffled my feet, contemplating whether to run. Uncertain, my boots kicked the leg of the desk, echoing in the quiet room.

Fuck.

I let out a small groan, pasting a false smile on my face. "Hey, girl, what's up? What are you doing here?"

She jerked to face me, growing pale. "Oh. Hello, Ember." Curling her hands into fists, nails like talons, she hid the drops of blood as she stepped away from the cabinet. "What are you doing in here?"

I shrugged, leaning against the ancient desk while I causally slipped my dagger into my pocket. "Just needed to escape the Coven for a few minutes, you know?"

She cocked her head, studying me under the candlelight. "Fleur told me about your adventure the other night. You know, Ember, demons are slippery creatures. I would be wary when dealing with their ilk."

I suppressed a sigh. If another witch told me how dangerous the demon was, I was going to revolt. My neck heated in aggravation at Fleur's loose lips. "Did Fleur tell you about Killian?"

Tabitha's eyes hardened. "No," she trailed off, raising her brow. "Hunt Boudreaux lodged a complaint against you for coming to their property uninvited. He shared you were with a demon asking questions about the recent murders."

Of course, this all trailed back to the pack. I would never be free of them, it seemed.

I bounced off the desk, needing to be anywhere but here. "Yeah, well, Hunt is a cantankerous dog who needs to learn some manners."

Though outwardly calm, my hands shook with unease. If Tabitha knew of my irksome evening at the den, that meant my grandmother for sure knew. "Is Fleur here?" I asked, my voice breaking off.

I needed a change of subject before I set the library on fire.

Her gaze grew suspicious before she shook her head. "She wasn't feeling great, so Dad let her stay home."

"Lucky. Well, I'll leave you to it. My sisters will wonder where I wandered off to."

Tabitha watched me flee without a word.

Yet, I ran like the Devil himself was chasing me, a prickle of fear spreading under my skin. This was becoming more complicated than I could have imagined, and I felt more alone than ever. I didn't know why Tabitha's judgement bothered me so much. Not too long ago, I would have been right there alongside her, making remarks over the demon's sketchy career and ties to Hell.

But I realized I did trust Killian. Now more than ever.

He could have left me in Faerie to die, severing him from the bond and my spell, but he put himself in peril to save me. And then he stayed the night while I suffered through the effects of the Fae wine and the traumatic aftermath of my attack without a word of complaint.

Would an evil demon with no moral code do something like that?

Instead of returning to the meeting, I veered towards the gardens, needing some fresh air. In the darkness, the hedge maze appeared villainous—a terrifying abyss of darkness. I followed the scent of roses and admired the bouquet with a deep breath.

"Ember Marie Belle."

I froze, my fingers outstretched to a pale pink rose, the thorn breaking through my skin like a sharp bite. Before I looked at my grandmother, I took a shaky breath, bracing for her anger. "I can explain," I started, but she cut me off with a look.

Grandmother strode towards me, her hair uncoiling from her elegant updo as she glared across the ivy trellis at me. "And what do you have to say for your actions?"

I couldn't very well tell her the truth. If she discovered what foolhardy mess I found myself in this time, she would force me and my sisters to remain in this estate until I died.

And so, the lies I told my sisters would have to continue.

"Killian and I met at the Bacchanal. We're sort of dating, and he invited me to the den to watch him fight in the ring. The unfortunate altercation with Travis happened because of the wolf's uncouth words about me. Killian protected my honor."

Grandmother pinched the bridge of her nose, shaking her

head. "Unfortunate altercation? Uncouth words? Ember, you humiliated me and our Coven by encroaching on shifter lands uninvited on top of socializing with such a ghastly creature. Carreau may be on the Council, but that doesn't mean you can trust demons. I forbid you from continuing any sort of relationship."

My irritation finally reached its peak. "Grandmother, I love and respect you, but this is bullshit. You can't tell me who I'm allowed to spend time with or date. Killian is twice the man Wren ever was, and you had no problem with the two of us."

She sighed, more from exhaustion than genuine anger. "Ember, what am I going to do with you? Allowing your relationship with the wolf was one thing because of his family's connection to the Council. Do you even know where your new beau comes from? He is the son of Satan himself!"

I squirmed under the weight of her disappointment, but my newfound trust with in the demon anchored me from spiraling. My words were soft but unwavering. "I trust him with my life. I will continue dating him, and that's final."

She tapped her nails against the glass table, considering my words. "Since you will do what you please, regardless of what I say, I will let this new development slide *for now*. But I don't want to hear another whisper of you sticking your nose in other creatures' business, most especially not anything to do with these murders. Am I understood?"

Crossing my fingers behind my back, I nodded. "Understood."

She glanced at the roses behind me, her face drooping with sorrow. "Your mother loved these flowers. I, for one, cannot stand the sickly fragrance of their buds, but Helene threatened to cut off her hair if I touched them. Even after her death, I can't seem to defy her wishes now."

I breathed a hoarse laugh, my heart aching. "Was she very

skilled with her magick? I hardly remember seeing her use her fire."

Grandmother chuckled. "Oh, she was one of the best witches I've ever known. Her and your father were powerful beyond measure, ensuring you girls were gifted as well. But they wanted you to grow up without the weight of such a burden."

A prickle of hurt lit within her eyes and from her tone, I knew she didn't agree with their methods. For once, she didn't look like the ice maiden High Priestess but my grandmother, a grieving woman who bore her own share of burdens thanklessly.

Biting my lip, I asked, "Is it possible for a witch to spell someone without trying? For a witch's emotions to create a spell from desire alone?"

Grandmother watched me, considering. "To conjure and cast effortlessly is a rare thing. Such magick is powerful and begotten from years of training. But with magick, anything is possible." She gave me a pointed look. "Was there a reason you asked?"

I shook my head, my heart deflating.

She let out a long-suffering sigh and shooed me away, the mask returning. "Go find your sisters. Dinner has already begun."

"Thank you, Grandmother."

I wished I could escape the rest of my problems as easily as this one.

19
KILLIAN

I shifted back into formation, my feet unsteady on the uneven plot of grass within the Belle's spacious backyard. Dead leaves and branches littered the ground, and the vestibules of a once-lovely garden lay untended and charred near the oak tree responsible for the bracken.

Regardless of our less-than-ideal training space, I continued to push Ember, uncaring of her fatigue and growing resentment. "Focus, witch. Eyes on your opponent. Distraction gets you killed."

She spun, attempting to dodge my fist as I struck, knocking her backwards once more. With her teeth bared, she lifted her fists. "You're such a dick. You know that, right?"

In her attempt at a stealth ambush, she rushed forward, her movements sloppy.

With ease, I dodged her pathetic attack and kicked out my leg encased in the leather trousers she seemed to love, knocking her back onto her ass.

She lay prone on the dirt, eyes flashing with annoyance as her breath wheezed out in shallow pants. Her moon and stars embroidered t-shirt with the phrase, "Support Local Witches," darkened with sweat, while her leggings stretched over her body in ways that made me stiffen.

I now realized why tight pants could distract in a fight.

"Okay, enough," she huffed, closing her eyes as she sunk further into the ground. "I'm going to become one with the grass now. We'll try again later."

I shook my head, holding my hand out to her and fighting a smile at her dramatics. "No, we keep going until I say otherwise."

Something flashed in her eyes, but she quickly waved the emotion away, concealing it through the bond.

"Bossy bastard," she hissed with another tortured groan.

For the first time in my life, the insult made me laugh.

Rolling her eyes, she let me lift her back up to her feet without further complaint, but I could feel her underlying frustration radiating through the bond.

"Loosen your stance," I commanded, rolling my eyes when she exaggerated her movements. "Not that loose. You're worse than the prepubescent demons my commander, Taliah, trains."

"First, I resent that. Let me loose and I could scratch and bite my way out of a kerfuffle. And second, Hell lets females command their armies? I guess it's not as primitive as I thought."

Oh, if she only knew....

My shoulders rolled back, and I refocused on today's mission. I wouldn't allow her flirting to distract me from teaching her skills to defend herself.

No matter how desperately I craved it.

I adjusted her stance once more, my mood darkening at the atrocities I had witnessed. "Oh, Hell is primitive alright; we just respect strength and power above all else. Try again."

"Lucky for me, I have neither," she grumbled as she squatted down, hinging on her foot as she punched.

Harder than necessary, my arm knocked away her fist before I kicked her back onto her back with ease.

"Oh, that's it!" she screeched, jumping to her feet with more energy than she had displayed in the last twenty minutes. "What the fuck is your deal? If you wanted to smack me around a bit, you didn't need to pretend to train me to do so."

Black dots coated my vision as my humor wiped away. Seeing her like this—frantic and defenseless—brought back all those buried reminders of how close she had come to death. Before I could stop myself, my hands seized her arms, pulling her closer to me as if crazed. "My *problem* is you almost *died*. In a miserable plot of Faerie, where you would be absorbed into the earth and made into worm meal. All because you couldn't defend yourself. All because you can't control your fucking impulses!"

Crimson marred her fair cheeks as her hands gripped my shirt, twisting it as she sought to get closer to my heated skin. "I don't see why that would bother you. You'd be free of me and my hex once and for all. That's the only reason you're here, remember?"

My fangs lengthened. "I can't determine if you actually believe the shit falling from your lips or if you are more disturbed than I realized."

"Oh, I am nowhere near as disturbed as you are." Her lips twisted with cruel amusement and my traitorous eyes dipped to them with hunger. She pushed against my chest, my body not giving an inch.

My emotions felt jumbled, blending with hers until I didn't know which emotions were my own. Inhaling her warm peach scent, I leaned down and wrapped my hand around her braid, pulling her neck to the side and baring her soft throat to me. "Is this how it's going to be, witch? Are you going to sit back and take it, or are you going to put in a little effort for once?"

Temper exploding, she dislodged my fist from her hair and

threw her braid behind her back with a sneer. "Demon, just because I haven't trained in Hell for the past however many years under Satan's tutelage in the fiery pits, doesn't mean I'm weak."

"Fiery pits?" I snorted, not at all amused. "Not so much in the Realm of Pride. And no, you haven't fought in battle, but last night, you put yourself in the position to be taken advantage of with no contingency plan to get yourself out."

Her eyes grew cold. "Victim blaming much?"

With growing ire, I stepped away from her. "I'm not saying it was your fault the Fae attacked you. I'm furious you keep putting yourself in dangerous and vulnerable positions, yet you refuse to work on harnessing your magick to protect yourself!"

"Pretty sure I've managed the past twenty-three years just fine without your guidance. I think I can manage a few more on my own."

A choked laugh escaped. "Gods, these past few months were you *managing fine on your own*? What about the night I found you puking into the Mississippi River alone and unprotected after the concert where any creature could have preyed upon you?"

Surprise rolled off her. "That was different. And I didn't even know you were there—"

"I took measures to remain in my shadows the entire time, but I ensured you made it to a cab and then home. A task your boyfriend should have carried out."

My lips curled at the word.

The wolf allowed his supposed female to wander off alone in such an inebriated state where anyone could have taken advantage of her.

And the idiot wondered why she ditched him.

With stilted, backward steps, she turned to flee. "I'm done with this. And you."

She would not escape her fears this time. I wouldn't allow her to.

Grabbing her arm, I forced her back, not releasing her until she glared up at me. "I don't think so, witch. You want to leave, then make me let go." My grip tightened to hammer my point.

With a growl, she lashed out, her nails scratching down my arms as she kicked my shins with frustration.

Pathetic. "Is that all you've got? It's no wonder the Fae took advantage of the situation. And you're not even under the effects of wine or the Faerie moon. Are you even a witch? Where's your power? Your skill? All I see a spoiled brat who gives up at the first chance."

Everything around us froze. She shook, her body radiating the locked away emotions she refused to release. Through her black lashes, her eyes glowed fiery orange. "Get. Off. Me!" she screamed, her magick exploding from her in a rush of smoke and flames.

I flew backwards, my wings catching my momentum before I fell. When her flames followed my movements, chaotic and unbridled, I dematerialized to avoid the sparking embers.

Instead of anger, I felt heart pounding relief at her show of power.

It meant she may make it in this world.

As soon as her magick spent itself, she collapsed onto the earth, tears staining her cheeks while she wept.

I approached her slowly, giving her space and watching her frenzied breaths. "Are you okay?"

She nodded, her lips trembling.

But she wasn't. After her loss of control, the walls she built up through the bond collapsed into ashes, revealing the truth.

More solidly, she answered, "Yeah, I'm okay. Sorry."

Confusion flowed through me at her words and the solemn curve of her lips. "Don't apologize. You should be able to defend yourself in any way you can. I'm sorry for pushing you too far. I've been under a lot of pressure and may have taken out some of it on you." I paused, clearing my throat. "I didn't mean a word of what I said."

The moment stagnated as we watched each other. Softening her frown, she held out her hand, and I immediately lifted her up.

Though I wanted nothing more than to crush her to my chest and whisper apologies into her hair, I released her, watching as she walked over to the back porch and collapsed onto the wooden steps.

"Regardless of my lack of skills, I appreciate you trying. You must have better things to do than train me."

I sat beside her, saying nothing. Even knowing her spell precipitated these feelings inside of me, I couldn't force myself to lie to her. Because there was nothing I wanted more than to be with her in this moment.

She lifted those dazzling blue eyes to me, and I thought I could get lost in those depths if I let myself. "Is it something I could help with? Whatever pressures you're under?"

I laughed without humor. "Not unless you can change the future."

Her lips quirked. "The key to not living up to expectations set out for you is to not try at all. Haven't you heard avoiding your problems is the best way to survive?"

"I forgot who I was speaking with. You *are* the Queen of Avoidance."

She pushed my shoulder, her smile infectious. "I resent that. I'm simply keeping my heart and mental state safe."

A sigh drifted free, and I glanced out into the yard once more. "No, you're hiding so you won't be hurt again. But some of us can't hide forever. You included, witch."

Her eyes glittered in the darkening sunlight as she caught me in her web. "And you know this how?"

"Because I am the son of Satan, and my destiny is to claim his throne and become one of the seven Lords of Hell. I know all about being forced into a life you don't want."

Her face shuttered, arms draping around the wooden stair beam. "When does this happen?"

She was too painful to look at, so my gaze swept down to my boots and remained there. "As soon as my business here is finished. After Samhain."

"And that's why you're so concerned about my spell? Because you won't be able to leave your realm, though your demon would clamor for his mate?" she choked. "You realize if I hexed you, it wouldn't last forever. It's not the same as a more intricate curse."

My back stiffened. "I can't have your hex over me when I return to Hell. That is nonnegotiable. Speaking of responsibilities, I have our meeting scheduled with Alexei."

Taking a deep breath, she dropped the subject. "I've never been inside the Vampire Court."

Gaze rivetted to her fingers brushing a trail over her leggings, I muttered, "And you won't tomorrow night, either. We're going to visit with the Vampire Prince at his club and interview him about his whereabouts and why someone would target Rosalind and Travis."

"Are you talking about Bite?" she gasped. "As in the vampire sex club?"

I pinched the bridge of my nose, forgetting about the vampire's establishment catered to depraved sexual proclivities. "That's the one."

She sputtered, "But we'd have to blend in... in a sex club."

A spark of humor settled through the cloud of frustration, and I huffed out a laugh, meeting her eyes with a lifted brow. "Yes, witch. Undercover means you try to blend in. Will this be a problem?"

"No. I'll do it." Her cheeks pinkened, and I fought a groan at the pulse of desire through the bond.

"Did you want to keep training or call it quits for today?"

"I'm down for more." She stood and held her hand out to me, nodding to my leathers. "All that medieval times training did you good, demon."

Eyes crinkled at the corners in a wry grin, I let her pull me up. "That's because I am an unstoppable force. The reckoning the mortal plane fears."

Rolling her eyes, she got back into formation. "I wouldn't go *that* far."

My lips pursed. "Want to put your money where your mouth is, witch?"

"Put up or shut up, demon."

20
KILLIAN

With one step into the elusive Bite, I felt as if I had transported myself into the Realm of Lust. Bodies swayed together as booze, blood, and sweat coated the air in a sheen of desire. After checking in at the front desk with the young, pierced vampire wearing a medley of chains and studded belts—and little else—we entered through the bolted doors that kept away curious mortal eyes.

I could see my reflection along the black marble floors, the crystal-spun chandelier sparkling in the shadowy dungeon like a disco ball. Whips and chains adorned the crimson walls, making the club resemble a medieval hall, with the vampires playing the role of conquerors.

If Ember felt shocked by the mass of nude bodies and sexual activities, she showed no outward sign of it. The hemline of her skintight, black latex dress cut in an over-exaggerated heart at her bust inched closer and closer to her ample ass cheeks with every move she made.

"Let's find somewhere to sit." I fought the urge to growl at the creatures who turned and gaped at her progression through the club. My hand clasped hers, and I pulled her through the sea of bodies to a secluded, empty leather couch.

She sank onto the buttery cushions, thighs pressed together, as she perused the crowd with interest. Glancing back up to where I stood frozen, she cocked a brow. "Are you going to stand there all night?"

My demon clamored inside my mind at her sensual display. Taking a breath of saturated air, I sat beside her, sending her a warning glare when she sidled closer to me.

Her long hair that resembled a sheet of silk brushed over my bared chest like water. She leaned closer, her lips grazing my ear as her fingers traced the springy dark hairs visible through my gaping shirt. "How long do we have to wait before Alexei arrives?"

The witch was playing her part perfectly. With her wanton dress and bedroom eyes, she blended in with the rest of the patrons as if she belonged here. Imagining her pressed into a booth by some unknown male had my aggression firing.

Chin angled down, the scarred skin of my cheek brushed against her softness. "I'll know when the prince arrives. For now, let's just watch the clientele for any suspicious activity."

Her glossy lips quirked, capturing my undivided attention. "No problem with that."

Eyes widened in surprised lust, she watched as a vampire and a nymph disappeared into the partition opposite our vantage point. The booth did little to disguise their activities, the sounds of the female's moans carrying over the pulsing bass. Ember bit her lip and blushed, glancing away as the nymph stood, straddling the male's face, his fangs visible through the gauziness of her dress pulled to her waist.

My hands clenched into my suit pants in reaction to Ember's sweet arousal. Before I could do something idiotic, like drag the witch over my lap and tongue the skin at her neck, a barmaid approached.

The blonde vampire's lips broadened into a saucy grin as she sauntered over. "Can I get y'all anything?" she purred, glancing between the witch and me with blatant interest in her eyes.

Ember's smile was tight. "I'll have a club soda with extra lime."

I hid my surprise and ordered the same before the vampire hurried away with a knowing smirk. The witch pretended to watch the dance floor, sinking deeper into the cold seat. But I could sense the sudden fire simmering beneath the surface of her placid expression. "What's wrong?"

Ember's eyes narrowed on mine. "She definitely wanted to fuck you."

I rasped a laugh, looking down at her with a smirk. "I think she wanted to fuck *both* of us. But she's not my type."

Ember looked at me with skepticism. "Her tits were bursting from her top and she's gorgeous enough to be a model. Isn't that everyone's type?"

I shrugged with nonchalance.

After a beat, she let out an amused snort. "I suppose we have a 'we like your vibe' kind of thing going. Sitting alone and searching for our next victim."

My lips twitched. "Perhaps," I murmured, leaning closer to breathe against the shell of her ear. "But one thing about me is I do not share. Ever."

Her heart hammered within her chest, the beat bursting through me. "What about the female from Low Road? Is she your girlfriend?"

It took me a moment to remember the scene Ember had stumbled into. Amarisa's arms and legs had wrapped around me like a boa constrictor as I delivered the payment for the information on the wolf. I reached my arm over the seat back, bringing our bodies closer together. "No, she's not my girlfriend."

"A hookup then?"

I shook my head, searching the crowd as the energy of the room shifted.

Her fingers twitched in her lap. "Well then, what—"

"Shh," I broke the witch's next question off as the Vampire Prince made his arrival. I stood, keeping him in my line of sight. "Stay here." I disappeared into the shadows, moving towards the mirrored bar top overflowing with creatures ordering drinks in shiny glassware.

Alexei Vasilyev's raven hair shone from a distance, rumpled from fingers pulling through the thick strands. Two stunning nymphs adorned him like jewelry, running sultry touches down his bare arms and chest. The Vampire Prince allowed their liberties, though he never paused his conversation with the burly centaur who faced him with an indignant sneer.

As I looked upon him now, I understood why beings in the city called him the Prince of Pleasure. His long black robe spilled open to display pale muscled pecs and a defined abdomen free of hair. Ruby eyes sparkled with mirth, the red blending with the warm coffee-brown shade of his irises. In his grip, Alexei held his infamous emerald serpent staff—another tasteless relic from his people in Slovenia.

"I'll have a demon brew if you have it," I spoke to the barmaid, cataloguing the argument transpiring between the irate creature and the bemused prince. Sipping on the frothy brew, I gave a false smile to the pretty female with barbs through her brows. "Busy night?"

Her laugh tinkered as she flashed sharp, needlelike teeth. "Demon, this is nothing. You want to see a truly busy night at Bite, then come on a full moon. It will be a night you'll never forget."

I raised my brows. "A full moon? Do the shifters spend their moon nights here with vampires, then?"

She snorted, refilling glasses for the creatures next to me. "Full moons don't just affect the wolves.."

She shook her head wistfully, and I realized whatever she thought of, I'd rather not know. I took another sip of brew, the foam bubbling across my top lip. "And what brought you here to Bite?"

Her elbows propped on the bar as she refilled the glasses of nearby creatures. "The Vampire Prince is generous. He offered me this position despite not having worked outside of my village as a seamstress."

From her appearance, I surmised she belonged to Faerie, but her words confirmed my suspicions. An interesting development. With a flirtatious grin, I admitted, "I've heard much about the prince and his exploits back in Slovenia. The New Orleans vampires are lucky to have such a male as their leader."

Her eyes dashed to Alexei before she leaned across the bar top to whisper into my ear, her breath a cool kiss. "One would think so, but his own people revile him. After his father forced him into exile, all the uppity, elitist vampires turned on him."

Before I could question her further, the prince waltzed closer, a drained cocktail glass in hand. "Bridgette, another glass of blood wine, if you please." He stood at my height, though his frame was lankier. I could still sense his hidden strength as he watched the patrons with a small smile, sharp, white fangs peeking through firm lips.

When he noticed my presence, his smile froze. Eyes hardened into slits, a lethal calm settled over his well-bred swagger as he sidled closer to my perch at the bar, claiming the empty stool beside me. "What are you doing here, demon? I wasn't expecting you until tomorrow night at my Court." His smooth voice belied the wrath rolling off him in waves.

The annoyance rippling off him justified my decision to crash his club instead of watching his performance at his Court. I wanted a true reaction from the vampire, not his carefully orchestrated façade.

"I won't take too much of your time, Majesty."

He raised his brows at my impertinence. With a roll of his shoulders, he muttered, "Everyone wants a piece of poor Alexei. Well, let's get on with it. I have business to attend to."

Doubtful. I looked around the crowded bar with a lifted brow. "Is there anywhere we could go for more privacy?"

Suspicion rose in Alexei's crimson eyes. Drinking from his glass, he tilted his head to the vampire guards around the room. "You see the vampires? Well, they follow my every move, so privacy is a bit of a nonstarter. Not to mention, I am not foolish enough to go anywhere alone with a demon during these uncertain times."

This time, there was no mistaking the threat in the vampire's tone.

My throat bobbed with annoyance. "Carreau arranged this meeting because the Council has selected me to investigate the murders. I wanted your input on determining why the killer may have dropped the shifter on your lands. Or, if your people had any insight into who may be behind the attacks."

Alexei's lips thinned, his dark eyes flashing with anger. "As I told the rest of the Council, I have never seen that shifter before in my life. The wolves come into my territory for a night at the club, but I have no qualms with the pack. Lest you forget, someone slaughtered my cousin near the Fae borders, so I don't see how my Court garnered suspicion."

"I'm not trying to suggest anything of the sort. Just trying to find answers, same as you."

He clicked his tongue with mock concern.

This was getting me nowhere. Undeterred, I pushed further. "What of Wren Boudreaux? Do you have reasons to meet with him outside of Bite?"

Alexei laughed low, the rumbling in his chest catching hungry gazes from across the room. "Oh, you are bold, demon. But I'm a busy male and my working hours are strictly defined, so if you want an official meeting, you'll have to find me at my Court." He stood, grasping another fresh glass of blood wine. "Don't stay too long. Things go bump in the night around these parts, and I'd hate for you to find yourself lost in the darkness."

The prince rejoined the nymphs, his arms thrown over their shoulders as he led them towards the private suites, his guards following closely behind.

What a waste of time. Downing my brew, I wandered through the writhing bodies back to our table, ready to get the night over with, but I halted mid-step when I found the couch empty. My fangs lengthened in my mouth as I searched the crowds before I stilled.

I watched the witch dance, her arms raised in the air, smiling breezily under the twinkling lights while her hips moved in delicate circles.

Memories from the night of the Bacchanal resurfaced like a tidal wave. Despite my mission and dislike of witches, she drew my attention like a moth to a flame. Even when she sparred with me, I had fought the urge to feel the rasp of her swollen lips against mine and her sweet, supple body curling around me the way she danced near the fire. And now, her spell acted just as powerfully, captivating me where I stood.

When a vampire moved closer and trailed greedy, umber hands over her slim waist, I growled low. His fangs grazed along the witch's neck, and my feet were moving before I could process the action. My ribs squeezed tight with seething jealousy though I fought my possessive reaction. "Having a good time, witch?"

Her vivid eyes opened, and her lips curved into a defiant smile. There was no haze of alcohol in her eyes, only passion, as she dislodged from the vampire's grip. "Bonsoir, Pierre." She waved to the male, who swept back into the melee of the dance floor without a backwards glance.

His disappearance saved the male's life.

The witch sidled closer, her perfumed skin surrounding me. "I've been having a great time for your information. I forget how *informative* Bite can be."

A nymph's sudden scream of pleasure seemed to emphasize her point.

My chest vibrated with vexation as she brushed her hand against mine, pulling me into the mélange. Sex tinged the air as supernatural beings submitted to their carnal urges. The lights had dimmed, concealing the ravenous mouths and hands wandering over each other in delight, only flashes of titillating images in the darkness.

She gazed up at me in amusement before she moved her hips.

Temptation plowed through me as I watched her. What could one minute hurt? Allowing myself to escape into my own desires, I pulled the witch flush against my body, reveling in her hitched breath. I leaned to her ear, breathing her peach spiced skin like an addict. "Did you enjoy dancing with that male?"

Her delicate hands fisted into my shirt, ripping the buttons free with the force of her movements. "Pierre and I are old friends. It meant nothing. Surely, you can understand such arrangements." A pinch of her own envy bled through her words.

Appeased, my hands slid down to caress her lush, generous ass, barely covered by the tight pull of her dress. "Is that how you dance with all of your friends?"

Lids gone heavy, she ran her hands up my chest before wrapping her arms around my neck. "Only my *very* good friends." She shifted out of my arms, making my eyes grow black with displeasure until she settled her back against my chest. She ground against my responding cock, throwing me a haughty glance over her shoulder as if to punish me.

I felt drugged as I watched her hands caress the tops of her bare thighs before sliding up her dress to squeeze her gorgeous tits nearly spilling free from the low neckline.

With a glance back, she bit her pouty lips. "How am I doing?" Her arms fell back around my neck, opening herself up for my greedy perusal. "Do you think I can seduce the male away from his date?"

"I don't doubt you could lure anyone into your bed, witch," I rasped into her ear, making her shiver.

"Does that include you?"

The hot lash of her tongue as she licked a small line up to where my scar ended caused my cock to pulse against the seam of her ass. A sheen of sweat formed atop my upper lip as we moved within the wall of dancers.

I refused to answer her question, the answer obvious enough by my reaction to her.

Moans and the crude slaps of flesh surrounded us in a cacophony of lust, but our eyes remained trained on each other. She dropped her hands from around my neck to pull my hands to her hips in invitation.

I gripped the fabric of her dress as I fought the desire to rip it from her and fuck her against the wall as I lost myself under her spell. My mouth hovered over her neck, her small mewls beckoning me closer. "Fuck yes, it does," I snarled, the worlds pulled from me.

She writhed closer to my hips, and we both moaned at the sliding friction.

The night took on a hallucinatory edge as I inched my fingers past her hem, brushing against the damp edges of her lace thong. She moaned low as I pushed the material aside, my fingers spreading her wetness along the seam.

"So wet for me," I murmured, my fangs grazing her shoulder. When I felt her wild response to my touch, my demon became feral, the need to claim my mate all consuming.

Her hands caressed my swollen shaft beneath the stiff fabric of my pants. I leaned down to kiss her neck once more, stretching my finger inside her for the first time as she moaned low in my ear.

Absolute fucking bliss.

21

EMBER

Goddess above, this was *bliss*. I couldn't recall how Killian and I ended up coiled around each other. Nor did I care to analyze my actions as my body sizzled like an electric wire. Killian's wicked touch felt both greedy and tentative at once.

Restless and hopelessly aroused, I turned in his arms to watch his golden eyes. When he didn't run screaming, I lifted onto my toes and brushed my lips against his firm ones. A moan escaped at how perfect he felt, my eyes fluttering shut as I continued pressing small kisses around his.

Like awakening from a spell, he groaned low, his hand winding into my hair and pulling me closer. He used the opportunity to brush his tongue against mine, his taste spicy and sweet from the demon brew. And then he *really* kissed me.

We tangled together, no part of our bodies separated. He cupped my mound, his warmth like lightning against my weeping flesh. A thick finger pushed through, and my core clenched on him in an attempt to absorb him whole.

He laughed low, removing his finger enough to add another. It pulled—the tightness foreshadowing what would come once he fucked me. His palm ground against my clit, rubbing in maddening circles until I bit his neck to suppress a groan.

Yet in the moment of chaos, he moved his palm away, teasing me when I wanted to devour him whole.

In retaliation, I lifted my lips back to his and bit down on his lip. My punishment only lit the flame in his eyes bright enough to scorch me whole. His tongue smoothed against mine, while his ministrations below began once more.

It was the most sensual kiss of my life.

And I knew with no doubt that Killian would be the best lover I'd ever had. He watched and listened for my body's response to his touch, becoming bolder as he sought to please me. To drive me mad with need.

And it was *working*.

I felt possessed, like I was no longer in control of my body now that Killian was its master. Briefly, I wondered how he would react if I dragged him back to the couch. If I mounted him and rode him until we both screamed with pleasure. Or maybe he would press my face into the leather seat, the smooth, cold fabric juxtaposed with the hard slaps of his hips and hands, marking my body as his.

I almost came from the thought of it.

A sudden flash of green hit the light, blinding me. I blinked as reality resurfaced drifting to the surface of a sunny day in the marsh.

I spun around, catching sight of the prince, his serpent staff shining as he exited through the door to the back alley. His perpetual grin was drawn into a fierce scowl.

Killian looked down at me with surprise, before he followed Alexei's. He removed his hand from me, putting space between our bodies.

I wanted to cry out at the switch he would flip, the blame he would wage against me. Just another witch using her magick to bespell demons to do their bidding.

But instead, he leaned down and brushed his unshaven, scarred cheek against mine. "Hurry, before he gets away," he whispered into my ear before dragging me through the orgy.

My lust—and knee-shaking relief—simmered beneath my skin as we followed the vampire.

The gust of fresh air filled my lungs as Killian and I crammed against the building's back brick wall. Our bodies remained hidden behind dripping water pipes, and Killian pressed his finger to his lips.

At an enraged shout, he looked out into the night to better see the fight unfolding.

From my vantage point, I could see Alexei, his pale skin luminescent under the moonlight. He hissed at the creature lurking in the darkness, his voice a whisper in the wind as the noise of cars and tourists around the block drowned out his words. Alexei's voice was a whip, slashing through the darkness. "This is your fault. I've let this go on long enough, but no more, Boudreaux."

I gasped at the vampire's words, but the demon's hand clasped over my mouth as Wren emerged from the shadows.

His shoulders hunched over with fatigue, and his tanned skin appeared deathly pale. The bright streetlight emphasized the crazed glint in his eyes, as well as the dark circles underneath.

Wren closed in on the prince with fury, his fangs elongated to sharp points. "Dis is as much your fault as mine. And now, Travis is dead."

Killian grew taut as a bowstring, his hand twitching over my face as my spine stiffened.

"That's a hefty accusation, and a pointless one. I'll give you some advice, pup. Casting blame for your own foolishness will lead you down a path you cannot turn back from."

Wren seethed, not cowing down to the prince. "You and Carreau helped us get dose drugs, and now I'm close to spendin' eternity in the pits of Hell for the effort. Not to mention, Travis is dead from da drug not working as it should've. Dis is as much on you as me!"

His words made a chill go down my spine.

Alexei's dark form closed in on Wren. "And who's fault is that, wolf? I merely provided you with a demon contact, nothing more. You're lucky one of your goons was smart enough to slash his throat to throw off the Council. If not, I would you sell you out faster than you can say, 'Sam vanjo pade'."

Enraged, Wren snarled. "The pack would never do such a thing to our own. It was your people who mutilated him!"

Brent appeared from the darkness, his face stoic. "Come on, Wren. Let's get outta here."

"I would listen to your friend, wolf," Alexei warned, his voice thick with the Slovenian accent he often hid, "or you won't like the consequences."

Wren's claw brushed against the vampire's robe with no fear. "I'll be seein' you again soon, bloodsucker."

"Perhaps it will be while you're chained up in my dungeons. Think through your actions before you embarrass your father more than you already have." Alexei inspected his nails with a bored expression before he stalked back to Bite's exit door, his eyes crimson with anger.

Before I could panic at being discovered, Killian dematerialized us into the shadow dimension. His inky ribbons embraced me like an old friend, the sensation silky and sensual. Now that I wasn't under the effects of Faerie, I could better appreciate the nuances of the shadows I was submerged inside. I lifted my hand close to my face, gasping as the light moved in and out of my flesh like a phantom.

Alexei passed by, none the wiser, cursing the vampire guards on the other side. And after a moment, Wren and Brent darted away from the alley, their voices trailing away as Killian returned us to the mortal plane.

"That was wild," I muttered, amazed Killian could use the shadows to his needs. "Do you spy on people using that?"

His brows pinched together, but I could detect the humor in his tone. "I *am* a mercenary, witch."

All traces of humor disappeared when I glanced back to where the wolves had stood. "You don't think this had anything to do with Rosalind's death, do you? Not after all that."

Killian flexed his hand, walking out from our perch along the dirty wall. "We can't eliminate anyone from our suspects just yet. Although this was an interesting dispute. Did Wren ever mention these drugs to you?"

I shook my head, my cheeks pink with shame. "I was on some wild substances during that time, but nothing out of the ordinary. And not in a while. What did he mean about remaining in the pits of Hell? Has he made a demon pact?"

Killian's face remained carefully blank. "Probably a figure of speech."

My mouth tightened as I sensed the untruth, my witch's intuition tingling with unease. What was he hiding? And why did it hurt so much to discover he was?

The night wore thin on my nerves, and I was eager to peel myself out of my plastic dress. "Should we leave?" I hinted, pulling my car keys from my bag.

We had parked nearby, and I only wanted some quiet and the candy bar I stowed in the center compartment. And then, maybe, once he revealed his secrets, more of the hot kissing from earlier.

He parted his lips to reply when, in a burst of violence, his body was suddenly slammed from the side. He flew into a parked car along the alley, crushing it under his massive weight.

Wren snarled low, his teeth inches from Killian's face. "You," he hissed. His frame grew larger and bulkier, with his wolf close to the fore. "You shouldn't have come here, demon."

The alarm blared, and I screamed as Brent pulled me into his grip. He pinned me to the brick wall, my teeth clattering with the harsh movement.

I struggled, fear sparking through me.

Brent shot me a fierce look as he wavered between guilt and disgust. His eyes were lined with dark circles, and I realized they were withdrawal symptoms from whatever drug they used.

Before I could open my lips to reason with the wolf, Killian exploded, his wings bursting into the car's windshield, shattering the glass and bending the metal further under their combined weight until they flattened the wolf to the ground. His fangs ripped at Wren's skin, tearing flesh from bones, letting his blood drip onto the black pavement.

At the sight of the gore covering the wet concrete, my mind fractured; all hopes of calm conversation out the window. I gasped, my hands scratching at Brent's forearms where he held me. "Let me go," I pleaded.

He shook his head, his sandy hair brushing into his eyes. "Be quiet and let Wren finish dis."

Remembering Killian's lessons, I struck out with my fists, my bones almost shattering against the strong bones of his face. Pain shot through me, but I stomped down on his foot, piercing his foot with my heels.

He yelped, his arms locking around my throat as he flattened me against the wall, the pipes digging into my back.

My vision bled, and memories played through my mind.

The blood coursing down my father's face, his glasses askew and coated with rain. My mother's hand reaching out for him, dying on the forest floor like an animal. The gruesome slash across their necks, nearly severing them from their bodies.

A low buzzing came from the back of my throat as my eyes flared with flames.

Brent's hand hesitated, the tendrils of smoke leaking from my skin, curling around my face, as if to offer me comfort.

Killian and Wren had moved away from the car and now wrestled on the pavement, their bodies covered in black blood. "Use your magick!" Killian shouted between blows, his voice distorted by his demon. "You won't win in a physical fight with a wolf, witch."

Fuck, I could use the Goddess damned amulet about now.

Pulling forth my true magick wouldn't end well, but it wasn't like I had another choice. My eyes lowered with determination as I pulled on the well inside me, past the surface-level magick I normally used.

Those flames were mere hints of what lived inside of me.

The well was the source of my fear and my self-loathing, but I called upon it now, only hoping I wouldn't fall apart after using it.

There was a second of eerie silence.

And then there was a light. A searing white that nearly burned through my retinas burst from me in a shimmering orange flame.

My power exploded in a rage, sending Brent's body flying backwards. The force of my detonation knocked him out into a cold heap of limbs against the pavement.

As I saw him lying there, bloodied and broken, it shattered whatever control I had.

I screamed as my power re-entered my body, the pain sizzling under my skin, causing my knees to collapse. My body hit the ground with a hiss before I desperately searched for Killian.

Now straddled on top of Wren—whose face was unrecognizable under the blood and swelling—Killian landed his last punch and the wolf collapsed down onto the pavement with a sickening thud.

At the sound, my eyes shut, and my body wracked with

sobs while I rocked myself. When I felt the demon's hand on my face, I peeked through my wet lashes to his blood-spattered face.

His face crumpled as he reached a finger to the blood seeping from my nose. With darkening eyes, he pulled me up, making me cry out in pain. "The wolf dislocated your shoulder," he snarled, glaring at Brent's body as if he would go and finish the job.

My sight wavered between consciousness and the promise of escaping into the black void. "Hurry and pop it back, so we can get out of here."

Killian focused back on me, before he braced his hand against my arm, his warm eyes finding mine. "Look at me, sweetheart." His voice became calm and reassuring, pulling me from the darkness. He jerked his hand, pushing my bone back into place with a loud pop.

I sucked in a breath before sagging against his chest, the relief immediate.

He wrapped his arms around me, lifting me off the ground into the circle of his arms.

"Thank you," I whispered, pressing my face into the damp crook of his neck.

His voice was the last thing I remembered before I surrendered myself. *"Brave witch. Rest."*

☽☉☾

Hours later, I jumped from my bed, reaching the toilet just in time to retch into the bowl. Hot tears streamed down my face as I coughed, my face pinching when I felt Killian's presence behind me. I hadn't been sick like this after magick use in years. My well felt depleted from my explosive detonation in the alley after years of unuse.

He wrapped my hair in his fist while the other rested on my back, rubbing soothing circles. "You're okay, witch. Let it out."

I sagged against my crossed arms, my body shaking under the strain of the dreams encompassing my mind. I felt the demon pulling me against his chest, rocking me as silent tears streamed down my face.

"Breath. Inhale one, two, three. Exhale one, two, three. Can you do that?"

I relaxed and melted into his grip, my chest rising and falling with the calming breaths he led me through. His body lifted and fell in time with mine as I calmed enough to stand.

Humiliated, I dropped my head to my chest and laughed darkly. "Bet you're glad you met me, huh, demon?"

He ran a hand through my gnarled hair, brushing it behind my back. "Don't be ashamed. All of those bitten by life's teeth and survived to live another day bear the marks on their soul."

My throat clogged at the tender earnestness in his words. Was I still dreaming?

I quickly brushed my teeth, swirling cold water around my mouth with relief, before climbing back under the covers with the demon at my side. "Thank you for staying," I whispered, propping my head in my arms as I turned to watch him.

His dark hair looked soft in the moonlight, and I wanted to run my hands through the strands as he held me close. Like the night after Faerie, he remained on top of the blankets, his arms and legs crossed like a resting knight. Already, his bruises from Wren's fists were healing and turning a sickly shade of yellow.

I noticed a book on my nightstand and raised a brow. "Were you reading while I slept?"

He flushed as I reached over him to grab the paperback, catching a whiff of his addictive masculine scent.

Eyes flickering over the title, I raised my brow. "I wouldn't have pegged you as a romance reader."

"The Princess Bride is not a romance. And you don't know

me, so how would you know what I enjoy?" He snatched the book from my hand, his voice defensive.

I pursed my lips, stung by his defensive retort.

His hand brushed over mine in silent apology just as swiftly as the words escaped his mouth.

Relieved, I muttered, "I would have assumed you read war strategies or creature's histories. It surprised me. And the Princess Bride is *totally* a romance."

His frozen scowl melted, and he chuckled, his grip on the paperback loosening. "My mother brought back mortal books whenever she ventured onto Gaia. It became the highlight of my week: the nights she would return with a handful of new books I could add to my treasure trove. We didn't have much, but those pages were something we shared."

The warmth in his tone made my lips curve in a small smile, but from the steely glint in his eyes, I knew the tale was not a happy one.

"She died when I was ten, forcing me to return to my father in Inferno. I no longer had time for such luxuries once I entered the regiment." His body grew tense, laughing without humor. "And now, as a mercenary and future leader of the Realm, I won't have time for much else other than my duties."

My stomach clenched as I pictured Killian as a child, alone and grieving, with only the Devil to comfort him. I knew he would hate me for pitying him, so I gave him the only thing I could offer in exchange for his vulnerable honesty.

I propped my back against the headboard, pulling the blankets over the goosebumps covering my arms. "In my dreams, I see my parents after their deaths," I rasped, focusing on my fingers fidgeting on the sheets. "After returning home and finding the back door swung wide open, I took a flashlight and my raincoat out into the back woods, drunk and afraid. I found them near my mother's garden. Their bodies were broken.

Horrifying. I stared down at them for what felt like hours before I could make my legs move."

My confession fell free from my lips deep and painful like a physical wound, but now that I had started, I couldn't seem to stop. "Jade was at Loyola, and Audra and Isla were upstairs asleep in bed. What could have happened if either of them woke up and ventured down to see what was happening? It keeps me up at night, the guilt. I should have been there."

The words spilled loose like poison. "My mother's grey face stared up at me and I could see her disappointment, even in death. I'm a failure as a daughter and a sister, and now, I can't help but continue to blunder through my life. A fuckup through and through."

Killian's finger lifted my chin, his eyes tender. He wiped away the tears with a gentle touch, as gentle as a butterfly's wings. "No one is perfect. You are not to blame for your family's deaths, the killer is. Don't ever forget that."

Our gazes held in the early morning, light peeking through my curtains like a warm glow.

I could see every shade of caramel as his eyes swirled with feeling. My gaze dipped to his firm lips, and I let out a small sigh, wanting to feel them against mine once more. Wanting to escape these horrific memories and feel something *good*.

Was it only tonight that we kissed? Mere hours ago, I felt his body and his spicy taste?

It seemed like a lifetime.

I lifted my gaze back to his, jolting at the desire within them. A shaking hand lifted to his face, and we both shifted closer. My eyes fluttered shut as I felt his breath, minty and cool, along my face, lingering in the space between us.

Audra's door slammed open next to mine, and we froze.

When I opened my eyes, Killian had shuttered his emotions, his hand dropping from my face. "I have much to do back in Hell. But I'll find you later. I promise." Without another glance, he disappeared into a cloud of smoke.

I lay back on the bed, feeling strangely cold. No longer could I deny it. *I wanted him.*

And with a sinking feeling in my gut, I knew I was the last creature on Gaia he would allow himself to have.

22

KILLIAN

From my perch on the rocky castle windowsill, I stared down at my father's army of soldiers training below, the cold prickling my bare arms. Twirling my silver dagger, I ran my finger over the sharp edge of the blade, savoring the bite of pain.

My mind whirled from my night in Gaia, and I felt more unsure than ever.

Ember's salty tears still lingered on my fingertips, and I pressed them to my lips like a fool. My emotions for her felt less like a spell or carnal desire, and more like something I had never experienced before.

I had to flee her bedroom like a coward, unable to allay her fears or offer comfort. Not when her sorrowful confession had torn through me as powerful as a blade. We mirrored each other, reflecting all the regret and shame we kept hidden inside.

Taliah's voice broke through my thoughts, her wild juniper scent slapping my senses as she wiped her glistening forehead with her forearm. "There you are. I've been searching for you." She glanced down at the training yard below, before her eyes refocused on mine. "What's happened now? The last time I saw you, you weren't quite this… unhinged."

She sat beside me, her face full of knowing, and I wanted to swipe it away. "Could it have to do with Hunt Boudreaux calling for your banishment from the mortal plane? It would appear you attacked his son in cold blood on the vampire's territory last night."

I cursed, standing from my crouch. This was just what I needed—more trouble from the pack. "The wolves ambushed me and Ember last night when we overheard their plans involving a drug the shifters have been using and spreading along the black market. I wouldn't doubt if it was the alpha and his vile pack behind the murders as well."

Her head whipped around to ensure we wouldn't be overheard. "My spies have not shared any of this. Do you have evidence we could use? Other than your word?"

I bristled, pacing along the empty hallway as I considered our options. The wolves were no doubt sloppy in their crimes, but Alexei was not stupid. If there was even the possibility this could be traced back to him, he would ensure it remained impossible to prove.

When Taliah's lips pursed, her pragmatic mind whirling, I threw an accusatory finger at her. "Do not hit me with logic now. If not the wolves, then who else?"

She leaned against the wall. "Why would Alexei let anyone who killed his cousin live? If there was even a miniscule chance the pack killed Rosalind, they would be six feet under by now. Something's not right."

I hissed, my fangs flashing at her in annoyance. "The wolves are unbalanced, full of self-righteous rage. Reckless and immature."

"And yet, that doesn't translate to murderers." She sighed, pity filling her cool depths. "Right now, you have a lot of *ifs* and not a lot of solid evidence your father and the Council will demand."

She lifted a hand to my shoulder, her brows pinching when

I knocked it away. "I know you're under a lot of pressure to complete this before Samhain. And I'm sure the witch hanging around your wrist like a ball and chain isn't helping matters. But you must keep a level head if you want to do this by the book and begin your reign with a clean start."

I knew her words held merit, but I was beyond reason. Not when memories of the previous night bounced through my mind in an endless loop. I spun on my heel, ignoring Taliah as I walked towards the training yard.

Bartholomew and the rest of his squadron followed my approach with amusement. "You've been hiding away, *my lord*," he sneered, pulling his sword free from the demon he tarried with. "Whispers say you consider yourself too good for us now that your succession is in sight."

His eyes glowed with spite as he watched me like a predator stalking its prey, his bulky body looming over the other demons in Satan's armies. Another high-born bastard in the realm, Bartholomew had risen through the ranks with Taliah and me, but not without a vicious rivalry between us breaking out. The demon had it out for me and the power I would soon hold over him.

I twirled the blade in my hand, straightening my spine. "Not hiding, just doing my job. Something I know you know little about. Responsibility, honor, duty—those qualities matter little to you."

An audience formed on the outskirts of the ring, the mirth spreading as they sensed a fight brewing. The melting snow dripped from dark green treetops, the sound of cracking branches deafening in the quiet yard.

At the sound, my spine stiffened. Confiding in Ember about my mother had been a mistake. The emotions I kept bottled inside were forcing their way to the surface, disrupting my calculated moves.

Bartholomew's eyes held a gleeful secret, and I felt a trickle of uneasiness as he circled me in the ring. "You forget yourself. Soon, I will be your lord. You should practice displaying a modicum of respect."

He balked, his own eyes growing black. "My respect?" he bit out. "Respect must be earned, and you know you will never bring this realm pride. Not with your ugly face and muddied bloodline. Perhaps you should worry more about securing your alliances here with your people instead of fleeing to Gaia at every chance you get, before it's too late."

"Is that a threat?"

The steely glint returned. "Only an observation. To survive in Hell, you must be merciless. Unrelenting. And we all know where you would rather be, Killian."

Taliah cleared her throat, giving me a pointed look at the growing crowd. No matter how badly I needed to bash in his face, I couldn't attack the general like this without proper provocation. The time would come when nothing would matter but my wishes, but that time wasn't now.

My teeth clenched at the victory I knew gleamed in Bartholomew's eyes. Raring with unspent tension, I portaled back up the mountain. I needed release, and I would find it. Even if the thought of the repercussions made my stomach twist with regret and a piercing stab of something I was too afraid to name.

)◉(

The brothels were quiet this early in the day, but demons still meandered in and out of the darkened rooms lit by heavy sconces flickering. The other males' clothing and hair were askew as the scent and sounds of sex lingered in the air. Some demons angled their heads at me with a silent show of respect, but the majority steered clear, somehow sensing the fire percolating under my skin.

I startled when Carreau swaggered out of one of the back bedrooms. As he re-buttoned his trousers, he caught sight of me, a slow smile spreading across his face. "Killian." He threw an arm around my shoulder and led me to the small bar area, pouring himself a tall, fizzling demon brew.

When he offered me the glass, I shook my head.

He shrugged and downed it himself in one gulp. With a contented sigh, he eased into one of the weathered leather chairs. "Didn't think I'd see you around here with the case in Gaia. You're so uptight, forgoing your passions in favor of hiding away like a damned monk. Good to see you giving in a little."

My hands itched with the need to fuck or fight, but I forced them to unclench and sat across from him. "Just taking a break to clear my head. But I'm surprised to see you in the realm. I thought you preferred to remain on the mortal plane now."

He shrugged, taking another sip of brew. "Oh, I still like to visit now and then. The creatures above can be so tedious in their moral superiority. I like to be reminded now and then of what I'm missing."

My brow quirked. I always assumed Carreau preferred his time in Gaia—the Council seat an escape from his father. The situation was familiar. Like Satan, Gressil left a heavy shadow to fill, and Carreau had never succeeded in making his father proud.

A twinkle entered his eyes. "It's been years since we spent time in the brothels together. Remember the busty demoness we once shared? Gods, that female was something else. It's too bad she found her mate and left us high and dry."

I hardly remembered the female he spoke of. My time in the brothels came at a low point when I thought loneliness and sorrow would consume me whole. Grimly, I admitted I was no better than the witch, drowning myself in fighting and strangers' bodies to lose myself for a single night. Voice thick, I muttered, "Some would find claiming your mate a worthwhile excuse to leave this hovel."

Carreau ran a hand through his blond locks, as if disgusted by the thought. "Please. I'd rather cut off my balls than be tied to one female for my entire life. Willem found his mate years ago, but he rejected the bond. Saved himself from a lifetime of pain and misery."

His chatter did little to ease the tension brewing inside of me, and the mention of mate bonds had my leg shaking against the table with unease. The absolute *wrongness* of being here radiated through my body like a pain.

When a female crooked a finger at me, I jumped from my seat, ready to get this over with.

"Have fun," Carreau called from his chair, laughing as another demoness dropped into his lap.

Emmeline didn't bother with chatter as she led me to her room. Shutting the bedroom door behind her, she leaned against the wood, her dark hair swishing as she pushed me to the bed.

I could smell the males and females who had rolled around in these sheets, none of which smelled like peaches and cinnamon, but I pushed that thought from my mind.

"Same as before, Killian?" she purred, walking over to stand between my spread knees. Her hands lifted to the straps of her nightgown, dragging them to expose her small breasts and narrow stomach, before dropping the material in a pool at her feet.

I closed my eyes, forcing my brain to slow.

Emmeline and I shared this bed several times in the past. Her reactions to my touch were honest and lacked the blatant fear my scarred face and reputation provided.

"Yes," I rasped, ignoring the stab of pain in my chest. "Just like before."

She pushed me backwards once more, climbing atop me the moment my head hit the pillow.

Perfunctory, she eased my shirt buttons open and crawled down my body to begin. When she reached for the buttons of my trousers, I halted her with a small touch.

"Wait," I groaned, my mind in torment. This was what I needed. A release. A distraction.

But Emmeline's sultry brown eyes weren't the same captivating blue shade as the witch's, her body not as supple, her smile not as bright. But any path with Ember in it only led to torment.

"Okay," I managed, my eyes clamped shut as I dropped my hand to the sheets.

Every instinct inside screamed at me to stop this. I couldn't understand what was happening to me. With my eyes shut, I could almost pretend I was in another room, another bed. With another woman.

When her lips brushed against my lower stomach, a gasp escaped. "Ember."

The demon above me froze before a hoarse laugh escaped. "I know it's been a while, Killian, but my name is Emmeline."

My blood ran cold. *I couldn't do this.*

Sitting up, I pulled her body away from mine. "Actually, Emmeline, I've forgotten something I have to take care of." With an apologetic smile, I dropped a few gold coins from my trousers onto her dresser before pulling the material over my body. "Sorry."

She leaned against the bed with a shrug. "Not a problem, my lord. Come find me whenever you want me."

My stomach lurched at her words. Sickened, I hurried back to my bedroom and ordered myself a bath. I needed her scent off me, and I needed to harness whatever this was inside me.

A ragged breath escaped as I scrubbed a hand over my face. Now I understood what denying your mate must feel like. How could Willem—or any other demon—suffer through this torment?

Nausea roiled at the thought of her discovering my evening here. It felt like I had *betrayed* Ember. I was so fucked.

I knew this story between us would end in tragedy and yet, as I stood from the bed, cancelling the bath, I knew I would tread down the path, regardless.

As much as I wanted to deny it, there was an undeniable thread tying me to the witch.

And I would have her for however long I could.

23

EMBER

After Killian fled my bed, I fretfully dozed for hours until I forced myself to leave the confines of my room. Sat at the kitchen table, I nursed a mug of steaming tea flavored with rosehip and elderberry. I listened as Isla chattered on about her friends and their plans for ritual night while braiding her long, blonde hair into an elaborate crown atop her head.

And yet, I hardly listened. My mind stewed over our steamy kiss inside Bite and Killian's surprising tenderness afterwards. Not to mention the shocking revelations about Wren and the wolf pack. There were too many puzzle pieces, and I couldn't find any logical way to put them together.

After such a turbulent evening, the only thing that could bring me back to the emotional living was copious amounts of sugar. Audra came barreling through the kitchen, her hair gleaming fiery red in the morning sunlight as she dropped bags of supplies before us with a proud grin. "I've got carrot and red velvet cake, pralines, pecan pie, and of course," she drawled, holding up the bag of takeout, "shrimp poboys and fries to soak up all those cavities."

I gaped at the feast Audra laid out and laughed, hugging her as Isla ran to find us plates.

"Where's Jade?" Audra asked, securing her carrot cake with a mutinous grin.

"I'm here," Jade shouted from the front door, her arms bursting with fragrant spell ingredients and stacked grimoires.

With a leap towards her, I helped carry all the materials for our Samhain booth onto the counter with a thud, a sprig of fragrant lavender tickling my nose.

She shot me a smile of thanks before observing the kitchen table piled with food with a sigh. "What's happened now?"

"Nothing's happened." Isla giggled. "We decided it had been too long since we had a family night. And it's *my* turn to pick the movie."

Jade's green eyes lit up, and I felt the love coursing through her as she watched Isla prance around the kitchen like a fairy. "I think that's a great idea, dearest."

Curled between Audra and Isla on the plush couch, I lazed back, eating from our stuffed plates of fresh bread and fried goodness as Isla started the movie. We groaned as The Lord of the Rings title flashed on the screen.

"I'm not committed to a three-part movie night. I have studying to do," Audra groaned, ignoring the piece of shrimp Isla flung at her face.

After the first break in the extended edition, I stood to stretch and refill my plate with dessert, my teeth preemptively aching from the amount of sugar I would consume.

Audra followed behind me, picking over the desserts before selecting a praline. "So, I have good news and bad news."

Panic surged, and a piece of red velvet cake lodged in my throat. "Yeah?" I choked, avoiding her eyes. Oh Goddess, what if she knew about last night...

"I know you haven't thought twice about it, so I made the

executive decision to take your new eyeshadow palette and hand it off to Grandmother for the ritual tomorrow night."

Her eyes twinkled with glee as I growled low, as much from relief as annoyance.

My hands reached out to shove her, but she spun away, laughing as she jumped over a cushion into Isla's arms, using our baby sister like a shield. "That was brand new. I hadn't even tried it yet," I groaned, already missing the bronze and amber shades I planned on using for the Samhain festival.

Audra laughed, unsympathetic to my whining. "Maybe next time you won't procrastinate and leave your sacrifices until the last minute."

Relieved, I stuck my tongue out and crashed back on the sofa while Isla restarted the movie.

There was a knock on the front door, and we all stared at each other in surprise.

"Did someone order more food?" Jade gawked, sifting through the piles of junk on the coffee table, the smells of tangy remoulade sauce and buttery brown sugar pecans wafting from our mess.

I shook my head, looking at Isla and Audra, who lifted their shoulders with equal confusion.

"Well, go answer it," Audra huffed. "We're almost to the best part, and I need a shower after all this vegging out."

With a sniff in her direction, my nose wrinkled. "Yeah, you do," I teased.

She huffed and pushed me, knocking me and Isla onto the floor.

We dissolved into peals of laughter as Jade rolled her eyes and walked to our entry-way.

"Children," she muttered. Peeking through the stained-glass window in the door, she growled. "Ember, your boyfriend is here."

At her words, we sat up in a blur. Isla began containing our mess while Audra and I tripped over our feet in our haste to reach the door. Glancing down at my sweatpants and stained t-shirt, I regretted every decision I had made that led me to this point.

When I pulled open the door, I ignoring the two nosy witches behind me who lurked like gargoyles, with mirrored expressions of suspicion and crossed arms. Lost in Killian's hardened eyes, I could sense the tension under his skin.

His hands reached for me before he curled them into fists and returned them to his side. At a noise behind me, he looked over my shoulder, his lips twitching. "Am I allowed inside?" His voice was gruff, thick with some hidden emotion.

I opened the door wider for him. "Of course you can. Right, girls?"

Jade and Audra's frowns deepened, their auras promising violence, but they stayed silent as he stepped inside the black doorframe.

Isla popped out from the living room, her smile wide and uncaring of their moodiness. "Hi, Killian. Come on in! Sorry, it's so messy in here." She dragged him by his arm, ignoring the steely glares my sisters threw at him as she deposited him on the couch. "Help yourself. We mean business on movie night, so whatever you like, I'm sure we have."

His expression looked dumbfounded as my baby sister handed him a bottle of root beer and an empty plate.

Any opportunity to interrogate him disappeared as my sister began explaining the plot of the Fellowship of the Ring.

Audra rolled her eyes and claimed her spot on the couch a safe distance away from the demon. "I don't trust creatures who haven't seen the trilogy before. Ember, are you sure he's welcome here?"

Isla's eyes flashed electric blue with her magick. "Be nice," she hissed.

Audra raised her hands in surrender.

I chanced a peek at Jade, who sat perched on the edge of her chair like she was Smaug, planning on squiring Isla away and hoarding her inside a locked room, so nothing could harm her.

The tension grew awkward. Uneasily, we settled in as Isla pressed play and darkness submerged us once more. Over the next few hours, after the start of The Two Towers, my sisters loosened their stiff postures and exasperation replaced their ire as we discovered the true depths of Killian's—and the residents of Hell's—cultural ineptitude.

"No, seriously, how can someone live in a world without having seen Pan's Labyrinth? I can't stand by this," Audra snapped, reaching for our overflowing movie case.

I curled my arms around a pillow, feeling a warm glow in my chest at the domestic scene. That part of my heart I had closed off years ago felt breached, and I couldn't decide whether I was pleased or terrified by that revelation.

In turn, Killian appeared baffled by the sudden shift in intimacy between him and my sisters, unused to having a bevy of witches tossing popcorn at his chest or teasing him with heated barbs.

"So, Killian," Jade began, her voice controlled with a gleam in her eyes, "tell us more about you. We know next to nothing other than you're a demon in Pride's realm and a *mercenary*."

Her lips curled on the word, and I fought an annoyed groan. "Here we go," I drawled, my fingers grasping my mug of coffee with a glare at my older sister.

Killian appeared unfazed as he faced off against her cool exterior, crossing his legs and relaxing back onto the couch. "What would you like to know?"

Jade narrowed her eyes at his measured words. She waved her hand and muttered with an irritated sigh. "You know, the basics. Where are you from? Who are your friends and family? Explain your *job*."

Killian pursed his smooth lips, considering. "I'm thirty, born to two seraphim. And as part of the Realm of Pride, I reap the souls of creatures who haven't made good on their deals."

His voice trailed off, and we sat in silence, waiting for him to continue with bated breaths.

When seconds passed in silence, Audra booed. "Lame. Come on, we could've Googled that information. Give us some juicy deets. Especially about the souls."

Isla shot him a sweet smile before glaring at her sister. "Maybe his past is painful and pushing him to share more than he's comfortable with is unkind."

"No, it's fine." He cleared his throat, looking hunted despite the assurance. "After my mother's death, I worked my way through the ranks, training and fighting within Satan's armies for nearly two decades. Now, I work as a mercenary, completing tasks for him on the mortal plane—and before you ask, I target souls of creatures whose crimes are foul or unforgivable. If that matters." His clenched jaw ended that line of questioning.

Something in me softened. I realized it *did* matter.

When I looked over his scarred face and dark hair curling at the ends brushing his chin, I felt a pulse of longing so powerful I lost my breath. I squelched it in case he could feel it through the bond.

Jade opened her lips to push, but I shot her a glare. "Enough. That concludes tonight's interrogation."

"Fine," she said through her teeth, not finished at all.

Isla yawned, and it shifted the tone of the room. Audra paused the movie, and we cleaned our mess in silence.

After finishing up, Isla wrapped Killian in a brief hug. "It was great to spend time with you. We hope you come and visit with us again. You still have Return of the King to look forward to."

He nodded his head, for once unable to speak.

Jade shot us a look over her shoulder. "Next time, I suppose you can just portal inside, demon. I already know you can get through our protective charms."

He raised an eyebrow, leaning close to my ear to whisper, "I think I'm growing on her."

She threw him a vulgar gesture over her shoulder, and I laughed, my upper body shaking as I tried to hold it in.

Audra turned to me, her lips stretched in a knowing smile. "See you two at the ritual tomorrow night. Don't be too loud tonight. I need my beauty sleep."

She ran up the stairs before the pillow I threw at her could land.

Killian turned to me in the darkness, a question in his eyes. "Ritual?"

I sighed and motioned for him to follow me to my bedroom. I could swear I felt something molten touch me through the bond, an answer to the question I had been wondering all day.

At my blush, I hid my face and locked my bedroom door. "Before a Sabbath, we give thanks to our Goddess, Hecate, and ask her for blessings. Like most witchy rituals, it requires a price. This spell requires a personal sacrifice and invokes powerful sex magick when we cast it. Obviously, none of the minors come—they have their own separate ritual—but it's generally a fun time."

He choked on air, and I felt a sudden thrill of excitement. Leaving the room in darkness, I lit the medley of white and black candles scattered around the room with the flick of my hand. My lips pursed with feigned casualness as vanilla sugar filled the room. "You're invited, if you'd like to come. Many of the witches bring dates and make a whole event out of it."

He watched me like I was a puzzle, a mystery he was desperate to solve. "Is that what you want? For me to... help you with the ritual?"

Energy consumed the air between us, desire and lust bleeding with exciting tendrils of newfound affection. It felt as if the Fates kept driving us together, and I knew better than to deny such a calling.

My voice was breathier than I intended when I answered him. "Only if you want to. Usually I bring a partner, but there's no one I felt like inviting. I guess I could pull a one hander, if you know what I mean. Though it's nowhere near as fun." I broke off with a laugh, my cheeks flaming scarlet.

This shyness wasn't like me; I was Ember Belle, not some blushing maiden. So, squaring my shoulders, I sauntered closer to where he stood, my body sensitive and buzzing with energy. "But then last night happened, and it was better than I could have imagined. We're not finished—not by a long shot, demon. We could explore this chemistry between us, release the tension."

A surprised chuckle ripped from his throat, the sound skittering down my spine like a caress.

The way he watched my body, I knew he was interested, though he clearly wanted to deny it.

My fingers dipped and curved into the muscled planes of his chest. "Do you deny it, Killian? That you don't want this?"

Ignoring my question, he leaned down to whisper in my ear, "Can a witch conjure sex magick with only herself to bring her to climax?"

My answering grin was positively wicked. "A witch can do much with only her intuition to guide her. But again—what's the fun in that?"

"Indeed," he purred. His finger caught a tendril of hair

that escaped my bun, and he tugged it, wrapping it around his finger.

My lips parted on a gasp. I pulled him closer as my other hand lifted to his scarred cheek, my thumb grazing the skin. I wanted him. *Badly.* "Yes," I murmured, answering his earlier question, somehow knowing he needed my raw honesty. "I want you to come."

Killian's hand tightened in my hair, and he pushed closer until I could see the flecks of bronze within his molten depths. "There can only be this," he rasped, his thumb dragging down my lower lip. "Nothing more."

My lips parted, biting down on his thumb before soothing the sting with the brush of my tongue. His smoky pine scent surrounded me as my eyes drifted shut and our lips grazed in the slightest of touches.

He pulled away, his intention clear.

"Just sex and after Samhain, everything will go back as it was before. Our deal done and whatever this is, put to rest," I managed through the haze of want coursing through me.

A flash of something mutinous simmered in his eyes before his lips were on mine.

Finally.

I gasped into his mouth, moaning low as he sucked my bottom lip between his.

His tongue brushed through my parted lips and languidly moved with mine. It was sultry and addictive as sin. He kissed like I imagined he would in my deepest fantasies. He kissed me like I was his salvation, like he thought this moment was fragile and he wanted to clamp down and hold it within him forever.

There was a flicker of emotion between us—a vulnerability that terrified me.

My fingers twitched with the need to pull him down and over me, letting him dominate me with his shadows like before.

But somehow, I knew I needed to let him have the reins, to not push him too far.

As if privy to my innermost thoughts, he dragged his lips away with a shuddered breath.

My lips tingled, and I brought my fingers to them.

His eyes glowed with desire, but he forced himself to step away from me, the leash he held over himself more than I could say for myself. "Then I'll see you tomorrow night, witch."

When he dematerialized, I laid back on my bed with a shaky breath. My thighs clenched together, wet with my desire. "Bastard," I breathed, as a relieved, sultry laugh slipped through my swollen lips.

The sparkling tingles of anticipation coursed over my skin like static. I knew when the demon finally fucked me, it would be unlike anything I ever felt before. And that was worth the wait.

24

EMBER

The walls of the Grave's estate burst at the seams with witches and warlocks pre-gaming for the night of hedonist rituals. Carafes filled with pre-mixed Sazerac cocktails made with real absinthe that came from plants in Faerie and overflowing trays filled with hand-sized muffulettas and bowls of crawfish etouffee were passed around.

Jade, Audra, and I wandered through the hallways, passing groups of witches stretching and moving through yoga poses to limber up for the night's activities, despite the cocktail dresses and pressed trousers they wore for the occasion.

I stared longingly at the cart stacked high with sacrifices to be brought to the bonfire behind the property, ignoring Audra's pinch on the back of my arm.

Bye forever special edition autumn eye palette.

Audra and I dropped our go-bags filled with emergency contraception tonics, wet wipes, and lube, while the rest of the Coven and their dates mingled inside the meeting room. Fleur's silver hair caught my attention from across the room and I weaved through the crowd to reach her, waving to get her attention.

She glanced up at me and frowned, her eyes rimmed with dark circles. "Ember."

My smile slipped at her cutting tone and the disgusted curl of her lips. Chagrined, I realized in the days since the Faerie party, she hadn't reached out to me—and neither had I. After shifting on my feet uneasily, I stammered, "It feels like I haven't seen you in forever. Is everything okay?"

She glowered. "You mean after you ditched me and ran off with some random Fae who attacked you and then sending a demon after me?" Her eyes held accusation. "The demon you're apparently fucking."

Curious looks from the other witches made my heart surge. A sinking feeling settled into my stomach as I dragged Fleur into an alcove adorned with portraits of my Salem ancestors. "Look, it's complicated. And I'm sorry about Faerie. It was fucked up what I put you through. I shouldn't have ever gone when I felt so out of it mentally."

Fleur crossed her arms, her face frozen with censure. "As if you're ever not in an unfortunate state of mind. And you're really calling your situation *complicated*? He's a demon, a minstrel of Hell, for Hecate's sake! What are you thinking?"

My eyes widened, and I shushed her, whispering, "Does anyone else in the Coven know?"

I don't know why I let their opinions bother me. But like my errant magick, this was just one more knock against me. Already, I could hear their whispers how much of a disaster I had become after my parent's deaths. And it stung.

Unconcerned with my apprehension, her expression hardened. "Of course they know. Hunt's been very vocal with the Council about the two of you. Word has spread, and the Coven wants answers." Fleur turned away and waved at Tabitha across the room. "I've got to go, Ember. See you around or whatever."

I watched her leave, sauntering over to her sister with a scowl.

What the Hell was that? Fleur couldn't stand Tabitha. Her brown-nosing and general distaste for fun soured most Coven gatherings, but now they were thick as thieves?

Feeling strangely exposed, I adjusted my burgundy silk dress and walked back to my sisters.

My phone lit up, and some of the tension loosened from my shoulders at the three words lighting up my screen.

See you tonight.

It was hardly illicit, but the promise fizzled in my stomach like expensive champagne.

Rebecca clapped to get the room's attention, her golden hair swept into a coiffed crown around her head. The gossamer silver gown hung around her like moonlight and emphasized her soft curves. Her lips twitched into her version of a smile before her clear voice rang through the estate. "Witches and warlocks, happy tidings. Let us take our places around the fire and begin our ritual for the Goddess."

The procession began filing towards the back of the property. I followed behind Jade, who stood out in the crowd with her jeweled emerald satin jumpsuit. She would most definitely be performing the rite alone tonight since she hadn't taken a lover since she became our surrogate parental figure.

"You okay?" she asked me, concern lighting up her green eyes.

"All good," I promised. Glancing back at Audra, I watched her kiss her date goodbye before she wandered over to us.

She linked her arm through mine as she leaned to whisper in my ear, "He's hot as Hell but kisses like a puffer fish."

Laughing, we approached the fire, slipping off our shoes and settling our bare feet into the grass as we formed a circle. The roaring bonfire at the center of the field reached ten feet tall—a fire worthy of Hecate. Unlike the rest of the Coven, the flames affected me strongly, my fire magick soaring beneath my skin.

Jade and Audra reached for my hands as we linked together, all our magick connected and offered to the Goddess.

The elders stood before the congregation, their gazes lifted to the moon. All at once, the sacrifices exploded in a cloud of shimmering smoke as Hecate accepted our offer. Yarrow and Enchanter's nightshade wafted through the breeze, and the elders beat on the ceremonial drums as Grandmother chanted the spell.

Accipere gratias deae meae.
Hecate, Crone Goddess, Keep us whole.
Dark is the Moon.
Quiet is the night
I ask Hecate, the Crone
To take Her throne.
And protect through the darkness.
Let thy wisdom fill my soul.
And in the circle binds us.
Accipere gratias deae meae.

Together, we repeated the spell. As the drums beat faster, our chanting grew louder and faster as well. We swayed, our hearts open and our eyes closed as the magick took effect. Our voices rose like a crescendo in the night. The cicadas, frogs, owls, and other night creatures grew silent as they could feel the pulse of magick in the shimmering air.

The pull felt like a thread unspooling from its tight bounds. The fiery lick of flame coursed through my blood, lighting my skin in goosebumps, and I let my head fall backwards as I siphoned power from the fire before me.

The fire opal strand around my wrist fit like a shackle, the stone controlling my power, holding me back from spiraling into chaos. I wanted to rip it from my body and burn through the world like a beacon of light—cleansing and destructive.

"Easy," Jade whispered, her grip pulling me back from the aether.

I bit my lip hard enough to draw blood as I floated back down to reality. Slightly less intoxicated, the energy spread, buzzing under my skin with small vibrations. Hecate's blessing filled me like spiced wine, seductive and sweet, and laughter broke out as delirium and euphoria spread through us like wildfire.

The music changed into a sensual rhythm, my core pulsating in tune with the sound, and we unlinked hands. From the corner of my eyes, I watched as witches and warlocks found their partners in the fog.

Nerves pulsing through me, I took a few steps backwards until I was out of sight of the others. Once inside the dark woods, I glanced over to an opening in the trees, a buzzing roaring through me when I saw him.

His bourbon eyes held mine as he strode with purpose. There were no words between us as he grasped my hand and dragged me further away from the bonfire and the moaning witches. His course was set on the sweeping branches of an ancient oak tree, the ground beneath it soft with moss and grass.

He turned to me, his gaze fierce. "If you want this to stop, tell me now and I'll return you to the estate. We can pretend this never happened and finish our mission as before." Hands drifted through my hair, wrapping the locks in a tight grip as he searched my eyes.

The thought of denying this pull between us was not a

possibility in my mind. My hands shook as I grasped his, twining our fingers together. "Please, Killian. I don't want you to stop."

At my desperate words, he groaned with surrender, his hungry mouth finding mine in a heated embrace.

My skin grew heated, the pulsating rhythm of the drums still beating inside me, drawing me deeper under its spell, like a drug. I reveled in the warm glide of his tongue as we fought for dominance, letting myself go in his arms. Here, in this corner of the woods, I could drop all my worries for the future or how I needed the amulet or what this would mean.

All that mattered was this.

My hands left his shoulders and found the buttons of his shirt, pulling them loose with rising urgency. After struggling with the first two, I tore at the material, his husky laugh fanning over my neck like a caress.

"Slowly," he breathed into my skin. "There's no need to rush." His fingers were gentle as he pulled the thin straps of my silky dress down to my waist and over my hips, the fabric spilling at my feet like a pool of blood.

I kicked the fabric away and squared my shoulders, letting him look his fill. My breasts felt full and aching, the tips peaked under the crisp night air. I thought I may die if I didn't feel his touch on them soon.

Eyes gleaming with awe, he lifted a large hand to the curve of my right breast, cupping it before molding it against his palm firmly. His warm breath fanned across the skin of my neck, making me shiver despite the warm October breeze. Soft lips trailed across the expanse of my shoulder, his fangs grazing, making me jump at the sharp pull.

"I've dreamed of these tits," he breathed, before he dropped to his knees. Level with my breasts, his lips grazed my nipple in a sweet kiss. And then, a tantalizing bite.

A heady moan escaped, my fingers dancing along the soft, thick strands of his dark hair.

He looked up at me, eyes following the lines of my body to my parted lips. Desire blew his pupils wide. "I knew you would be like this. Even when you foolishly tried to kill me, I knew in my bones you would eventually destroy me." To punctuate his impossible words, the warm sweep of his tongue brushed along my sensitive skin until my knees grew weak.

He felt destroyed? My body quacked in the aftermath of his earnest confession, breaking me down on a cellular level. Even still, my lips quirked with amusement, remembering my disastrous summoning. "Figures you would fantasize about fucking me while also threatening to kill me. It's very on-brand for you, demon." My voice broke off in a gasp as his tongue lashed at my other nipple, dragging it between his teeth.

"I never considered killing you, witch. Tossing you over my shoulder and giving that ass a firm spanking, maybe, but never death."

His words were not a confession of anything but his desire. Yet they tugged at my heart, warming me from within all the same. Especially knowing through all our clandestine meetings across the city, he was there to watch over me.

He rumbled, "I've heard that witches love nothing more than having their pretty tits played with. Is that true?"

His filthy words skittered across my chest like a whip, shocking me enough to pull away. I laughed low, delight curling in my stomach. "Witches love anyone who will adore us the way we show reverence to our Goddess. I'm always open to some worship, demon."

His breath warmed the cooling expanse of my chest as he began trailing wet kisses down my navel to where I wanted him the most. "How am I doing? I aim to please," he purred.

Dazed, I swayed on my feet. "You're doing okay, I guess."

An arrogant laugh was the only warning I got, before he

licked up my center in one broad sweep of his tongue. "And now?" he rumbled.

Stars exploded behind my eyes, my nerves jumping under my sensitive skin like live wires. I dug into his shoulders, my hips writhing against his tongue.

With a low chuckle, he paused his movements. "Oh, I've just begun, sweetheart." He squeezed the flesh of my ass, while his inky shadows emanated from his body. "I've imagined how I would take you a million times these past months, and I won't let you rush me before I'm good and ready."

And then his shadows were upon me, locking my legs and arms.

Shock rolled through me, the lick of desire that fanned through me at being held down like this, a revelation. By the way his eyes blackened, I knew he could see the wetness dripping down my thighs, revealing how much I needed this.

His clever tongue returned, sweeping inside me, hot and frenzied.

I screeched like a banshee, trying and failing to buck onto his face as sensations blinded me. Fire exploded within me, seeking an escape, while my arms fought his hold to drag my hands over my body, through his hair, *anything*.

He groaned as if in pain, and his shadows tightened further over me, halting my movements.

He forced to simply *feel*.

Through my lashes, I watched him run a hand over the tent in his trousers, and I grew desperate to feel his impressive cock. In my hands, my mouth, my body.

I nearly came when his coarse tongue curled inside of me, making me clench.

"You taste exactly as I knew you would." His voice was roughened as he circled my aching center with the slightest touch. "Do you want to know what you taste like, witch?"

Without waiting for me to answer, he dipped one broad finger inside me, stretching and pulling.

When he removed them, my body rebelled, squeezing him tighter to make him stay and finish the torment he wrought.

Killian ignored my whispered pleas for more, and brought them to my waiting lips. His gaze grew hooded as my tongue dragged the wet digits into my mouth, sucking them before releasing them with a pop. "Fucking beautiful."

My core clenched with longing, my legs rubbing together to ease the ache.

With a huffed laugh, he loosened the shadow bonds, only to drag a shaking leg over his shoulder. There was reverence in his eyes as he looked at my body until I could not deny this was anything other than worship.

Tightening his shadow bonds once more, he commanded, "You are not allowed to come until I give you permission. If you disobey me, then I'm going to punish you. Do you understand?"

I was so close... too close. There was no way I could hold back from my release. But maybe he knew that, maybe he *craved* my disobedience. Just as I craved his punishments.

"Say the words," he commanded.

I was helpless to deny him. "I understand."

"Good girl," he breathed, before he *really* tasted me.

I bit my lip, trying desperately not to come. A keening moan escaped my gasping lips while my hands twitched with the need wind through his soft hair. A prickle of regret that he wasn't in his demonic form surged through me. Visions of his dark wings cocooning me as I grasped his horns, forcing him to service me, blasted through my mind.

Smack.

Never stopping his kisses on my wet flesh, he slapped my ass, hands already soothing the stinging skin before he moved to the other cheek. "Does my witch like to be punished?" His tongue flicked across my clit as he slapped my ass again.

"Yes," I moaned. "I love it." I shook like a leaf above him, his dominance feeding something inside of me I didn't know was there.

Inhaling my scent, his scarred cheek brushed against the smooth skin of inner thigh. "You smell like a heady summer night under the stars, and you taste like peaches and sugar snaps. I could devour you all night long."

My body broke into a sweat, increasing the bottled emotions inside of me to a near tipping point. He was ruining me, never to be the same. And yet, I craved *more*.

Sensing my need, Killian's tongue danced over my clit as his fingers thrust inside me, curling and pumping in time with his unyielding licks across my sensitive bud.

"*Killian*," I screamed, my hips jerking as my orgasm coursed through me. He refused to relent his pace, and my vision darkened as a second orgasm ripped through me, coating his face with my desire.

Time drifted, and I swayed under the stars, unaware of anything but his unyielding tongue.

The magick I created from my pulsating orgasms erupted from me in an explosion of swirling orange and blue energy soaring into the night sky, feeding the Coven's combined power.

My breath sucked in as my head tilted up to the moon.

Oh, Goddess, I was utterly screwed.

A hoarse laugh burst free from my throat. Nothing had felt nothing like this before, this feeling of connectedness. All my past experiences were obliterated by this one evening, and I wasn't ready for it to be over. Not by a long shot. "Is that all you've got, demon?"

Amber eyes crinkled with affection as he rasped a laugh, his voice coated in darkness. He lowered both of us to the soft forest floor, his hands never leaving the curves of my body.

Giddy, I caressed my hand over his face, drawing my thumb down his scar, feeling a wave of tenderness for the demon despite the dirty things he had done to me with his mouth.

But instead of dignifying the sweet moment between us with words, he pushed my shoulder down to the ground and fitted his body over mine. He ran his tongue back over me, sending shocks throughout me. "Then I suppose I'll have to keep trying to earn your approval, witch."

Despite the impossibility of a future between us, I still felt the burning impulse coursing through me to have any part of him he would give me. I would take these moments and I would savor them, knowing in the end it would utterly shatter me.

25

KILLIAN

The witch's broken cries rang out in my ears, her voice hoarse from the number of times she had screeched into the night from her pleasure. I couldn't help myself. I felt drugged, *consumed* by the small noises she made and the way her body came alive under my touch.

"Oh, Goddess, I can't anymore," she gasped.

Satisfaction like I had never known coursed through me as I looked up to her flushed cheeks. Like a kitten, she stretched her arms above her head, her skin luminous under the moonlight with the enhanced magick flowing through her veins.

And yet I craved more.

She shook her chestnut curls with a laugh before leaning forward to kiss the center of my bared chest. "Do you want to know what I thought when we first met, demon?" she breathed against my skin, her deft fingers unzipping my trousers, my length springing free.

Not waiting to hear my response, her fingers teased across the dripping head, spreading it before she grasped me fully. "I thought you looked like a tortured angel—beautiful and tragic all at once with the most beguiling eyes I had ever seen. Like expensive whiskey or fine-sun gold."

"Is this a part of your ritual, witch?" I groaned, spreading my thighs wide as her tongue swept over my neck, her soft hands caressing me. Need barreled through me, fusing with her own through the bond.

She looked like a lustful enchantress with her long mane of hair tangled from her fingers and the forest floor. When she gave me a sinful grin, I feared I would embarrass myself and explode before she held me fully.

"Even surly demons deserve worship. We've only begun making some magick tonight." Leaning forward, her wet lips suctioned around the weeping tip of my cock, her warm tongue licking away my taste before sliding along my aching length with a throaty moan.

My world froze at the pleasure roaring through me. Unlike anything I had ever felt, and unlike anything I feared I would feel again, I sought to absorb her touch. My demon growled low, hands threading through the strands of her silky hair to guide her over my cock. "That's it. Just like that, sweetheart."

At my fervent praise, she moaned, glancing up at me through half-lidded eyes. Her mouth stretched over my length indecently, her ruby-red lips glistening.

I had to look away or I would be finished.

My soul splintered, broken down before emerging anew. Tormented at the pleasure, I reasoned this had to be her spell at work. Nothing could feel this powerful. Nothing this right.

Her movements became faster and harder, her hands joining her mouth to wreck me.

Through the fog of lust, a crack pierced through me. Fangs extended, I hissed, warning away whoever dared interrupt us. When another branch snapped, closer this time, I dragged Ember's lips and hands away from me with clenched teeth.

Blanketing us in shadow, I concealed her nude body as the intruder stepped into our little sanctuary.

Her apologetic sister crashed through the foliage, a hand

clapped over her eyes. "Em? Sorry to interrupt, but something's happened. You need to come. Now."

Caught in between my demon rage and sanity, I forced myself to not respond with a scathing retort. Ember, however, thought the situation extremely humorous, giggling in my ear as her hand gripped me once more.

Through the wave of desire, I considered throwing her to the forest floor and finishing this, fuck the consequences. But instead, I forced her hands away from my cock and willed my body to cool.

After a moment of silence, Ember's eyes gleamed with mutiny, but Audra let out a pained groan. "Fucking Hell, Em. Please vocalize you heard me, so I can leave."

Ember rolled her eyes. "Yes, we heard you. We'll be right behind you." She stood and searched for her abandoned dress after pressing a quick kiss to my lips.

With a swallowed groan, I found the fabric stuffed behind a bush and brought it over to her. She lifted her arms, letting me drag the material over her perfect body, hiding the love bites spotted over her pale skin. With a laugh, she ran her fingers through her hair, pulling twigs and leaves from the warm brown tresses.

Amused, I couldn't help but grin at her efforts. "I'm afraid there's no hiding what happened here, witch. With your dirty dress and bee-stung lips, you look like a forest nymph cavorting in the brush."

"Cavorting? Is that what we're calling it?" she snorted, wrapping her arms around my middle. "Not to mention the pulsating glow of magick flowing through me. I feel as if I've been amped up like a charger."

Unbidden, I let my lips graze her hair before I pulled away. "Let's go see what new mess the witches have gotten into now."

Before the night held an air of excitement and wonder, but now the fog appeared ominous. The quiet unnerving. We emerged onto the field and gaped. The fire's roar had dimmed and a group of witches hovered in a circle, blocking whatever laid beyond.

A young witch noticed Ember, and screeched, "It's Rosemary! Someone tried to kill her."

Ember paled before she ran, pushing through the witches, until I heard her gasp of horror.

Over the heads of the Coven, I gazed down at the witch, who lay on the grass like a sleeping angel. Her greying black hair fanned around her forehead like a halo, which made the telltale slash of red along her dark neck stark. A male with similar features to the witch fell to his knees beside her and lifted her hands into his, his eyes haunted.

Ember stood frozen with shock, her lips quivering. "It was the killer. They were here."

Gasps broke out, and a new tinge of panic coursed over the crowd.

The High Priestess stepped forward, her perfect appearance ruffled. "Rosemary still lives. The cut was not deep enough to sever her artery. We stopped the bleeding, but we put her in a spelled coma to help her body heal." As she spoke, her gaze flitted to each of the witches, until she noticed my presence and paused. "Demon, what is the meaning of this?"

My gaze lifted from the trickle of blood and narrowed at the High Priestess. In my haste to follow Ember, I had forgotten to shift back into my shadows.

Ember stepped forward, her face still deathly pale. "Don't freak out. He's here with me."

The Coven noticed me lurking behind Ember and broke out into sounds of outrage, their faces twisted with revulsion.

The mask of the Scourge unfurled over my expression. "I will leave you to deal with your Coven, High Priestess."

Ember opened her mouth to stop my retreat, but Rebecca

turned to her granddaughter with irritation. "Enough, Ember. You have done quite enough tonight."

Ember's eyes flashed with fire and she stepped closer to me, as if I was the one who needed protecting. After a muttered oath, Jade dragged her away.

In a wisp of smoke, I dematerialized. Instead of leaving this realm, I hovered in my shadows, following the witches as they moved Rosemary back into the estate. As they wandered through the high-ceilinged hallways lined with portraits and Carnival masks, I weaved in and out of the crowd, listening to their muttered conversations for any clues. Other than their disapproval of the High Priestess's lack of action and their disgust at my appearance on their land, I learned nothing of value.

Gathered around the guest bed, Ember and her sisters stood alongside the Coven, their expressions tormented.

My heart ached to see them suffering. In the short time I spent with the Belles, they had weaseled their way past my defenses with their ridiculous pop culture knowledge and sugar intake.

They were a shining beacon of how life could be if things were different.

If I was different.

My brows furrowed as the witches' protests grew louder, the energy in the room shifting as they turned on their leader with menacing scowls. "This has gone far enough, Rebecca. How many more attacks must we endure before the Council acts?"

Rebecca eye's glittered, but the Coven was not finished. A warlock stepped forward; his arms wrapped around the curvy witch beside him, his voice holding a thick French accent. "If the Council won't act, then we must. This is personal. Someone attacked her on our own property, under our protection."

After a heavy silence, the woman beside him spoke up, her voice full of pain. "Rosemary could have been killed. It was sheer luck that we stumbled upon her, causing the killer to flee like a bandit in the night. This is a targeted act of violence, and we appear weak if we do not act."

The elders rallied beside Rebecca, a show of force against the rising tensions. "We must remain calm and let the Council do their job. Without a stable governing force, this city would descend into madness. We must trust they know what's best."

"You mean what *you* think is best?" The female frowned.

Another young witch pushed forward; her eyes narrowed on Ember while her chin elevated to the ceiling with her disdain. "I say we investigate the demon on our lands tonight. He would have reason to kill one of our own, and Ember allowed him through our protective borders!"

My shoulders stiffened in reaction to her threatening finger pointed at my witch. But Ember needed no one to save her.

Ember ignored Jade's grasping hands and stepped nose to nose with the witch. "You want to point fingers, Tabitha, then let's air it out. *Yes*, I'm fucking a demon. *No*, he wasn't the one to attack Rosemary. How do I know this? Because he was with me during the ritual. Y'all can whisper and gossip all you want about who is inside my bed, but don't come at him for something he had nothing to do with."

My face blanked at her words. The witch stood before her entire Coven, fresh from the brink of her trauma, to defend my honor to her people. I let out a shaky breath as wonder coursed through me. I didn't deserve her. Not by half.

Rebecca glared at her granddaughter. "That's enough, Ember." She turned back to the Coven, her hand clapped her forehead. "My granddaughter is right. If the demon had an alibi for the attack, then someone else is to blame. So, unless one of our own tried to kill Rosemary, someone else broke through our borders."

They froze as realization hit.

The elder's voice brokered no argument. "We must work on imbuing our protection with more magick. There must be a hole in the field or a slip in our power."

Rebecca nodded. "Deal with that immediately. As for the rest of you, go home and rest. The elders will remain by Rosemary's side until tomorrow, when we'll plan the best way to present this to the other Council members. We need their support on this."

The witches and warlocks grumbled but followed their High Priestess's orders.

A young witch hung back, and I realized it was Fleur—the witch from the night in Faerie. She appeared pale as she kept glancing from Rosemary to the floor with panicked breaths. "Tabitha, let's go please."

The witch, still glaring daggers at Ember, sighed and led her sister out the door.

Jade leaned close to her sisters. "We should leave soon. It's late, and there's not much we can contribute tonight."

With a brief nod, they walked past my shadowy form. Ember's fingers danced as if she could feel me here beside her, though I knew it was impossible.

I wanted to trail back out of the eerie estate with the sisters, but I remained behind, watching the High Priestess with a cocked head. I couldn't read the witch, her face a cipher as one by one witches fled the room.

When she was alone at last, she glanced up to where I stood, a glint in her eyes. "You and I have much to discuss, demon." Her voice was glacial, a stark contrast to the fire blazing behind her blue-green eyes.

My face remained stony as I shifted back into my physical body. She watched me like one watched a pet inside of a terrarium, with grim fascination and a prickle of disgust. "How are you able to see me through my shadows?"

Her face revealed nothing. "What is going on between you and my granddaughter?"

Unhurried, I approached the witch with a bored air. "Does it matter?"

"Of course it does, you swine. My granddaughter deserves better than a mercenary demon, begotten of Satan. Not to mention you are supposed to solve this case, not frolic on my estate. Or was your promise to Carreau all a lie?"

My jaw ticked. "I'm working on it. Even mercenaries must do their due diligence. And you underestimate your granddaughter. Ember is braver than you give her credit for."

A flash of pride flickered in her eyes before she quelled it. "I'm no fool. You could have solved this case already if not for your distraction with my granddaughter. I know who Ember is, which is why her interest in *you* concerns me."

She settled against the armoire near the window, her gaze settling on the rosebushes creeping inside with a wistful expression. "Ember is brave, but she is also impulsive and struggles through immense grief. It makes her unpredictable and dangerous."

Bitterness colored my tone. "Having some sort of purpose and someone who believes in her has done wonders for her self-confidence. Fancy that."

"Confidence is not what Ember lacks," Rebecca snorted with fondness. "Caution is what she needs. Before it gets her, or her sisters, killed. She does not need you endangering her with this murder investigation. What if it had been her tonight the killer wanted?"

My chest heaved with violent emotion before I could school my expression.

I would fucking burn the world to ash if any dared to harm her.

"Then I would have protected her," I grated.

Rebecca shook her head sadly. "And when you're not there? What will stop the killer then? Someone walked straight into my daughter's home and butchered them like cattle, leaving them behind for young Ember to find." Her eyes misted. "That is not something one easily recovers from. She's flailing and latched herself to another dangerous distraction."

My respect for the witch deepened. I could not fault her for protecting her own. Nor would I suffocate Ember in a protective bubble, like Rebecca longed to do. "She can make her own decisions."

Frustration lit in Rebecca's eyes, and she turned to level the full force of her resentment on me. "Stop her. Do whatever it takes to keep her away from this case. Or her blood will be on your hands, demon. And I'll make you fucking suffer for it."

Filled with contempt, I portaled away from the estate, the need to punch something roaring through me. For once, I was unsure where I should be. I wanted no part of Hell, nor was I capable of facing Ember in my current state. Flashing to my townhouse in the Quarter, I asked myself how I had found myself in this twisted mess.

Ember and I were already in too deep.

No matter how badly I wanted to, I could not shelter her from the fallout. We were barreling towards the end of the line with no brakes to pull us back from the edge. And if the time came where I would have to reap her soul, I don't know how we would ever recover.

26
EMBER

Before the sun had fully risen, I watched the warm peachy glow crest through my window, and I settled deeper into the covers. Despite the warmth of my blankets and the smell of coffee brewing downstairs, I still felt unaccountably cold, processing the events from earlier.

Though Rosemary and I were not particularly close, her near-death had submerged me into the depths of my painful memories once more. Only now it felt more real. This wasn't a vampire or a pack member, this was one of our own. If anything happened to Jade, Audra, or Isla, I would... *No.*

Swiftly, I put a halt to that line of thought and jumped from the bed, desperate to move my body. All my reliable tricks to slip away from the past wouldn't work this time. I needed to be fully sober and present to deal with this murder and stop them before anyone else was hurt.

But all those feelings felt exposed and raw with no outlet to express them.

Hands shaking, my intuition pulled me towards the demonic grimoire nestled amongst my things. What a mistake, stealing this monstrosity. Like every time before, I idly thumbed through the pages, ciphering the strange text for any solution. Instead, it only reaffirmed how idiotic it was to summon a demon and enter a pact with one. I truly was the dumb bitch who died first in every horror movie.

Before I slammed the book shut, my eyes fluttered over the name Gressil—Carreau's father. With a huffed laugh, I skimmed over the details of his family lineage and the demonic possessions they were infamous for. Unlike his magnanimous son, Gressil had spent decades waging wars under Lucifer's tutelage—a terrifying thought.

My eyes glossed over the Realms of Hell until I found the page describing Pride and the mantle of Satan. This section was one I read thoroughly in my quest to better understand Killian, yet I only discovered more questions that I wanted answered.

The original Fallen parceled out Hell into nine realms, and each had held their prospective thrones for thousands of years. Passed down through the ages to their legitimate children, Satan's crown found its way to Killian's father. What Killian didn't mention was why he had to reap souls. Unlike my previous notions, it wasn't a choice; the demons *relied* on their pacts and reaped souls to survive. Without them, they would be utterly lost.

Chills crept over my skin as I read about the horrifying lengths demons went to ensure they continued to reap souls, and the price for those who dared renege on a pact.

Soon, I could be a part of their numbers.

Worrying about our pact would not help my situation. What I need was to stop fearing my magick and find a way to undo the hex I cast over Killian. My witch's intuition flowed once more through me as if approving my sudden determination.

Decided, I dressed and hurried down the stairs.

In the chilly kitchen, Jade sat at the table, her dark hair

pulled into a loose ponytail with a cup of steaming coffee in her hands as she looked over stacks of bills.

She glanced up as I walked over to the coffee maker to pour myself a cup. I sat across from her, pulling my feet off the floor and curling them around me. "Do you do this every morning?" I asked, glancing at the scattered envelopes.

She huffed a tired laugh. "What do you think?"

The world wasn't fair; Jade should be out living her life, enjoying the successes of her hard work in the Coven and beyond. Yet here she sat in her family home, taking on responsibilities she never asked for.

"Stupid question," I muttered.

She set aside her laptop and rubbed her eyes. "You're up early. Trouble sleeping again?"

"I slept fine last night. But there was something I wanted to talk to you and the girls about."

Her brows raised as she leaned back, crossing her arms with suspicion. "What now?"

Bracing myself, I took a deep breath. "I want to train my magick. It's time. I've let my power go unchecked for too long already, and with everything going on, we need to be at full strength."

Jade sat straighter, shocked by my answer. Her eyes grew misty, and her hand found mine on the table. "I think that's the best idea I've heard in a long time." She glanced at the clock on the wall behind me with a slight grimace. "We still need to finish up our spells for the festival, but we can practice in between batches."

Relief coursed through me. "Perfect."

She stood and began packing away the kitchen table to make room for ingredients. "Why don't you go wake the girls? I'll gather some tools to help."

I stood from the table, kissing her on the cheek. "I love you, Jade-bug."

Her surprise at my childhood endearment morphed into a broad smile.

The time would come when I would have to open up to her and be honest about everything. When the time came that she discovered the depths of my lies, she would unleash her disappointment on me. But that time wasn't now.

☽☉☾

The morning felt bright and promising as we crowded around the wide back porch. Before our parents died, it had been our hangout spot in the evenings. Now, the rusted furniture doubled as storage for the amassed junk from our childhood.

Isla jumped off the porch step to help, but Jade shot her a dark look. "You and Audra stay on the porch until we know how flammable Ember's going to be."

Isla rolled her eyes but wrapped an arm around Audra's shoulder, settling back on the steps.

As Jade walked a safe distance away from the house to set up our workstation, I followed, kicking leaves and branches. Without thinking, I wandered to the charred section of the yard where I had discovered our parents' bodies. Days after finding them, a swell of overwhelming grief and anger roared inside me, and my fire destroyed my mother's garden. It marked the moment when my magick turned tumultuous.

"Ember, let's go."

I jumped and returned to the plot of grass, my anxiety growing by the second.

Jade placed her hands on her hips, blowing out a breath as she surveyed the crystals, candles, and herb bundles forming a circle on the dewy grass. "Okay. I'm going to start by using my magick to summon yours and see what we're working with. Since you seem to have some sort of block, it's won't feel pleasant, but it'll be safer for everyone involved if you can try to let it come naturally."

My eyes drifted shut as I focused on the well inside my chest that housed my magick.

Jade's hand brushed mine, leaning closer to whisper, "Are you sure you're ready for this? I'll warn you now—it'll be difficult and most definitely painful," she cautioned.

I gulped. "Like on a scale of one to ten, how would you rate it?"

Her lips turned down. "I'm not sure, having never experienced it. But magical blocks are no joke, and whatever caused it will react defensively, not wanting anyone to remove it."

"You act like it's a living thing."

She shrugged. "Isn't all of our magick alive in a way?"

Thinking about my magick in those terms put it into perspective. Rituals and casting came from intention. Without a spell or a witch's guide to channel the magick, it had nowhere to go. Our witch's intuition perceived those emotions and expressed its wishes through us. Almost like Killian and his demon.

After a brief moment of hesitation, I took a deep breath and closed my eyes once more, focusing on the task at hand. "Alright, let's do this."

Tendrils of her earth magick touched my skin like raindrops, palpable, but not painful. The droplets of magick seeped beneath my skin, forcing their way inside my body as they tried to infiltrate the cage I kept around my power source.

My magick prickled with unease before it fought to defend itself, the sensation sending tiny shocks through my blood.

"Focus, Ember. I'm almost there," Jade's voice bled through my bubble of concentration.

Focused on my meditation breaths, I tried to picture myself on a beach somewhere tropical with coconut sun oil and a pina colada. It worked for another second before the next wave hit.

My breathing picked up to panicked pants, the air around me heating with energy.

The next spike was definitely more painful than a shock. I crouched over, clutching my ribcage as my magick retaliated, sending stabbing wounds throughout my body as it searched for the source of the attack.

"Okay, maybe that's enough." Isla's worried voice trailed to me from the porch like a whisper on the wind.

Through clenched teeth, fighting the blistering pain, I gasped, "No. Keep going."

Another wave hit me and a choked scream escaped my lips before I could suppress it.

"Almost there," Jade promised, her voice a lifeline as my eyes blackened at the corners.

One second, I was with Jade in our yard, feeling the unbearable pain of my magick, and in the next, there was nothing.

I lost consciousness and dropped to the ground, flames erupting around me as I burned alive.

Drifting in the darkness, untethered. Like a ship lost at sea, detached from its moorings, floating in the Black Sea of my consciousness.

Until, in the next ragged breath, I rose to the surface once more.

"Maybe you should smack her?"

"Are you kidding? Her skin is like a million degrees right now. I'm staying over here, out of the fire zone."

I blinked open my eyes, blinded by the bright sun overhead. Easing onto my elbows, I glanced around the backyard and breathed a sigh of relief when I saw nothing had burned to a crisp. Their gave me anxiety, so I held up my hands. "Can you guys give me some space? Y'all are freaking me out."

Jade glared at me. "*We're* freaking *you* out? Ember Marie, I swear to the Goddess you will be the death of me. Sooner rather than later, I'm sure."

"Are you alright?" Audra asked, his lips flattened with concern.

"Fine, I think," I whispered as I lifted a hand to my sweating forehead, my skin hot to the touch.

"Here, try this." Isla tipped a glass of iced lemon lavender tea to my lips, and I drank it down gratefully, the kick of her healing magick soothing the flames under my skin.

With my focus returning to Jade, my heart pounded anew. "Well? Don't leave me in suspense. What's the verdict?"

Jade held out her hand, and I delicately gave her mine, cognizant of my burning skin. She pulled me up with pursed lips. "Do you want the good news or the bad news?"

"Obviously, the bad. Break it to me—I'm broken, a dud."

Her finger traced the lines leading from the center of my palm to my wrist. "You're not broken, and your problem isn't about control."

Audra snorted. "What do you mean? We all saw that, right? Her magick has gone AWOL."

Jade continued, ignoring Audra, "The only thing between you and the full use of your magick is *you*. And it's no mere block. This is serious shit, way beyond anything I've ever seen."

I bit my lips hard, needing the slice of pain. "What's that supposed to mean?"

Jade's eyes held as she enclosed her hand around mine in a tight grip. "It means until you work through whatever blocked you in the first place, or we figure out how to break it with magick, you won't be able to teach yourself control or master your abilities."

After Jade's revelation, we scattered to do our own activities. Deciding I needed a break from the chaos, I snuck away to the estate to check on Rosemary. As if seeing her alive and fighting would flush the darkness away.

With my purchase from the florist in hand, I wandered up the gravel driveway lined in swooping oaks. At the door, Mr. Rollings barred my entrance. "The Coven is very busy today dealing with the Council. Your grandmother has advised me to keep anyone out who is not a part of the committee."

Though I wanted to argue, I knew it would be pointless. The old bat was as stubborn and cantankerous as a bull. "Sure thing." I mock saluted. I waited until he slammed the door shut before slipping around to the back of the property.

The gardens were quiet. My eyes dipped to the hedge maze with a shiver before I inhaled the fragrance of the sweet air with a cleansing sigh. I placed my hands in my jeans pockets and watched the surrounding air with amusement. "Are you going to hide in your shadows all day?"

In the next instant, Killian materialized next to me, his face flushed with surprise. "Could you see me in my shadows?"

My gaze drifted over his rumpled, dark clothes and the inky swoop of his hair, brushing his scar. A sudden wave of shyness coursed through me, and I flushed at the memory of last night with his face between my legs, devouring me like he was a starved man seeking salvation.

Sheepish, I turned away from his unwavering attention. "I can feel your presence through the bond. Lately, I can also sense when the air around me bends with your shadows." I shrugged, embarrassed to admit how often I searched the space around me for signs of him when he was gone. "Are you following me because you don't trust me or because you fear I'm going to do something foolish?"

His lips quirked, his whiskey eyes warm in the afternoon

glow. "Neither. I wanted to discuss last night with you, but couldn't find you at your house."

My heart stuttered and my grip on the flowers grew taut. "Did you learn anything about the attacker?"

He shook his head. "I searched the shadow dimension for hours but couldn't find any traces of Rosemary's attacker. After I left the estate, I worked on mercenary business, tracking souls through the Quarter. With my succession approaching, I'm under a lot of pressure to have everything in line."

"Hm," I murmured noncommittally. Weary from the knowledge I discovered in the grimoire, I pushed aside thoughts of reaping souls.

The gate to the Coven cemetery creaked as I entered the hollowed grounds. Our footsteps were silent as we wandered through the plots until I stopped at my parents' tombstones. Perched next to them, I arranged the bouquet in between their plot. White chrysanthemums and marigolds for eternal love after passage into the Beyond, along with a few sprigs of my mother's favorite flowers: purple hydrangeas.

Killian sat beside me, his hand covering mine as I shuddered out a heavy breath.

I plucked a weed from the plot absently. My voice sounded empty, even to myself, despite the emotion swimming inside my chest. "My mother used to say happiness was a floating speck of dust in the aether. It was meant to be seized with both hands and anyone who waited for it to happen to them would never find it. That's how she lived her life—full of joyous excitement for everything."

My lips quirked with amusement. "Even with the looming title of High Priestess over her head, she denied her family's wishes and married my father, a powerful warlock, but one without a prominent family name. We lived a quiet life, away from the rigid expectations she lived under as a child. But if they had been more involved with the Coven, maybe they wouldn't have been without the protections of the estate."

I continued, my throat constricting despite the rein I tried to control within. "Not only was I not there that night to protect them, but I have spent the nights since their deaths living in ways they would be ashamed of."

Killian's fingers wound through mine. A sturdy rock I crept closer to.

His voice was soft but firm. "You are far too hard on yourself. You're twenty-three and allowed to make mistakes and grieve your losses."

His mouth hardened into a flat line, eyes haunted by his own pain.

"You don't have to talk about this."

After a moment, he lifted our joined hands to his face. He dipped down to run his nose along the delicate skin of my wrist before pressing his lips in a light kiss. "My mother would have loved you. You have her fiery spirit and her compassion."

My chest grew warm at the praise I knew meant more than any flattering comment about my body or face. When I thought about his feelings towards me being tied to whatever spell I may or may not have placed on him, I felt icy fear shoot down my spine.

When my pulse of dread escaped through the bond, Killian stood, pulling me to my feet. The heat from his body felt delicious as he pressed me closer to him. "I don't know about you, but last night was the best night of my life. We have little time remaining on this plane together before Samhain. We shouldn't waste any more time."

A gasp slipped through my lips at his earnest confession. I nodded my head, his pine scent soothing my worries. "I feel the same."

He caught my chin and lifted it until his lips brushed mine, a mere touch before he pulled away. His cheek lifted in a crooked smile. "Your place?"

My pulse raced before I nodded.

With Killian's arms around my shoulders, I wondered how bad it would be to renege on a demon pact and have my soul indebted to him, if it meant I could have this feeling sweeping through me forever.

27

KILLIAN

As Ember and I stepped inside her home, anticipation growing thick between us, we skidded to a halt at the scene before us. Her sisters sat around the kitchen table bagging fragrant tea leaves, thwarting any hopes of amorous time alone.

Ember shot me a wink before pulling me into the kitchen for a kiss.

"Do not have sexy time in the kitchen, Em," Audra shouted, before her voice abruptly broke off with a giggle.

Ember stepped with a sigh of longing and grabbed a bag of salt and dark glass bottles of herbal tinctures. "Well, come on, then," she grumbled. "Before they send in a rescue party."

Surprising myself, I ended up enjoying my afternoon with the Belles, learning much about their individual personalities and tastes, as well as how they worked as a unit. When one sister spoke, it was as if the others were in tune with more than just her words. They shared an almost hive mind dynamic where they could finish each other's sentences or understand the words left unspoken and what they meant. Audra and Isla were by far the most vocal, with Audra complaining about the competitive sorcery school in Wales that rejected her application once again, and Isla dreaming of traveling the world.

Jade turned an alarming shade of green at the mention of faraway places.

I could understand her concern. If I had a family like this, I would do anything to keep it protected and safe from outside harm. Whether or not I smothered them with my love.

They insisted I stay and finish Return of the King, and I was helpless to refuse.

After hours of movies and junk food, I portaled back to Hell, conflicted emotions tugging me in different directions. My initial wrath at Ember for hexing me had dwindled to mere flickers of confusion. I no longer doubted the suffering her past trauma and inconsistent magick caused her, nor did I blame her for lashing out.

But no matter how I felt, the pact was binding.

Our only hope now was limiting the fallout when Samhain came. So, instead of venturing to my rooms or the fighting rings, I sank below the castle to Charon and the prisons.

The dungeons were quiet for once. Charon watched me with the lift of his grey brow. "No souls today, my Lord?"

I hissed, warning him I was not to be played with today. "Has her name appeared?"

He sighed and lifted the Scroll of Debts onto his desk with a clanging drop. Flipping through the thick, worn pages, he settled on the latest sheet depicting the pacts made by demons in the Realm.

Impatient, I looked over his shoulder, sifting through the hundreds of names until I spotted the name I dreaded most.

Ember Belle.

"Fuck!" My fist shook with the need to punch something. "When did her name appear?"

He shook his head with displeasure. "This is the first time I have seen it, but you knew this would come. You entered a pact with her, and the time draws to a close on your agreed terms. Soon you won't have a choice but to reap her soul."

My hands were around his throat before he could blink. "That will not be happening. I'd kill every demon in this cursed plane before my father took her soul."

Soldiers entering the prison halls paused before rushing away from my volatile anger. The tale was likely to spread to the rest of my father's court, inciting more incursions. A ploy of my father's I had no energy to deal with currently.

I pushed Charon away, forcing my breath to calm.

He watched me, unbothered by my outburst. "As soon as your father realizes what she is to you, he will stop at nothing to see her destroyed."

"And what is she to me?" I asked, staggering away.

"Your mate, of course." Charon rolled his eyes. "Anyone who watched your reaction would know."

Fucking Hell. She may have spelled me to believe she was my mate, but the falsehood would make no difference to the demons of the realm. If anyone discovered she was even potentially my mate, they would use her to punish me. Hurt her in despicable, unthinkable ways.

Sickened, I turned on my heel, my demon clamoring to return to her.

"Killian," Charon shouted, halting my steps. "You must finish this before Samhain if you want her to live. Once the deadline has passed, there will be nothing you or I could do to stop this. And you have more than her life riding on the upcoming succession."

Dread settled through me and I portaled back to my townhouse. There was much to do, but first, I sent a quick text to Amarisa—the nymph who knew everyone and everything going down in NOLA.

It was time to finish this. Rebecca's warning would not come true—Ember would not pay the price for these crimes, nor would I give up without a fight.

28

EMBER

Moretti's Italian Kitchen sat on the corner of Decatur in the heart of the Quarter. It had the best Italian fare in the city with the added benefit of an outdoor courtyard that hid behind an eight-foot-tall red brick wall piled high with potted plants—and a magick protection spell keeping mortal eyes and ears away.

Trumpets bursted from street performers and the lilting sounds of an opera singer inside the restaurant floated towards us in the slight breeze, along with the heady scent of magnolia from the tree growing at the center of the patio.

I took a sip of iced sweat tea as I watched Killian. The demon had cut his hair, the ends of his black waves now reaching just under his ear. The cut made his butterscotch eyes and silvery scar more noticeable that usual in the soft evening light.

As if afraid he would disappear in a snap of smoke, my eyes wandered over him before skipping away to my phone. Fleur had texted me, asking me where I was—a surprising turn of events after our last interaction—but she hadn't responded when I gave her the same excuse I told my sisters, that Killian and I were on a date. Though as I cozied up to the handsome demon with stars in my eyes, the excuse was hardly a lie.

"So," I murmured, glancing around the empty courtyard, "when was Amarisa meant to show?"

Killian's brows furrowed deeper, his leg dancing under the metal table uncharacteristically. "She should have been here half an hour ago, but I don't mind waiting longer."

I pursed my lips to fight a smile. "I don't mind, either."

We ordered some food, the courtyard filling with creatures from around the city as the afternoon sun slipped away. Twinkling lights flickered to life as I propped my chin into my hands and watched him take a hesitant bite of the squid ink pasta with fresh Gulf prawns.

The bliss on his face was almost as delightful as the dish itself.

Amused, I scooped a portion onto my plate and savored the succulent scent of garlic and herbs. As I chewed, my attention dragged back to his cheek. The scar never bothered me; in fact, I thought it was pretty hot. My imagination spun through the possibilities of how he acquired such a mark. He must have been young. Young enough that his immortal healing hadn't settled in. Like mortal puberty, the transition was both powerful and awkward. It ensured a supernatural creature would possess the strength to survive in our world, though some grew to lament it.

Curiosity churning, I swallowed the bite of food and chose to be bold.

The demon once claimed I didn't know him, and I wanted to change that. It scared me how much I wanted to know every detail about him—his passions, his fears, his dreams for the future. I wanted to hoard all those nuggets of what made Killian, *Killian* and never surrender them.

"If you don't mind me asking, and please tell me to shut up if this is rude or if you don't want to talk about it, but how did you get this?" I rambled as my fingertips lifted to brush against his cheek.

When his shoulders stiffened, I rushed to assure him of my intentions. "Seriously, I shouldn't have asked. It's by no means date night conversation material. Not that this is a date!" I rushed to add as my cheeks flamed crimson. "I'm going to shut up now."

Killian's lips twitched, and the icy tendril of hurt melted into dew. "It's ugly as Hell, isn't it?"

My relief was short-lived as his words rippled through me. My mouth opened in shock. "Um, no. It's actually really fucking sexy." When that irresistible smirk flitted across his face, my thighs clenched together. "Though don't let it get to your head. You still lack even a modicum of charm, demon."

He snorted, his eyes glowing with mirth. "You weren't saying that the other night, sweetheart."

His hand brushed over my cheek, his thumb parting my lips before he sobered. "My father gave this to me the night I arrived at his palace following my mother's murder." His voice was quiet and controlled, empty of all emotion. "I was always a disappointment, the unwanted bastard weakling he tried to beat into submission. But no matter how far he pushed me, my fury kept me going strong."

An evil smile curled his lips, and I shivered at the promise of violence in his blackening eyes.

"Being forced to pass down his most prized possession, his crown, to me, is the sweetest revenge I could ask for. Revenge that will be reaped once this mission is concluded."

The food in my stomach soured. "Your father sounds like a grade A asshole."

"Oh, you don't know the half of it." He frowned.

Before I could ask another question, he moved the conversation to safer topics.

We brushed past the moment of awkwardness and before

long, he was making me giggle as he shared stories of his soldiers back in Hell, including Carreau.

Killian swirled his glass of demon brew, a hint of a smile on his face. "So, he flew over to the chieftain of the village, who pretended to obey his every command, until later that night. Carreau was deep in his cups and their army evacuated cargo loads of the crops Carreau tried to steal from them. Taliah swooped in at the last minute and saved the alliance and the remaining supplies. Now, she goes and visits the village every year with a gift. She claims she does it for our realm, but secretly she loves to dance around the fire with the other demons, with no one from our army to see her let loose."

His fond smile as he talked mention of his oldest friend had both fiery jealousy and relief soaring through my body. "And have the two of you ever—?"

A twist of horror curled his lips before he laughed. "Absolutely not. She's like a sister to me after the years we grew up together in the barracks."

My immediate relief must have shown, because his hand twirled through mine.

I cleared my throat. "You tell Taliah she can hang with us anytime she wants to dance. My sisters will show her how it's done on Gaia."

But then, my mind shifted back to his story with Carreau. The idea of Carreau following in his father's footsteps, possessing creatures and causing mayhem, made me uneasy. "You said the chieftain pretended to follow Carreau's orders? What is his gift again?"

Killian's lips thinned. "It's an ability than runs through Gressil's line of demons. Carreau's gift is not as pervasive as his father's, but no less dangerous. He can see inside a person and feel their greatest hurts—all their regrets, their losses, their fears and humiliations—and he brings them to the fore. If the person isn't strong enough to deny his call, he could influence them."

My blood turned cold. "Like kill someone?"

He nodded, his fingers flexing around the handle of his brew. "I've seen Carreau use his gift when it serves his needs, but I haven't seen him force someone to commit anything truly heinous. Not like Gressil."

With the power to shape the people around you to your will, I wondered what I would do. Perhaps I would force Wren to eat slugs and then have him beat Brent to a pulp. At the unbidden thought of the pack, I bit down on my fork hard enough to make me wince in pain.

"What are you thinking about?" Killian watched me like he wanted to crack open my head like an egg, so he could discover all my secrets. Even the ones that hurt. *Especially* those.

"Just imagining the destruction I would bring to the Boudreaux pack if I possessed such a gift. Not that they need any help to bring about their destruction," I muttered.

Killian's face transformed to biting anger. "They deserve your ire. I think if I ever see those filthy mutts again, I may kill them."

I brushed my hair over my shoulder, feeling strangely turned on by his threat. "I suppose I have brought enough drama and chaos to their pack over the years. Maybe I could let their behavior slide. After a small beating or two."

Still playing with my hand resting on the table, he wondered, "So, how did the jock shifter break your heart, witch? I promise not to be too unmerciful in my judgement of your terrible taste."

I drained my glass before laying out our sordid history. "He was my first real boyfriend. I partied a lot in high school—and after high school. I decided it was time to try being a respectable daughter and find a nice guy to bring home to mom and pop. It was fine... boring. Then, I found him with his tongue down a sexy vampire's throat and the rest is history."

He pursed his lips. "There's a lot to unpack here. No pun intended."

I burst into laughter. "Oh, you have no idea what kind of mess you've bound yourself to."

Killian didn't smile or laugh. His eyes smoldered until I feared he would burrow within me and ruin me forever. "I know exactly who I'm bound to. And I don't regret it."

I shivered as I felt the honesty in his words through the bond that tied our souls. Leaning closer together, the tension between us sizzled. His eyes dipped to my lips, and I licked them subconsciously.

The moment shattered when the waitress popped over my shoulder, her voice snapping us out of our trance. "How was your meal? Can I offer you two desserts?"

"No, thanks. Just the check." Killian gazed up at the darkened sky with a deep etch between his brows.

"Maybe Amarisa got caught up in something and couldn't text you."

He nodded, but the concern remained in his eyes.

A plan formed in my mind, and I offered him my hand. "Let's walk around. I know the perfect place."

<hr>

Strolling through the busy streets filled with costumed tourists celebrating Halloween, the city came alive. Mortals with skeleton painted faces and striped tights strolled through the cemeteries with the desire to see ghosts, without realizing how real the supernatural world was.

Killian held my hand as we found our destination: Cypress Treasures. The bookstore resembled an expensive department store, the stacks arranged in hidden mazes of bookshelves that made me feel like I was entering Narnia.

I pulled him to the romance section with a grin. "You must get at least five new books. I'm sure Hell's libraries leave much to offer. Especially in the romance department, which I know you secretly love."

His grin widened, displaying white teeth and a hint of fangs. "Hell's libraries certainly lack good fiction, none of which would be considered romantic. Tomes on the long history of the fallen and their conquests over the realms? Hell Hounds and how to locate your enemy? We've got miles of books on those topics. But an action-adventure romp through the Amazon? Not so much."

"Hell Hounds?" I gulped, my eyes widening with twisted delight. "Like Cerberus?"

He laughed. "Not quite. Satan keeps them locked in hiss private dungeons, only released for the truly terrible miscreants. That's what I'm for."

We wandered around the store like children, flirting as we squirreled away books from each other and stole forbidden touches. A glimpse into what life could be like if things were different.

The fantasy of such a future floated between us like snowflakes, and I let myself open my mouth and touch them with my tongue, knowing it would only leave me cold and alone in the end.

When I couldn't bear not to touch him any longer, I dragged Killian into a dimly lit corner and pulled his lips down to mine.

He chuckled into my kiss. This evening was the most I'd heard him laugh since I first met him. Hand fused to his soft locks of hair, I tried to climb him like a tree, my legs wrapping around his hips. He flicked my tongue with his like I was his dessert, devouring my desperate moans.

I was utterly smitten. Ensorcelled by him. Maybe it was him who put the spell on me, forcing me to desire and crave him more than anything before in my life.

His hands gripped my ass before pulling my body closer, and I ground down against his hardened length.

The moment was broken when the bookshop owner's small tabby hissed at Killian, its claws swiping out at his pant legs as if sensing a fellow demonic entity.

Killian broke away from my lips to hiss back with fangs extended, sending the cat flying back around to safety.

A laugh escaped as my gaze wandered over his raven hair, mused from my rough hands to his swollen lips begging to be bitten. I couldn't hold myself back. With my heart in my eyes, I leaned down and kissed him again. Once. Twice. Lingering touches I wanted to freeze in time like a photo and hold to my chest forever.

"Let's get out of here," he murmured against my cheek. "My townhouse is only a few blocks away."

I slapped his chest, jumping back to the floor unsteadily. "You have a secret bachelor pad here in Gaia and you haven't told me about it? For shame."

He intertwined our hands. "You'll like it. Especially my bed. It's big, soft, and wide enough for me to show devious witches how to behave."

My core clenched with desire.

Walking back to his place, our hands trailed over each other, our giggles echoing in the quiet, empty street. So distracted, I almost missed the sudden shift in the air.

Killian became instantly alert and pulled me to a halt.

"Wha—"

He threw his hand over my mouth, dematerializing us into

the shadow dimension. His eyes were hard, moving towards the ill-boding juncture of the street, as if he wasn't sure he wanted to keep me close to him or protect me from whatever lurked around the corner.

I knew almost immediately I had made a mistake in looking.

The body lay broken, a leg snapped, eyes opened wide in horror, while a pool of blood emptied onto the pavement from the sickening slash along the female's throat.

Blood and fear suffocated me where I stood. My legs gave out, and I would have hit the concrete had Killian not wrapped me closer to his side. "That's—"

"I know," he cut me off, his eyes blazing black as his demon raged under his skin.

Amarisa's beautiful face was nearly unrecognizable underneath the bruises, as her mouth screamed open in pain.

I felt my stomach contents rising, but forced myself to remain calm, to swipe away the images from that night. "Should I call my grandmother?" I whispered.

The lines of his face appeared stark in shadow. He shook his head, eyes never leaving the nymph. "I'll handle the Council, but not with you here. I don't want you involved with this anymore."

When I opened my mouth to argue, he shot me with a snarling glare and I froze under his sudden anger. In a blink, his fury was gone.

"Apologies," he stuttered out, his eyes returning to his normal pupils with remorse. "I shouldn't have snapped at you. My demon is screaming at me to protect you, but that's no excuse."

I shook my head, pulse returning to normal. "It's okay. I'm shocked too. Just get me to your place so you can deal with this. Then, come back to me."

Eyes dark, he nodded.

As we portaled away, I chanced one last look at Amarisa and promised her I wouldn't let her killer go unpunished. Nor would I allow anyone else to fall prey to their villainy.

29

KILLIAN

The summons from the Council was not a surprise, but I felt the slap of resentment all the same. I studied the pretentiously scrawled calligraphy on the parchment courtesy of Carreau, my brows furrowing at the building designated for their affairs. Situated at the epicenter of the three creatures' boundaries, the small white church, enchanted with a concealment spell, had been renovated to fit their needs. Ironic and blasphemous, though it may be.

Taliah stood beside me, her wings and horns hidden away, though her skin looked far too perfect and luminous in the mortal realm. "I'm sending my spies underground once this is finished. We've don't have time to deal with Gaia's troubles when we have so many of our own," she hissed.

Though I wanted to deny her words, I knew time was running out, and we still had no answers. Through the colorful stained-glass windows, I could sense activity within. Whatever this summons was about, it was bound to be tedious, and Taliah was right—the rebellions in Hell needed immediate attention.

"Feel free to leave, Tal. Who knows how long this will take? Besides, I trust you implicitly to deal with the matter."

Her brows furrowed with concern, her hand flexing around the hilt of her blade strapped to her waist. Her weapon was an alarming sight in Gaia, but any mortals who passed merely snickered, thinking she was in costume rather than an actual threat. "Can we trust these people?"

I barked a dark laugh, nudging my shoulder against hers. "I wouldn't trust them with my greatest enemy, but I doubt they will be foolish enough to harm or imprison me with Satan and the rest of Hell ready for war at any moment. Plus, I have the benefit of being innocent of any crime they may lodge at me. But if it makes you feel better, I'll portal away if need be."

"Very well then." She sniffed at the dirty street with a grimace. "I'll find you and your witch later to discuss my findings. You can finally introduce us."

I didn't like the evil glint in her eyes. "Be careful, Tal. Satan is smarter than he lets on. Don't get yourself harmed or in trouble because of this."

"I'll keep that in mind." She saluted me with a smirk and portaled away in a wisp of smoke.

Alone once more in the quiet street, guilt soured my stomach. Amarisa's horrified scream seemed burned into my vision, remorse consuming me for dragging her into this case. And I knew this was not the end. Fear for Ember's safety kept me awake most of the night after I returned to my townhouse. Asleep in my bed, she looked as if she belonged there.

The cathedral doors creaked open with a muffled groan, and I forced myself back to the present. Stepping inside the cavernous space, a petite sprite with a broad smile and electric-green hair greeted me. She guided me through the main high-ceilinged room, removed of pews and altars, to the Council's meeting room.

Her voice rang like a chime that grated on my ears. "If you need anything, call out."

Unenthusiastic, I sat on a wood chair at the center of the

raised circular platform. With a glance around the barren room, I snorted. They certainly loved the drama of it all.

The door burst open once more and the Council members filed in, taking their prospective seats without a word. Alexei, Rebecca, and Hunt watched me with silent anger while Carreau's face was blank, his fingers steepled together.

After a stilted silence, Rebecca demanded, "Let's get this meeting started. I have much to do."

A chuff came from the alpha. Hunt's wolf looked near the surface, his eyes flickering in the overhead lights. "As if you're the only one who has responsibilities to their people."

"Can we please not? Especially in front of our *guest*." Alexei ran a hand over his eyes, the lighting painful in the fading daylight hours.

I hid a sly grin. It would be far too easy to rile the alpha up. All it would take was a single word. A mention of his son's dark secret and Hunt would be ruined, along with the smug vampire, who simply appeared bored.

Only Rebecca remained silent, her blue eyes watching me in that calculating manner that made my fingers itch. "Let's begin with the first order of business—your presence on Coven lands the night of the attack."

My eyes focused on hers. I wondered how much she had shared with the others about my relationship with her granddaughter. The shame of it would be something she intended to keep secret. But I would not shove Ember under the bus to these pricks. "A witch invited me, and I provided my services for the ritual."

Hunt snorted, disgust rolling off him in waves as he ascertained what sort of ritual I spoke of and who would have stomached my servicing.

Ignoring him, I spoke to the others. "When we discovered the witch's attack, I searched through the shadow dimension but could not find evidence of the killer. Whoever was behind it knew to hide their trail from me."

My eyes swept over to Hunt, my accusation clear.

Smoke practically blew from his ears as his face grew purple with anger. "How dare you imply one of our own could be behind these crimes. Especially after you attacked my son on the vampires' lands. I knew it was a mistake involving you in this."

My eyebrows inched closer to my hairline. "I'm not surprised you feel that way. But your son attacked me after I overheard a conversation between him and the Vampire Prince. About some suspicious activity the pack dabbled in."

Alexei leaned forward in his chair, his face cleared of his previous humor. "While I appreciate the lengths of espionage you have gone to with this case, I can assure you what you overheard had nothing to do with the murders."

"As if the word of a vampire means anything," Hunt muttered under his breath, causing Alexei's head to snap to his with disdain.

Rebecca gritted her teeth and raised her hand to silence the two.

This was pointless. The Council themselves could barely stand to be in each other's presence and yet they were the glue binding the city together?

Carreau spoke up, his voice firm. "Regardless of past issues, what matters now is ensuring there are no more incidents before the Samhain festival. We only remain in control if we have the illusion of power. Killian, will you be able to find the killer before then, or do we need to find someone else?"

"I have it under control."

Rebecca raised her brows. "I'm sure you do. But in case you don't, know that we will have no issue blocking off your realm, ceasing all interference from the demons if this isn't solved."

My stomach clenched as I realized her meaning. "You would cut the Hell plane free from Gaia?"

Hunt's anger cleared as he grinned with growing excitement.

From my vantage, I could see Carreau's outrage, but I forced my gaze to remain on the High Priestess. "And how exactly would that help solve matters?"

Rebecca's eyes hardened. "We will do whatever it takes to stop these crimes, and to avenge the killer's victims. I don't care if anyone from your realm is responsible. We will block entry to the city from every outside plane until we sort this out. So, if you value retrieving souls from Gaia, you will get to the bottom of this."

I seethed as they stood.

Rebecca sniffed like a queen staring down at a peasant. "You're dismissed."

⁕

Instead of portaling away, I walked through the claustrophobic streets covered in confetti and beads to clear my mind. Body odor and other foul substances lingered in the air, but after that shit show of a meeting, and the High Priestess's threat, I didn't notice.

Though my time in Gaia would be at an end after Samhain, we would still need access to this plane for souls that fueled our realm. Not to mention, that would mean no more Ember.

I kicked myself for my foolish hope. Some part of me dreamed of a future where our lives could intertwine despite my new role as the Lord of Pride, but my time in Hell had taught me one thing: There were no happy endings for creatures like me.

Walking back to my townhouse, I felt my chest expand, knowing that Ember still remained in my home. Before, I worried anyone entering my sanctuary would disturb the small sliver of peace I imbued inside those walls. But it just seemed right for Ember to be there.

Music reached me from the door. Ember's eyes danced with amusement from her perch on my couch with her legs curled beneath her and a mug of coffee in hand. A stack of books from my shelf nestled beside her, revealing a busy morning of snooping. "Are you going to tell me that you're not a romance lover now that I've recovered the evidence?" She smirked.

"You caught me, sweetheart."

Her eyes danced with glee. "I earmarked a few pages I think would be very interesting. We could have a dramatic reading... or maybe try out some of the moves. For scientific purposes, of course."

My body responded to her sultry purr, my cock throbbing with need.

Unfortunately, Taliah chose that moment to portal inside my home. "So, this is where you hide during your excursions in Gaia. Not going to lie, after living so close to you these past years, I was expecting something rougher."

Arms crossed, my friend wandered around the space, ignoring Ember altogether.

"And how exactly did you find me?" I asked through my teeth.

"Oh, I had my spies following you, of course. Didn't need our future lord to be wiped out by a ridiculous council of creatures before you're crowned." At her threatening pronouncement, she turned to assess Ember. It was predatory and protective.

And completely unnecessary.

I shot her a look that said *play nice*. "Well, as you can see, I'm alive and well."

She rolled her eyes but complied with my unspoken command. Face neutral, she sat beside Ember with a sniff of disdain.

"Ember, this is Taliah. She and I work together in my father's court. Taliah, this is Ember." I leaned against my door, preparing to referee between the two females in my life.

Ember's brows furrowed, likely sensing my unease through the bond. After a beat of silence, she squared her shoulders. "Nice to meet you, Taliah. Killian's said great things about you."

When Taliah merely watched her before sliding her gaze away with annoyance, Ember gripped the mug of her coffee. Hurrying towards the couch, I saved the glassware, prying open her white-knuckled fingers. I lifted the steaming drink to my lips, wincing at the sugary taste.

Her lips twitched in amusement before falling back into a frown.

The moment stagnated as the two women remained silent.

This wouldn't do. I blew out my breath. "Let's air everything out in the open. Taliah, you're pissed at Ember because she placed a spell on me against my consent. Ember, you fear Taliah because of her skill in battle and general demon heritage. Now, let's focus on what matters."

Both Taliah and Ember glared at me, united in one thing: their irritation with me.

I could work with that.

Taliah rolled her eyes, laying her smooth hands flat on her thighs. "If we're being honest, then I'll share some truth bombs. Whatever hopes you had of discovering the killer are for naught. This city is far worse than past years, the infighting and death toll higher than I've ever seen. The Council pretends everything is fine, but the black market trades have ramped up, weapons and magick-laced drugs being transported across state lines."

Not meeting Ember's gaze, I muttered, "We figured out as much at Bite with the wolves. That leaves us with Wren and the shifters as our prime suspects. Perhaps they are targeting creatures tied to their underground business. Regardless, they hate being forced to play nice with the Council and would be chomping at the bit to create havoc."

Ember snorted, but her face paled.

Taliah dragged a hand through her dark hair. "The wolves are powerful, well-stocked, and loyal to their own. My spies have not discovered anything to tie them to these murders yet, but we'll continue searching for evidence."

"It may not necessarily be the pack," Ember muttered, her lips thinned. "I've been thinking about the night of the ritual when Rosemary was attacked. With the exception of you, only the Coven remained on our lands. So, either someone broke through our magicked protections, or—"

"Or the killer was already on the estate grounds," Taliah finished, her eyes sparking with respect as she took in Ember with a new light.

My head tilted. It wouldn't be out of character for the witches to dabble in murder, but what would their motive be? The Coven's place on in the Council and their continued concealment from mortals mattered most to them. Not to mention the near-death of one of their most valuable witches.

Ember grew flushed, her leg shaking under the table. "When everything went down with Killian, I stole a forbidden book from the estate with demonic runes in it. I can read some of it, but the majority is gibberish to me. Maybe there's something in their we can use to discover the killer."

"Would you allow me to view this book?" Taliah perked up, her skin vibrating with anticipation.

Ember shot me quick glance before she straightened in her

seat. "Yes, you can stop by the house. Anything to help stop this."

"Even if the creature responsible is one of your own?"

Ember swallowed twice before she could answer. "I don't care who is behind this. They are murdering innocents and need to be stopped."

My chest expanded, warming with affection and pride. I grabbed her chilled hand and held it against my leg like a lifeline. Though she spoke truthfully, it would kill her to hurt one of her own. And my witch had suffered enough heartbreak.

I glanced over at Taliah and found she was already looking at me with a strange expression.

Her eyes lowered onto our joined hands, her brows furrowed. She cleared her throat and stood, adjusting her weapon straps. "Okay, then, there's much to do. I'll find you later for an update and the book." Her smile was friendlier than before as she held a hand outstretched to Ember. "Don't hurt him too badly, witch."

Ember gripped it firmly, her lips twitching into an answering smile. "No promises, demon."

30

EMBER

The days leading up to Samhain comprised either magick training with my sisters, fighting lessons with Killian, or tedious shifts at Get Hexed. I woke energized each morning, bursting with renewed purpose. My progress was slow, but every time my muscles ached less the morning after a training session or my magick wasn't as quick to lash out, I considered it a win.

There were also the nights curled in my bed with Killian. That night at the townhouse illuminated how lonely his life had been. The space was cold and meticulous, with no evidence of a life lived beyond his weapons, books, and the lone photo of a beautiful demon with dark hair and gold eyes. My heart ached every time I thought of it.

"Ember, *focus*."

My attention returned to Audra and Jade across from me in the backyard. Despite the magical block and the lack of answers on how to break it, we continued our attempts at a breakthrough. Audra had gathered different herbs and crystals with incantations that may help me overcome my issues.

"You're doing great, Em," Isla shouted from the porch with an encouraging smile.

"Thanks, sweetness," I murmured, redoubling my efforts.

With another deep breath, I focused on my well of magick. It was easier than weeks ago, but sweat still lined my forehead as I struggled under the weight of my suppressed power. Like before, I could feel myself tap into my power, the warmth and comfort dwindling into a sharp, defensive reaction as it turned against whoever tried to summon it, including myself.

My shoulders collapsed under the weight of my efforts. "This is useless."

Audra circled me, considering. "Maybe we're going about this the wrong way. Whenever we get too close to your magick, it lashes out. We need to find ways for it to release, like with your past mishaps. Then we can understand the nature of your block."

Jade cracked her knuckles, approaching me from behind.

I didn't like the gleam in her eyes and glanced over at Audra for help. She looked as if she was trying to swallow a laugh as I inched away from the two witches on the prowl. "What are you doing?" My voice rose at the end as I felt a lick of flame respond to my fear.

"Helping you," Jade promised as she raised her hands, her quartz amulet glowed as she channeled her magick.

The surrounding dirt vibrated, the crunchy, dead leaves tunneling into a whirlwind from Audra's air magick, trapping me behind a wall of bracken. Their lavender and cranberry scents reached me as they worked the powerful spell to trap me inside the cyclone.

My magick awakened, my flames stretching past its tightly woven box to reach out and tangle with the power encroaching on me. I gasped as I tried to fight my initial instinct to hold it down, control it. A sharp inhale helped empty my mind, allowing my muscles to relax.

"That's it," Audra's quiet voice reached through the torrent. "You're almost there."

My jaw clenched against the intoxicating pull, feeling detached from myself—like an out-of-body experience—watching the torment unfold around me. A pulse from my fire opal bracelet blazed through me, and I screamed as my magick exploded out of me. My flames attacked the earthly objects surrounding me, the leaves turning to ash and the dirt charring and falling around me like sand.

Jade reached through the tornado of leaves and fire and grasped on my bracelet, the burn grounding me back into my body and mind. She screamed in pain, and it pushed me free from the fog.

My knees collapsed, and the flames sunk back into my chest.

"Well, that was unnerving as Hell," Audra huffed out a laugh.

Jade's hand was bright red but not blistered as she turned it this way and that. Her smile was strained, but she held her unburned hand out for mine, gripping me in her form of a hug. "You can say that again."

Isla ran over and poured some of her healing tonic onto Jade's wound, her sigh of relief calming my deafening pulse. She joined our hug, squeezing my shoulder affectionately. "I'm so proud of you, Em. You pulled back all on your own this time. This is progress."

Audra came to my other side, her arm reaching to pull on the hair in my ponytail. "And don't think we haven't noticed your efforts to quit drinking and staying out all night. I may have had my qualms about the demon at first, but he's been a good influence on you."

Their praise was everything I had wanted, and yet it tasted like ash in my mouth with the bitter truth lurking beneath the surface.

Inside, I felt sick.

Tears prickled at the back of my throat. "I'm so sorry.

Maybe we should stop. I appreciate your help, but if it's an internal issue, what good will forcing it out do? I won't have you girls hurt over my magick. What I really need is that amulet."

Jade froze. "Amulet? What are you talking about?"

Realizing my mistake, my heart thudded.

I had lied to them time and time again, hiding the truth about Killian and the deal I made, and now we were almost out of time. With only three days left, I knew the time for honesty had come, despite the inevitable fallout and disappointment.

I summoned my newfound bravery as my sisters looked at me with growing confusion. "I haven't been entirely truthful with y'all," I breathed out. "Another reason I decided to work on my magick is because I made a demon pact with Killian."

Gasps rang out as they pulled away from my embrace.

My fingers fidgeted with my t-shirt. "I summoned him after the Bacchanal when I realized Alexei was offering the amulet in exchange for finding Rosalind's killer. I figured with such a magical item in my possession, I could finally take control of my magick and not be a fuckup."

My eyes misted, but I choked the emotion down. "While Killian was inside my circle, I somehow hexed him. He agreed to bargain with me and help me find the true killer for removing it before Samhain."

With a wince, I pulled up my long-sleeved shirt, exposing the inky evidence of my idiocy. I could feel it buzzing under my skin like bees, my vow and the imprint of Killian's soul tied to mine.

Audra and Isla turned my arm for a better glimpse of the tattoo, but Jade shook, her face contorting with silent rage. Audra sighed, dragging Isla away. "Now, you've done it."

"You *what*?" Jade screeched.

The oak tree we stood under swayed as the windows and

doors of the house opened and shut, the hinges squeaking. Wind blew dead leaves from across the yard around us like a tempest, while Jade's quartz amulet glowed bright as she harnessed her earth magick.

My magick was spent, but I could still feel my power flicker in response. I grasped her hand in mine once more. "Jade, please listen to me. I know I fucked up, but it's not actually that bad. I've done way worse, though I can't think of a single thing at this current moment."

"Pacting with a demon isn't *that bad?*"

As the earth the whooshed around us, my eyes squinted with tears as I tried to open them against the torrent. "Okay, bad choice of words, but this isn't a hopeless situation. We still have time before the deadline of our pact to fix this."

Isla's hair whipped around her as she grasped Jade's other hand. "Jade, please stop and listen to Ember."

Jade's gaze focused on her, and she breathed a deep, calming breath, sending all the debris and dirt back outside where it belonged.

I felt a pang of jealousy at how easily she could contain such a tremendous show of magick, her casting effortless and elegant as it should be.

Jade's previous fury dimmed to a low simmer. "I knew something was off with you and the demon. How could you lie and keep something like this from me?"

"That psycho piece of shit. The next time he rolls up in here, I'm going to toss him on his demonic ass," Audra growled low.

I rubbed my temples as a pounding migraine came on. "Look, I'm the one that forced Killian here and spelled him. He's been understanding considering everything I've done. And things have changed between us—it's not just a pact between us."

Jade harrumphed, but Isla ignored her. "How were you

able to cast an intricate spell like that anyway?" Isla wondered. "Your magick is unpredictable and reactive. I don't see how you managed a complex hex. No offense."

It was a valid question and one I still had no answers for.

Jade and Audra paced in the yard. "What were the spell's terms?" Audra asked.

My shoulders lifted. "We kissed and a pulse of something went through me. I wasn't intentionally trying to spell him, but my magick triggered a response in him, making him consider me his mate. It just happened."

Isla watched on with a dip forming between her golden brows. "I've never heard of spells manifesting like that. Certainly not something as permanent and sacred as a mating bond."

Audra perked up. "Precisely. Without proper incantations or ingredients, such a spell would be impossible for a young witch in control of her magick. What if this was his plan all along and he's playing you? When the bastard returns, we'll demand answers from him."

Isla's eyes brightened with excitement. "What if there wasn't a spell and Killian isn't trying to trap you? What if you are his mate and your enhanced emotional state and vulnerability triggered the bond?"

Isla was an idealist, a romantic, but I doubted such a thing would occur.

Surely, I would feel it if we were mates?

Audra let out an amused chuckle, rolling her eyes at the thought. "The Goddess would not shackle Ember with one of their ilk for eternity. The most logical conclusion is that Ember hexed him after she lost control of her magick. We need to focus on removing it before he can collect his prize. Considering only the witch who cast the spell can remove it, we have a lot of work to do."

My stomach tightened with anxiety. "Finding the creature

responsible for these deaths is more important than anything else. They didn't finish the job with Rosemary, so they may find another witch to claim. Plus, if I had the amulet, I could better fight them off *and* undo the spell."

Jade straightened. "The last thing we need is you throwing yourself into a murder investigation and getting yourself killed."

My retort was cut off as Killian appeared from the shadows, not knowing the war zone he had wandered into.

His eyes glowed warmly. "Good evening. How was training today?"

Jade's face flushed an alarming shade of puce before her magick exploded, slamming the unsuspecting demon against the porch railing, tethering him with serpentine roots like ropes against the black wood beams.

Goddess above, it was going to be a long night.

⊃☉⊂

"You know she was going it easy on you, right?" I mused, leaning forward to scrub away the drops of blood from Killian's brow. "If she wanted you dead, you'd be floating in a swamp somewhere being eaten by the non-shifter alligators. Never to be found again."

Killian glared at me, sinking deeper in the bespelled healing bath I had forced him into.

After subjecting the poor demon to my sister's wrath, it was the least I could do. He took little convincing once he realized I planned on joining him in the heavenly, eucalyptus-scented water.

He shifted in the tub, pretending to be uncomfortable with me tending to his cuts and scrapes, but through the bond I could feel his vulnerable delight at being cared for.

It made my heart hurt to realize these moments were so few for him.

Satisfied with my work, I settled into the water across from him, sighing in contentment as my smooth legs brushed his much larger, rougher ones.

He leaned back and grabbed the box of spelled chocolates I had brought inside the bathroom. Holding out the small, delicate truffle dusted with red magick in front of him, his eyes gleamed with mischief in the flickering candlelight. "Open those pretty lips for me."

My insides fluttered with excitement. I parted my lips, letting them close around his fingers as he dropped the truffle on my tongue. The chocolate tasted like magick, silky, dark, and laced with desire. I moaned, my eyes rolling back into my head as the spell took effect.

"Good girl," he breathed, his hand clasping my face as his tongue tasted the sweetness on mine. "You witches sure are creative when it comes to your pleasure."

Amused, I grabbed another truffle between my wet fingertips, the chocolate already melting against my warm skin. Settling into his lap, I ran the truffle against his lips, my eyes intent on the sharp planes of his face.

He groaned low, his cock straining against my belly as he let me place it into his mouth. When I pulled away, his hand caught mine, his tongue tracing each of the digits. "Delicious."

Sighing, I brought my lips to his, our tongues tangling. I melted into him, my core clenching around nothing as I trailed wet, lingering kisses along his neck, breathing deeply his clean, masculine scent.

His touches were slow when I wanted fast and hot and *now*.

Within his arms, I felt like I belonged. And I knew I shouldn't feel this way, that I should remember what this was— hot, filthy sex with the unavailable demon who would leave soon, possibly with my soul.

His arms wrapped around me, my peaked nipples brushed against the hard planes of his chest. Being held like this was a newfound ecstasy, and I found myself as needy for his comforting touch as I was for his body.

"There was something I wanted to talk to you about," Killian's deep voice broke through the fog of the spell, his own words slurred as he fought to think of anything but the pounding desire between us.

"Hm," I murmured, my eyes drifting shut as I huffed in another breath of his woody scent like an addict.

He leaned forward and bit my lip, his scar catching the light. "Focus, sweetheart."

When I sat up to study his eyes, my core grazed his cock. We both froze and moaned low.

My hips shifted, seeking more friction as I moved in small circles. "You were saying?"

Eyes half-lidded, he rested his hands on my hips but didn't stop my movements. His voice grew hoarse at the pull of the spell's magick. "You drive me mad, Ember."

I was on fire; his honest, broken words, the match.

And yet, I felt the trickle of unease and doubts. How much longer could we make this work? In less than three days, everything would end, and I would be left picking up the pieces. Or worse—a soul sucked away and harbored in Hell for eternity.

His molten eyes watched my face as the furrow between my brows deepened, my worries clear through the bond. His hands spread over my thighs as he pulled me closer to him. So close, I was hovering at just the right angle for him to slide inside of me.

Arms cocooning me, his lips moved up my neck. "Stop stressing. We can focus on all our problems tomorrow," he whispered into my ear, his warm breath causing me to shiver. His tongue flicked out and then he let his teeth graze my skin. "And we'll enjoy our evening and pretend for another night."

Good enough for me! I wrapped my arms around his neck and brought my lips to his in silent agreement. My heart felt like it was vibrating with the effort to not expand out of my chest.

He must have felt the aching tenderness pulsing through our bond because he wound a finger around a springy lock of hair, twirling it around his finger.

Our lips were like magnets.

Never before had kissing felt like I was fusing my soul with another. Like I would die if I didn't have his taste on my tongue.

He groaned as his hands slid over my slippery body to rest on my ass. When his fingers sought my folds, they glided effortlessly, coated in my wetness.

I was rabid, desperate for his touch. If I wasn't so needy, I may have felt embarrassed by my body's reaction to him, but I knew my lust only added to his own desire by the flickering black in his eyes.

His tongue circled a spot on my neck that had my eyes rolling back in my head. My hand grasped his hard length and stroked him, loving the growls he let loose against my skin.

When I couldn't deny my urges any longer, I rubbed him against my center, letting my eyes fall shut at the sensations.

My body throbbed, the spell and my own lust spearing through me. Through the haze, my eyes opened, catching his.

His cock pulsed against my clit and he nodded.

Lips joining, I inched his cock inside of me, wincing at the sheer size of him as he stretched me. My thighs tensed as I lifted, emptying my sheath before trying to take him again. "Fuck, you're big. You may not fit."

His hand fisted my hair, dragging my head to the side for his soft bite at my neck. "Don't worry. You'll take me well, witch."

The effect was immediate. Embarrassingly, I could feel myself drip onto him. Something inside me gave, and I took him whole. My ass smacked against his thighs, absorbing him to the hilt.

Our breaths whooshed out, and his hands on my hips became vices, holding me still as he fought against whatever needs coursed through him. By the black tendrils of smoke radiating around me along with the inky jets of his eyes, I knew his demon must be clamoring to be freed.

I didn't want him to struggle. I wanted him to take what he wanted. My hands wound into his dark hair, pulling hard enough to sting his scalp. "Don't hold back," I commanded throatily into his mouth. "Let your demon take me how he wants. I need it just as bad."

He shook his head, his eyes feral. "Not enough room," he gritted out. "I'll destroy the house."

My toes curled at the wicked threat, and I wanted nothing more than wild destruction as we fucked each other into oblivion.

He felt my answering clench and thrusted his hips, the broad expanse of his hands spanning my ribs. "You want me to fuck you so hard the walls collapse?" he ground out through clenched teeth. "You want to me to own you so thoroughly, you won't remember any cock but mine?"

"Oh, Goddess, yes," I moaned, my voice reedy.

Through the bond, I felt his soul's desire and longing, the same as my own. I came to my feet, hovering over his cock as I began to *really* move. My hips lashed back and forth, water sloshing over the edge of the tub.

When his shadows anchored my feet, I laughed low, swinging my head back so my hair became saturated in the warm, soapy water. My throaty chuckle sputtered out as the shadows played along my skin, incorporeal, and yet I could feel them like caresses.

His shadows tweaked my nipples, pulling and tugging until they burned. Shaking hands dragged into my hair and bared my throat once more. His fangs grazed the sensitive skin, teasing me as if he was going to take a claiming bite.

I shouldn't like that thought as much as I did. It was primal and possessive, the way I felt about him. The way I wanted him to feel about me.

His bite turned into a suck, his lips and tongue and teeth working together to torture me.

My thighs shook, and I knew it wouldn't be long until the wave inside of me crashed to the surface, uncontrolled and wild. Especially when his shadows added delicious vibrations against my clit, moving so fast it felt like a vibrator, before branching off to caress my lips stretched around his cock as he moved within me.

Our lips met once more, halfhearted and sloppy, distracted by our wild fucking below.

When he adjusted his hips, his cock hit a spot inside me that made my vision blur. I screamed, and his mouth silenced the sound. My orgasm was continuous, his shadow touches prolonging the sensations as his hips rocketed beneath me.

After my first orgasm slowed, he still moved as if possessed. His lips and shadows were incessant, as if he couldn't slow even if he wanted to.

I pushed forward to lean on his shoulders to give him a deeper angle to hit, whispering every filthy thing I could imagine into his ear. When he reached his peak, he roared, his head flying back against the tub.

The hot jet inside me was all it took to set me off into a second orgasm, even more electrifying than the first.

Our hearts pounded as one, tied together more than physically.

We held each other as if we could pause this moment in time and never leave the lukewarm waters again. But reality waited for no one.

I came back to the surface, my eyes taking in the darkened

bathroom with only a flickering candle casting shadows over my walls. Then, I inhaled the scent of his skin mixed with sex and the silky tendrils of mint and vanilla from the bubbles.

Meeting each other's eyes, something passed between us, a thick cloud of questioning emotion, as if neither of us had intended to share a piece of ourselves.

This was casual sex, and yet this was undeniably something *more*.

Before either of us could speak it into existence, a noise broke through my haze of swirling emotions. The pounding continued as Jade's voice reached us through the fog. "You two have five minutes to dress and get down here. Samhain is in two days. We don't have time to fuck around. And yes, I mean that literally."

As the banging on the door became louder, Killian leaned forward, our foreheads touching. His voice rumbled, "Your sisters definitely know how to ruin a mood."

"I'm going to kill her." I lifted my hips away from him, causing him to hiss as the cool air hit his body.

"Not if I get to her first," he muttered, catching the towel I threw at him before dragging me back for a sultry kiss.

31

KILLIAN

My dreams were the same as always: mud-splattered boots and blood running down my face as I cried out for my mother, knowing she would never return. I gasped awake, hearing a voice call my name. Hands shook me and I growled low in warning. My horns extended to sharp points as I lashed out, slicing the pillow beneath me and shredding it to ribbons.

I was going to go fully demonic.

Staggering to my feet, I stumbled inside the unfamiliar bedroom, ramming into a bench.

"Killian, Killian," the witch kept calling my name, her soothing voice dragging me away from my memories and back into my body.

I glanced down at my nude form and shuddered, collapsing back onto the bed with a low groan. The nightmares had returned like wildfire, surging my fears and sorrow to the fore.

Transported back to that weak boy who could do nothing but take his beatings. Who did nothing but watch as his grandfather murdered his mother.

"You're okay. It was a dream," she whispered.

With her body wrapped around mine, the emotions I

fought to bury swept through me. The last thing I needed was her feeling them through the bond and pitying me. My eyes hardened. "I shouldn't have stayed tonight."

She shushed me, lifting my face to hers. "I believe I recall a few nights when you didn't shy away from me when I was in pain. There are even vague memories of you holding my hair while I puked for hours, so I think I'm good for it."

I must still be under her spell, because I didn't materialize away.

Her hold on me soothed like a balm. And gods, I wanted a reprieve from this torment.

After a minute of quiet, she leaned her head against my shoulder. "Do you want to talk about it?"

My eyes burned. The thought made my stomach roll, but I felt as if my chest would rupture unless I released it. Of their own accord, my hands tangled into her hair, crushing her to my chest. "My mother's name was Marguerite. She was a peasant girl with next to nothing, but demons across the realm took notice of her beauty."

"Is that whose photo you have in your townhouse? She looked lovely."

I nodded, my lips brushing the top of her head. "When she was eighteen, my father saw her and took her, damn the consequences. He got her pregnant, and she knew he would seek to kill any bastard children, so she hid the pregnancy from everyone. When her family discovered her treachery, they abandoned her and sent word to my father."

I laughed hollowly at the memories of our struggle. "It wasn't so terrible at first. We would swim in the lake and eat meat pies she stole from the tavern. And of course, there were the books. She resorted to making pacts with mortals and creatures from different planes. Anything for an extra meal. She stole and cheated, but I loved her."

Ember's vivid eyes welled with unshed tears at the grim tale of my youth.

I shook my head. "I don't want your pity."

Before I could move from the bed, she lifted her hand to my cheek, her thumb rubbing over the scar. "It's not pity. It's sorrow for your mother and for the boy you once were. I can understand the pain of losing your family. It wasn't fair for either of us."

Pain skittered down my spine. And then my rage replaced it.

I stood from the bed and dressed, avoiding her eyes. "The day my grandfather killed her, I swore to hurt everyone who caused her pain. It wasn't until after I murdered him and joined my father that I realized it was at Satan's bequest he acted. I vowed to take everything my father loved and tarnish it forever."

Ember froze at the edge of the bed, finally understanding.

"I risk losing the chance to seek my vengeance, the chance to avenge my mother if I don't return to Hell after Samhain. Not that I have a choice in the matter—the succession is compulsory. The realm will bind me for a century as its lord. Once and for all, I will take the thing my father loves most. I can't let anything get in between me and that future."

Her face in the moonlight looked like an angel, but her words glittered with pain. "And what would your mother want? Surely someone who loved you and dreamed of a future beyond Hell would want more for your life than vengeance."

My face turned to stone. "You know nothing," I hissed. "There could be no happy ending for us, Ember. There never was. With or without your soul, I will return to Hell."

She stood on shaky legs, her long, silky hair falling around her bare body like a shield. "So, that's it? Last night was just sex? Business concluded and now we never see each other again?"

"Yes, like we agreed. We released the tension between us as we tried to solve these crimes. Which, I must admit, the Council urged me to complete. There is no longer any reward from Alexei or earning your city's respect. Whatever you do now, it'll have to be on your own terms, witch."

The slash of pain and shock across her face made my heart bleed.

But that too was a lie. Any emotions I felt came from a spell.

Before I portaled away, her hands grasped my arm. "You're just going to leave? What about the killer?"

"Do you really think we'll find them now? With Samhain so near? I have to focus on my own problems, which right now is the rebellions forming over my throne." Dematerializing into my shadows, I realized I would do anything to destroy my father.

Even betray the witch whose eyes made me want to fall to my knees in forgiveness for crimes I had yet to commit. But that I *would*.

***

As I waited for the emergency meeting called forth by Satan, I tuned out Carreau and the war generals as they discussed their latest conquests on the battlefield. An anxious desire to return to Ember and mend whatever I had broken during my outburst, but I fought it, burying it inside with the rest of my emotions.

Taliah materialized beside me, her braids pulled back in a leather tie. "You've missed much excitement here in Hell, my friend," she said lightly as she pulled up a chair next to me.

I didn't dare show a reaction. Satan's spies were everywhere. "Oh?"

She laughed and punched me in the shoulder. "Oh, you know. Just your typical demon drama. Makes me wish I spent more time in the mortal realm like you. Hell grows wearisome after years of the same conflicts and tedium."

"Hm," I murmured.

Before I could question her further, Carreau waltzed over, leaving behind his boisterous audience to join me and Taliah at the far end of the war table. "Why are you two hiding over here? Come and listen to Bartholomew's stories of the latest scuffle in Gluttony. The tales will have you shivering in your boots."

Taliah wrinkled her nose. "I think I'll pass. How goes the mortal realm and your precious Council?"

Carreau smiled at her steely tone, wiggling his eyebrows. "Don't be jealous, Tal. Just because I escaped this pit doesn't mean Gaia is a cakewalk. The mortal plane is so dreary after my years spent here."

I fought an eyeroll. Carreau's hunger for esteem and power was the only reason he accepted the position in Gaia, and I doubted he would give it up for anything less than the position of Lord of the Realm. Now that Rebecca had threatened to cease contact with Hell, I wondered where his true loyalties lied.

In a gust of smoke, Satan entered, and we all stood as one, bowing low. He preened under the show of propriety before urging us to sit. "We have much to discuss tonight. First, Killian, tell me of the progress on the mortal plane with the souls. Our stores have not raised in days."

I clenched my teeth as the room grew deadly silent. "My work above continues."

Murmurs broke out, but Satan silenced them with his hand. He glanced at Taliah. "You were in Gaia. Is Killian just terribly lazy at his job? I would think there are plenty of souls ready to be reaped."

I bit back a rude retort. It would do me no good to lash out. I needed these demons on my side when the transfer of power happened, especially with the rising whispers of rebellion Taliah and I sought to destroy.

Taliah didn't spare me a glance, her expression fierce. "Killian speaks true. There are fewer pacts to be made with the mortals or creatures with the witches using their powerful magick to hide supernatural happenings from the mortals' eyes. If you want another opinion, you could ask Carreau. Gaia is his playground, after all."

Carreau leaned back in his chair, his feline amusement apparent by the wicked gleam in his eyes. "'Tis true, Satan. Gaia has become most dull. Across the globe, creatures are getting smarter to remain hidden, which limits the souls available to reap. Short of the current murder streak, there is hardly any deceit or treachery to enjoy. Killian over here found himself the only slice of cake worth having, and the granddaughter of the High Priestess at that."

I froze, my blood rushing from my head.

Hunt's outrage from the event on their lands had garnered the Council's attention, but the question remained whether he knew of the bond. As long as our deal—and her hex—remained a secret, I could still keep her safe.

Satan hissed and turned his fury on me. "What witch does he speak of?"

Carreau looked between us with growing delight. "Oh no. Was she a secret? I'm terrible at secrets. I was down in the prisons, and I read through the Scroll of Debts. It was more than a little surprising to see her name."

Darkness spread through me with violent intent.

Taliah positioned herself at my side. "There is some other grim news, my Lord. My spies have heard whispers that the killer in Gaia plans to strike during the Coven's Samhain festival. If we can intercept them, we will keep the peace between our realm and Gaia, so we may continue harvesting souls. Unless Carreau hasn't shared the Council's edict that they will block our realm from their plane."

My father stood, eying the room in disdain. "Carreau. I want to speak with you privately on this matter. Be sure your ridiculous Council does nothing to block our people from entering the mortal plane until then. Do I make myself clear?"

I opened my mouth to object, but my father shot his glare towards me. "You will bring me more souls by midnight tomorrow, or you will bring the witch to me as payment. I'll toss her into the dungeons and feed off her soul until you realize the levity of your failures. Maybe I'll do so anyway as punishment for your insubordination. Or for fun. I care not anymore."

Goblet of wine in hand, he exited the room in a wave of perfumed oil while I fought to remain in control. My eyes flooded with black, and I tensed as if to follow.

Taliah's nails dug into my arm hard enough to draw blood.

Demons sent fearful or amused glances my way, but I felt nothing. With a growl, I spun on my heel and stormed out of the throne room, seeking fresh air and quiet.

Taliah leapt after me, her hand gripping my arm. "You must calm yourself, Killian. We can solve this if we stay logical and move quickly."

I snarled, sending my fist into the marble column again and again.

She pulled my bloodied hand away from the stone. "You must get ahold of yourself," she hissed, eyeing the frozen maids and demons wandering the halls. Leaning close to me, she whispered, "If we can warn the witch, remove her spell, and find the killer before tomorrow night, we can still turn this around."

A violent shudder rolled through me. "*No.*"

"What do you mean, no? This can still work—"

I pulled away from her grip. "No. The witch's magick is

blocked, meaning the spell remains. I'll be compelled to surrender her to Charon and my father, no matter what we find." Stalking to a window, I sought clarity in the forest. "How did he know to look in the Scroll of Debts?"

Her scowl deepened. "An excellent question, but not the one that needs our attention right now. Why is your father so adamant he gets souls before your coronation? The succession is a done deal, so why continue this farce?"

I ground my teeth. "Because he's a corrosive dick who gets off on causing me pain."

"And if he's not just doing this to hurt you?" she growled low. "What if this is tied to the rebellions? My spies learned they began soon after your pact with the witch. Whatever is happening above could be tied to this too."

My breath sucked in. "Now we're just reaching because we want this to be easily cleared away. The simplest explanation is that my father hates me as much as I hate him and is seeking a means to thwart my succession. Not everything is a conspiracy."

"And if it's not a coincidence? Then what? We'll be trapped down here with no way to reap souls." Taliah's eyes flashed with irritation. "What about your mate? What will you do when your father discovers that tidbit?"

My fists clenched at my side. The thought of the horrors that would befall her if he discovered the truth... *Fuck*.

She threw her hands in the air. "All I must do is speak her name and your eyes fill with black, your demon under the surface. When I watched the two of you, I could sense the bond between you. And before you argue with me, it is *not* the pact. I have made my fair share of bargains and I have never looked at a soul like you looked at her."

Dazed, I shook my head. "No. It's impossible. If not the bond, then it's her spell. Even if she was my mate, it would never work. I will have to reap her *soul*, Taliah."

"You mean the spell from a witch whose magick is unstable and blocked? You always think in absolutes, and it will be the death of you. Do what you want, Killian, but I'm going to save as many innocent creatures as I can. Even if you can't be bothered. Enjoy your evening."

She portaled away before I could mutter another word.

Collapsing against the column, I muttered a dark oath.

She couldn't be my mate. Not when she would grow to hate me beyond any other soul in existence. If she didn't already.

32
EMBER

For the first morning in weeks, I stared up at my ceiling, fighting a wave of immense sorrow and regret. Nightmarish visions plagued my dreams. For once, not my own. Killian's broken admissions had shattered me. His pain so visceral. While his words sliced me deeply, I still wanted to hold him close and protect him from enemies I'd never know.

The sun hid within the clouds, the day promising grey gloom and storms. I wanted nothing more than to wrap myself into the blankets once more and disappear from the doom of the day, but I forced my feet onto the cold hardwood.

Downstairs, Jade was already awake, the dark rings under her eyes a glaring tell of the stress inflicted from my latest impulse. She said nothing, only held her arms open to me.

With a sob, I collapsed within them.

She let me weep, making soothing sounds as she ran her hands up and down my back soothingly until I lifted my wet cheek from her shirt.

"Sorry," I whispered, feeling utterly useless. Without Killian's help, we could hardly search for the killer alone. Whatever kept my magick at bay seemed a lost cause as well.

With no other options, I felt defeat rise within me, as destructive as the storm raging outside.

She smoothed my tangled hair from my face and offered me a handful of dried flowers and twine. "Don't give up yet, Em," she whispered, before straightening with renewed purpose. "Work will help distract your mind. So, let's get to it."

Audra and Isla made their way downstairs and joined our workforce to complete the spells and goods we would sell during the daytime mortal-friendly portion of the Samhain festival later this afternoon. Small glass bottles of tinctures and tonics and an assembly line of white dried sage, lavender, mugwort, and thistle covered the kitchen island.

No one mentioned the demon pact or the killer still on the loose. Instead, Isla turned on her music playlist and we enjoyed a last moment of peace together, our shoulders brushing with comforting domestic familiarity.

After a few hours of work, Audra announced it was time for a break and wandered to our kitchen table transformed into a library with stacks of grimoires and ancient tomes. She had glued herself to books she'd taken from the estate, as well as some resources her friends at Dragomire expedited to the house.

I winced at the pile. "Have you learned any more about what kind of spell I could have used on Killian?"

She rubbed her temples in exhaustion. "Nothing yet. This will take time to sort through, but it's not looking good. It would be easier if we had a fire witch to help us."

My stomach tightened.

Audra shot me a sullen glare, her auburn hair a tangle as she ran her hands through it with frustration. "If you had confided in us sooner, we could enjoy the pre-Samhain festivities instead of rushing to fix this mess."

I knew her anger came not from missing out on celebrations or revelry but out of deep-rooted fear for me. "I know, I'm the worst," I mumbled.

Suddenly, like a lit flame, my witch's intuition tingled, guiding me upstairs. It would be pointless to resist, so I bolted up the stairs until I stood at my parents' door, their belongings still untouched.

After a heavy breath, I stepped inside. The fragrance of their clothes and skin washed over me, offering me comfort and torment. I sat on my mother's side of the bed and grabbed her Book of Shadows from her nightstand. The leather felt worn and soft. Familiar.

I forced my fingers to open the crisp, yellowed pages. My mother's flowery handwriting sent a wave of tears to my eyes. I thumbed through the pages until my fingers settled on one. Reading my mother's words, my heart cracked.

I slammed the book shut with a gasp. I couldn't do this.

Not ready to separate from my mother's prized possession, I clenched the book to my chest and brought it to my bedroom. I set it on my dresser next to the ominous, demonic grimoire.

My neck tingled at the feel of magick buzzing from the book. Taliah had not come to investigate the tome, nor had I discovered anything new in the days since I stole it. But somehow, I sensed it was important to figuring this out.

Determined, I lifted it into my arms and rushed downstairs.

Dropping it onto the table with a thick thud, Audra startled from the text she immersed herself in. "What in the Hell is that?" she gaped. As if drawn to the book, her fingers reached for the tome to study the sigils.

The chair groaned as sat next to her. "Well, don't freak out, but it's something I borrowed from the estate's forbidden shelves to investigate demonic pacts. I can't make out much because of the runic language, but maybe you'll have better luck."

"Ember Belle. I didn't know you had it in you." Audra

laughed. "I'm only annoyed I never thought of that."

Jade walked towards us with an outraged gasp. "You stole from the Coven's sacred texts? Do you know what Grandmother would do if she found out?"

Audra rolled her eyes. "She didn't steal; she borrowed without permission. And none of the consequences will matter if it helps us find what we need." She flipped through the well-worn pages, the smell of patchouli and musty vanilla filling the room.

Jade rolled her eyes and cleaned up our mess.

Audra's brow furrowed, and she leaned closer to the book. "Did you do this?"

She spun the book around to face me, and I glanced down in confusion. "Is there something I'm meant to be reading? Because that looks like gibberish to me."

Her fingers pointed to the neat tears along the spine, looking at me expectantly.

"Um, book destruction is *bad*."

She threw a piece of twine at my face. "No, you idiot. Someone tore out the pages describing the spells for demon summonings and bindings."

"How do you know that?" My eyebrows furrowed as I flipped through the grimoire.

"Because some of us paid attention during our magick lessons. This is Latin. Most of the book looks to be outlining the different realms of Hell and their individual strengths and weaknesses. But these are spells to prevent demonic harm—and cause some in return."

A growing sense of dread built inside me. "Who would do such a thing?"

"That's what I intend to find out."

My hands grasped her arm, preventing her from fleeing. "You will do nothing dangerous. Do you hear me?"

She snorted. "That's rich coming from you."

My throat grew tight as I hugged my sister close, her lavender scent as familiar as my own. "Please. I can't lose any of you. Why do you think I made this stupid pact in the first place? I will protect you three. Always."

Jade shook her head, coming to stand behind me. "You don't have to do this by yourself, Ember. We're big girls, and we won't let you fight this alone. No matter how dearly you might wish to."

A knock on the door disrupted the choked emotion rising in my throat. I stood on shaky legs, needing some space. "I'll get it."

Rushing to the front door, Taliah's dark, worried face stared back at me. "What's wrong? Is it Killian? Is he hurt?" I urged, growing more alarmed by the second.

She shook her head, glancing behind me. "Killian is fine. But you won't be unless we figure out how to fix this mess you and my idiot friend have created."

Jade and Audra came to stand behind me, their arms crossed. A united force, unwilling to allow anything or anyone to harm me.

"And who is this?" Audra asked with narrowed eyes.

I opened the door wider. "She's a friend. Taliah, you may as well come settle in. We could use all the help we can get."

☽☉☾

The estate grounds resembled a village of yore, with booths filled with bewitched merchandise, trinkets, and delicious treats. I munched on a candied, caramel apple, while steaming cider, hot spiced wines, and roasted meats filled the autumn air.

The hours following Taliah's arrival had passed in a blur. We had yet to discover what the missing pages entailed, nor could we discover a way to break a demon pact. Instead, I resigned myself to enjoy my last night on Gaia and deal with the aftermath when it came.

Curious mortals wandered around with wide gazes and laughter. At our booth, Jade, Isla, and Audra simpered and charmed, their dresses unmistakable from a distance with the brilliant shades of purple, blue, and green making them appear like shining jewels.

We sold all of our wares; the time flying by too fast for my liking. Once the sun set, the Coven ushered the mortals away, and the estate's concealment spells clicked back into place. Booths were cleared away to make room for the tables of delicious foods and creature-approved beverages.

The night descended, my deadline fast approaching. My skin itched with anxiety, and I smoothed the bodice of my dress. If I was going out tonight, I would do so in style.

My dress would do little to help me if the need came to run or fight. The corset top laced at the front, pushing my breasts together over the short peasant shift beneath. The skirts were rich gold with silver moons and stars stitched into the fabric and felt soft and luxurious.

I *definitely* hadn't chosen the color because it reminded me of Killian's eyes.

"Have y'all seen Grandmother?" I asked my sisters, looking around the emptying field.

"She's probably busy working on last-minute details in her office," Jade answered from beside me. "What about Killian? Wasn't he supposed to be here already?"

I glanced down at the time. Less than an hour away from midnight.

Although I had sworn to be honest with my sisters, I hadn't shared the aftermath of the night he left. What did it even matter anymore? The last thing I needed was more outrage when I only wanted to spend my remaining time with those I loved.

"Not sure where he is," I murmured. My fingertips dragged the skirt of my dress past my calves, revealing my stockings and garters, as I avoided a muddy part of the field. "I'm going back to the estate to find Grandmother and visit with Rosemary. Mr. Rollings hasn't let me inside since the ritual."

Unease radiated from Jade. She nervously adjusted her quartz amulet to fall along her exposed neckline, looking composed and regal as a queen. "Are you sure? Maybe you should stay here. With me."

A small smile curled my lips. "I love you, Jade, but I want to see them one more time. I promise I'll try not to get whisked away to Hell without coming back to say goodbye first."

"Not fucking funny," Audra growled.

Tense silence followed.

"I know, you're right," I whispered.

Clearing our throats, we avoided each other's eyes as we summoned our strength.

Isla pulled us into a tight hug and we clutched each other for dear life. She tugged on a loose tendril of my hair and kissed my cheek. "Be careful, Em. No sacrificial lambing it tonight, no matter how dicey it gets. Promise?"

I nodded, though I knew it was a lie. I would do anything to protect them. "Promise."

We released each other with a broken laugh, wiping our eyes surreptitiously.

"Well, I'm going to find Jeremy. See you girlies later." Audra adjusted her breasts in her low-cut dress before sweeping into the crowd.

With a final squeeze of Jade and Isla's hands, I wandered through the melee. From my peripheral, I noticed Edward Harlow hunched over his baskets and Fleur's white hair braided into a crown above her head.

On a whim, I changed the direction of my footsteps, my false smile in place.

Fleur hadn't spoken to me again since my text, and it was the longest we had gone without seeing each other since middle school. When she caught sight of me, her eyes dimmed to grey slits. I tried to not let her disappointment with me sting.

"Hey, guys." I waved.

Edward straightened, his grey, bushy eyebrows jumping like caterpillars as he noticed who stood before him. "Oh, Ember. You startled me. How are you and your sisters doing?"

Warmed at his concern, a more honest smile spread along my cheeks. "We're doing alright. I was just going to visit with Rosemary before the actual party kicked off."

His eyes clouded, sympathy rolling off him in waves. "I'm sure her attack brings up a lot of painful memories."

"Yes, I hope she recovers soon. And that the killer is found and punished."

Fleur stood frozen, a scowl on her face. "I'll walk with you to the estate, Ember."

My brows furrowed with confusion. "Sure, sounds good."

As we walked through the gardens, the silence between us grew taut. Lit up like a fairy tale in the twilight sky, the aromas of the fresh herbs and flowers were potent in the night air.

From the corner of my eyes, I watched her face and noticed the darkness under her eyes, her expression weary. Swallowing my pride, I reached a hand to her. "Fleur, I'm sorry it's been so weird between us, but I miss you. Can't we put everything behind us and move forward?"

Her eyes flared with hurt. "*Weird?* You're sleeping with our enemy! You've kept so many secrets when we're supposed to be friends."

Defensive and annoyed, my words held more bite than I intended. "I'm sorry you don't agree with my choices. You never did. And I'm sorry I've let our friendship fall apart over the years, but I don't want it to stay this way between us."

Her feet came to a halt. "I stood by you when no one else

would. When everyone whispered nasty lies about you or when they shared ugly truths; I stood up for you. But you only ever think about yourself."

With a sinking feeling in my gut, I watched her retreat.

Another fuck-up I would need to mend. If I even survived the night.

The Graves estate was alight with candelabras glowing in the darkened sky, a beacon for me to wander to in the darkness. Stepping inside, I wiped my dirty shoes and watched the line of hired staff stuff carts full of food and wine for the evening's revel.

My stomach grumbled at the scent of savory beef, but I forced myself to creep towards the back wing of the house, slipping through unnoticed. I glanced at the grandfather clock, and my shoulders grew tense. Less than thirty minutes now.

At the door to Rosemary's room, I paused. More than ever, I wished I had been brave enough to ask her for help before her attack. Had she known what would occur? How terribly I would mess everything up? She *was* a seer, after all.

With a deep breath, I opened the door, skidding to a halt at what greeted me.

Tabitha stood over Rosemary with a strange expression that sent the hairs up along the back of my neck.

"What are you doing?" The words burst from my throat with suspicion.

Tabitha jumped, cat-like, her wide eyes shooting to mine. Instead of guilt, relief shone through her expression. "We don't have much time. *Hurry.*" She pulled my hand and dragged me down the stairs, back outside.

Frozen with shock, I could do nothing but follow her, the grip of her hand hard and unyielding.

What the *fuck* was happening?

I fought to keep up with her long strides, my gown slipping

around my ankles like restraints. As we approached the dark hedge maze, my intuition prickled with unease. "Wait—"

Her grip turned feral, nails digging into my skin in red crescents.

Realization hit, and my feet stumbled again. "Was it you? Did you tear out the pages in the grimoires?" My eyes bled with terror as we disappeared further into the dark maze. "Were you in on the murders, too?"

Her brows furrowed together. "What? I don't know anything about a grimoire. And the murders weren't because of me, but it's happening. Tonight. You must get to the cemetery and stop them before it's too late."

Vines tipped my feet, and I almost went sprawling. "The cemetery? What's happening tonight?"

She ran faster, our movements quick and silent in the moonlit night. "I can't say any more, Ember." From her agonized face, I realized she was just as fearful as me. "Heed my warning and *hurry*. Don't stop for anything. I must return to Rosemary to keep her safe."

She pushed through the hedge, forcing us outside of the thick foliage at the edge of the maze. "Go," she whispered, turning on her heel and fleeing back inside the maze without a glance back.

I glanced around the empty field with a shiver. Now what? Was this her idea of a joke?

A shadowy figure emerged from the fog, entering the cemetery, and I let out a shaky breath.

My body tensed with unease. Grasping my fire opal bracelet, I tried to think through this rationally instead of resorting to my typical impulsive responses. It was unthinkably stupid to wander into a quiet, dark part of the estate alone with a murderer on the loose. But this may be the best chance to stop whoever was behind this, ending it once and for all.

"I'm probably going to regret this," I whispered to myself as I hurried towards the back of the property.

The rickety, black gate creaked as I stepped over the small plots of my ancestors. Almost immediately, my gaze found the demon who stood before my parents' tomb. I crouched behind the mausoleum of my great aunt, my eyes finally noticing the witch standing before him.

"You're late," Carreau hissed to her.

Fleur's eyes glowed silver in the darkness with terror, but she said nothing.

He tilted his head down to her forlorn face, his eyes furious and cold. "Where is the witch? I need to finish this task before it's too late."

Fleur stood resolutely, her eyes pained as she bit her tongue to hold back the words fighting to escape.

Dread consumed me as I realized the truth.

The creature behind the deaths was Carreau. And Fleur.

Carreau laughed low. "Cat got your tongue, witch? *I said*, where is the witch?"

Her body shook, possessed. When her back arched at a sharp angle, she gasped in pain. "She's inside the estate. Her room's wards are down, so you can enter unnoticed by the Coven." Fleur slapped her hands over her mouth, eyes tortured. Her knees collapsed, and she let out a sob, tucking her head into her knees.

Carreau stood over her, his hand dragging through her pale hair. "Now, was that so difficult? You have almost earned a place in my city, along with your pitiful father and sister. Just one more task, little dove."

I could feel it in the air, *taste it*. It was bitter and ugly—the control he had over her. His power of manipulation forcing her to do his bidding. Nausea churned, as well as my need to protect her, but I forced myself to remain hidden.

Carreau continued, his hand dropping to her cheek. "And

once the witch dies, you will return to your Coven, and you will tell them who you saw entering the estate."

Fleur shook her head. "I won't."

His fingers knotted along her scalp, pulling her face up to his. "You know I can make you. Why must you make everything so difficult for yourself?"

At her yelp, I couldn't stop my gasp from escaping.

Fleur and Carreau whipped their heads towards me.

Her face crumbled in a broken cry. "No, Ember. Run away before it's too late."

It was pointless to hide. Stepping forward, I pulled my fire to the fore. My hands flickered with flames, my magick tumultuous with my rising emotions.

Gone was the smooth, carefree face of my friend and, in its place, a chilly deadness. Her eyes sunk into her head, her skin clammy with sweat. She was weakening, her soul withering within her body under Carreau's influence.

I had to get him away from her.

"It was you?" I asked Carreau. "You killed all of those creatures?"

All signs of his pleasant charade melted away. He cocked his head to the side, shifting away from me like I was a worm beneath his boot. "Naughty witch." He clicked his tongue. "You shouldn't have snuck up on me like that."

My tongue felt heavy in my mouth. "Why would you do this? Why—"

"Why do you think?" he interrupted, his mouth turning down in a cruel sneer. "Do you think I enjoy being trapped on this cursed plane with you creatures? I decided if I couldn't rule in Hell, I would bring Hell to me, finally showing my father and all the demon lords my strength. You and Killian made my job so much easier."

Chills raked down my spine like nails as all the stories I had read about Gressil—Carreau's father—flooded to my mind. I took a step backwards, not daring to glance at Fleur. "So, you murdered the creatures to show your people you're strong? Surely, murdering a handful of creatures is trivial to the lords of Hell?"

He laughed low, his eyes twinkling with wicked delight. "I only continued what I started five years ago. Tonight I'm going to finish this with your whole ridiculous Coven finally under my power."

No. No, no, no.

My blood froze in my veins, my breath stuttering out. I grew numb as his words processed through my fog. "No," I mouthed.

"When I first started this, I chose random creatures. However, the Council ignored the murders, sweeping them under the rug. I knew I would need to choose victims closer to home. The High Priestess's daughter would cause quite an uproar. So, I waited until your car disappeared into the storm before luring poor Helene out of the house. Your father, of course, followed her to their doom. It was unfortunate but necessary to get the Council's attention."

My stomach heaved.

Sickened, I barely noticed Fleur's grim face behind Carreau. Her magick formed a silent torrent of broken slabs of bark and wilted flowers whirling behind Carreau.

"But why kill the creatures you want to rule over? *My parents were innocent,*" I choked on a yell.

"Innocent?" he hissed. "The creatures on this plane are more prejudiced than the demons in Hell. Other than my lone seat, the Council gave us no opportunity to grow our own community on this plane, just awarded us blind hatred and meager toleration. Witches are to blame for that more than any other creatures in this city."

Hatred simmered under my skin. I could barely look at his face without wanting to claw the skin until he bled. "Yet your plan didn't work, did it?" I taunted him, my anger a reprieve from the harrowing sorrow. "You gave up and played the dutiful Council member until now. What changed?"

He snorted, creeping closer to where I stood. The crunch of dead leaves echoed in the cemetery. "I didn't have the resources I needed back then. I realized soon after the murders that I wouldn't be able to stage a full attack alone. But now, things are different."

Bile filled my throat.

If Carreau was monologuing his entire evil plot to me, he must have dangerous plans in place to devastate the entire city. We had to stop him before it was too late.

My eyes briefly flicked to Fleur, and I hoped she understood my silent message. "What about Killian? He's taking the throne soon; he could have helped you if you wanted a better relationship with the Council."

His fangs extended in a grotesque smile. "Killian will never claim the throne. His vengeance has blinded him. He won't be coming to save you this time, witch. Satan has tasked to reap your soul and feed it to the realm, which will power my conquering of your precious city."

Fear and anger flooded my system as my mind rebelled against his words. "It isn't true. Killian would never hurt me."

"Wouldn't he? He had no trouble servicing the whores in Hell's brothels while bonded to you. Nor has he been back to help you fulfill your pact, has he?" Carreau's grin twisted. "Killian only pretended to care about you because of the demon pact, you fool. He is a being from *Hell*—he can't feel love or compassion."

Hurt and frustration reared out of me in a cloud of smoke.

When Carreau pounced, I screamed, my heart ripping open. Fire sparked out from my fingertips, scorching the grass below my feet.

My magick exploded out of me like a bomb, throwing

Carreau back against the stone mausoleum hard enough to crack the stone. His eyes focused on Fleur, and I felt the compulsion take effect.

Fleur gasped, and my attention broke for a second. But a second was all Carreau needed.

His power then seized onto me, sending me backwards. My head sliced open against the corner of the crypt, the smell of my blood filling my nose. Groaning, I lifted my hand to the back of my head, my fingers coming away wet.

Carreau's amusement faded as he lifted a sword conjured from his shadows. "Rest easy, Ember. This will all be over soon."

He moved in a flash, but Fleur was faster.

Carreau screamed as she yanked him through the air with the bracken tornado she amassed from the grounds. Spinning and thrashing through her spell, a crack sounded. He fought her power uselessly before his wings erupted in a snap of muscle.

I lifted my hands and sent a deluge of fire towards him. My aim was off, but like the coward he was, Carreau portaled away, leaving the two of us alone in the cemetery.

On shaky legs, I stood and ran towards Fleur. She sagged onto the ground, drained from Carreau's compulsion and her magick use. We needed to find Grandmother and the elders before it was too late.

"Can you run?" I asked her, dragging her alongside me anyway.

"Just go. Rosemary and the others will be targets. He won't just stop with one death tonight. He wants total chaos and destruction." Her lips quivered. "I'm so sorry, Em. I couldn't stop myself; he did something to my mind."

I shushed her. "It's okay. I know it wasn't you."

Shame coated me as I realized if I had been a better friend,

I could have figured this out sooner. So much death and suffering because I was too afraid to be honest.

From a distance, I could make out the vampires. Alexei Vasilyev's gleaming ebony hair flickered under the lanterns, his arms gesticulating to the Fae creatures scattered on silk rugs with wine-stained lips. Even the wolf pack stood to the side, their presence a requirement for the night's events.

If Carreau's plans worked, everything would be laid to waste

Running into the estate, I froze as the grandfather clock chimed midnight. My demon mark sizzled on my skin in warning, and my feet stuttered to a stop. "Get to Grandmother and tell her everything. I'm going to be forced to go to Hell, but I *will* return to help you."

Her eyes widened, and she clutched my hand tightly. "No way. I'm not leaving you, Ember."

I shook my head. "It's too late for me. But we can still help the others. Please, Fleur. For me."

Tears streamed down her pale cheeks, but she nodded. She brushed her lips against my cheek before turning and running with renewed effort.

With a sinking feeling, I glanced around and waited.

His woody scent reached me before his shadows did. Like the grim reaper, Killian stood before me, his demonic form flickering in and out of the shadows. His eyes held mine with regret and resignation.

The sight should send fear through me, but I only felt blind fury.

Releasing my breath, I stepped towards him, knowing this night could only end in one way: my soul lost to him. My wound still stung, and I grimaced in pain.

His nose flared as he scented my blood, and wrath rose over him like a thunderbolt.

Before he could pretend to care, I bared my teeth. "It was

Carreau. He used Fleur to help him kill all those creatures. Including my parents."

He opened his mouth, but I wasn't finished. Not by a long shot.

"He also told me plenty of interesting details about your father commanding you to capture my soul and how you were fucking around in brothels. Do you deny it?"

His eyes grew cold, unreachable. He stepped closer, his boots scuffing along the wood floors. "I deny nothing. From the brand still upon your arm, it appears your deceptions loom over us as well, witch."

With the murderer's identity discovered, that meant my spell was the only broken term of our pact, condemning me to my fate. A crazed laugh escaped.

And I had thought this might be real... No longer would I hide from the truth.

The grandfather clock still tolled, the only sound whirring in my mind other than my frenzied heartbeat. My eyes sparkled with rage as I reached out my hand. "Let's get on with it, then."

After only a moment's hesitation, he gripped it, pulling me closer.

Despite my anger, his presence still soothed my fears, his touch familiar and comforting. "Will it hurt?" I asked through my teeth.

His voice was gruff. "I don't know."

Now he chose honesty? *What a dick.*

He pulled me closer to his body, his wings cradling me protectively. And then we dematerialized into the shadow dimension, falling into the world of madness.

Yet his grip on me never wavered.

33

KILLIAN

Ember glanced around the ominous Realm of Pride, her breath puffing out at our vantage point from the castle walls. The land appeared enchanting, with its snow-kissed forests and surrounding mountains looming over the gilded castle like the inside of a snow globe. She stiffened as she noticed my demonic form, her eyes trailing over me with awe.

My chest expanded, bulking up, while my horns and wings sprang free from the shadow dimension. Like this, I felt like a gargoyle, coming alive to snatch a beauty away to the underworld.

But I bit down on my fear and my longing and let the visage of the Scourge settle over my face. My mask of indifference was impenetrable as I forced her to move into the castle gates. "Come along."

I dragged her to my side, ignoring her squirming as we walked through the castle entrance towards the throne room. Satan's court watched with hungry eyes at our quiet approach. From their plush seats, they whispered gossip and shouted insults at her.

Her expression wavered between wide-eyed marvel as she

took in the bejeweled surfaces, swimming in wealth, and revulsion as she bared her flat teeth at the creatures.

Her lack of fear infuriated the court, who enjoyed torturing those from other planes. Demons spat on the ground near her feet, attempting to rip at the skirts of her dress in retaliation.

With a low snarl, I warned them away, and the demons broke away in fear.

Soon, I would be their leader, and I would make them pay for this insult.

After what seemed like a lifetime, we stood before the Lord of the Realm, his golden hair laid flat against his emerald crown in oily waves. His skin was more gaunt than usual, his face lacking the vitality and luminosity of the other seraphim.

I fell to my knee in reluctant subjugation, my dark head tilting to the floor.

A fallen knight. Tortured and full of regret.

My father cocked his head, raising a brow at Ember's insolent smirk.

Pride boomed in my chest at her jutted chin. Her false confidence was impressive, but ultimately pointless. I could feel her tendrils of fear through the bond. My demon reacted to its mate's panic, and I fought to cage the demonic rage.

Before, reminders of her spell brought on rage, but now I felt only the need to comfort Ember. When the pact compelled me to portal her away, I realized I didn't care if she lied. I felt no anger towards her, and I would do anything to keep her safe.

I loved her, gods help me. And I had delivered to her to Hell on a silver platter for my father and his people to consume.

Satan's attention returned to me, glee simmering within his cold eyes. He leaned back into his golden chair with the click of his tongue. "I suppose, if nothing else, you are a loyal dog, Killian."

I stood, towering above my people below the dais. "More

loyal than your puppet, Carreau. I discovered his part behind the attacks on the mortal plane. He has been using his gift on creatures to create disillusionment with the Council and chaos within the city. All to better his position on Gaia, which will spell our doom."

The room of demons reacted with outrage. Shouted insults and threats whirled at my back like weapons. Satan's serene calm deteriorated as he surveyed the ire of his subjects with growing annoyance. "Carreau acts out of loyalty. He seeks to forge a sanctuary for demons in the mortal plane while you cry and moan about a few measly creatures?"

The last piece of the puzzle fell into place. Taliah was right —I *was* a fool.

"You knew."

My father rolled his eyes. "About Carreau's mere murder spree in efforts to secure our territory in New Orleans? Yes, I knew. And yet you think you have what it takes to be the Lord of the Realm? You cannot stomach what must be done for the good of our people."

Black seeped through my vision, but I fought it easily enough. My voice echoed through the cacophony of broken yells grew deafening. "The good of our people?" I chuckled. "My succession is not up for discussion. Accept your losses and fix this mess before we lose everything. His plan will cause unfixable dissent between our people and the mortal realm. Rebecca Graves and the Council will ward the plane from us, barring us entry after this night if he succeeds."

Ember stepped forward, her eyes as hard as diamonds. "If you stop Carreau, as granddaughter to the High Priestess, I will swear an open passage between our realms. Even though the bastard killed my family."

My spine stiffened as my father turned to me with shocked outrage. "Why does the creature deign to speak to me?"

The hall grew silent, every demon's rabid attention focused on the witch.

Satan crooked a finger at her. "Come closer, witch."

She approached the demon lord with her head held high, her face set.

My fists clenched at my sides with the need to stop her progression and take her away from this wretched realm. And as my father leaned closer to her, my demon roared in my mind loud enough that I winced in pain.

His black claws reached forward to grab her chin, forcing her face closer to his. "You are nothing here, witch," he whispered. "Your presence here is a blight, a pest we must endure. And now, you will pay for your foolhardy pact with my son."

Fury assailed me as my eyes narrowed on his touch upon her precious skin.

His eyes lingered on her lips with a covetous glance. "Guards, take this beauty to the dungeons. If the wards rise between the mortal realm and she survives the night, we'll see how loudly we can make her scream."

The demon hordes broke out in guffaws and sharp whistles as the armed soldiers stepped forward. When the demon guard grabbed her arm, tearing at her flesh hard enough to make her cry out, I snapped. My demon charged, enraged with every foul touch they placed upon her precious skin. Ripping the demon's hands from her body, I pulled her into the protection of my wings. They stretched over her, creating a shield as I swung my wild gaze to the other soldiers.

My father's fangs lengthened, his hands gripping the edge of his throne. "You dare get between my guards and my prisoner, Killian? You are not Lord yet. If you ever will be."

My demon did not care for his tone. and for a second, I nearly stalked over to the throne and tore my father's throat out.

Taliah appeared out of the corner of my shadowed vision, her hands lifted to me. "Stand down," she mouthed.

Reason settled into my discombobulated mind. If I attacked him here before all, Ember and I would both be dead. As the black faded, my aggression bled out like a sigh. My wings still held Ember, and I felt her fingers dragging across the membranes in a soothing caress.

From the dais, my father approached me. "Bring the witch to the dungeons while Killian and I discuss this matter further in the war council room. It appears my son needs a reminder of his place in this realm."

Taliah stepped forward, and I almost succumbed to my demon once more. I took a deep breath and let my wings fall along my back, revealing the witch, who appeared sturdier than before.

Ember hissed an oath as Taliah lightly constrained her within her grip. Looking up at me, the beautiful contours of her face crumbled, her lips trembling. "You asshole. I trusted you."

Her scorn cut deeper than any wound. My heart seized as she disappeared away from the throne room and down to the cold, underground dungeons. I exhaled a pent-up breath.

"Seize him," Satan ordered.

Bartholomew portaled next to me in a flash, his fist colliding with my face in a ringing punch that made my vision blur. Stumbling, I caught myself before I fell, but the demon was already before me, slamming the hilt of his ax into the back of my head.

I dropped, eyes falling shut as my blood coated the golden floors.

My eyes peeled open at the sound of my father's shouts. A pounding drum echoed in my head, and as I lifted my hand to the wound, I assessed my situation. Through slitted eyes, I determined I was lying on the cold, golden floors of the counsel room. My hands were tied behind my back in metal chains, but they kept my legs and mouth clear. A mistake they would come to realize.

"Prepare the armies. The portal opens within the next hour." Satan's command broke through my confusion.

The room bustled with demons who supported my father's coup, their task—readying for war. Stealthily, I sat up from my dormant position only to be pushed back down by Bartholomew, who watched me with a menacing grin.

"Oh good, you're awake," my father sang, his face bright. "I want you conscious and suffering as you watch your world fall apart."

With a glower at Bartholomew, I released an amused snort. These demons loyal to my father would pay for their crimes. Bartholomew's victorious smile only rubbed salt on the wound, and I promised myself his death would come soon after my traitorous father.

More alert, I turned back to my Satan. "I never thought you would have the balls to question the succession knowing how the laws work. How do you plan on thwarting the throne's rules?" I wondered.

Satan's smile dimmed. "If Carreau's plan works, I may not have use for this cursed plane any longer. I have you to thank for this, my son. If not for the steady contributions of souls, we could never make this large of a move on the mortal realm. But now we have enough power to wage war."

My pulse ticked, and I felt a ragged flame of disgust for both him and myself. "It'll never work. The Council is strong, the witches most of all. Not to mention the allies Alexei has."

Satan shook his head, admiring his crown in a mirror with

a wistful expression. "It will be too late for that, I'm afraid. If the vampires choose to exact revenge, we'll deal with that, too."

"What about the mortals?" I asked through my teeth. "If you garner attention, you risk outing supernatural creatures to the public, which would spell disaster. For you included."

"Why do you think I agreed to Carreau's plan? His gift will make domination of Gaia effortless once we deal with the foolish creatures who dare stand in the way."

This plan was rooted deeper than Taliah had feared. This was the end of days kind of talk, and no one would win if such a conflict erupted. Visions of Ember's family and the other creatures in the city I had grown to know and care for rushed through my mind, and my resolve turned to stone. Behind my back, I pulled at the chains, while my father distracted himself with his war plans.

Bartholomew's attention focused on his ax, which he sharpened with a small grin. "Once I finish on Gaia, I may find your witch and discover all the goods you sampled for free. I hope you're still alive to witness it."

My eyes turned black, my demon no longer willing to be held back. With a snap, I tore through the metal, my wings popping out and slicing Bartholomew in the side with a sharp talon. Demon rage went beyond any laws of physics or physical strength and now my demon fought for Ember.

At Bartholomew's shocked yell, Satan and the other demons pulled out their weapons, charging me. I was forced to relinquish my hold on the demon as I dodged a flying blade, dematerializing a few feet away as I reclaimed my sword and weapons.

Satan's cold eyes gleamed with rabid anger, and I smiled at him as we faced off. "I think I'll enjoy this very much," I murmured to him, as visions of my mother swam before my eyes, mixed with Ember's fearful eyes gaze and hatred as she discovered my treachery.

As if I conjured her with my thoughts, I felt a pulse of powerful emotion through the bond.

Sorrow, fear, hatred. And then… nothing.

My feet staggered, my tie to her soul sliced away in a flash. I roared with fear and fury, charging at the smirking demon who crept up beside me. My sword pierced through his throat, and black blood sprayed across my face as my horns gorged through his chest.

With a mournful growl, I shot one last look to my father and dematerialized. My focus settled on finding Ember in the dungeons. Whatever befell her, I would ensure everyone in this gods forsaken realm paid for the crimes against my witch.

And then I would follow her wherever she went.

34

EMBER

"Move it, witch," Taliah spoke from beside me, her hands pushing me harder than necessary. "I don't have all night here."

The guards surrounding us laughed, their eyes gliding over my exposed skin and my bloody wound with lascivious desire. Instead of lashing out, my hurt and anger towards Killian became a visceral thing inside of me. It brought me the presence of mind to not act on my emotions.

I held my tongue as we wound our way down to the lower levels of the castle, the air dropping to below freezing temperature. I tried to keep track of every turn and hallway we walked through in case I made it out of here to escape, but after another winding turn, I knew it was hopeless.

Water dripped through gaping crevices, and rat-like creatures scurried along the path ahead of me as lanterns flickered. Deep inside the castle, it was pitch-black, with only a single lantern near the entrance to give off any warmth or light.

A skeletal creature looming in the distance halted my feet.

Taliah stepped closer to me, her voice low in the echoing cavern. "That is Charon. He is the jailer of reaped souls and will ensure you are undisturbed until it is time."

As we walked closer, I could make out the creature better. Charon's skin was gaunt in the flickering lamplight. His cold, soulful eyes watched me as closely as I watched him. A flicker of a smile crossed his harrowing face, and a bony hand smoothed his grey beard.

"You have brought me Killian's prize," his wearied voice traveled in the empty cave. "I'm surprised he let her out of his sight for a second in this realm."

I stumbled under my own feet.

Cognizant of the guards, Taliah stepped forward with a breezy smile. "Matters above grew tense. The witch will remain in the dungeons until Satan has need of her in the morning."

Charon's intelligent eyes revealed nothing. "Hm. Very well. Taliah, I believe you know the way?"

I breathed out a quiet sigh of relief as the guards remained behind to talk with Charon. He removed an ancient tome from behind his desk and used a feathered quill to cross out a line.

My name, I realized.

Thankfully, the dungeons were empty, so I wouldn't share a cell and waste precious energy fighting off a grotesque prisoner. *Small mercies.*

Taliah cranked open the metal door to the small cell and shoved me inside. My feet slipped on the oily surface of the floor that I didn't want to contemplate the origins of. I took in the bunches of stiff hay for sleeping and the two buckets leaning against the wall—one empty and the other filled with murky water.

A barred open window loomed above my cot, allowing a sliver of moonlight to penetrate the gloomy, barren room. I shivered, almost wishing this realm resembled the fire and brimstone I imagined when I thought about Hell, instead of the endless cold.

With a puff of air, I turned back to Taliah. Cognizant of the demons' advanced hearing, I whispered, "So, what now?"

The beautiful demon's lips dipped into a frown. "Now, you wait until Lord Satan has use for you. Or we hope Killian takes control of the throne before then, so he can pardon you."

"Hm." I wasn't feeling too hopeful about the latter coming true after the shitshow I witnessed above in the throne room. "Can I at least get a blanket? Hell is as cold as a witch's tit."

She watched me as if she could see through my facade, like my attempt at lighthearted jokes, even now, was something fascinating. "You know, most in your place would not dare to speak to Satan in such a way. I can't decide if you're incredibly brave or foolish."

I snorted, sitting back on the straw. "My sisters have been asking the same question all my life. I'd like to think it's a charming mix of both."

Her eyes grew hollow. "You remind me of my sister. She had your feistiness and impulsiveness. It got her killed, along with my parents, before I reached young adulthood."

"I'm sorry," I murmured, my heart cracking at the thought of having to lose Jade, Audra, and Isla on top of my parents' deaths. It would be unbearable.

Taliah sighed. "And like me, you refuse to forgive yourself. To let yourself move forward knowing that although the blood may not be directly on your hands, your actions brought you shame. And you imagine the looks of horror on their faces as they see who you've now become."

My throat filled with unshed tears at her uncanny reading of me. "How do I forgive myself when they'll never be here again? When I can't tell them I'm sorry?"

Taliah stepped away from the cell. "Just because they have moved to the Beyond doesn't mean they can't watch over you. You're a witch; surely you know that better than I. And you honor their lives by not wasting what time you have left to do better." She turned on her heel to escape back above.

Alarmed, I gaped at her retreating back. "You're just going to leave me here?"

Over her shoulder, she laughed throatily. "If I release you, I'll lose everything I've built for myself. If you want to be free, believe in yourself. I'm sure once you let go of whatever's holding you back, you'll figure a way out."

As she disappeared, I growled low, smacking the bucket of water with my fist.

I wanted to lash out, to scream she was wrong. That I deserved to rot in this prison.

From the pocket of my dress, I pulled out my mother's Book of Shadows. My intuition hadn't led me astray, and a sense of rightness flowed through me as my fingers cracked open the pages. Like before, her scent wafted over me, comforting and torturous all at once.

Did she know about her future—that she and my father weren't to be long in the world? Or had she awoken that fateful day full of dreams and happiness for a life that wouldn't continue past that night? It mattered little now. My mother's life's work, her desire for a quiet life and independence from her duties, was wiped away by Carreau's blade.

Hunched over, I sobbed. The cry wrenched from my chest as my pain and rage reached its peak. I wanted to claw my skin, to make myself bleed because that would be less painful than my heart being crushed into a million pieces. My voice broke as it bled into a wail, pouring out all my pent-up grief and loss. For years, I had suppressed my parents' death. And it was all for nothing—one demon with a world domination wish had upended my life forever.

I pulled my arms around myself to keep all the ragged parts together. Laying my cheek on the scratchy hay, my vision blurred as I looked up through the small window. Eyes on the full moon, I prayed to the Goddess for guidance. For a path to lead me from my destruction.

The stilted, cold air inside the lonely cell blanketed me like death. My fingers brushed over my pale skin, tracing the demon mark. When I died, would he would feel my soul entering the Beyond? Would he even care?

No. The thought entered my mind, cutting through my self-pity and regret.

Get up. Brows furrowed, I sat up, obeying the strange call inside my mind. A quick glance around my cell proved I was alone, but then I lifted my gaze to the moon once more.

Forgive. My hands shook as I pushed my palms into my chest, feeling my well of magick pulse in reaction. I bit my lip, the sharp sting grounding me as copper filled my tongue.

A memory of Killian entered my mind. I remembered his pain as he recounted his mother's death, the guilt and shame for not protecting her. Would I blame him for his mother's death when he was an innocent? When he was merely a child who suffered the fate of having a terrible father? Would I continue to punish my sisters with the fallout of my shame?

I had to let this guilt go, or it would kill me.

I had to stop Carreau from destroying peace in the mortal realm.

I needed to help my Coven heal Rosemary and keep my sisters safe.

And I couldn't do that sitting in a cell in Hell, hating myself for things I couldn't change.

Not when my actions now could make all the difference.

A breeze whipped through the open window and danced around me like a caress. I gasped, as the full scale of my magick unleashed itself inside my body. Fire burned in my veins, my blood, my skin as the block inside unleashed. With a panted breath, I watched in shock as the demon brand disappeared from my flesh, and the full weight of my power settled inside me. Unwrapping itself from the chains I had forged around it, it burned clear and true in my heart.

All at once, the pain was over. A calming energy flowed through me like a balm to ease a wound. Staggering to my feet, to my feet. I felt lighter than I had in years.

More than a mere mystical block, my power worked to protect me from lashing out. There was no spell cast over Killian, after all. It was *me* who was hexed.

The terms of the pact never specifically mentioned removing the spell from *Killian*, I realized with a choked laugh. Whatever Killian felt about me, it had nothing to do with a false spell. Now I was free.

I would not sit here and wait for my death.

I was getting out of here and returning to Gaia to save my Coven.

Instead of attempting to channel the small lick of fire from the lantern, I sourced the energetic force from within. It was more potent than anything I had ever felt. Energy pulled from my soul, and I let my power do what it was intended to. My magick siphoned out of me like gunpowder, blasting open the cell door, the door hanging from the hinges and melting into a molten core on the cold stone.

My shoulder collapsed against the cell wall. The sensation of using my magick unhindered for the first time since I had reached adulthood was more intense than I had expected. My power greater than I ever imagined.

The fire opal against my wrist gleamed as I stepped out of the cell and glanced back once more at the cell door. I had much to do, and the first step was getting the Hell out of Hell.

35

EMBER

Like a frozen rabbit being chased through the dark mountainside by the fox who wanted my blood between its teeth, I ran through the forest, my dress whipping through the snowy air.

After sneaking out of my cell, Charon had smirked, eyes dancing with mischief as I slipped through the dungeon's entrance and back to the main hall. Most of the guards remained inside, their echoing laughter and clinking glasses piercing through the corridor. As I approached the armed soldiers with weapons gleaming under the moonlight, I whispered a spell under my breath, sending them running from the sudden flames erupting at their feet. I didn't consider the consequences of my chosen path as I darted down the rocky mountainside, skidding towards the tree line with panicked breaths.

My lungs burned, but the shadows of the forest created a camouflaging cover as I ran for my life. I knew from the hours spent studying the demonic grimoire that there were wards around each realm's borders. If I could make my way to one of them, I could spell one of the few demons guarding the territory to portal me back to the mortal plane.

However, after an hour wandering through the woods, I doubted my ability to reach one before I froze to death. My initial euphoria at breaking through my magical block had long since dulled to intrepid fear as howls and screeches echoes in the imposing woods.

My surroundings weren't as disturbing as the Autumn Court, which kept me from spiraling out of control, but the quiet beauty was somehow equally unnerving. The path became rougher with spiked thorny overgrowth plucking at my skin. My hands and knees stung with scrapes and cuts.

The cover of trees became sparser, and the chilling bite of the wind sunk into my bones, making each step more painful than the last. A frozen lake sat in the distance, the deep purple waters iced over by the freezing temperatures, shimmering like amethyst.

I felt a moment of peace as I entered the idyllic scene—one I would enjoy more if I were in a cabin with a fire roaring and a mug of hot chocolate in hand. My breath puffed out with steam as I shivered in my gown, rubbing my bare arms for friction.

A broken tree stump lay ahead, and I walked over to it, collapsing into a heap of satin.

What a fucking disaster. I would freeze long before I made it to my destination. My situation felt like the old tale of Baba Yaga. Like the maiden, Vasilia, I was trapped in the forest, doomed to death, unless I found the redemptive fire that would save me. Only, there wasn't a witch in these woods to help me—only myself.

Wearily, I leaned down to gather some twigs and dried leaves to form a small fire. I blew an ember from inside my well of power and smiled with overflowing pride as it lit without my hands exploding in fireworks. My fingers prickled as they unfroze, and I wondered if I could warm all my extremities with the small wood pile.

A sickening thud sounded, and my hands froze, extended over the fire.

Of course, I nearly groaned. My streak of bad luck seemed endless.

With a grim frown, I turned towards the frozen lake where the sound had echoed.

Silence. Not a creak of a branch or the flutter of wings. The air itself seemed to freeze, with only my flickering flames piercing the night's quiet.

The fire had been a mistake.

I glanced around the forest when the thud sounded again from behind me. As I turned back to the lake, a gasp of horror escaped. A massive crack had appeared at the center, spreading closer to the shore. I squinted, trying to make out the cause when, through the crack, two icy blue eyes appeared, watching me with desperate hunger.

My feet glued to the ground as a literal nightmare emerged from the icy depths. Petrified, I took a shaky step back out of instinct.

From out of the depths, the creature broke through the frozen lake like a nuclear blast, shaking boulders of ice from its massive scaled head. It was like something out of folklore—a tale of an ancient mythological beast whispered around fires intending to frighten children. Blue scales fanned out around its face like icy whiskers, and rows of razor-sharp teeth emerged from its snarling mouth.

I watched in horror as its sickening claws, as long as my arms, sunk into the ice to pull its body out of the depths. The monster's tail whipped out and swung in the night air, propelling its body forward. Crouched low, it slithered across the lake towards me, breaking whatever terrified trance kept me tied to the broken stump.

"Fuck," I gasped, ducking behind the tree line. My feet kicked and fought the billowing skirts of my dress. With a look behind me, I choked on a scream when I realized how close behind me it was. The beast was far more dextral than any water monster should be.

Its hot breath saturated my dress with moisture, the particles reeking of rotting sewage.

I spun around and shot two fire balls at its face, too frazzled to concentrate and whisper a targeted spell in an attempt at searing its vulnerable eyes.

It let out a ground-shaking roar, screeching in pain, before it whipped its claws out at me in retaliation.

I ducked just in time as the sword-like fingers whizzed over my head, the tips scratching into my shoulder. I bit my tongue, tasting copper at the sharp sting. Though its body slowed, the trajectory of its tail smacked me off my feet. As I hit the hard ground, I sucked in a painful breath and turned over to my stomach to crawl further into the thick brush.

My body moved purely on survival instincts as my breath panted out with fear. The beast's furious screams were deafening, piercing my eardrums and sending droplets of blood down my neck. I hid behind a giant gnarled tree trunk before glancing back.

Where its blue eyes once sat, there were two burned sockets, the retinas damaged beyond repair. I felt a flicker of regret as I watched the beast squirm in pain, however those emotions faded as its nostrils flared, scenting me nearby.

It snapped its jaw with irritation, teeth gleaming as it slithered to where I crouched.

Oh, fuck this.

The sound of its body crushing debris giving me some idea of its closeness, I shaped the tendrils of fire, molding it into a blade with my mind, channeling all the training Killian had taught me on stealth attacks. And then, I waited with bated breath.

The moment the beast was in my line of sight, I struck, my magick sending the spelled dagger hurtling towards its throat. The beast lunged at me, its teeth snapping into the satin train of my dress as I tried to thrash it away. Scratching onto its thick scales, I sought a patch of vulnerable skin. Along my back, I could feel its burning breath, and gooseflesh crawled over my skin. Mindless, I kicked backwards, desperate to hit any part of its body.

This was just like the Fae beast from before, trapping me and planning to eat me while I thrashed around uselessly. I screamed as it dragged me backwards, sharp teeth snapping through the material of my dress. Panic seized through me when it began pulling me back towards the water.

I was *not* going out like this.

Flames trickled over its head after I shot out a blasting spell. As it lifted its claws to swat away the flames, I slipped free from its grasp. My dress ripped to hang along my exposed back, and I pulled the hem up to my thighs and ran.

Branches tore into my stockinged skin like claws. I made it past the edge of trees, backtracking to my ill-advised fire. The beast would return and, with my wounds, I would leave a bloody trail straight to me no matter where I attempted to flee. With the fire behind me, I would be stronger, the additional energy source giving me more vitality through my pain.

I pressed my opal bracelet into the delicate skin of my wrist and summoned a wall of flames to protect myself as the dragon beast sprung from the trees. It crept closer, ears twitching as it listened to my panted breaths and the licks of fire. Another wail shattered the quiet, this time its breath and tail wafting my flames.

They flickered, and I grit my teeth as I tried to keep them firm.

When a gust of wind added to the beast's offensive attack,

it stretched a claw through the dwindling flames, testing for any weaknesses.

My eyes watered with frustration as I tried to summon more fire. But I only just rediscovered my magick, and I had used much of it in my attempts to escape. If defensive action would not save me, I would have to take the offense, no matter how much it frightened me.

"Come on, fucker. Let's do this," I growled.

Its ears twitched at the sound of my voice.

When it lunged in a whirl of teeth and scales, I summoned my fire blade once more. My eyes shut as I waited for the impact, a trickle of regret washing through me as I awaited my doom.

But the impact never came. Instead, I felt a breeze against the side of my face, and a sense of comfort, like everything would soon be okay. Steel was the first thing I noticed when I peeked open my frozen eyelashes, followed swiftly by the beast's black claw inches from my face.

Killian stood over me, his eyes wild and black. In a whoosh of cold air, his wings surrounded me in a protective wall of tendons as he roared at the beast with extended fangs.

Pure relief radiated from me. And then a shocking torrent of affection and love so intense, my knees nearly buckled. All the betrayals and hurt drifted to the foreground of my mind as I watched him place himself between me and the creature. My magick responded to his guttural roar, the well inside me purring with contentment.

I shook my head. What had gotten into me? Now was not the time to swoon over the demon.

Refocusing on the furious beast, I squared my chest. "Demon, I had this covered. I don't need or want your help. But now that you're here, what's the plan?"

His eyes flickered with amusement, though the lines of his

face showed his weariness. "I think we're past the point of plans, sweetheart. I'll stab while you cast. How's that for a plan?"

The deep purr of his voice, combined with the sarcasm I had grown to love, wrapped around my heart like a warm embrace. I could have kissed him had there not been a horrific monster about to eat us. Or if I hadn't wanted to kill the demon myself.

"Good enough for me." I crouched low and sent two fire balls at the monster's face, spinning as it lashed out.

Killian took the beast's moment of distraction to slice his sword in a downward arc at the arm reaching out for me. The beast screamed as its amputated claw crashed into the forest floor with a sick thud.

My eyes searched its massive frame for a weakness, catching on the spiked scales around its neck and face. "I think this is a Tauntaun kind of moment," I yelled to Killian, who had flown around the beast to hack at its back.

"What the fuck are you talking about?" he yelled back, his voice echoing in the wind.

I dashed behind the beast's eye line, my fire dagger retreating inside. "You know, guts spewed, hiding inside the belly for warmth?"

From above, Killian's eyes met mine. I could read his utter horror and confusion. "Have you struck your head? I believe you've gone mad."

I choked on a laugh. "We really need to expand on your cultural education. We need to focus on its belly, where the skin is the most vulnerable and thin."

He shook his head with bafflement, ignoring my sage advice as his sword dragged through the upper layer of the beast's scales, breaking them off like popcorn.

The dragon beast's bellow thundered through the forest.

An opening presented itself as it fixated on Killian. I made my move, dashing towards the creature with my fire molded into a long sword. With a brutal yell, I dragged it down its belly, the height difference hindering me from aiming at anything vital.

Wings would be so *handy* right now.

"It's too tall, and its skin is too thick. I can't get through," I shouted, before squeaking as its massive teeth snapped at me.

Killian head-butted it with his straightened horns, stabbing it in the neck. "Run, Ember. Towards the center of the forest. There's a hunting cabin you can hide in until this is finished."

The beast squirmed, almost crushing me from where I stood beneath it. "Not a chance, demon," I spat with annoyance. "You'll never kill this thing alone."

Heedless of my commands, Killian flew down and grabbed hold of me, flying me a distance away. I slapped his face, my elbow digging into his stomach. "You are not putting me in timeout, demon. We do this together." I glanced back as the beast lifted from the ground, its wings snapping like the sound of crunching bones. It would reach us before Killian found the cabin.

Killian's dark eyes surveyed my bloody wounds with growing ire. "You are injured and weakening. I will not let you kill yourself trying to prove a point. Let me protect you, witch."

The beast was getting closer, despite Killian's jerky movements to evade it.

I grabbed the hilt of a dagger from his belt and summoned fire in my other hand. "I can almost guarantee I'll be in trouble for the rest of my life, but I'm done hiding or letting others fight my battles for me. Either you bring me back or I'll find my way in the snow."

His brows furrowed and his breath huffed out in frustration. "If you so much as injure your—"

I covered his lips with my hand. "Let's go."

Killian's gaze hardened, but he flew us towards the beast, his arms wrapped around my shivering body. We soared over the creature, circling it, before he dropped me onto its back. "Sever its neck while I keep it busy!" he yelled over the roar of the wind.

He lowered back to the safety of the ground, the beast following in a mountainous rumble that nearly jerked me off its back.

My nails dug in for better purchase as I climbed up the scaled spine of the beast. Killian's blade remained clasped beneath my armpit. The growls from below my treacherous grip vibrated my entire body, but I latched on for dear life as it lunged towards Killian.

Killian was right. My magick grew weary from the heavy usage after so long without siphoning it. But as I straddled the beast's neck and dove the blade inside the thick, meaty skin, I realized I didn't need magick to decapitate it.

The beast screamed, and my thighs gripped its body. I rode the ice dragon like a mechanical bull as it tried to buck me off. It seemed my nights wasted at the bar were actually paying off.

Tirelessly, I sawed through the muscles and tendons, attempting to avoid the spurts of thick, sapphire blood, to no avail. Killian yelled out, but I couldn't chance looking away from my task. My arms were exhausted, aching as I continued to cleave the monster's head from behind, but I refused to slow.

It shook me, nearly unseating me with the movement. But I was almost there—only another foot of meat left. In the next beat, the beast moved, dragging me with it, back to the depths of the frozen lake. "Um, Killian. Some help here!" I shouted.

My grip on the water dragon turned vise-like as it slithered back onto the ice that was crushed beneath its weight. The spray of frigid water pierced me like knives, and I gulped as I stared down into the murky purple water.

Killian flew above me. "Move back!" he yelled.

My body slid backwards down its spine as Killian dropped onto its neck; sword drawn to make the killing blow.

The beast's head severed from its body and thudded across the ice.

"Killian!" I tried to stop my downward slide, but couldn't get any traction. Screeching, I fell towards the hard, icy surface below when the demon caught me in his arms.

"I've got you," he breathed, flying me away as the beast's body sunk through the broken ice and submerged in the depths once more.

)☾☾(

Killian clasped me in his arms as I looked down at the treetops below. From a distance, I could make out a small cabin at the edge of the woods. As he descended, my stomach bottomed out as we whooshed towards the snowy ground.

"This is a hunter's cottage. It is unoccupied during this time of year, so we won't be disturbed." His voice had returned to his normal, controlled tone, though I admitted to myself I enjoyed the guttural sounds of his demon just as much.

Free from imminent death, all my anger returned like a slap, my body shaking from the force of my suppressed fury. Though I wanted to lash out at the demon who held me close, I knew any action on my part would have my ass falling to the trees below.

Not that Killian would let me get that far. As if he understood my inner dilemma, his face pressed into my hair, inhaling the tangled locks like I was a lifeline.

The wind stung against my skin as we landed on the

creaking porch of the log cabin that looked more likely to exist in the Colorado wilderness than inside a realm of Hell. I stepped away from Killian's masculine scent, putting some much-needed space between us. With a snap, I sent a flicker of flame towards the lantern at the door, illuminating the inside of the cabin.

There wasn't much to it—a small bed, a copper tub, a kitchen with a worktop and an empty fire pit. When I turned back to face the demon, his eyes were watching my movements, tensed as if I would flee into the night. I crossed my arms against my chest. "Are you here to take me back to your father?"

He shook his head. His eyes seemed unsure where to land as he took in my shredded gown and the cuts and blood over most of my exposed skin. "Your wounds need tending to."

I took a deep breath, letting it out with annoyance. "We don't have time for this. My family needs me. I've been gone too long already. And don't pretend to care now—you've made it more than clear how you feel about me."

He scrubbed a hand over his weary face, his scar starker here in this realm than in Gaia. "We will return to your family and deal with Carreau, but my demon is going a bit insane. You need to be at full capacity to face the battle above, so let me tend to you and then we will go."

A humorless laugh sputtered out. "Oh, and is this the same demon who determined I was your mate with no spell or treachery from me and yet you didn't listen to him? Fancy that. Was that your plan all along, Killian? Use me and my ignorance to attain your vengeance?"

I had intended the words to sound detached, but my hurt leaked through. Like nothing else, I wanted to hate him, to rage on him and never see his face again. And yet I couldn't lock away my emotions any longer and let them fester inside. Not now. Never again.

He stepped forward, his boots scuffling to a halt on the wood when I put more distance between us. I felt ragged, a raw wound exposed. But damn him, he wasn't wrong. Until my magick recuperated enough to not be a hindrance, I couldn't return to the mortal plane.

"Fine, let's get this over with."

Relief shone through his eyes, and he nodded.

On the patio lay a bucket, and he grabbed brought it to the well to fill with water. While he focused on his task, I sent fire to the pit, lighting the cabin in a warm glow. I stripped the beautiful, ruined dress from my stinging skin, blood and dirt coating me like a pagan.

He returned and set the bucket of water near the fire to warm.

As he worked on filling the tub, I meditated on my breath, assessing the state of my magick. I had used a lot of energy in my escape and the battle with the dragon beast and could feel my well of power was low. Unfortunately, there was only one surefire way to recover in a short amount of time. And I was in no mood for sexing up the demon.

"Come." He gestured for me to get inside the tub with an outstretched hand.

I hesitated before removing my garters and undergarments, stepping into the lukewarm water with a sigh. At least the water wasn't ice cold.

His eyes stayed averted from my nude body as he brought more water from the fire. "Lean back." Voice gruff, his fingers brushed over the marks at my neck where the beast's claws had seized my skin.

As commanded, I sunk into the water, hissing at the prickles spreading over my frozen skin as it thawed. My eyes screwed shut, not wanting to feel his tenderness or care. Not when I now knew it had all been a lie.

He repeated the process a few more times, and the tub filled with grime and blood.

Through half-lidded eyes, I watched him. Meticulously, he scrubbed under my nails and around my wounds. All the while, my ragged heart shattered further. My throat clogged with tears until I feared I would suffocate. "You hurt me."

His hands paused in his ministrations before he sifted through the strands of my long hair. "I know," he sighed.

A moment passed, and I waited with bated breath, for once thinking he would expand on what lay inside his heart. But this was Killian, so of course he didn't. He was as emotionally constipated as ever.

My anger burned, heating me more than any amount of water ever could. "That's it? That's all you can say—*I know?*"

His finger trailed down my forearm where his brand once lay. "My father explained his coup after I awoke in the throne room. While I followed orders collecting souls, he was using me to halt my succession. All that time and energy wasted. And yet when I felt the pact between us snap, none of it mattered. I didn't know what to think; I thought you were dead."

His haunted eyes darted to mine, the icy fear still swimming in his molten depths.

With that look, I'd had enough of this sham. I stood from the tub, sending droplets onto the floor of the cabin.

He froze for only a moment before he stood from the perch of his knees.

Dripping water onto the floor, I drew on my dwindling magick, forcing it to the fore. "How could you leave me when I needed you? If you were there like you promised, we could have stopped Carreau. But you hid away, too afraid to face that there was something real between us." I broke off with a bitter laugh. "Then to discover that you planned on letting those monsters torture me? How can I believe the words out of your mouth when your loyalties will forever be tied to your revenge?"

His hands clenched into fists at his sides. "I'm sorry, Ember. I really am. But for the past twenty years, all I've had to my name is my desire to destroy my father. It is what I solely lived for—no love, no future beyond my revenge. I never expected this to happen, for *you* to happen."

He swallowed thickly, taking a hesitant step forward. "I used your spell as a crutch. Anything to deny what was right in front of me because I knew it would be the end of everything. And a beginning I could never claim." A broken breath escaped, but his eyes never wavered. "I fucked up. I'm sorry that I hurt you when you're the last person in the world I want to."

My chest ached from his fracturing words, his visceral pain felt through the bond that somehow remained between us despite the pact being demolished. "So, there was never a spell between us, despite your adamant insistence. What about you other betrayals? You knew how much I needed the amulet, and you let me believe it was still within my reach. What about Carreau's claim that you fucked demonesses in the brothels, all the while pretending to care for me?"

Nausea churned with sick jealousy. All his countless acts against me hurt, but that one? That one felt like knives lodged in my heart.

His jaw clenched, his eyes dropping from mine, confirming my worst fears.

I wanted to claw his face, to shred him as thoroughly as he eviscerated me.

He shook his head. "It wasn't like that. It was before the ritual night, before there was more between us. And I couldn't go through with it. Nor could I go through with turning you in to my father. I would never have given you to him, no matter what you may think."

I snorted, brushing my damp hair over my shoulder as I advanced on him. "Assuming I believe a word you say, how do you expect us to move past this?" A bark of laughter expelled from my lungs. "*Of course*, because you still plan on returning here and taking your crown regardless of this so-called new beginning between us."

When he stepped towards me, I forced my knees to lock and not retreat away from him.

His eyes burned as he grasped a wet tendril of hair along my neck. "A firecracker of a witch summoned me to New Orleans. She looked at me like she didn't know whether to stab me or kiss me. With these dazzling blue eyes and an even more lovely heart that endured heartbreak and sorrow, she still held kindness and compassion for others in her heart. Her inner strength showed me how wrong I was to live only for my hate and not for my love. Whatever happens now, know that it's with you in my heart."

He looked at me like he could see into my soul, and he liked what reflected back at him.

He looked at me like I was the most beautiful person he had ever known.

Like he was undeserving of my love despite the ugly, secret parts of myself I let him see.

My vision blurred as the love glowed in his eyes. If only I could continue raging. But my heart already belonged to him. I knew it as surely as I knew my name. And I couldn't let him live the next century in Hell thinking I hated him when that was the furthest thing from the truth.

I stepped closer and lifted a shaking hand to his chest. The fire in the pit of my stomach withered away to mere embers as I clenched my fingers into the fabric of his shirt. "Then there's nothing left to say." Lifting onto my toes, I brought my lips to his.

He dislodged my grip and staggered away, his eyes wild. "What—"

"You wanted to help me, to ensure I'm strong enough to fight Carreau. You know what charges my magick, demon."

His body shot tight, eyes flooding black.

I nearly laughed at the equal measure of panic and desire in his eyes.

The demon was mine, and I would take what I needed.

36
KILLIAN

My mind fought to keep up with Ember's sudden shift in mood. Especially when my own emotions felt like a torrent inside my chest. From realizing the realm hated me so vehemently that they would dishonor traditions to thwart my succession, to Ember's pact snapping and her near-death by ice dragon, I was having a fairly shit day.

Unbidden, my lips returned to hers like a man starved. Yet I couldn't help but think this was a trick. If I had learned one thing about Ember during this past month, it was her single-mindedness. I broke away from the kiss and groaned at her body in the flickering light of the fire.

Her lips were wet and swollen as they quirked into a half smile. "I want you and you want me. Are you going to deny me?"

My mind struggled to remember why this wasn't a good idea. Why we needed to wait.

"It wouldn't be right," I argued, hoping she would have the strength to realize the truth of my words because with every dip of my eyes upon her lovely face and body, my resolve weakened.

Her eyes twinkled. "Only you and I get to decide what's right, demon. So, unless you want me to sacrifice you to Hecate, this night *will* end with us together."

Gods, save me. She was right. To survive, she needed what I could give her. But my guilt and shame still suffocated me. I had fucked everything up, and if this was what I needed to do to give her a fighting chance, I would. Any part of her I could get, I would take gratefully. No matter how much it fucked me up in the long run.

Resolved, I stepped forward, grazing my fingers down her shoulders and crushing her to my chest. My arms grasped her like she was treasured, like I was trying to imbue all of my love and my silent promises with every sweep of my hand over her slim back.

Though at first, she appeared surprised, she soon melted into my embrace, returning my hug with feeling.

"I love you," I whispered into the wet strands of hair I buried my nose within, not needing her to say it back, but feeling as if I'd die if I didn't voice what was coursing through my veins like my lifeblood. "I love you so fucking much, Ember."

Her breath hitched before stopping altogether. She lifted her head and the raw, unrestrained emotion in her eyes soothed many of my worries. Not all was lost. There was still hope for a future, though I had no clue how.

Disentangling herself, she walked over to the bed, laying back for my perusal.

Helpless to deny her, I fell to my knees once more, my hands forming shackles around her ankles. "I'll make sure you're strong enough for the battle ahead. I'll give you everything I have. Anything you need." My lips trailed up her smooth legs to her warm center, my tongue finding the spot between her upper thigh and stomach.

"Please, Killian," she begged, her hands squeezing her tits together. "Please touch me."

Not needing to be told twice, I dove in, growling against her as my tongue sought her most sensitive places in a broad stroke. She shot off the bed, mouth open in a silent cry. Her hands wound around my horns, and I growled savagely as she lifted her hips, steering me at the pace she wanted.

Fuck, yes. I snarled against her flesh, my eyes blackening at the taste of her sweet honey on my tongue. Her petite hands clasped my horns tighter, her nails digging in, sending shockwaves of nerve-tingling pleasure straight to my aching cock.

Lost in my desire, my finger slid against her wet opening, sweeping inside and curling with a silken caress. Her orgasm quickly approached. She bit on her lip, moaning when I added another finger.

"I want your cock. Give it to me. *Please*, Killian."

Instead of succumbing, I added a third finger and moaned at the view of her arching off the bed. My shadows began seeping towards her, my mind imagining all the ways I could make her scream. I groaned and thrust against the bed, halting my hips with an internal shake.

This was not for you, Killian. Tonight was about giving, not taking.

Arms wrapped around her hips, I opened her wider while my shadows gripped her thighs, pushing them up and into her chest. The visual of her wet and shaking, immobile under the inky swath of shadow, would remain with me forever.

When I scraped my fangs against her clit, it was over, far sooner than I wanted.

"*Killian!*" she screamed, eyes rolling back as she writhed against my all too eager mouth.

My shadows stilled her hips to help her better absorb the pleasure.

Though I was nowhere near ready to stop, she yanked on

my horns once more, forcing me up to her seeking lips. I moaned as her tongue caressed mine, her taste sweet and addictive as spiced wine. She hooked her leg around mine and pushed me onto my back, settling over my hips like a woman possessed. She ripped my clothes from my body, seeming to enjoy the startled look in my eyes.

But I couldn't help my delayed reaction. Her drying curls and glowing skin mesmerized me.

I huffed out an awed breath and my eyes grew hooded. When she grew tired of waiting for me to act, her hips began to descend on me. My hands grasped onto her hips, stopping her movement. "No. This is about you tonight," I gasped as she jerked, the magick renewing her and lighting her up like fireworks.

Her hand clasped my cock in her soft palm, her thumb spreading the moisture leaking from the tip over my thick, velvet length. "What about what I want? Don't I get a say?"

I could no more deny her than I could deny the blood pounding through my veins or my heart from beating. Looking into her shining, beautiful face full of joy and desire, I was helpless to do anything but give her anything she wanted. "Then fuck me like you need to, sweetheart," I rasped.

She needed no further encouragement. Fitting me inside her, she moaned at the tight pull, her body stretching to fit around me. "Oh, Goddess."

My fangs tore into my lips as I fought the need to fuck her. To claim her. To push her onto all fours and ram into her, my fangs seeking her flesh in the bite that would make her mine.

Somehow, I held myself back and let her take the lead. My hands didn't push or guide her to take me harder. Instead, I let her control the movements, my chest arching up so my mouth could latch onto her rosy, peaked nipples glistening in the firelight.

My hand smacked her ass with a muffled groan. "Take me like the good girl you are, witch."

At the sweet drag of my tongue over her stiff peaks and the stinging slap on her other cheek, she slid down to the hilt, taking me whole. Our breaths puffed out the moment our bodies joined.

I knew then that there was no going back for me. My heart would belong to her forever, just as my body was hers. My face lifted to hers, eyes naked and sure, and the same truth reflected in hers.

We moved together as one, grinding until we found a rhythm that suited the fire burning brightly between us. I fell back to the bed and lifted my arms behind my head, watching as her hips shot back and forth, chasing her orgasm.

My hand reached forward to brush against the wetness covering her swollen clit and rubbed the bundle of nerves with my thumb, while my shadows began moving over every inch of her skin I could reach.

Her eyes rolled back into her head, and she screamed as she buckled down onto me, her pussy clenching me while I urged her hips to move faster. Her orgasm seemed to go on endlessly, toes and fingers twitching as I prolonged the heady sensation with whispered words of love and my unrelenting touch.

When she collapsed onto my chest with a broken sob of pleasure, I flipped her onto her stomach, my hands dragging her lower body off the bed. Standing behind her, I lifted the tendrils of drying hair into my fist, as she arched her back in a crescent moon. I drove my hips back to hers with a snarl. The deep stab of my cock at this angle was almost too much for her, but she moaned at me not to stop, so I kept up my punishing thrusts until she screamed out once more.

"That's it." My hands grasped onto her shoulders to pull her deeper into me.

She glanced back, her blue eyes glowing with need. "Do it," she commanded me, her brows reaching together as she reared back onto my cock with her hips. "Claim me."

Gods, she tempted me! Shaking my head, my cock pulsed within her as if readying for the pleasure of my bite. "No. Not until you're truly mine."

She bared her teeth once more at me. A challenge and a smile blurred together. "Well, considering you're *mine*, it's only fair you claim me as yours."

My breath grew tortured, my head and my heart at war.

She tilted her head, baring the milky skin of her throat, and I could not deny myself.

My demon would take its due.

The heat of my chest hit her back as my fangs latched onto the curve of her neck. I gave her a moment to change her mind before my fangs pierced her skin. Like electricity, I jerked, my eyes rolling back with pleasure.

"Killian!" Her magick exploded when she came.

The surrounding air shimmered, and her skin glowed like lightning. The sight of it was my undoing. My roar shook the foundation of the cabin as she wrapped her arms around my neck from behind, her hips meeting my thrusts as my mouth loosened its hold on her pretty skin.

Our lips met. Panting together with one shared breath.

On an exhale, I released her body and dropped onto the bed, soothing the places where hands gripped before pressing a lingering kiss to her damp spine. As she lay satisfied on her stomach, I told her with my hands and my lips how much I loved for her.

She rolled over to sear my eyes with hers. Twining our fingers together, she dragged me down until my body pressed into hers. "If you hurt me again, I will make you pay, demon."

My voice was gruff with emotion. "If I hurt you again, I

will make myself pay and then spend the rest of eternity making it up to you."

Her lips met mine once more and though she didn't say the words, I could feel the love pouring through her touch.

I stood on shaky legs and pulled her up to her feet. The magick glistened over her skin from within, ready for the battle ahead. "Let's go finish this once and for all."

37
KILLIAN

We materialized back into the mortal realm to utter chaos. Ember pulled away from my arms, coughing smoke from her lungs. A flying dagger soared near her face, nearly nicking her skin if not for my quick reflexes. Taking stock of our surroundings, I watched in horror as the armored group of demons fought through the crowds of creatures. Splattered glassware and shredded tapestries covered the grass already seeped with black blood.

Ember caught sight of Jade, Audra, and Isla, who were facing off against Satan's armies, alongside the other creatures of New Orleans.

Her legs tensed to run towards them when I grasped onto her arm, halting her movements.

She shot an angry look up at me, but I only pulled one of the many blades from my belt and handed it to her. "Be safe, witch. I don't want one single mark on your body. Do you understand?"

She nodded, her gaze fierce. "Always am, demon." She gave me a saucy salute before running towards the creatures, fire radiating from her palms.

I faded into the shadow dimension, stalking towards the

field when a demon portaled into the space beside me. Relief coursed through me at Taliah's appearance, thankful she was here to fight alongside me once more.

She smirked, twirling her blades. "Looks like you finally grew a pair. I'm proud of you, Killian. Though, I don't think I can say the same for our people."

"I can deal with their disappointment," I grunted as I sent my dagger flying into the back of a demon's head.

We raced towards the horde, a force of deadly intent, as we faced off against our own.

Taliah's voice echoed in the field, a paragon of justice and power. "Traitorous demons, lower your weapons and leave this place or you will pay for your treasonous crimes by the end of my blade."

Carreau stepped forward from behind the wall of demons. "Taliah, I'm wounded. Why don't we play nicely? We are fighting for the same cause here."

She hissed, her fangs lengthening in outrage. "You fight for only yourself. You spread your corrosive filth to any who will listen, and now you have brought them to their doom. Release their minds, or you will pay the price."

Carreau clicked his tongue, his golden air gleaming under the moonlight. "Everyone assumes I force those under my influence to act against their will, but the seed of dissension must be there for me to call upon it. The demons here come willingly under Satan's order, and it won't be to their doom but their deliverance."

The skies opened, covering us in sheets of rain as lightning speared the night like Zeus's wrath. Winds whipped hard enough to clatter against their armor and, as the horde approached, I twirled my sword in readiness.

Carreau drew his own blade, his charm falling away as icy determination took its place. "It's a shame you went this way, Taliah. You could have helped me rule here on the mortal plane. But now, you will die with the rest of them. Especially *him*."

I grinned impishly at his glare.

The horde raced forward, moving half through the shadow dimension and half on the mortal plane. It would make them impossible to kill for the creatures without the use of shadows. Taliah and I yelled out a battle cry as we ran, meeting the warriors head-on in a dance of metal.

Alongside us, vampires, witches, shifters, and Fae fought together against our enemy.

With a roar, I rushed towards Carreau. Like the coward he was, he kept back, letting the masses die by blade instead of facing me himself. I was nearly upon him when a dagger sliced me from my shoulder, down my back. With a hiss of pain, I whirled and caught the blade's downward arc with my sword, snarling at Bartholomew, who swung his axe down.

Enraged, I spun, kicking out the brute's feet, his heavy weight dropping into the mud.

Lightning quick, he jumped to his feet, avoiding my blade. Malice coated Bartholomew's bloodied grin. "I told you, you wouldn't be my lord, Killian."

Shielding his axe, I dodged another strike. I didn't have time for this. "Tal! Need your steel over here."

She ran through the battle towards me, cutting through demons as she moved. As Bartholomew advanced on me, he never saw her blade. With a mighty swing, she missed his neck by a mere inch, debilitating him on the ground. "Go get Carreau. I'll deal with him."

Dogged, I sought the demon prick who started this entire mess.

Carreau fought stealthily, moving within his shadows, with a witch and warlock who I recognized from my time spent with Ember's Coven.

In a burst of muscle, I let my wings expand and flew

towards them. My sword aimed true as I knocked Carreau away from the pair. "Go help the others," I grunted at them, circling Carreau with a hard glint in my eyes.

He grimaced at the mud coating his clothing. "You know what your problem is, Killian? You can't see the bigger picture. You're so fucking focused on your rules and your petty vengeance that you miss what's right in front of you."

We circled each other, our vision clouded by the sheets of rain and blood. From the corner of my eye, I could see Ember and her sisters fighting a demon beast, trampling through the festival on a bloody rampage. Before I could tense to follow, Wren Boudreaux stepped forward, protecting Ember with a flash of fangs and claws. Some of my ire against the wolf softened. Perhaps I wouldn't steal his soul after all.

Shaking myself, I focused on the enemy before me. He moved as quick as a snake, blade clanging against my own. The blow was swift but unpracticed. He spent more time in the training yard gossiping than fighting. He threw his head back and laughed, unhinged as he dodged my sword.

"My priorities may be out of order occasionally, Carreau. But you're right—I would never have imagined you were capable of this." I kicked him in his stomach, and he collapsed into the mud on his knees.

Though I could slay him now while he kneeled before me, I paused my blade. My demon rage slipped to the surface, and I did little to control it, wanting him to feel my ire and know I would make him pay. "Why did you do it?"

"As if you have to ask?" he growled, eyes slanted with defeat. "If anyone should understand, it's you. The pressures our fathers put on us, the unending disappointment. This was my chance to finally be worthy of his approval. But you never cared about approval; you gave that up long ago."

My fist moved faster than his eyes could track, pummeling the smile off his lips. "Why fight for assholes who will never accept us for who we are? We could have worked together with me as Lord to make things different, but now it's too late to turn back."

He spat black blood on my boots. "In case you hadn't realized, I have no intention of returning to Hell to sit in the prisons. I find I much prefer the mortal realm, especially now that I'll hold dominion over these foolish beings."

My breath stuttered. "I never pegged you as delusional, Carreau."

"Lower your sword," he bit out, attempting to use his persuasion on me without effect.

I pulled him by the collar of his shirt, my fangs grazing the vulnerable patch of skin peeking through the material in warning. "You know your filthy gift never worked on me."

He wiped the blood from his face. "If you let this go now, I will go back on my promises to Satan and ensure you sit on the throne of Pride. Just let me finish this and you'll get your revenge and take his crown. We can go back to how life was before the witch."

I shook my head, amazed by his nerve. "I don't think so."

"It's too late," he hissed. "I've already compelled another horde of demons who will arrive to massacre all these vile creatures. Your precious witches, the vampires, the Fae—all of them—will perish, freeing New Orleans for my domain."

"You lie." My fangs tore into his neck.

He screamed and writhed until I released him from my grip, spitting his blood onto the ground. Fear finally cracked through his armor.

I raised a brow, teeth gleaming in the darkness. "You've lost, and you'll spend eternity wishing you could join the Beyond instead of whatever punishment gets doled out by your precious Council."

My blade nicked his throat, but he appeared unbothered, mirth dancing in his crazed eyes. "I may have lost, but you will never win. You can't have both the witch and your precious crown. No matter which you choose, you will regret the choice unmade."

My demon raged inside at the truth of his words.

Many of the demons lay slain, leaving behind wearied creatures, searching the dead for their parties. A breach in the air shimmered, and as one, everyone looked to the source of the disturbance.

Carreau's eyes lifted to the portal, a feral grin spreading across his face. "You've lost, old friend."

Another wave of demons burst through the shadow realm, weapons raised in righteous anger. Howls echoed in the field, and I felt my stomach plummet as Satan's Hell Hounds shook their black fur, the rain steaming off their heated skin.

They weren't here for Carreau, I realized with grim understanding.

They were here for me.

With the coronation hour upon us, soon I would be dragged back down to Hell to assume my mantle. And away from Ember forever.

This ended now. I lifted my sword, my body framed in the storm like an avenging angel. "Goodbye, Carreau." And then I swung.

38

EMBER

My breath wheezed out in shock when I noticed Alexei Vasilyev and several members of the Boudreaux pack fighting alongside my sisters. Before I could gape at seeing my ex fighting on behalf of my Coven, a flash of wings sprouted across the sky as Killian and Taliah dove towards the demon horde.

Red coated my vision with my need to punish Carreau for all the suffering he had caused me and my family. But first, I needed to focus on saving my own. Without a backward glance, I harnessed my fire and sent it straight at the massive demonic beast with gnarled horns and a slimy body.

My fire landed along its back; its head reared back as it screeched before it turned its attention towards me. In the moment of distraction, Alexei and the others shot forward, the clanging of their weapons and claws slicing into the demon's belly.

High-pitched sounds blasted from the creature. The direction of its assault shifted, with Isla in its periphery. Faster than light, I ran towards her, grasping her hand and dragging her away as the beast's snarling mouth emitted tusks that pierced the dirt where she once lay.

Like with the ice-dragon, I forged my fire into a dagger and circled the beast until I found my opening.

Wren watched me with shocked yellow eyes. "New party trick, Belle?"

With an arrogant grin, I waved the dagger. "Don't say I do nothing but lay on my back, Boudreaux." Turning to his pack, I yelled out. "Can you guys get the thing's attention? I'll sever its neck with my cool fire blade."

Alexei Vasilyev snorted, his coiffed hair and impeccable clothing askew. "We'll do whatever you say, witch, so long as we kill this thing soon. The expense it's going to take to cover up this mess from the mortals makes my fangs hurt. I am far too old to be dealing with monstrosities such as this without ample time and alcohol."

Jade shot him with a glare. "Typical vampire—more concerned with your comfort than with helping others. Can't say I'm surprised."

His grin became a leer, eyes heated as he stared at my sister like she was a decadent dessert he couldn't wait to sample. "Don't over flatter me, darling, or I'll think you're flirting with me."

She cursed in response, lifting her hand to give him a one-finger salute.

His laughter echoed into the night as I refocused on the battle before me and gave the wolves my cue. As one, they growled low, attacking the beast from the front, leaving its back exposed. With a scream, I threw the fiery blade into the back of its neck, falling to my ass with my momentum.

Without scales or protective tissue, the blade sunk through its skin like butter. It squealed, writhing and jerking wildly before sinking into the mud beside me, dead.

Relieved, my head fell forward. Wren was the first to reach me, and he held out his hand. After a moment's hesitation, I grasped it and let him pull me to my feet. "Thanks."

His eyes were warm but cautious, an apology written over his face. "You're welcome. You did good, Em."

"I did, didn't I?" I nodded, not bothering with false humility.

Audra snorted as she collapsed next to me, wrapping me in a hug.

Jade stalked toward us, ignoring the Vampire Prince who watched her with a coy grin before searching out his crew.

With a glance around the field, I realized we had slayed most of the demons, their bodies scattered across our property. "We need to go find Grandmother and Killian. The new concealment spells should have hidden away the events of tonight, but who knows how far the demons have gone past our borders? And then we're going to deal with that fucker once and for all."

Their brows furrowed, and I realized much of the sorry tale was still unknown to them.

I sighed. "Long story short, Carreau is behind everything —the demons, the murders." When Jade and Audra's eyes widened, their mouths opening to spew questions, I raised my hand, already feeling my throat tightening under the revelations from earlier. "Carreau is the one behind Mom and Dad's deaths. It was him who killed them that night, along with the other creatures five years ago."

Jade's eyes glowed silver, and Audra's wind lashed around me, tearing at my skin.

Beside me, Isla's face leached of all color. I grasped her hand, letting her pull me to my feet. "I know, so we're going to take all of this pent-up rage and sadness and we're going to kill that motherfucker. Sound like a plan?"

My sisters' eyes gleamed with menace, and I gripped my dagger in response.

A sudden shout shattered through the field, and I gasped as I realized it came from Killian.

Like I was possessed, I ran, uncaring if they followed behind me. When I found him, my eyes searched his form, breathing a quick sigh of relief that he was unharmed beyond minor scrapes. Then I noticed the demon on his knees before him and the portal with hundreds of demons emerging behind him. When three wolven dog creatures with glowing red eyes emerged from the portal, terror rushed through me. *Hell Hounds.*

"Wait."

Killian glanced back at me and my sisters. Stark relief transformed to understanding as he sensed the emotions seeping out of us. He knew this wasn't his kill to make. After a beat, he lowered his sword and stepped back. "He's yours to do as you see fit," he rasped, his eyes taking in my unharmed body. "Be quick before we're overtaken."

With that, Killian turned and rejoined Taliah to fight off the new demons.

The demon on his knees appeared broken, but his pernicious spirit still lingered in the way his eyes fumed with disdain.

Coming closer, I crouched down towards his angelic face. It was the face of someone I had thought I could trust. Someone who should have protected our city instead of causing untold harm. His eyes lifted to mine, and the wrongness inside his cool depths sent a chill down my spine. But there was a lash of clarity in them as well, as if he knew his time was over.

Jade and Audra fanned out beside me while Isla remained behind. Her gentle nature was at odds with the reality of his evil, but the strength in her eyes was clear and bright. We dropped our weapons and grasped hands, forming an unbreakable chain.

My smile twisted bitterly. "You should have never returned here, Carreau. You may have gotten away with it had you stayed away. But now you *will* pay for your crimes."

Uncaring of the crowd gathering behind us, we closed our

eyes and channeled our combined elemental energy. Fire, water, earth, and air. All focused together and coexisting in a beautiful harmony. Swirls of light and sparks of energy heated the air, shimmering with the current we were building together.

A shift reverberated around us, and I opened my eyes in shock at the spirits surrounding me and my sisters.

It was All Hallows Eve, and we had somehow channeled the fifth element with our combined magick. Our combined *spirit magick*.

"What the actual f—"

Audra's words cut off as our ancestors and the souls of creatures who died by Carreau's vicious attack surrounded us. Desperately, I searched for my parents. With a sinking feeling in my gut, I realized they were not here among the rest.

I muttered the words we were all thinking, "Did we do that?"

"Of course you girls did." Pride beamed in Grandmother's voice as she stood beside us. Her hand reached for Isla, who clasped it tightly. Affection shined through her blue eyes as she watched the spirits. "How many times did I try to get you girls to train? The spirit element runs in our family, and you four possess the gift. So, yes, Ember, you girls did this. And now, we finish it."

Overwhelmed, I nodded, and we refocused on Carreau.

Together, we sent forth every ounce of our corrosive grief. Sleepless nights swallowing our sobs into the fabric of our pillows, endless bottles of wine to drown the shame and guilt, and the ever-present false smiles. Spinning down the rabbit hole without an end in sight.

And then we let him feel our *anger*. Corrosive and ugly. Tinged with every what-if that tormented us for a future that would never be.

The demon's body seized on the forest floor, mud coating his body in a slimy coffin. With every sliver of magick coursing through his blood, lightening stab wounds appeared over his once-perfect body, piercing him from within.

"I would say go to Hell," I whispered to him, "but where you're going... you will wish for it."

His eyes lifted to mine with pain and fear while his body leached itself of color.

In a final push of magick, he exploded. His body scattered in hot, bloodied pieces across the ground, misting us in his fiery blood.

Through the film of red, I peeked open my lashes. A euphoric sense of justice rolled through me, but I could not linger on our victory.

The chaos unfolding around us reached a fever pitch. Though Carreau's hold over the demons was over, the creatures still fought just as recklessly as before. The Hell Hounds' bellows penetrated the once entertaining night. There was no earthly way we could fight them off, and the Council members surrounding Rebecca seemed to come to the same conclusion.

"Rebecca, it's time. No more waiting," Hunt growled from behind me.

When I glanced up, I caught her haunted eyes, already watching me. "I'm sorry," she mouthed. "It won't be forever."

And then I knew.

From her pocket, she drew forth the ripped piece of parchment from our stolen spell book. A page describing the means to perform a demon summoning. And their banishment from the mortal plane.

My heart hammered in my chest as she and the elders spoke the words that would undo everything I had let myself hope for.

On a gasped breath, I ran for Killian, heedless of the battle before me, or the death and violence. Like he could sense me, his eyes found mine and tracked my movements through the battle. With a brutal yell that moved the ground beneath my feet, he flew to me, clasping me to his chest and flying me away from the immediate danger.

Wracking sobs shook my body. With all the events from the past few hours, I felt torn apart. Things were moving too quickly. I thought we would have time—time to figure out the next step for us. But now, everything around me came crashing down.

He placed his hand over my racing chest, searching for injuries. "Are you hurt? What's happening?"

Anguished, I caught his face in my hands and dragged him down into a surprised kiss.

It wasn't sweet or soft. It was savage.

Our tongues tangled as he lifted my body up, my legs winding around his waist in a vise grip. My lips dragged away when I could no longer breathe, though at that moment I didn't care if he suffocated me in his kiss. "They're performing the spell to banish the demons from Gaia. I don't know how long the spell will last, but by the time it opens, you will be back in Hell, forced to remain with your throne."

His eyes watched my face with tender calm. "It's the only thing your people can do to stop them, sweetheart." His forehead dropped to mine, his wings furling around us like a cocoon, blocking out anything other than the two of us. "I only regret we didn't have more time."

Another shuddered breath slipped free at his words. Goddess, I loved him. I loved him so much, I didn't know what to do with myself without him. How could I have been so stupid to not realize? How could I have let this adorable idiot waste the time we had?

My tears slowed by sheer will. Leaning forward, I pressed my lips to his once more, so he could feel everything within me. "I love you, Killian."

His eyes flickered with emotion, and the smile crossing his face was brighter than the heavens.

But then a distant howl broke through the night, and his smile dimmed.

"So, this is goodbye, then?" I made myself unfurl my legs and jump away from him, the cold rain prickling like needles along my overheated body. More than anything, I tried to be strong. To not make this harder than it needed to be. But Goddess, it hurt.

Shrieks and yells sounded around us as the spell took hold. Demons zapped away from the lands like lights being tampered out, wisps of smoke all that remained of them.

Killian's attention never wavered from me. "The hounds won't cease until I sit upon the throne. My reign will be the same as the other lords. A century until I am free."

A small smile curled my lip. That tendril of hope was too strong to die. "I could come back to Hell and be with you. Long distance dating between realms. We can make it work."

He was already shaking his head. "You saw how the demons reacted to your presence. There is already too much uncertainty within my reign and my enemies will stop at nothing to hurt me. Plus, you have your sisters you must think about. Your Coven."

He stepped closer to wrap a hand around my head, pulling me into his chest. His heart beat slow and steady under my ear.

Like a silk, his voice crooned into my ear, "I won't ask you to wait for me, but know that my heart is yours eternally."

Tears threatened. I lifted my head to look at his face one last time.

A whisper of wind blew between our bodies as chaos unfolded around us. Taliah appeared in a wisp of smoke. She turned to us with a grim frown. "Sorry to interrupt, but it's time, Killian. We need to flee before the hounds get to you and drag you back. An appearance of strength will be critical to seize the realm from your father."

My heart galloped. I almost begged him again to let me follow him, but I held the words inside.

His lips lifted his scarred cheek into a small smile for my benefit, but the torment in his eyes matched mine. "Goodbye, witch."

My throat ached like shards of glass lodged inside. "See you later, demon."

Moisture misted in his eyes, but he turned, giving me his back as he picked up his sword and walked to Taliah. Her gaze shot to me with concern and gratitude before she gave me a small nod. Killian never turned back to me, and I was thankful for it as my heart shattered to pieces. He whistled, the sound piercing the night, and the Hell Hounds turned, seeking their prize.

In a flash of smoke, the demons and the beasts were gone. With the demons purged from our lands, the battle slowed. Creatures cheered, their raucous yells and heartfelt cries a cacophony in the wind.

The rain slowed to a fine mist, and I felt a ray of moonlight shine down on me like the Goddess herself was giving me strength. Shattered, I walked back towards the field, finding my sisters.

At the sight of me, they rushed over, tears shining in their eyes. Jade's hand gripped mine, and she stared down at me with anger. "Don't you ever do something like that to me again, Ember Marie," she hissed before pulling me into her arms. Her body shook with silent sobs as she held me tighter.

Audra wrapped her arms around my shoulders, forcing her way into our hug. "We can't lose you too, Em."

Isla let out a choked cry and came to my other side. Jade opened her arm to allow her into our huddle. "No sacrificial lambing it, remember?" she whispered into my ear, and I huffed a small laugh.

Grandmother cleared her throat beside us, and we lifted

our gazes to her and the rest of the Council members. Alexei stepped forward, blood and gore coating his skin and clothes while Hunt stood stiffly with newfound respect radiating in his eyes.

"It appears we have some business to take care of," Alexei groaned, his body twitching as if he'd rather be drunk and staggering away to a bedchamber. "Let's get on with the clean-up, shall we?" As he walked towards the estate house, he grinned wickedly, eyes catching Jade's with a sultry wink.

She flushed and scowled, turning her back on him, which only seemed to amuse him more.

Grandmother stood taller and cleared her throat. "Come, girls, we have much to do."

Jade followed behind her, though from the look on her face, she was loath to do so. Audra and Isla set out to find the other young witches and warlocks to clean the field and tend to the wounded.

Nearby, Edward and Tabitha stood together, with Fleur under their arms. She flashed me a small smile that I easily returned. There would be time later for us to talk, to mend the broken fences, but for now, all I cared about was my demon.

My face lifted to the moon once more, and I let the rain wash away Carreau's blood and my hot tears. Had it been hours ago that I had looked to the same moon, begging for the Goddess's help? Now I sought her guidance once more.

Like before, I knew the answer lay inside me.

I had much to do, and I would not let this second chance at happiness slip away.

39

KILLIAN

Pride's court was bustling with harried soldiers on guard as demons ran through the castle grounds, preparing for the mass trial over my father and Carreau's treacherous coup. The golden crown on my head felt as if it weighed a ton, the pressures just as heavy as my grief.

Though my chest ached with longing and my demon prowled around inside my head, screaming at me to return to Ember, I forced my steps towards my new quarters, ready for this to be done so I could wallow alone.

"He's in here." Taliah's hand touched my arm, bringing me back to the present. Her presence was the only tether against my wrath. And for my sorrow, that seemed to consume me whole.

Inside Satan's quarters, my father sat in the middle of a disaster—shredded linens, turned over furniture, and spilled wine covered the suite as the reek of demon brew and stale air made Taliah cough with disgust.

When he turned to us, his eyes were red and dazed with booze. They narrowed with disgust at the crown now sitting on my head. "It's all over," he sighed. "It appears you've won, Killian."

It didn't feel like a win.

How could I savor his misery when my own seemed to swallow me whole? My brows furrowed as I considered my father. This very moment fueled every decision in my life for so long that I couldn't remember not wanting to destroy his happiness. And now my victory felt hollow.

He belched, groaning as he stood and staggered to the window facing out to his kingdom.

A breath of relief escaped as he opened the balcony doors, sending a wave of fresh air into the chamber.

"I suppose I should prepare for the trials." Taliah's eyes glittered. With a final glance back at my stony face, she left me and my father alone.

Satan turned to me without his usual armor of cool disdain. In its place was pure hatred. "You may have won, Killian, but you'll never be happy. 'Tis the life of a demon lord to have everything taken from you."

There was no smooth retort to his cruel words. The other demon lords would soon take him prisoner for his crimes and sentence him to the Pits, a fate far worse than death.

And yet I felt nothing. No joy or relief. No lingering regret or sadness.

His words echoed in my ears, deafening me. I swallowed and realized I was done with him. All the energy I had wasted on my revenge was now gone. My mother's soul could rest knowing that the villain who cursed her to misery would pay his due.

Turning to my guards, I gave them the nod to begin his transfer to the prisons. At the door, I turned back one more time to watch his pitiful visage. "Goodbye, Father."

And as I walked away, I allowed his bitter silence to clear from my mind. Finally, I was finished with Satan once and for all.

Two weeks into my reign as the Lord of Pride, I believed I would lose my godsdamned fucking mind. My days passed in long, grueling meetings and trials. Not even Bartholomew's punishment put a smile onto my face. It would be another hundred years before I could feel true joy again, which only sent me further into dark despair.

"How long are you going to stare out into the forest, my friend?" Taliah stood at the doors to my chambers, her arms crossed.

I shrugged, too exhausted to manage much else.

She rolled her eyes and approached my side, knocking into my shoulder. "I spoke with Gaia's Council this morning. After their banishment spell ended, we discussed damages and negotiated a truce between realms under your leadership. Apparently, they owed you a favor and consider this your payment."

She waited, watching my face for any emotion, but I had nothing to give her.

"This is good! It means we'll keep our supply of souls. We can make changes to our laws to ensure we only pact with beings who make ill-intended bargains. And your witch can come visit you here in Hell—putting us *all* out of our misery," she quipped.

At the mention of Ember, my chest seized, and my fangs lengthened mutinously. "*No*, she will never step foot in this realm again."

Taliah's brows furrowed. "But why? All the demon traitors are gone."

A ragged breath blew out, and I forced my demon to calm. "So, she comes to the realm, and then what? What happens if another rebellion surges? Or if a demon visiting from another realm senses her witch's blood and wants a closer look? It's a risk I cannot afford."

The forest below that once offered clarity and peace now only brought back memories of her and I tangled together in the cabin. Pain skittered down my throat at what I had lost.

"If I re-open this wound, Ember will spend her days here in Hell instead of where she belongs—on Gaia with her family. I won't force her to live this way, broken between the two halves of her heart. She deserves someone who can give her everything."

"And what about what she wants? Have you asked her?"

With a glare, I stalked away from the window. "Leave me."

She held her ground, her hands on her hips. "No. I'm not going anywhere. Ember is an adult and deserves a chance to make this choice for herself. You're fucking miserable, and you don't have to be."

I laughed without humor. "As long as I'm Lord, I'll be miserable. My father was right; it is a death sentence."

But then, the idea came to me, like a spark of genius. *What if I wasn't Lord any longer?*

The realm had forced me to accept the crown, but there was nothing in the law saying I couldn't step down and give my seat to another. Such a thing was unheard of, considering Satan's line was a proud bunch of demons who reveled in their power. But I couldn't care less about the throne and knew who should sit on it instead.

My eyes found Taliah's, and she frowned at the hopeful glint in my gaze. "I don't like the look you're giving me. Whatever it is you're thinking, the answer is *no.*"

Pulling her into my arms, I breathed, "I want you to rule in my stead. I think it's about time we had ourselves a Lady of Pride, don't you?"

She grew rigid. "But I'm not noble. And you can't give me

your throne. What about the other demons and the laws? You're obviously not thinking clearly."

I squeezed her. "Neither was I before Satan acknowledged me as one from his bloodline. With the line of Satan dead, the realm could use someone new. My first act will be transferring power to you before I abscond."

She sputtered a laugh, her eyes full of affection. "The other lords will never go for it, my friend. But I thank you for your confidence in me, regardless. And, for the record, I still think you're a fool for letting your witch go."

I brushed a soft kiss over her head, releasing her with a grin. "Leave the other lords to me. And the witch won't be without me for much longer now."

Hustling towards the doors, I sent her a relieved grin. My first genuine smile since Samhain.

40

EMBER

The weeks after Samhain flew by faster than I expected, though my heart seemed to be permanently bruised from the loss of Killian. After he had disappeared with Taliah and the Hell Hounds, my sisters and I had stayed long enough for the clean-up and for Fleur to explain how Carreau found her after our night in Faerie and worked his gift to lead her astray. I couldn't bear to watch the pain in her eyes as she recounted the horrific deeds the demon forced her to take part in. Her journey to healing, like mine, would be a long road.

My sisters and I worked around the clock, sharing chores and shifts at Get Hexed to give Jade a break. After some convincing, I'd agreed to therapy sessions with a vampire at Alexei's court who specialized in trauma and grief. Though the sessions were painful and most of the time filled with tears and magick-singed tissues, I could feel the small shift inside myself after every meeting. I wasn't healed, but I was trying.

My training at the estate with the Coven resumed now that I had freed my magick. Now that my power was unhindered by a block, I realized I *loved* casting. Learning new spells and mastering techniques I once feared brought me joy on days when little else could.

Jade was beside herself with joy that I found my place within the Coven. Surprisingly, she was more than happy to step aside and allow me to take her place as Grandmother's protégé. There had been grumbles about rules and tradition, but Grandmother could see how well I took to my new role.

We hadn't spoken about our strange connection to the spirit realm the night of Samhain, but I knew it was a question lingering in our minds and something we would have to deal with eventually. Especially now that I was no longer hiding from my power.

The only part of my life that felt unfinished was Killian. Without him, I couldn't put the pieces of my heart back together.

On a chilly Saturday afternoon, my sisters and I lounged on our outdoor furniture, wrapped in cozy blankets as we surveyed our finished backyard setup. Jade poured us glasses of Pinot Noir while Isla spread a charcuterie board covered in delicious cheeses, olives, and spreads, along with my favorite pralines.

I took a sip of the berry and plum wine and allowed myself to enjoy the fruits of our labors. The garden was a task suggested by my therapist to get some closure. It was far past time to clear away the destruction and make it into something beautiful.

We spent laborious hours at twilight pulling out weeds and dead plants, our arms scratched and itchy by the end of the evening, with piles of trash bags stuffed to the brim lining our driveway. It became our new ritual every afternoon after Isla got home from school. Critters and small Fae creatures who had escaped Faerie and wandered through the bayous and marshes would explore now and then, luxuriating in the oasis our elemental abilities seemed to foster.

The silver new moon shone through the clouds, and I brought a cracker stuffed with brie and fig jam to my lips. My mind wandered, as it always did, back to Killian.

Had he claimed the throne? Was he happy? Did he miss me at all?

The questions clamored inside my mind, but I tried to silence them. My sisters missed him just as much. The weeks in October had fused us together into a unit, and now it felt like a phantom limb, his absence felt keenly.

Audra huffed, tossing back her glass of wine and nearly spilling the jars of water Isla placed under the light of the moon to infuse with magick. "This mood is far too gloomy for me. Are we going to stop pretending everything's peachy keen and finally discuss the big—with wings—elephant in the room?"

Jade snorted and glanced over at her with a smirk. "Like the fact that you have been hoarding all the cinnamon apple muffins in your room as you study like an old monk?"

Audra threw an olive at Jade's head. "No, more like why Killian hasn't sent word for Ember, so she can come see his new digs in Hell? The Council agreed to their terms and the portals are open once more. What's his deal?"

My throat closed as heartbreak speared through me. Lately, I wondered the same thing.

It had become my new, secret tradition these past few weeks to cast summoning circles, attempting to bring him back to Gaia and have it out with me once more. If not to tell me he still loves me and wants to make our relationship work, then to once and for all tell me it was over between us. But every time I lit my black candle and whispered the spell, only silence greeted me.

Audra sighed, her anger dying as her hand reached to enclose mine. "Until he's with you once more, he'll never be truly happy. And neither will you."

"Is that something you read in one of your romances?" I wiped a piece of jam from my lips, deflecting the words I knew were true.

She harrumphed. "*Yes*, but that's not the point."

Isla laughed. She turned her startling blue eyes on me and smiled sadly. "Take time if you need it, but don't wait too long to rebuild those bridges. Don't let your fear of opening yourself up to pain keep you from experiencing life. Would you leave this world behind without the love of those around you to keep you warm at night?"

I huffed a surprised laugh. "When did you get so wise?"

The wind sent her hair flying around her, and she caught it with her fingers. "I may be young, but I see what you hide from yourself and others. Don't be afraid to be happy, Em. You deserve it as much as we all do."

"Well, I'm more interested in what you're planning on doing with the prize Alexei awarded you." Audra grinned, breaking the tension with a wink. "The prize he insisted on hand delivering when he knew Jade would be home."

I groaned, not wanting to consider the ominous onyx amulet Alexei had reluctantly handed over to me. Whenever I touched the cold metal, shivers ran down my spine like spiders. The Amulet of Davorina was powerful, but sinister. I preferred its current location at the bottom of our kitchen pantry and intended on keeping it that way.

Jade stood with rosy cheeks, her blanket falling to the cushion. "How about leftover crawfish gumbo and French bread for dinner? And then we can watch a movie. My pick tonight and I'm warning you, I'm feeling a bit like some gloomy historical dramas."

Audra and Isla giggled, letting her escape from comments about the Vampire Prince's new obsession with her, which she preferred to ignore. "Fine." Audra stood, stretching her arms above her head. "I'll take Victorian romance over more cleaning. Upstairs reeks of incense and it's giving me migraines."

For a moment longer, I stayed outside, watching lightning bugs light up the darkening sky. I stood on uneven feet and glanced inside the warm glow of the house. Soon, our little unit would change, our lives branching off from the roots that bound us. But I didn't want to be afraid of living. So, tonight I would try again. And if Killian didn't come to me, I would find a way back to him.

***

As always, I waited until nightfall, when I knew the girls would be out at the coffee shop getting their weekend fix of sugar and caffeine. With a flick of my wrist, I lit the black summoning candles and placed Killian's forgotten leather trousers at the center of my altar.

I refused to admit how many nights I lay in bed, tears streaming down my neck as I held those ridiculous pants to my chest, remembering the way he watched me with that incongruous, perplexed brow or the way he held me close in his sleep, like he was afraid I would slip away into the shadows.

With a deep breath, I whispered the words I had now memorized. The Latin flowed easily off my tongue, and my magick sizzled as I finished the spell and waited.

When only quiet darkness greeted me, disappointed tears splashed across my cheeks. I wiped the wetness from my face and muttered an oath.

But then, in a wisp of smoke, he was there.

Shirtless in a pair of low-slung boxer briefs, his hair was mused as if he had just rolled out of bed. His tired, red-rimmed eyes met mine, and he froze.

My breath stuttered out as we stared across the salt circle at each other, taking in each other with hungry eyes. Gone was the stony mask, the hard edges I had grown so used to. Warm, molten eyes watched me with surprising tenderness.

He glanced down at the circle containing him and lifted a brow. "A summoning, witch?"

My lips pressed together to hide my relieved smile, my heart feeling as if it would burst from my chest, before his words registered. Then, my eyes narrowed on him with annoyance. "Well, considering I've tried to summon you every other night since you left, I'm surprised it worked."

His eyes darkened. "As Lord of Pride, I wasn't so easily summoned." Lips pursed, he took in my glowing skin—a result of hours spent outdoors and having my magick freed from its cage. My eyes were brighter, my skin less dull. Cutting out excessive alcohol and long, restless nights seemed to work wonders. "You look good, Ember."

I shivered at the timbre of his voice, at the way he spoke my name like a vow. "I wish I could say the same, demon, but honestly, you look awful."

And I meant it. He looked exhausted. As if he hadn't slept a wink since Samhain.

But apart from the red eyes and pale skin, he was still the sexy demon I loved. "How are you here this time, then?" I asked, fighting the urge to run to him.

A rueful smile brightened his face. "I wore the crown and tried my hand at ruling, but found I was unsuited." He stepped closer to me, his feet touching the salt line. "*I'm* unsuitable without you. You're lucky I came to my senses before I ended up setting this plane on fire in my desperate attempts to get back to you."

A husky breath sucked in. "I *am* terribly miss-able, demon."

His eyes softened, and he lost the veil of humor. "I missed you more than words can express." His voice was gruff, underlining the longing he felt towards me, though I could feel it through the bond, loud and clear.

I stepped closer, my feet disrupting the circle holding him off. My fingers brushed past the boundary and grazed his. "I love you. And I don't want to waste another moment not having you in my life. Are you okay with that, demon?"

He wound his fingers through mine, dragging me into the circle with him. "You're mine, witch. I don't plan on letting you go now."

Killian's eyes held a promise, and my heart jumped inside my chest, my magick lighting me up from within. He watched with something like awe as I lifted my hand to his face. "I'm counting on that, demon."

His lips collided with mine, and I felt the hole inside my chest close. As I fell deeper into Killian's arms, I knew I was ready to face whatever came our way. Together.

41
EMBER

Six Months Later

The demon at my back pounded into me as I bit into my lip, trying not to scream out. My hands fought for purchase along the sink top, my gaze half lidded as I watched him through the fog of the mirror. His magnificent body seemed made for battle and giving me pleasure.

"You like to watch me fuck you?" he rasped. He lifted my leg to the counter, opening me for our joint perusal. His shadows reached out to hold my leg suspended while the other pinned my arms to the sink top.

I moaned at the feeling of immobility and the sight of his thick cock sliding in and out of my core. One hand dragged over my clit in teasing circles while the other came to my throat, squeezing lightly. He forced my head back against his damp chest, leaning down to smell my skin. A hint of a smile teased across his lips, and I shivered in response. "Answer me, witch. Or I'll punish you again."

My eyes twinkled with fiery mischief. I *did* love ignoring his orders and reveling in his punishing smacks. But I was *so* close, and nothing would come between me and my orgasm.

"Yes," I moaned. "I love watching you fuck me like this." Biting my lip, I let my eyes drift closed as his wet circles grew firmer. My hips lifted to help him move deeper inside me. For my acquiescence, his shadows caressed my tits, squeezing them together before they pinched my nipples roughly.

My eyes glared back at him. "Now, make me come, demon."

His laugh skittered across my spine, and his eyes were wicked as he pulled out of me with a wet glide.

"Nooo," I groaned, breath panting out in hectic gasps as my hands fought against his shadows to trail to my center to finish myself.

He chuckled before he grasped both of my arms behind my back, pushing me forward to lean, bent over the sink. His shadows held me immobile on the counter as his firm hand met my right ass cheek, the sting hitting me like a vibration.

When I tried to wiggle for more friction, he smacked the other cheek, giving it the same attention. "Now, are you going to behave?" His voice held arrogant laughter.

"*Yes!*" I screamed, uncaring of who heard me.

He didn't make me wait any longer, filling me once more, deeper at this angle. His thrusts were hard and teeth-clattering as his hand found my bud once more. "Killian!" I screamed as my climax found me, my legs shaking with the strain to remain standing as he obliterated my senses, sending shockwaves through my blood.

He groaned as he came, his hot finish coating my walls in warm spurts, making me see stars once more. His head met my back, shaking back and forth as he chuckled. I felt the brush of his hair like a silken caress and I lifted a freed hand to caress his face.

"We're going to be late," his silky voice purred into my ear.

Content to lie here in the aftermath, I managed to mutter, "Worth it."

Audra pounded on the door, breaking through my post-orgasm haze. "You two hurry up or Jade will murder you!"

Killian rolled his eyes and dropped another heated kiss on my lips.

With a sigh of defeat, I fished my robe from the hook above my door and wrapped it around my glistening body. Walking through my bedroom, I creaked open the door an inch and met her wrinkled nose and crossed arms.

"You two need to spend more time at Killian's townhouse," she complained, but a small smile slipped onto her lips, belying her annoyance.

My sisters relished having his presence back around the house. Movie nights and family dinners felt more exciting with his surly but tender affection, providing us with endless opportunities to share our wealth of pop culture knowledge.

My eyes filled with mock accusation. "Why do you care? You're leaving us, anyway."

Audra beamed, her excited green eyes lighting up with the endless joy her acceptance had brought her. She was only the summer away from her first semester at Dragomire, and though I couldn't be happier for her, I would miss her like crazy.

She winked. "Don't be jealous. I promise to send you postcards detailing every delicious morsel I can get my hands on. Food or otherwise."

"That's just cruel." My lips curled, imagining the delectable pastries she would get to enjoy in the countryside of Wales where the sorcery school resided inside a spelled, ancient castle. Not to mention the hot men she would no doubt explore.

Audra glanced at her watch, her brows furrowing. "It's almost time. And you know how awful parking's going to be."

Though we knew it was coming, Isla's high school graduation seemed to creep up on us. The notion that our baby sister was officially an adult and about to enter the world was a terrifying but exciting one. Isla's summer holiday with her friends backpacking across Europe took days of begging to convince Jade, but my sister knew it would be pointless to hold Isla back from what she wanted. To say Jade was on edge because of this development was an understatement.

I winced. "We'll be fine. We can always spell a mortal into giving up their spot if need be."

Audra's lips quirked with humor as Jade popped around the corner, her dark hair frazzled as she attempted to complete all our tasks before the party this evening. "Why are y'all standing around? We still have so much to do. Ember, leave Killian alone for like five seconds and focus on your baby sister."

Audra and I shared a look, and I ducked back into the safety of the bedroom, leaving her to deal with Jade's meltdown. When I took over the mantle as High Priestess in training, I assumed she would mellow out and choose a path to bring herself happiness. But instead, she was more high-strung than ever.

Her hours spent working inside the Vampire Court as a liaison between the Coven and the vamps altered her moods into tumultuous storms, yet she refused to quit. She claimed it was out of stubborn pride that she remained as the Court's mystical guide rather than interest in Alexei's rakish flirting. But I had my suspicions.

Leaning against my bedroom door, I narrowed my eyes at the demon, fully dressed, and laying on my comforter. "This is your fault," I told him with a pointed finger in his direction.

His golden eyes crinkled at the corners with amusement. "And what am I in trouble for now?"

"You know exactly what I'm talking about. Don't play games with me. All your hours away have turned me into a hedonistic harlot, in need of ravishment at inopportune times. Jade's going to erupt eventually, and we'll be to blame."

He stood from the bed, his arms coming around me as I secured my dangling gold earrings into place. "Your sister doesn't scare me, and I'm afraid the good of the city must sometimes come before my lusty mate." He bit down on my ear. "And don't pretend this is a recent development in your personality. You've always been a harlot."

I pursed my lips, but my eyes danced with mirth.

As the new Council member on behalf of Hell, he took his job very seriously. The creatures of the city were more unified than ever before. After dealing with Wren and Alexei's drug fiasco, he cut off the black-market trade and brought some level of peace to our community. It also helped that under Taliah's reign in Pride, the demons who now entered our plane were less likely to cause trouble.

He nipped my ear once more, making me gasp. "But no matter how busy I become, I'll always get the job done in the end, sweetheart."

Turning in his arms, I buried my nose into his pressed shirt. "Just imagine, we could be the new King and Queen of New Orleans. Me, on the seat as High Priestess, you as Gaia's Demon Lord. We would be unstoppable."

"Oh, gods, please no." He groaned low at the mayhem I would reap on the city.

Laughing, I jumped into his arms wrapping my legs around his waist. "No take backs now."

Killian's warm gaze lowered to mine, his lips gentle and searching. "No take backs ever, Ember Belle."

"Feeling's mutual, demon." I smiled before taking his lips once more.

THANK YOU

Thank you so much for reading! I hope you love the world and characters as much as I do. If you loved Bewitched Shadows, please consider leaving a review on Amazon.

Continue to read the **BONUS CHAPTER**.
Check out Jade's story, Blood Enchanted, out September 2023.

You can also connect with me on social media:
Instagram @authorautumnblake
TikTok @authorautumnblake

Love,
Autumn

JADE

From the upper-level booths of Bite—New Orleans' vampire sex club—I watched the show of brow-raising, over-the-top lust with quiet interest. My cheeks were a violent shade of ruby, which I hid behind my dark hair, while Ember and Audra giggled at my side, whistling and catcalling the vampire males performing below on the black marble stage.

Ember leaned over, her chestnut curls sloshing into her glass of red wine, waggling her brows at me. "Is this what you do all day working for the Vampire Court? If so, sign me up too."

"Goddess save us." Audra snorted, her hair fiery under the warm lights as she shimmied in her sparkling sequin dress. The movement sent rainbow shadows down to the various creatures seated below us.

A flicker of annoyance rolled through me at the mention of my new job and the infuriating male I worked under. My teeth ground with frustration as I fought the urge to glance around self-consciously.

Alexei Vasilyev, the Slovenian Prince who was better known in the city as the Prince of Pleasure, had made it his mission to make my life a living Hell.

After our unfortunate meeting at the Battle of Samhain last October, he had taken every opportunity to become a thorn lodged in my side. When Ember decided she wanted a chance to train for the role of High Priestess, I gratefully stepped down. It was never a role I truly wanted, and this left me open to explore my true passions. Only, after five years ignoring my own desires in favor of taking care of my sisters, I hardly knew what I wanted.

And like a knight in shining armor, Alexei swooped in and offered me a lifeline as mystical guide to his Court. Only now, his honorable armor slipped away near a cozy fire and he crooked a finger at me from the animal-skin rug, beckoning me closer.

Which I hated. Completely.

From the corner of my eye, I saw a shadow emerge. The male's towering frame and dark raven hair tousled as if he had just emerged from a lover's bed caught the attention of every creature in the club. Unbothered, he began walking through the space as if he owned it. Which, unfortunately, *he did*.

Ember's nose twitched at the irritated scowl on my face. She and Audra crept closer to me, so they wouldn't shout their next words over the screaming crowd. "So, how exactly are Alexei and the Vampire Court, Jade? You never talk about what you even do in that creepy manor house all evening."

Twirling her cherry stem, Audra glanced at me with a coy smirk. "Please tell me they all traipse around in silk robes like your boy-toy over there."

"He's not my boy-toy," I snapped through clenched teeth.

Ember brushed her hands over her pink velvet corset, attempting to appear innocent. "You can be honest with us. It's not as if you and Alexei roll around his expensive silk sheets all night, anyway."

My cheeks flamed as I shot an accusatory glance at her, which only made her burst into delirious giggles.

Audra frowned, pointing at us in drunken annoyance. "What's happening? Secrets are so uncool. Spill."

I bit down hard on my straw, forcing myself to calm. "Tell your idiot demon to mind his business. And I wasn't *rolling around in his bed*. He tricked me into his bedroom and has horrendous cleaning habits, so I tripped over a pile of clothes and into the bed. Which he laid in. And he assumed it was some sort of come-on."

Audra spat her gin and tonic across the booth, her hand clasping her mouth as tears sprung to her eyes. "Oh, my Goddess. Please tell me this is true."

Their laughter echoed in my ears. "Laugh it up, you two, but it was humiliating and annoying as Hell. Not to mention Killian materialized at that moment for important Council business and saw the whole unfortunate event transpire."

Ember's laughter died down, and she wiped the mascara tears from her cheeks. "He said you were fuming, and I quote, 'gave Medusa a run for her money when it came to revenge on male sycophants.'"

The whole situation had been a disaster.

When I received the note in his handwriting to find him in his chambers at sundown for an important task, I had assumed it was strictly business. What I hadn't expected was for the new fledgling to misdeliver the message meant for his second in command, Silas, to me.

With a pitch-black vampire bedroom meant to allow no sunlight through, and an entitled prince who never had a female not beg for a night in his bed, me falling face-first into the canopy bed atop a very naked, very muscled Alexei seemed very much a planned seduction.

His crimson and coffee eyes had opened in surprise, only to smolder as a dark smile spread over his face once he saw who lay in his grasp. His pale arms stretched up before winding behind his head as his brow arched. "If you wanted to get into my bed, darling, all you had to do was ask."

After a mad scramble out of the bed, I fled, my cheeks cherry-red like they still were weeks later whenever I thought about it. I had yet to look Alexei in the eyes since and I would rather never again.

As he made his rounds around the club, he glanced up at me and my sisters, that damned infuriating smile stretching wide over his face as he caught sight of me.

I shot Ember and Audra warning glances as he beelined for our table.

False smile in place, I leaned my chin on my propped elbows, my gaze never leaving his chest. With his black rope opened dangerously low on his taut abs, that was somehow even worse than his laughing eyes.

"Ladies, are you all having a good evening?"

That fucking accent. My thighs clenched despite myself.

Ember's smile widened, her eyes shiny with suppressed glee. "As we always do. You've done a great job on the renovations. I'm loving the upper levels. It's naughty to eavesdrop on the carnal activities below and partake in some of your own."

Alexei snorted, "As if you and Killian care about subtlety."

She shrugged, unembarrassed, and I felt a lick of jealousy at how confident Ember had always been with her sexuality.

As the perfect elder daughter, I had repressed all of my wicked tendencies in order to meet the expectations placed on me by my parents, my grandmother, and the Coven. Now that I was no longer in line to lead as High Priestess, I felt adrift, with no guide or map to steer me on my new path.

"And what about you, Jade? How are you enjoying the night's entertainment?"

With a jolt, I realized I had missed the last few minutes of small talk as I lost myself in my daydreams. I shrugged. "If one enjoys debauched displays of lust, I suppose it's been an acceptable show."

"Acceptable? Darling, my club is many things, but acceptable isn't one of them."

My teeth bared into a semblance of a smile. Foolishly, I let my eyes wander up to his for a moment. His eyes grew heated, his desire plain to see as he looked over the tight black dress Ember forced me into that cut a deep v past my cleavage to the top of my abdomen. By the way his tongue flicked across his fangs, he liked the dress *very* much.

I whipped my eyes away, catching Audra and Ember's knowing grins. They looked like maniacal Cheshire cats rather than the innocent sisters they pretended to be. My hands clenched around my glass of wine, fighting the urge to sling it at his face.

Then, lick the droplets away.

"If that's all, we would like to enjoy our evening in peace. My hours on the clock don't start until tomorrow night."

He pursed his lips, and I thought I saw stark disappointment flash in his eyes before he gave us a small bow. Performative and sly like always. "I bid you ladies adieu. Be sure to find Sergei for a ride. He will ensure you ladies get home safe."

Ember nodded, a wide smile stretching over her face when it became clear I had no intention of speaking or acknowledging him again.

As he stalked away, I glared at my sisters, who giggled like the traitors they were. "I'll kill both of you if you speak a word of this to anyone. Especially Isla."

Audra rolled her eyes and picked up her bag, pulling out some cash and throwing it on the table. "You're such a spoilsport, Jade. You need to loosen up."

Ember jumped from the booth, holding her hand out to

help me in my ridiculous heels. "And as for Isla," she began, "you know she's so busy having a blast in Italy with the other witches that she won't have time to worry about our drama."

My heart ached when I thought about our youngest sister alone, across the world. She hadn't mentioned the bags of willow, cedar, and moonstones I had placed in all of her luggage for protection, but it gave me some peace of mind knowing that she wasn't unsafe.

Arms looped together, we walked out of the club before the night descended into sexual madness. At the exit, I glanced back into the red haze once more and caught Alexei's dark eyes from across the room. Sat alone with Silas, his eyes held mine like a predator, never losing sight of me.

Trapped within those depths, I let myself remember how it felt to be held against his chest. The pulsing desire I felt from him every time we were together. But then, a group of nymphs wearing beads of pearls along their slender, nude bodies ran to him, squealing with excitement. Not bothering to watch his reaction, I turned and cursed myself for ever thinking Alexei would desire me when he had the attention of thousands within the city.

And worse, I hated myself for *wanting* him.

He was the Prince of Pleasure after all, and I would not be one among many.

My shoulders straightened as we walked into the boisterous chaos of the French Quarter. I could put aside this fantasy and treat him as any other creature in the Vampire Court. *I would.*

If it was the last thing I did, I would show Alexei Vasilyev how little I thought about him.